The Treading Water Series

Book 1: Treading Water

Book 2: Marking Time

Book 3: Starting Over

Book 4: Coming Home

For the millions of people facing recovery one day at a time.
You have my respect and admiration.

AUTHOR'S NOTE

This is another book I didn't plan to write. When I began work on *Marking Time*, I had no idea I'd meet yet another character whose story would need to be told. When I was looking for a name for Clare's love interest in *Marking Time*, my friend Julie and I batted around a bunch of options. Travis was one of them (we ended up using that in *True North*). When we settled on Aidan O'Malley, I decided to give him a big, boisterous Irish family full of the joys, trials and tribulations that go with it. When we met Aidan's brother Brandon in *Marking Time*, he was in the process of hitting rock bottom in his struggle with alcohol. His story needed to be told, and thus, *Starting Over* was born. During the writing of this book, I attended an Alcoholic's Anonymous meeting that ranks among the most powerful experiences of my life. I read *The Big Book* from cover to cover, and immersed myself in all things AA and Al-Anon. And while Brandon's alcoholism is a central theme in this book, it's not the prevailing theme. I like to think this book is about love—the sustaining love of a family, the love between a man and a woman and the love of a man for a little girl who quite literally saves his life. I hope you enjoy reading this book as much as I enjoyed writing it.

CHAPTER 1, DAY 1

Brandon O'Malley lay on the narrow bed, counting the cinderblocks that made up the sterile room. Ten up and twenty across, painted a boring, flat shade of tan. In addition to the bed, he had a beat-up dresser and a tiny bathroom adjoining the room. A small window overlooked the parking lot of the Laurel Lake Treatment Center, home sweet home for the next thirty days.

When his brother Colin brought him here two hours earlier, Brandon commented that the place looked more like a country club than a dry-out facility.

"It's not a country club," Colin had snapped. "The place costs a fortune, so don't forget why you're here."

Leave it to oh-so-perfect Colin to cut him down to size. He was sick to death of all three of his brothers and the way they talked down to him just because he liked to get loaded every now and then. Brandon touched the bridge of his nose, tender since his older brother Aidan's fist connected with it the night before.

To hell with them, he thought as a vicious burst of pain from his battered face stole the breath from his lungs. *They don't understand me. None of them ever has.*

Brandon checked his watch. After the most thorough physical of his life, he'd been brought to this boring room and told someone would come to see him in half an hour. That was forty-five minutes ago.

What I really want is a beer and a shot of whiskey. Brandon broke out in a cold sweat when he realized that wasn't going to happen. Suddenly, the ten-by-twenty room felt like a cell, and he wanted out of there. He sat up too quickly. The room spun, and the meager contents of his stomach churned. Bolting for the bathroom, he vomited and was splashing cold water on his face when he heard a knock at the door.

Still holding a towel, he opened the door to a balding man of average height and build.

"Yeah?" Brandon grunted.

"Hi, I'm Alan. May I come in?"

Brandon shrugged and stepped aside.

"Do you have everything you need?" Alan asked with a smile on his round, friendly face. He wore a starched light blue dress shirt and pressed khakis.

Brandon gave him a withering look.

"Towels, sheets, that stuff," Alan clarified.

"I guess."

"Well, just let us know if you need anything."

"Do you work here?"

"I volunteer on Fridays."

"My lucky day."

"It sure is." Alan sat on Brandon's bed. "In fact, one day you may look back and realize this was the luckiest day of your life."

"Yeah, *right*," Brandon snorted, pressing a hand to his throbbing face in a desperate attempt to find some relief from the pain.

"What happened to your face?"

"My brother punched me."

"Why?"

"He says I hassled his girlfriend."

"Did you?"

Brandon shrugged.

"You don't remember?" When Brandon didn't answer, Alan pressed on. "Why are you here?"

"My brother said it was either this or his girlfriend would press charges against me. Nice, huh?"

"It was nice of him to give you a choice."

"I can see whose side you're on."

"Actually, I'm on your side, Brandon. I was once right where you are today. I'm an alcoholic."

"Whoa, man! I'm not an alcoholic. I just like to have a few beers after work. I don't know why everyone thinks that's such a big deal."

"Have you had blackouts before last night?"

"No."

"You're sure?"

Brandon looked away from him.

"How old are you, Brandon?"

"Thirty-eight."

"Ever been married?"

"No."

"You mentioned a brother. Do you have other siblings?"

"Three brothers and a sister."

"You're lucky to have such a nice big family."

"Yeah, well, they've kind of let me down today."

"Do you really think so?"

Brandon shrugged.

"What do you do for work?"

"I'm an engineer. My family owns a construction business."

"That's impressive. Has your drinking caused you problems at work?"

"No," Brandon said as his patience ran out. "What's with the twenty questions?"

"I'm just trying to get to know you. I'd like to help you."

"I don't need your help."

"Perhaps not, but I need yours."

"What could I possibly do for you?"

"Part of my recovery involves helping others who're struggling with alcohol. Would you help me by listening to my story?"

Brandon sat on the floor. "Do I have a choice?"

"Always."

"Fine." Brandon's stomach lurched again. "Have at it."

"I started drinking when I was thirteen," Alan said. "I fell into a group of rich kids who had easy access to booze. We always had the good stuff—vodka, gin, rum. I couldn't say no to any of it, but I had a particular fondness for vodka. I drank every day of high school, college, and law school. No one ever called me on it, so I thought I was getting away with it. I got married a month after I graduated from law school, and it didn't take my new wife long to realize I was drinking all the time. If I wasn't at work, I was drunk. She hadn't signed on for that, so she left me two months after the wedding. I found out much later that she was pregnant when she left. I have a fifteen-year-old son I've never met. You see, by the time I finally hit rock bottom and admitted I was an alcoholic, I'd lost my job, I was broke, my ex-wife was remarried, and another man was raising my son."

Despite his best intentions to stay detached, Brandon was moved by Alan's story. "I'm sorry."

"Me, too. I go to my son's football games just so I can watch him for a few hours. Lucky for him, he looks like his mother, and I can tell just by watching him that he's popular with his friends. He thinks his stepfather is his real father, and since I'd never do anything to mess up his life, I have to be satisfied with a few glimpses every now and then."

"That must be really hard."

"It is, but I've managed to find a good life for myself. I'm married again, and I have two little girls who are the joy of my life. I've been sober for twelve years, five months, and thirteen days."

"You count the days?" Brandon asked, incredulous.

"Every sober day is a victory to be celebrated."

"Yeah, well, I'm sorry about everything that happened to you, but I don't see how it applies to me."

Alan stood to leave. "You will, Brandon. Maybe not today or tomorrow, but one day soon you will." He took a card out of his wallet and put it on the bed. "If you ever want to talk, feel free to call me any time. You're going to discover an enormous network of people who want to help. If you don't want to talk to me, talk to one of them. All you have to do to gain access to all this help is take the most important first step you'll ever take in your life."

"What's that?"

"Admit you need it." He turned back when he reached the door. "Oh, and you'll want to remember today's date."

"Why?"

"Because your new life begins today. Good luck to you, Brandon."

After Alan left, Brandon got up from the floor and reached for the card he'd left on the bed. Printed on the card was only the name Alan and a phone number. Brandon studied the card for a moment and then tossed it into the trash.

Brandon stood in the circle holding hands with the people on either side of him. He fixated on a spider web in the corner of the room while the others recited the Serenity prayer: "God grant me the serenity to accept the things I cannot change, courage to change the things that I can, and the wisdom to know the difference."

When the twenty or so people took their seats, the group leader, a young guy named Steve, looked around for a volunteer to go first. Brandon kept his eyes down so Steve wouldn't connect with him.

The room reeked of burnt coffee, and the walls were papered with slogans like "Live and Let Live," "Easy Does It," and one Brandon had heard often in the last five days: "One Day at a Time."

"Danielle?" Steve said. "Would you like to share with the group?"

Danielle blushed to her blonde roots and cast her blue eyes downward. Brandon wondered if she'd been a cheerleader thirty or forty pounds ago.

"Um, my name is Danielle, and I'm an alcoholic and an addict." She twisted her hands on her lap.

"Hi, Danielle." The group replied so loudly that they startled Brandon. After five days in bed suffering through detoxification—or the DTs, as it was known here—this was his first time in group, and he had no idea what to expect.

"I, um, I've been clean and sober for twenty-two days now," Danielle said to congratulations from the others. "I know that's not very long, but it's a lifetime to me. I never thought I could go a day without drinking or getting high, so twenty-two days is a big deal. I'm just hoping I can keep it up when I get out of here. It took me the first two weeks I was here to admit my life had become unmanageable. I'm very much afraid of what's ahead for me when I get out of here. I've hurt so many people." One of the other women passed a pack of tissues to Danielle. "I'm so ashamed of the things I've done..."

"You'll have the opportunity to make amends," Steve reminded her, referring to the all-important eighth and ninth steps in the twelve-step program.

"Yes," Danielle said. "I've made my lists. I'm quite certain, though, that my husband won't want to hear my apologies. I had... I'd turned to prostitution to feed my addiction, and I know he'll never forgive me for that. I can't say I blame him."

Brandon held back a gasp. This pretty, ex-cheerleader type was a *hooker*? *Come on! No way.*

"I'm going to do everything I can to stick to the program, to stay sober one day at a time, and to try to get visitation with my kids. That's my goal, and every day I ask God to help me get there."

While the others nodded in agreement, Brandon resisted the urge to roll his eyes. *Yeah, count on God. That'll get you far.*

The group turned next to a middle-aged man with a potbelly and a red face full of broken blood vessels. "I'm Jeff, and I'm an alcoholic."

"Hi, Jeff."

"Today's my last day at group. I'm getting out of here tomorrow. It's time to face the music, as they say. I'll be going to court next week to be sentenced on the embezzlement charges. Fortunately, the bank where I worked asked the court for leniency, but I could still be facing two years in prison."

Dismay rippled through the group.

"The upside is that at least I won't be able to drink while I'm in jail," Jeff said with a grim smile. "I'm ready to face whatever's ahead. This time I'm committed to staying sober, and I've given God the keys to my car. Whatever He has in store for me, I'll willingly take. Anything is better than where I've been, even prison. I just want to thank you all for listening to me all these weeks." His voice caught with emotion. "You've saved my life, and I won't forget you."

"Just keep going to meetings, Jeff," Steve said. "Even if you end up in prison. There're groups everywhere."

Jeff nodded. "I will."

Steve checked his watch before he called on two other people to share their stories. There were similar threads to each of them—they were powerless over alcohol and drugs, their lives were out of control, and once they accepted the presence of a higher power, they found a peace they'd never known before.

All this God talk was a major turnoff to Brandon. *Leave it to Colin the Pope to find the one program on the Cape that was all about God.*

"I want to thank everyone who shared today," Steve said. "We have a few new members with us. Let's welcome Phyllis, Frank, and Brandon."

"Welcome," the group said in unison.

"I'd like to invite any of you new folks to speak, if you wish to," Steve said, scanning the circle to include each of them.

Brandon again looked away. *There's no way I'm talking to these people. They're all drunks and druggies. What the hell do they know about me?*

Phyllis broke under Steve's gaze and began to sob uncontrollably.

Brandon bit back a groan.

"I need a couple of volunteers to stay and talk with Phyllis when she's ready," Steve said, standing to lead the Lord's Prayer. When they were done, they said together, "Keep coming back."

Brandon couldn't get out of there fast enough. He walked through the double doors that led to a patio off the cafeteria. Breathing in the cold winter air, he tried to get his hands to quit shaking by jamming them into the pockets of his worn jeans. They said the shaking was part of the detox process.

"Hey," the other new guy, Frank, said as he stood next to Brandon and lit a cigarette.

Frank offered him one, and Brandon shook his head.

"Some crazy shit in there, huh?" Frank said.

Brandon watched Frank's hand tremble when he brought the cigarette up for a drag. "Yeah," Brandon said. "I couldn't believe it when that chick Danielle said she was a hooker."

"Believe it. I've seen people do everything—and I mean *everything*—for the next fix. This is my third time through this place. I'm hoping the third time's the charm."

Great, Brandon thought. *All this and it doesn't even work.* "What happened before?"

"I failed to commit fully to the program and to my sobriety. This time I'm going to do it, though. My wife said she'd leave me and take my kids if I don't. I can't let that happen."

"Well, good luck. I hope it works."

"What about you?"

"What about me?"

"Still in denial? Most people usually are the first week or two."

Brandon shrugged. "I was never as bad off as those people in there. I get loaded every now and then, but I wasn't like them."

"You're sure of that?"

Brandon watched a group of patients walk along a trail on the back end of the property.

"Let me give you a little piece of advice I wish someone had given me when I was first here," Frank said. "Give in to it, man. Let these people help you. It'll save you a lot of time and your loved ones a lot of suffering. Both times I fell off the wagon harder than the time before. I left some serious carnage in my wake."

"I appreciate the advice, but I'm doing my thirty days and getting the hell out of here. And I won't be back. You can be sure of that."

Frank shook his head. "Keep thinking you don't belong here, and you'll be back. Mark my words." He ground out the cigarette and tossed it into the butt bucket. "See ya around."

"Yeah. See ya."

CHAPTER 2, DAY 6

Colin O'Malley drove his green company pickup truck through the picturesque town of Chatham, Massachusetts, on his way to his parents' home on Shore Road. Once a poor fishing village, Chatham had become one of Cape Cod's most affluent communities.

As on all the trucks belonging to O'Malley & Sons Construction, the company name on the door of Colin's truck was encircled by five gold shamrocks—one for each of the O'Malley siblings.

While driving, Colin replied to several pages from crews in the field on his two-way phone. With his father recovering at home from a mild heart attack and his older brother Brandon in rehab, Colin and his younger brother Declan were running the family's construction business with the help of their sister Erin's husband, Tommy.

Colin pulled into his parents' driveway, and as always, he cringed at the fanciful pink-and-yellow paint job his mother had commissioned several years earlier. What she intended to be a gingerbread house looked more like a three-story cake, as Colin's father often said when his wife wasn't listening.

The phone beeped again as he reached the front door, and Colin took care of two more crises before he went inside.

"Mum?" He removed his Red Sox ball cap and ran a hand through his too-long strawberry blond hair. Like Declan and Erin, he resembled his mother, but the three of them had their father's light blue eyes. With their wavy, dark brown hair, Aidan and Brandon favored their father in his younger years but with their mother's dark green eyes.

Wearing an apron over a wool sweater and jeans, Colleen O'Malley came from the kitchen to greet her third son. "Hello, love," she said, planting a kiss on his cheek. Her thick Irish brogue seemed heavier than usual that day. "Have you had lunch? I made your Da some chicken soup, and there's plenty."

"Sounds good, Mum," Colin said, even though he couldn't really afford the time. But she'd been so sad over everything with Brandon, including the awful fight he'd had with Aidan, and so worried about her husband that Colin wanted to spend some time with her. "Let me just go up and see Da first. He said he needed to see me right away. I don't want him fretting about work when he's supposed to be taking it easy."

"Neither do I, but I don't want you running yourself ragged either, Col." Her green eyes softened with concern. "I know you must be overwhelmed at work without Da and Brandon."

"We're coping," he said as he headed for the stairs. He didn't think she needed to hear that it had been a long time since anyone relied on Brandon at work. "Don't worry, Mum." Colin had vague memories of the house before the second and third floors were added on. His father had worked nights, weekends, and holidays for more than two years to expand the former ranch house to fit his growing family.

Colin knocked on the door to his parents' bedroom.

"Come in," Dennis called in a voice that was already stronger than it had been the day before. He was propped up in bed, resting against a small mountain of pillows. The room was full of the flowers he had received from friends and business associates.

"Hey, Da. How you feeling today?"

"Cooped up and coddled," Dennis grumbled as he ran a hand through his snow-white hair. "Your Mum's making me nuts."

Colin chuckled. "I don't doubt it." He reached into the pocket of his green O'Malley & Sons coat, pulled out a Snicker's bar, and slid it under his father's pillow. "Don't tell."

"Have I mentioned you're my favorite kid?" Dennis asked with a big smile.

Colin snorted. "Yeah, right. I'm your favorite kid at this moment."

"Why would you say that? Have I made you feel that way?"

"What way?" Colin asked, surprised to find sincere concern on his father's usually jovial face.

"That you weren't my favorite. I love you all the same. I hope you know that."

"Of course, I do. Even though I'm the one who never went to college. I'm not a doctor like Aidan was or an athlete like Brandon. I can't sing like Aidan and Dec can, and, of course, Erin gave you five grandchildren. Nope, I'm just good old Colin."

"You're the one I see myself in more than any of the others."

Taken aback, Colin said, "You do?"

Dennis nodded. "From the time you were old enough to walk, all you ever wanted was to come to work with me. You loved everything about the trucks, the yard, the men, the gravel, all of it."

"But you were mad I didn't go to college," Colin reminded him.

"I wanted more for you—for all my kids—than I'd had. I wanted you to go to school before you came into the business so you'd have something to fall back on if you ever needed it."

"You've worked seven days a week for forty years to make sure I'd never need it."

"I'm proud of the business, but nothing makes me prouder than having my sons and son-in-law working with me."

"You're awfully sentimental today, Da. What's gotten into you?"

"The fear of God in the form of a heart attack," Dennis confessed. "Listen, Col…"

Colin sat on the edge of the bed and took his father's work-roughened hand in his. "What is it?"

"I'm not coming back," Dennis said.

"What do you mean?"

"Mum wants me to retire, and I'm going to do it. She's been waiting for me to slow down for a long time, and there're things she wants to do. I owe her some of my time before I'm too old and sick to be any good to her."

Astounded, Colin had no idea what to say. "I figured you'd put up a fight when she was ranting in the hospital about you retiring."

"I'm tired. I think I'm ready."

"I can't imagine you not being at work with us."

"Oh, you don't need me. You all have been running the show for years now. I was just there to keep you guys from bickering."

"You do a lot more than that, and you know it."

"I want you to take over for me, Col."

Shocked, Colin stared at him.

"Someone has to be in charge, and I've decided it should be you."

"But what about Brandon? He'll blow a gasket over this when he gets back."

"He won't be in any shape to take on this kind of responsibility for some time, and even if he was, he's not the one I want. I want you, son."

Colin released a ragged deep breath. He hadn't seen this coming. "I don't know, Da."

"It was Aidan's idea, actually."

"You asked him first, didn't you?" Colin made no attempt to hide his disappointment.

"I only asked him first for one reason—all you boys respect him so much. I knew no one would fight him as the authority figure. You'll have a tougher time with that than he would've had as the oldest."

"Why did he say no?"

"He's getting his life together in Vermont. His restoration business is going well, and he's finally got a new woman in his life. Coming back here wouldn't be good for him after everything he's been through. It was wrong of me to even ask him—for all those reasons and because the most obvious choice was the one who's been here all along."

"Good old Colin."

"Just because you flew under the radar doesn't mean I didn't notice you, son. You've never given me an ounce of grief. And when a man has five high-spirited children, you'd better believe he notices the one who never gives him any trouble."

Colin smiled. "I should've raised some more hell."

"Your brothers and sister did plenty of hell-raising, believe me. So will you do it, Col? Will you take over my business and make it your own with the help of your brothers and Tommy?"

"You really think I can do it?"

"I have no doubt and neither did your brother. 'Take another look at Colin,' Aidan said. 'He's the best of all of us. Sarah always said so.'"

Colin's eyes burned at the unexpected reminder of the beloved sister-in-law he'd lost to cancer ten years earlier. Aidan's wife had died two days after giving birth to the stillborn son they named Colin, after him. "That was nice of him to say."

"He's right and Sarah was, too. You're everything that's good about the O'Malleys, and you've earned the respect of the men. It might take a while to bring your brothers around, but you can do it."

"I'm honored that you have such faith in me. If it'll give you some peace of mind, I'll give it a shot."

The relief showed on his father's face. "Thank you, Col. We'll do this right. I'll talk to Dec and Tommy myself, and then we'll have a meeting with all the guys so they know there's been a changing of the guard. I think it'll be important for them to hear it from the horse's mouth."

"What about Brandon?" Colin asked.

"When he gets home, we need to ease him back in slowly. In fact, I have an idea I wanted to run by you."

"What's that?"

"You know that apartment building I bought on Old Queen Anne Road?"

"Sure. You're just going to flip it, right?"

"I was planning to, but I'm thinking if we put some work into the place, it might make for some nice extra income for Mum and me in our retirement."

"You don't need money, do you, Da?" Colin asked with concern.

"No, no, but the apartment building might be a good project for Brandon, to get him back into things without the responsibility of leading a crew. After what happened that day with the loader, it'll be a while before the men trust him, anyway."

"You're probably right."

Brandon had narrowly missed dropping a load of gravel on two of the men a week before the blowup with Aidan sent him to rehab. Colin knew the workers suspected Brandon was drunk at the time.

"I'll talk to him if he gives you any trouble," Dennis said.

"No, I'll deal with him at work. If I'm going to do this, I have to do it myself. I can't be bringing you in every five minutes to bail me out."

Dennis smiled.

"What?"

"I knew you could do it, but now I'm sure."

"How do you think he's doing?"

Dennis shook his head. "Hard telling. I'm sure he's fighting with everyone."

"No doubt. That's what he does best. I sure hope it works, though. I don't know what we'll do if it doesn't."

"Mum and I are going for the first visiting day next week. We'll see then how he's doing."

"We did the right thing, didn't we?"

"We did, son. We absolutely did, and we should've done it a long time ago. I can't believe what he did to Clare," Dennis said, referring to Aidan's girlfriend.

"Did you write your letter?"

Dennis nodded. "How about you?"

"Yeah. Not the easiest thing I've ever done, but the truth hurts. I wonder if he'll ever speak to any of us again after he reads them."

"Hopefully, he'll hear what we have to say and take the treatment seriously."

"I hope so. Well, Mum said there's soup downstairs, and I'm starving. Call me if you need anything?"

"I will. You, too."

Colin grinned. "Oh, you'll be hearing from me, don't worry."

"I'm counting on it. I love you, son. I'm proud of you, and I know you're going to do a terrific job."

Overwhelmed, Colin leaned in to kiss his father's cheek. "Take care, Da."

"Wow, that was good, Mum," Colin said as he finished his soup and reached across the table for her hand. "Are you doing all right?"

Colleen shrugged. "I guess. I haven't been sleeping too well. I just wish we knew how Brandon is coping. I picture him all alone in that place…" She looked away from him as she struggled for composure.

Colin moved to sit closer to her. "We had to do something." He put his arm around her. "We're lucky Aidan didn't kill him."

"I know." Colleen wiped her face on her apron and leaned into her son's embrace. "I just can't figure out how this happened. I go over it and over it in my mind. I know he always drank, but how did it get this bad? How did it get to the point where he'd do what he did to a woman in this house and then not even remember it?"

"It's been this bad for a long time. We just covered for him and tried to keep him out of trouble."

"What else were we supposed to do?"

"Maybe we shouldn't have tried so hard. Maybe then he would've reached this point sooner, without practically attacking Clare."

"But he could've done something even worse."

"I've been doing some reading about it. Alcoholism is considered a disease—like diabetes or cancer. They say it's not just a disease of the body but a relationship disease, too. What we've been doing by cleaning up his messes has enabled him to continue drinking without worrying about the consequences. We can't do that anymore."

Colleen sighed. "No, we can't."

"I've been thinking about going to an Al-Anon meeting. They help people like us who have someone in their family struggling with alcohol. Why don't you come with me?"

"Oh, Col, I can't imagine talking about our family's troubles in public."

"You don't have to say anything, and if you do, it's completely anonymous. No one would ever talk about what happens there. It might help us to help him, and to feel better ourselves, too."

"I don't know..."

Colin kissed her cheek and stood up. "Think about it. You don't have to decide anything now. Do you mind if I go to a meeting? I feel like I need to do *something*."

"Of course I don't mind. I appreciate all you've done to help your brother. I know you've probably had it with him, yet you still help him."

"He's my brother," Colin said with a shrug.

"You're a good boy."

Colin laughed. "I'm thirty-six years old, Mum."

"And you're still my boy," she said with a spark of feistiness that was much more like her than the sadness.

"I've got to get back to work. Thanks for lunch."

"Thank you for what you're doing for your Da."

"You know about that, huh?"

She held his coat for him. "There's not much that goes on around here that I don't know about. You'll be just fine, Col." She zipped his coat for him like she had when he was five. "Follow your heart, be fair, and do the right thing. The rest will fall into place."

"I hope you're right."

"I'm always right."

He smiled. Truer words were never spoken. "Call me if you need anything."

"I will."

"Think about coming to Al-Anon with me."

"I'll do that, too."

CHAPTER 3, DAY 8

Brandon sat across from his counselor, Dr. Sondra Walker-Smith, and waited for her to say something. This was his third session with her in as many days, and the other times she'd led him through a basic discussion of his life, his family, and his work. This time, though, she seemed to be waiting for him, and he squirmed in his seat under the heat of her scrutiny. Her office was the nicest room he'd seen yet at the austere facility.

"Brandon?" she said, her inquisitive pale blue eyes trained on him.

Dr. "Call me Sondra" Walker-Smith was a babe. The big diamond she wore on her left hand said she was someone else's babe, but that didn't stop Brandon from feasting his eyes on the best-looking woman he'd seen in longer than he could remember.

"What?" he asked sullenly. Even for her, he couldn't pretend he was happy to be there.

"Nothing to say today?"

He shrugged.

"How's group going?" she asked with a sigh.

"Bunch of cry-babies. I've never seen so many tears in my life. It's pathetic."

"Most people think crying is cathartic. Don't you cry?"

"No."

"Never?"

"Not that I can recall."

"Surely there had to have been *something* in your life that's moved you tears."

Just one thing, but you're not getting that out of me. No way. "No."

"Hmm." Sondra stroked her chin and sized him up, her gaze full of wisdom, as if she had all the answers and wasn't about to share them with him. "You've told me about your family, but you haven't spoken of any other relationships. Have you ever been in love?"

Brandon hadn't seen that one coming and kept his face neutral to hide the burst of pain that exploded inside of him. He never had learned how to brace himself for it. More than any time in the last week, he wished for a drink—something—*anything*—to dull the pain.

"Brandon?"

"No. I've never been in love." His expression dared her to challenge him.

"You know, if you lie to me, you lie to yourself."

"I'm not lying."

"You're thirty-eight years old, a reasonably good-looking guy, and you're going to tell me you've never had feelings for a woman? Or a man?"

He laughed. "I'm not gay, so you can cross that off your list of issues to explore with me."

She smiled. "There's no list."

"So I'm only reasonably good-looking? That's somewhat disappointing."

"He has a sense of humor. Another facet is revealed."

"I'm very complicated," he said with mock seriousness, enjoying the banter despite his desire to stay detached. He'd forgotten how much fun it could be to go a few rounds with a hot-looking woman.

"Part of our treatment program involves our patients' families," Sondra said, changing gears on him. "People come to us at different points in their addictions. Some are so weary and so tired of being ruled by their demons that they immerse themselves in the program and commit fully to their recovery. Others, for whatever reason, resist. They're not ready to admit they're powerless over drugs or alcohol, they don't see their lives as unmanageable, they don't think they need help. They see themselves as victims of a conspiracy by disgruntled family members."

"Gee, which group do I fall into?" Brandon asked with a smirk.

"I think you know."

"So are those of us in Group B untreatable?"

"Far from it. They just take a little more convincing." She got up to retrieve a pile of paper from her desk.

"What's that?"

"Letters."

"From?"

She sat back down across from him. "Your family."

Something that felt an awful lot like fear twisted in Brandon's gut. He wanted to get up and leave but was frozen to his chair. "I don't want to read them."

"Then I'll read them to you. Where shall I start? I have letters from your brothers, your sister, your parents, and your ex-girlfriend Valerie."

Brandon exhaled a long deep breath and finally managed to push himself out of the chair. He had reached the door before she spoke.

"Brandon."

He turned around and was stunned to find steel in her usually compassionate eyes.

"Sit down."

He held her gaze until he realized she wasn't going to let him escape. She wasn't his mother, his father, his sister, or any of his brothers. She didn't love him and wouldn't make excuses for him. This woman had nothing to lose by playing hardball with him. When he couldn't bear the disappointment on her pretty face any longer, he returned to his seat.

"We'll start with your brother Declan. What's the age difference between you?"

Brandon cleared his throat and took another deep breath in an attempt to slow his racing heart. "He's three years younger than me."

"Are you close?"

Brandon shrugged. "I guess."

"Maybe you used to be?"

He looked down to study one of the old Nikes at the end of his long, denim-clad leg.

"Dear Brand," she began. "I hope you're doing all right in there. Colin said it's a nice place, and I hope they can help you. When you get back, I want us to go fishing like we used to. Remember how we'd go out all afternoon and then fry what we caught on the beach? Those were some of my favorite times with you. Why did we stop going fishing?

"When we were kids, everyone thought of me and Colin as a pair and you and Aidan as a pair. I guess that was because you and Aid came first and looked alike, and I looked like Col. But to tell you the truth, Brand, I always liked being with you the best. I used to love going to your swim meets when you would totally kick ass, and I'd get to say: that's my brother! You tried to teach me how to swim like you did, but I wasn't born with whatever it was you had. None of us were.

"I've been thinking a lot about this drinking thing of yours, trying to figure out when it got so out of control. I can't really decide when it happened. All I know is when I watched you almost drop that load of gravel on Simms and Lewis (and couldn't get there in time to stop it), I knew we couldn't ignore it any longer. Then Da had the heart attack, and the whole thing with Clare happened. Well, I guess Aidan and Colin saw to it that you got the help you need. Please get better, Brand. I miss my fishing buddy. I love you. Dec."

Brandon sat riveted to his seat and struggled against the tears he claimed to never shed.

"This one's from Valerie." Sondra moved on without skipping a beat. "Dear Brandon, When Colin called to tell me you were in treatment I was so relieved I cried all day. Even though I'm happily married now with a little girl and another baby on the way, I still think of you almost every day. I loved you so very much, and leaving you was the hardest thing I've ever done. But after five years of hoping you'd one day love me even half as much as I loved you, I couldn't put your needs ahead of my own any longer.

"You always kept me at arm's length, and no matter what I did, I could never penetrate that wall you keep around your heart. The four years we lived together were some of the happiest and most difficult years of my life. When I think of you, I remember the nights we'd make dinner and then snuggle together on the sofa to watch a movie. I don't think I've ever been as content as I was at those times. But then you'd disappear for two or three days, and I'd be terrified that something had happened to you. I reached a point where I couldn't live like that anymore, but that doesn't mean I stopped loving you. I hope you know that.

"Somewhere deep inside of you, there's a source of pain that keeps you from giving yourself fully to another person. I think you drink to dull the pain so you can pretend to live a real life. You know as well as I do that it doesn't work. Do yourself and everyone who loves you a big favor, Brandon. Take down that wall around your heart, and get the help you need. Find the Brandon we all know is in there and let him out. I will love you and miss you for the rest of my life. And I'll pray you get well and find it in you to give away the love I know you have inside of you. I'll always be sorry you couldn't give it to me. Take good care of yourself. Love, Valerie."

Tears ran unchecked down Brandon's cheeks, but he didn't notice as he stared out the window.

Sondra continued with an almost relentless determination. "This one's from Aidan. Dear Brandon," she read. "This isn't a good time for me to be writing to you, but Colin said it's part of the program, so here goes. I'm so furious with you that I seriously wonder if I'll ever be able to forgive you for what you did to Clare.

"I haven't told any of you the whole story of what she'd been through before I met her. I've already told you and Colin that she was raped. What I didn't mention is the guy who did it said if she told anyone he'd kill one of her kids. She has three beautiful daughters, and keeping them safe was her only concern, so she told no one. Not even her husband. She was hit by a car a few months later. Her daughters said she let the car hit her on purpose, but no one could understand why she would do that. She was in a coma for three years after the accident. A few months after she recovered, she realized she'd let the car hit her because she couldn't live anymore with what'd happened.

"It hasn't even been a year since she recovered to find her husband of twenty years had fallen in love with someone else and was expecting twins with her. Clare came to Vermont looking for some peace after the hell she'd been through. That's when I was lucky enough to meet her. She hasn't even been able to work up the courage to tell me all this yet. Her daughters told me. I'm hoping one day she'll be able to tell me herself, but even if she never does, I don't care.

"I love her. For the first time since I lost Sarah and the baby, I've found someone who fills the empty spaces inside of me. For ten long years, I walked around like a zombie, and the day I met Clare, I felt better. It happened that fast. I wanted you to know, really know, the woman you backed into a corner and terrorized in Mum's kitchen.

"You've done damage, Brandon, real, serious damage—to her and to your relationship with me. Not that you probably care about the latter. We haven't exactly been close since we were kids, have we? I don't remember when it happened, but you suddenly stopped wanting to hang out with me the way we used to. Why was that? What happened to the closeness we'd always shared? I've never understood it, but now I'm not even sure I care. I do hope you get better, though, because I can't stand the way your illness (and it *is* an illness—I believe that) affects Mum and Da. Think about them and accept the help I'm sure you're resisting. Do it for them. Aidan."

Sondra folded Aidan's letter and put it at the bottom of the pile. "How do you feel?"

Aidan's letter had dried up Brandon's tears. "Great."

"It's a lot to swallow all at once."

"You're on a roll. Why stop now?"

"Let's talk about some of what they said. I think we could spend a whole session on Aidan's letter, but first I want to know if Valerie is right. Do you have a secret source of pain inside of you?"

He'd carried the pain around for so long he didn't even recognize it as pain anymore. It was just a part of him. "I don't know what she's talking about."

"You didn't love her?"

"Apparently not."

"How did you feel when she left?"

Should I admit she was gone for two weeks before I even noticed? "Things between us had gone downhill in the months before she left. I wasn't surprised when she finally moved out."

"You didn't care at all that your girlfriend of five years had left you?"

Brandon decided to be honest for once. "No. I didn't care. I liked her—a lot. But I never loved her."

"Did you tell her you did?"

"No. I've never said that to anyone, because I've never felt it. I don't believe in saying something I don't feel."

"She must've loved you an awful lot to stay with you for five years without ever hearing the words in return."

He shrugged with indifference.

"Were you ever sorry you couldn't love her?"

"All the time. She's a terrific girl, and she deserved better than what she got from me. I'm glad she found a nice guy to marry and have kids with. She always wanted kids."

"Do you?"

"What?"

"Want kids?"

"Not really. I'm not much of a kid person. I have three nieces and two nephews, but they don't like me very much."

Sondra shifted through the pile of letters. "Want to know why? I have your sister Erin's letter right here."

Brandon was hit with another sharp stab of fear.

"Hi Brandon," Sondra read from Erin's letter. "How are you holding up? I hate that we can't have any contact with you for the first ten days. We all hope you're hanging in there—and getting better. Oh, Brand, how did this happen? It makes me so sad to see what a mess you've made of your once-promising life. You had it all—athletic ability the rest of us could only marvel at, great grades, and every girl in school falling at your feet. Where has that boy gone?

"You're so angry all the time that my kids are afraid of you. I know that's a terrible thing to tell you, but you need to know it. You make them nervous, so I keep them away from you. On the other hand, Colin and Dec babysit for me all the time. Did you know that?

"I've been blessed with a wonderful husband (who truly likes you, by the way) and five amazing kids you barely know. My hope for you is that you find a way to live without alcohol so I can bring you into my children's lives. I want it for you as much as I want it for them. I want my big brother back. I love you with all my heart. Erin."

Brandon leaned forward, rested his elbows on his knees, and shook with sobs.

"I'll let you take your parents' letters for when you're ready to read them, but there's one more I want you to hear now."

He wiped his face. "I've heard enough. If you want me to admit I'm an alcoholic, then I'll do it. I won't argue anymore. That's what you want to hear, right?"

"It's not about what I want, Brandon. It's about you finding the truth within yourself. It's about step one, admitting you're powerless over alcohol and your life has become unmanageable, and step four: the fearless and searching personal inventory. You need to hear this last letter. It's from Colin."

Brandon kept his elbows on his knees and his head bent.

"Dear Brandon, I'll cut to the chase and keep this short and sweet. Da's been paying your mortgage for the last year because you never got around to it, and the bank was going to take your house. Mum has cleaned your house for years and does your laundry. If you're wondering where all your secret stashes of booze disappear to, she can tell you.

"I've paid your bar tab more times than I can count and bailed you out of jail twice—once for a fight you had at Louie's and another time for public drunkenness. Da made the charges go away both times, so you didn't even know about them. Declan has taken it upon himself to cover your ass at work—so often that you would've been fired a long time ago if you didn't work for your father. So you see, I blame us as much as I blame you. We've created an environment where it's possible for you to be a drunk—a falling-down, irresponsible, dangerous drunk.

"But we're done now. You're going to have to keep your life straight on your own from now on. While you're in there, you might want to get sober so you can handle the responsibilities of an adult life. I love you as much as I love anyone in this world, and there's nothing I wouldn't do for you. But our efforts to clean up your messes have helped you to create an even bigger one. You can lean on me, you can call on me, and you can count on me. Always. As long as you stay sober. Colin."

Brandon was reeling. How could all of this have happened without him knowing about it? How much money did he owe his father? Thousands. How much did he owe Colin for posting his bail? *Twice?* He'd been arrested *twice? Jesus Christ,* Brandon thought as he frantically tried to process Colin's letter. He had no memory of it—any of it. How many days, weeks, *months* of his life had been lost to alcohol-fueled blackouts? Nothing in the other letters had hit him quite as hard as Colin's cold assessment of how his drinking had affected the rest of his family. He looked up to find Sondra waiting for him.

"Are you all right?"

He shook his head. "No," he said softly. "No, I'm not all right."

"We can fix it, Brandon. We can help you, but first you have to help yourself. You have to take the first step."

Understanding settled over him like a warm blanket, giving him the courage he needed. "My name is Brandon," he said haltingly. "And I'm an alcoholic."

Sondra reached out to take his hand. "Hi, Brandon."

CHAPTER 4, DAY 10

Brandon lay in his narrow bed, listening to the birds chirping outside his window. After ten nearly sleepless nights, he knew the chirping began about an hour before sunrise. Turning on his side, he watched his small piece of sky turn pink. On the bedside table, the letters from his parents waited for him to work up the nerve to read them after the emotional firestorm created by the others. His parents were coming to visit today, and he figured he should read their letters before they arrived.

He flipped on the bedside light and sat up. In the four days since his family's words led him to acknowledge his alcoholism, Brandon had wept more than in the previous thirty-eight years combined. He hadn't yet shared anything with the group, but their stories had taken on new meaning. One touching, heartbreaking tale followed another as they confessed their utter failure to control their addictions. They'd made him into one of the pathetic bawlers he'd once scorned. He felt raw and unprotected from what he expected to find in his parents' letters.

Sure enough, his eyes burned at the sight of his mother's familiar handwriting. "Hello, my love. I'm sure you've gotten an earful from everyone else, and you're no doubt expecting one from me, too. I'm going to disappoint you there. All I'm going to say is I love you, I hurt for you, and I miss the Brandon I used to know. I want him back. No matter what you do or don't do, though, I'll love you until I draw my last breath on this earth. Mum."

Brandon brushed a hand across a cheek wet with tears. His fierce, uncompromising mother had given him exactly what he needed, despite the terrible thing he'd done to Aidan's girlfriend. Knowing he'd caused his mother such heartache hurt him more than almost anything ever had.

After he absorbed her simple message, he forced himself to read his father's letter.

"Son, I want you to know I blame myself. I set a terrible example for you, your brothers, and your sister. You saw me drinking every day of your lives growing up. A few beers after a long day of work, it was just what I did. I showed you how to be this person you've grown up to be, and I'm sorry. I feel like I have failed you.

"You're a good man, Brandon, a strong man, and until these last couple of years, I always knew I could count on you. When you finished college, you came home with your degree, just like you promised me you would. You knew I was counting on you to bring your education into the business, and you didn't let me down. That I could've let you down haunts me.

"The proudest thing in my life is having you and your brothers working by my side in the business I built from nothing. We've made a hell of a go of it, haven't we, son? The business means nothing to me, though, when stacked up against your mum and you kids. You're the world to me, all of you, and the only thing I've ever really cared about was keeping my family safe and happy. They say there are times that try a man's soul. Watching your brother lose his wife and son was one of those times. Watching you struggle with this beast I introduced you to is definitely another.

"You're my son, and I love you. There's nothing I wouldn't do to help you. We're going to beat this thing, Brand. We're going to get through this like we've gotten through everything else. Together. Love, Da."

Brandon rolled his face into his pillow and wept. His poor, sweet father blamed himself. The tsunami of pain paralyzed him, and there was nothing, absolutely nothing, available to dull it.

***

Brandon showered and shaved in preparation for his parents' visit. In the mirror, he saw a face he barely recognized. Bags under his eyes and a sallow skin tone made him look ten years older than his thirty-eight years. The facility physician reported that Brandon's liver was functioning at only 80 percent, and his blood pressure was elevated to the point of concern. The doctor had assured him that both conditions would right themselves if he stayed sober. The athlete in Brandon was disgusted by what he'd let happen to his once finely tuned body. He could tell from his baggy jeans that he'd already lost about ten pounds since he entered treatment, and he'd sent word to his mother to bring running clothes from his house so he could start working out again.

The intercom buzzed, and he pulled on his shirt as he went to answer it. "Yes?"

"Brandon, your parents are here."

"Thanks, I'll be right down." He buttoned his shirt and checked his appearance in the mirror one last time. "Well, here goes," he said to his reflection. Someday he hoped he would recognize that face again.

Brandon went down the two flights of stairs to the small lounge off the lobby. Another of the inmates—as they jokingly referred to themselves—visited with his family in the far corner of the room.

Colleen and Dennis stood when they saw him coming, and his mother held out her arms to him.

Brandon battled a huge lump in his throat as his mother clung to him. When he finally pulled back from her, she reached up to caress his face.

"How are you, love? You've lost some weight."

"I'm okay." Brandon reached for his father. "You look good, Da. Are you feeling all right?"

"Much better," Dennis said as he hugged his son. "The doctor says I'll live forever."

"That's a relief." Brandon gestured for them to have a seat on the small sofa and took a chair across from them. "Thanks for bringing my running stuff, Mum. How is everyone?"

"Good." The crossing and uncrossing of her fingers told Brandon she was nervous. "They're anxious to hear how you're doing."

"I feel bad you're all so worried about me. Not that I haven't given you good reason to be."

Colleen reached for his hand. "You've been sick, and you're getting better. That's all that matters."

"I'm trying to get better. They've helped me see that, well…"

"What, love?" Colleen asked.

"I'm an alcoholic, Mum. I can't drink the way other people do, because I can't stop myself once I get going. I'm so ashamed of everything I've done," he whispered. "I'm so sorry."

Colleen's blinked back tears as she reached for him again. "It's all in the past now. Let's concentrate on getting you better and out of here, okay?"

Brandon pulled back with great reluctance. He would love nothing more than to let his mother try to make it all go away. "It's not that simple, Mum. I've done things that have hurt people. Bad things. I can't just pretend none of it happened. A big part of my recovery will be making amends to them, even to you."

"Don't be too hard on yourself, son," Dennis said gruffly. "Everyone's pulling for you."

"The people here talk about the rest of our lives being a journey. I'm just at the very beginning."

"Then that's where we are, too," Dennis said. "We're right there with you, Brand, every step of the way."

"Thanks, Da." Brandon appreciated their support but knew he couldn't rely on it the way he had in the past. He had to do this on his own.

"Are they treating you all right in here?" Colleen asked, looking around suspiciously. "Is the food okay?"

"It's fine. No complaints. Listen, um, have you talked to Aidan?"

"He called the other night to say they were back in Vermont," Colleen said. "I guess they went to Clare's house in Rhode Island for a couple of days after they left Chatham."

"Did he say anything? About her? About what happened?"

"No, love," Colleen said. "He didn't mention it."

Brandon shook his head. "I just can't believe what I did to her. He'll never forgive me."

"He will," Colleen said. "Give it some time."

"Do you think it's the real deal with them?" Brandon asked.

"I do," Colleen said with a smile. "I really do. It's high time your brother had some happiness, don't you think?"

Brandon hated the flash of anger that question sent through him, but he hid it from his parents the way he had for most of his life. "Of course." He checked his watch. "I hate to say it, but I have to go to my group session at three."

Colleen and Dennis stood up to hug him. Colleen's eyes were bright with tears when she pulled back. She reached up to cradle his face. "We love you, Brandon."

Brandon felt the burn of tears in his own eyes. "I love you, too, both of you. I appreciate you guys standing by me even though I don't deserve it."

"You're stuck with us," Dennis said, putting an arm around his wife to guide her from the room.

Brandon saw them out the main door and then went back to work.

"Let's talk about your brother Aidan," Sondra said a week after Brandon first acknowledged his alcoholism to her. He'd been unable thus far to speak to the group but knew his day was coming. No one escaped.

Brandon groaned. "Do we have to?"

"What's the objection?"

He kept his expression neutral. *Oh, I have objections, all right.* "No objection. What do you want to know?"

"He's older than you?"

"Just over a year."

"His letter said you were close growing up but not so much anymore."

"He lives in Vermont. I live in Chatham. We don't see each other very often."

"How long has he lived in Vermont?"

Brandon had to think about that. "About ten years or so. He moved up there after his wife died."

"What happened to his wife?"

Brandon took a deep breath and reminded himself to be careful. "Sarah had breast cancer," he said softly. "She died when she was twenty-nine, two days after their son was stillborn."

"That must've been a terrible time for your whole family."

"I guess so." When he noticed her raised eyebrow, he added, "It was."

"Did you like her?"

"Sure. I'd known her since I was eleven. Her family came out to Chatham from Boston every summer. It was really hard on Aidan when she died, especially because she put off treatment to save the baby. Then he died, too."

"This gives Aidan's letter new meaning."

"Yeah, he's seriously pissed with me. He was alone for years until he finally met this new woman, and after what I did to her, he's probably all set with me. Whatever. As long as Aidan's happy, everyone else is, too."

"Why do you say that?"

"No reason in particular. It's just true."

"Did your parents treat him differently than they treated you?"

"No. Not really."

She sighed. "Brandon, I can't help you if you don't level with me. Your whole demeanor changes when you talk about Aidan. Do you realize that? Are you angry with him for some reason?"

"He's angry with me, remember?"

She stood up. "When you're ready to talk about this, you know where to find me."

"You're kicking me out?" Brandon asked, incredulous. She'd been a relentless pain in the ass, getting him to talk about stuff he never talked about. And now she was kicking him out?

"We're getting nowhere," she said with a wave of her hand. "So we'll try again another day." She sat down at her desk and busied herself with some paperwork.

Brandon was stunned by her dismissal. After a long period of quiet, he finally said, "Yes."

She didn't look up from what she was doing. "Yes, what?"

Brandon gritted his teeth. "I'm angry with him."

"Why?"

"He got to leave."

Sondra put down her pen and glanced at him. "What do you mean?"

"All our lives it was made clear to us that our father expected us to join him in the family business. He wanted us to go to college, but we had to come home after. Sarah's father was a big doctor in Boston. He convinced Aidan to give medical school a try, and like everything else Aidan did, he was hugely successful at it. He was well on his way to becoming a cardiologist like his father-in-law."

Sondra came around her desk and returned to her usual chair. "What happened?"

"After Sarah and the baby died, he couldn't stand to be in a hospital anymore, so he quit his residency. He has a restoration and construction business in Vermont now."

"So why are you angry with him?"

"Because!" Brandon exploded. "He got to do what he *wanted* to do! He was almost a doctor when he quit. He had everything he wanted, and he *quit*! And then he didn't even come back home to work with us. He went somewhere else. It must be nice to be him." Brandon slumped in his chair, exhausted by the outburst.

"What did you want to do, Brandon?"

Brandon's heart began to race, adrenaline cruising through him. These were big confessions. "I wanted to be a Navy SEAL," he said for the first time. Ever. No one else in the world knew that.

Sondra waited for him to go on.

"I was a great swimmer. It was the one thing I was better at than anyone else. When I was a junior in high school, my coach, Mr. Coughlin, told me there was a Navy recruiter coming. He told me about the SEALs, but I didn't even know what it was. I went to the library and looked it up. And then I was hooked. It was all I thought about."

"What did you do about it?"

"Nothing. When Aidan went to Yale as a pre-med major, I realized he'd been given the one and only pass. He wouldn't be coming back to the business. There was no pass left for me."

"You couldn't have known that for sure."

"I knew it. The only reason my father let Aidan go was because he had three other sons coming up behind him. The 'Sons' portion of O'Malley & Sons Construction was going to be me, Colin, and Declan."

"Brandon, you had two other brothers. Why didn't you ever say anything to your father? Why didn't you tell him what you wanted?"

"Because," he said softly, "as proud as my father was to have a son who was a doctor, I could always see a hint of disappointment that his son had chosen to follow in his father-in-law's footsteps rather than his own father's. I didn't want to let him down, too."

"So you let yourself down. How long ago was all of this?"

"Oh, jeez, I don't know. If Aidan's almost forty, he went to college twenty-two years ago, I guess."

"Twenty-two years. That's an awful long time to carry around that kind of anger." She paused, tapping her pen on her chin. "I'm curious, though."

"About what?"

"Why was your anger directed at Aidan rather than your father? He's the one who had all these supposed expectations for you, not Aidan."

"Aidan always got whatever he wanted." Brandon knew he sounded like a petulant child, but he didn't care.

"What else did he get? Besides this?"

Brandon shook his head. He couldn't say it.

"Before our next session, I want you to read about resentment in the *Big Book*," she said, referring to the Alcoholics Anonymous program bible. "More than almost anything else, resentment is the enemy of the alcoholic." She picked up her dog-eared copy of the book and flipped it open to a marked page. "With the alcoholic, whose hope is the maintenance and growth of a spiritual experience, this business of resentment is infinitely grave," she read. "We found that it is fatal. For when harboring such feelings we shut ourselves off from the sunlight of the Spirit. The insanity of alcohol returns and we drink again. And with us, to drink is to die." She put down the book. "Chapter Five."

Brandon got up, moved to the door, and stood there for a moment with his forehead resting against the cool, dark wood. He was tired—so tired of holding on to the secrets and the pain that he dragged around with him like a cement block attached to his ankle. "Sarah," Brandon said softly. "He got Sarah." With that, he opened the door and walked out.

Chapter 5, Day 18

Once his heart and lungs stopped protesting Brandon settled into an easy—albeit rusty—stride along the well-traveled path. "I was glad to hear you're a runner," he said between breaths. "But I'm slowing you down."

"You'll probably leave me in your dust when you get back in shape," Alan replied, adjusting his stride to match Brandon's.

"I had to get your number from the office," Brandon confessed. "I threw your card away."

"That's all right. All we can do is offer help. It's far more important that you ask for it."

"The people here are getting me to say and do all kinds of things I never imagined I'd say or do."

Alan chuckled. "They find a way to crack even the toughest nuts."

Brandon laughed. "Bad pun."

"Feels good, doesn't it? To unload that heavy stuff?"

"Yeah, but some of it's pretty bad."

"I imagine it is, or you wouldn't be here."

At the three-mile mark, Brandon slowed to a walk and wiped the sweat from his brow. His heavy breathing left a cloud in the frosty air.

Alan fell in beside him.

"I've told Sondra some stuff that no one—and I mean *no one*—knows about me," Brandon said.

"She has a way of getting people to talk. She's famous for that around here."

"Let me guess: she gets the toughest nuts?"

"You got it."

"I can see why."

"What made you want to call me, Brandon?"

"I've been reading a lot about AA. I'm surprised by how interesting the *Big Book* is."

"The one thing I still remember from the first time I read it is the analogy about alcoholics who think they can go back to drinking. The book says it's like someone who loses their legs thinking they're going to grow back. I've never forgotten that. It's compelling stuff, isn't it?"

"It sure is, and with millions of people saying it saved their lives, it's pretty clear it works, too."

"It only works for those of us who commit ourselves to it completely. I've seen a lot of people with good intentions go back to their old lives because they had some misguided idea that they were different from the rest of us or they could somehow control it. They thought their legs would grow back."

"I don't want to be one of the failures," Brandon said. "I've had enough of that. I want to do this right."

"I'm glad to hear you say that. You've come a long way from the day we first met."

"I know a lot more now about how I hurt my family and other people in my life. I can't do that anymore."

Alan stopped walking and turned to him. "That's very admirable, Brandon, and you're well on your way to achieving steps eight and nine by realizing it. But you can't do this for your family. You have to do it for you. First and foremost, it has to be for you."

"I want to stay sober for me, too. I do. I can't believe what I've let happen to my body. I was an All-American swimmer at Notre Dame. Back then, I ran ten miles a day without breaking a sweat. Now, I'm almost dead after three."

"You're getting old," Alan chuckled. "It happens to the best of us."

"I'm thirty-eight years old, Alan, and I have almost nothing to show for it but a beer belly and a bad liver."

"You're on the right path. I think you're doing great. You look a lot better, too. I almost didn't recognize you without the shiners and the busted-up face. What matters most, though, is your attitude has improved dramatically."

"I'm afraid I won't be able to stick to the program when I get out of here," Brandon confessed.

"Why?"

Brandon kicked at a grungy pile of old snow. "All the God stuff is a problem for me. A big problem."

"How come?"

"I don't have a good track record with God."

"He's let you down?"

"I guess you could say that. My parents are as Irish-Catholic as it gets, and we were force-fed religion as kids: Catholic school, altar service, sacraments, the whole nine yards. I haven't set foot inside a church since I was old enough to decide for myself."

"AA doesn't expect you to go back to the church. The program only suggests you open yourself up to the *idea* of a higher power, something greater than yourself. For some in the Fellowship, that higher power is AA itself. You have to find your own higher power and give over control of your life, because you've found when you try to go it alone, it doesn't work."

"Were you like me? Did you find all this talk of spirituality to be off-putting?"

"At first. But like many of the people you'll meet through the Fellowship, I've found all kinds of reasons to believe. I've seen it work. For me, God is the person running my show now, and I know He's got my back. It's one less thing for me to worry about every day."

"Did you have one of those 'ah-ha' moments people talk about when you were able to embrace this spirituality stuff?"

"I did. When my son was six, he had meningitis and almost died. My ex-wife called my mother to tell her she needed to come to the hospital right away. I'd been sober about three years then, and when my mother called to tell me, my first impulse was to find a bar. But instead, I dropped to my knees and asked God to save my child. Since I wouldn't have been welcome at the hospital, it was the only thing I could do. I prayed for hours, all night, in fact. The next morning, my mother called to say his fever had broken, and he was expected to survive. I guess you could say I never questioned God's existence again."

"That's amazing."

"It's really quite simple. I had a choice that night: find a bottle or put God in charge. There have been many other times since then when I've had the same choice, and I've never regretted choosing God over alcohol."

Brandon glanced up at the gray sky where puffy white clouds signaled the probability of snow. "I used to pray to God that my brother would die."

"I take it He didn't answer you?"

"No. Instead He took my brother's wife, the girl we both loved. Until I came here, no one has ever known that I loved her, too."

"So you blame yourself. You think because you prayed for your brother to die that God played some sort of dirty trick on you?"

"Something like that."

"God doesn't work that way. If He did, why would He allow murderers and rapists to continue walking the earth? Why wouldn't He punish them if He were going to punish you like that?"

Brandon thought about that. He didn't want to admit it made sense. If he did, he'd have to let go of some of the things he had believed for most of his life.

"Do you still want your brother to die?"

After a long moment of silence, Brandon said, "No."

When they reached the end of the trail, they sat on a bench that overlooked the ocean.

"If your brother had died when you asked God to take him, how do you think you would've felt?"

"I don't know. I've hated him for so long I don't remember what it's like *not* to hate him."

"I'm wondering if maybe you really hated yourself, and he was just convenient."

Startled, Brandon looked at him. "Why do you say that?"

"What did he do to make you hate him?"

"I met her first." Brandon drifted a million miles away as he remembered that fateful day. "Aidan and I were inseparable back then. We were playing football on the beach. I dove for the ball and landed face-first in the sand right at her feet. I looked up, and it was like a punch to the gut. I was eleven years old and still thought girls were gross, but in that moment, it was like all the mysteries of the universe had been solved, and I finally got what the hoopla was about. I didn't recognize it then for what it was, but as the years passed and the feelings I had for her became more intense, I came to understand what happened to me that day on the beach."

Alan stayed quiet and let Brandon talk.

"She laughed because I had sand all over my face, and then she bent down to pick up the football. I must've looked like an idiot because I just froze. She handed me the towel she had around her neck, and I stood up to use it to brush the sand off my face. She said her name was Sarah Sweeny. I think I probably told her my name, but I don't really remember what I said. Even at twelve, she was gorgeous, with long dark hair and these soft brown eyes that always twinkled like she'd just heard a good joke. I talked to her for a few minutes before Aidan came to find me. She took one look at him, and she never saw me again. I just disappeared. That night was the first of many nights I asked God to make Aidan go away."

"Did you think she'd turn to you if he was gone?"

"I looked just like him back then. I guess I still do in a lot of ways. People used to ask our mother if we were twins when we were younger, so I never got what was so special about him that she just stopped seeing me when he came along."

"Isn't that one of life's great mysteries? Why are we attracted to one person but not another? Brandon, she chose him. That wasn't his fault. And it probably wasn't just because of the way he looked."

"If he hadn't been there, maybe she would've chosen me. Maybe my whole life would've turned out differently."

"You still would've lost her," Alan reminded him.

"But at least I would've *had* her. She's the only girl I've ever loved. How pathetic is that? I had her for ten minutes before he showed up and ruined everything. Then I had to spend the next sixteen years watching them be madly in love. Every summer, she would come back to Chatham, and they'd pick right up again. They went to college together, got married, got pregnant. He got to have *everything* with her. I just got to wear a tuxedo in their wedding and had to act like I gave a fuck."

"He also had to lose her. How did you feel when that happened?"

"Like the world had ended," Brandon said simply. "It was fast. She was dead six months after she was diagnosed. By then she couldn't even stand me. I was a jerk to both of them because I loved her so much that I didn't know how else to handle it. For years that's how I coped with it, but while I was busy nurturing my feelings for her, I failed to have a genuine relationship with anyone else. After she died, something in me shut down. It was like I couldn't go through that kind of ordeal again."

"You've missed out on a lot. There's nothing like being in love with someone who loves you back."

"I wouldn't know about that," Brandon said. "I realize now I always drank too much, but the day she died was the first time I cried as an adult. It was also the first time I drank enough to black out. I woke up the next day in some girl's bed and had no idea who she was or how I'd gotten there."

"I'm sorry for your loss."

"It wasn't my loss. It was Aidan's."

"It was yours, too."

Brandon turned to him. "Thank you. Thank you for getting that. My mother has never forgiven me for not going to Sarah's funeral. She was furious. Aidan didn't go either, but everyone understood that. I just came off looking like an unfeeling asshole."

"But you weren't unfeeling; you were devastated. You know that. That's what has to matter here, not what anyone else thought. They couldn't have known what losing her meant to you."

"I couldn't very well admit to being in love with my brother's wife."

"Not then, maybe, but now might be a good time."

"I'm going to have to tell him all this, aren't I?" Brandon asked with a wary glance at Alan.

"Your feelings toward him have been a cancer in your life, and you've used alcohol as medicine. If you want to stop drinking, really stop, you have to get out from under all this negativity and resentment. It's smothering you."

"I can't imagine telling him this without a fifth of whiskey and a six pack in my belly."

"Ask God to show you the way. You don't need the booze. When the time is right to tell Aidan, you'll know. For now, don't worry about it. Worry about getting through today."

"One day at a time," Brandon said, repeating a basic tenet of the AA philosophy.

"That's right."

"Thank you," Brandon said, reaching out to shake Alan's hand.

"Glad I could help. Race you back?"

Brandon laughed. "Only if you give me a serious head start."

CHAPTER 6, DAY 21

Colin downshifted to ease his big Harley into a space at the far end of the Congregational Church parking lot. When he cut the engine, the bike let out one last gasp before it went quiet.

He'd taken his mother's concerns about airing the family's laundry in public to heart when he decided to take the bike on a rare midwinter outing. No sense advertising his connection to O'Malley & Sons by driving the company truck.

The motorcycle was one of the few secrets he kept from his mother, who'd have a stroke if she knew her two youngest sons owned Harleys and—even at thirty-five and thirty-six—went to great lengths to keep them hidden from her.

Taking off his helmet, Colin watched the clusters of people moving toward the door that led to the church hall in the basement. The group seemed to be well acquainted, and he wondered how they'd feel about a newcomer.

Before he could lose his nerve, he tucked the helmet under his arm and crossed the parking lot.

Inside he stuffed his gloves in the pockets of his brown leather coat and stashed the helmet on a table in the back of the room. Colin was relieved when he didn't recognize any of the dozen or so people who were helping themselves to coffee and brownies. Until that moment, he hadn't realized how concerned he was about running into someone he knew. A middle-aged man with a comb-over and a friendly smile approached him.

"Hi, there." He reached out to shake Colin's hand. "I'm Hugh. Come on in."

"Colin. Nice to meet you."

"First time?" Hugh asked, raising an eyebrow.

"Shows, huh?"

"No worries. Everyone's welcome here. Hey, guys," Hugh called out to the others. "This is Colin."

"Hi, Colin," they said in unison.

Minutes later, he was in possession of a steaming cup of coffee and a home-baked brownie. The group slowly made its way to the table in the middle of the room. A pretty brunette who Colin figured was in her early thirties appeared to be the leader. She said her name was Meredith. After she went over the meeting procedures, she asked who would like to go first.

Hugh raised his hand. "This has been a good week, but I'm worried about my friend." For Colin's benefit, he added, "I ran a business with my best friend from childhood until his alcoholism made it impossible for him to work anymore. I did everything I could to keep him out of trouble until he landed in jail, and I ended up with an ulcer. I've come to realize, thanks to these people right here, that I couldn't do it anymore." Hugh paused and cleared the emotion from his throat. "He's homeless now, and I'm not even sure where he is, but I'm as powerless over his alcoholism as he is. I realize now I can't help him. So I'm doing what I can to help myself."

Meredith's soft brown eyes were full of empathy as she listened to Hugh, and Colin wondered what—or *who*—had brought her here.

"Thank you," Hugh said when he was finished.

"Thank you, Hugh," the group replied.

Listening to five other people share their stories, Colin was fascinated to notice that few of them talked about the alcoholic—or their "qualifier" as some referred to it—in their lives. Rather they focused on themselves and how alcohol affected them.

Colin's gaze traveled to a sign on the wall: "I didn't cause it, can't control it, can't cure it." He'd seen the saying in Al-Anon literature, but the words took on new meaning as he listened to the group talk about the challenges they faced in their lives and the role alcohol and alcoholism played.

The ninety-minute meeting went by quickly, and Colin was surprised when Meredith said they were almost out of time. "Before we close tonight, we'd like to welcome you, Colin. I hope you found the meeting helpful."

"Very much so. My brother is in rehab, and everyone in our family is anxious about how he'll be when he gets home. I heard a lot of myself in what you all were saying tonight—about trying to keep the really bad thing from happening. Well, it did anyway, and I've come to the conclusion that a lot of what myself and other family members have been doing can't continue. So that's why I'm here."

"Keep coming back," an older woman named Leslie said. "It helps."

Colin nodded. "Thanks. I will."

When they stood in a circle around the table, the people on either side of Colin reached for his hands to recite the Serenity Prayer. While he was helping to put away chairs, he watched Meredith place a comforting hand on Hugh's shoulder and whisper something to him.

After the meeting, Colin called Declan. "Hey. Are you home?"

"Yep."

"Alone?"

"No," Dec said with a chuckle. "But you're not interrupting anything. Yet."

"Spare me the details. I was going to come by, but I'll see you tomorrow."

"Come on over, Col. We're just hanging out."

"You're sure?"

"Positive."

"I'll be there in fifteen minutes."

Colin drove the Harley through the deserted town. White lights twinkled in the windows along the winding row of shops and restaurants that made up Chatham's quaint Main Street. The winter had been cold, but so far there hadn't been much snow, and the streets were dry or he wouldn't be on the bike. He loved the big, powerful motorcycle and the way its rumble vibrated through his chest. Chatham's seven thousand year-round residents tended to hate noisy motorcycles, but the dark face mask on his helmet allowed him to roar around in anonymity.

Declan lived in a new townhouse in North Chatham, almost to the Harwich town line. He had turned on the porch light for his brother.

"Hey," Dec said when Colin walked in. Declan and his girlfriend Jessica were sitting together on the sofa and had paused their movie. "Did I hear the bike?"

"Yeah. I went to an Al-Anon meeting tonight, and in the spirit of anonymity, I left the truck at home."

"Watch out for ice," Dec warned.

"It's too warm for ice tonight."

"Want something to drink?"

"No, thanks," Colin said.

"How was the meeting?" Jessica asked. Dec had been seeing the cute, friendly physical therapist since Christmas.

"Good. It's amazing how many people are in the same boat we are."

"Da said Brandon seemed really good when they saw him," Dec said.

"Yeah, but the real test begins when he gets out of there," Colin reminded his brother.

"I hope he can do it."

"I think he knows by now that he has to, but whether or not he will remains to be seen." Colin paused before he said, "So, you talked to Da?"

Declan nodded and took a sip from his bottle of Sam Adams. "I hear there's going to be a changing of the guard, boss man," he said with a twinkle in his eye.

Colin groaned. "Don't start that crap. I'm counting on you and Tommy to help me out. We're going to do this together."

"Of course we are."

"So you're not mad?" Colin asked, relieved that Declan didn't seem to begrudge him the promotion.

"Hell, no. My first thought when Da told me you were taking over was better you than me. You've earned it, Col. No hard feelings from me."

"I appreciate that. What do you think Brandon will say?"

Declan snorted. "He's gonna be pissed, but what does he expect? No way any of the guys would work for him, the way he's been the last couple of years. But he won't like coming home to discover his little brother is his new boss."

"True," Colin said. "But I'm glad to know I can count on you to back me up."

"Always."

With that one word, Declan reminded Colin of the close bond they'd shared since childhood. As close as they were, though, they were as different as two people could be. While nothing seemed to faze the laid-back Declan, Colin took everything to heart, which had caused him nothing but grief where Brandon was concerned. But those days were over now. They had to be.

"Well, I'd better get going. Are you guys going to dinner at Erin's on Sunday?"

"We'll be there," Dec said as he got up to walk his brother to the door.

"See you, Colin," Jessica said.

"Bye, Jess."

"Hey, Col," Dec said quietly when they reached the door. "Everything's going to be okay. He's gonna make it. The Brandon we know would never do what he did to a woman. That'll stay with him. It'll keep him straight."

"Let's hope so."

Colin wiped mud smudges off the chrome fender, stashed the Harley under a tarp, and pushed the button on the wall to close the garage door. He entered the house through the kitchen, where the dim glow over the stove created a narrow swath of light. Moving through the dark, he flipped on a lamp in the living room and sank into an easy chair to pull off his boots.

The house was small, but when Colin thought about the wreck it had been when he found it, he was deeply satisfied by how it looked now. He'd spent two years working nights and weekends—while living in the midst of chaos—to renovate the place. There wasn't an inch in the house that he hadn't stripped, sanded, painted, or polished. He still felt like there was something he should be doing when he was home, but it was finally done. With some help from his mother and sister, he had comfortable furniture and tolerable curtains that he'd agreed to under tremendous female pressure. He usually kept them open to maximize his view of Oyster Pond.

He sat back and flipped up the recliner's footrest, suddenly tired down to his bones. At times like this, the house was too quiet. He'd expected to be married with kids by now. Six years earlier, he'd come close, but his fiancée Nicole called off their engagement a month before the wedding. The blow had devastated him, but in time, he'd come to see that she'd done him a favor. Something had been missing between them. He didn't know what it was, but he hoped he'd recognize it if he was ever lucky enough to find it.

His mother lamented that three of her sons were late bloomers in the love department. Only Aidan had been different. He'd been married at twenty-two and widowed at twenty-nine. Colin had known of no other woman in his brother's life until Aidan brought Clare home when their father had the heart attack.

He wondered if Declan had finally found his mate in Jessica. She was a nice girl and seemed well suited to Dec, but it was still hard to imagine his younger brother married with a family. He was still such a big kid in so many ways.

The whole family had been disappointed when Brandon's lovely girlfriend, Valerie, left him, but they couldn't blame her. She'd hung in with him much longer than she probably should have. His drinking got much worse after Valerie left, and without her keeping tabs on him, Colin had been sucked more and more often into the daily drama of Brandon's life.

As Colin gave in to the exhaustion and closed his eyes, he thought of Meredith, the woman he met at Al-Anon. She'd been so sweet and sympathetic to everyone, and it was clear they all adored her. There was something so comforting about being on the receiving end of that kind of empathy from people who'd been there and understood. His last thought before sleep took over was that he looked forward to going back for more.

Chapter 7, Day 28

On the last weekend before Brandon was due home, the O'Malleys invaded Boston to celebrate Aidan's fortieth birthday. His girlfriend Clare surprised him by inviting his family to meet them in the city for the weekend.

After dinner on Friday night, Colin sat with Aidan and watched the others tear up the dance floor in the hotel's nightclub. Erin's five kids were right in the middle of the action, and Aidan smiled when eight-year-old Josh spun his grandmother around. The expression on Colleen's face was priceless.

"Looks like Mum's met her match," Colin said, taking a sip from his bottle of Sam Adams.

"He's going to be a heartbreaker," Aidan said.

"For sure. It was nice of Clare to do this."

"I was so surprised when I answered the door and you were all there. She really got me."

"That's not easy to do."

"I must be slipping in my old age."

Colin thought his brother looked better than he had in years. Some of the hard edges he'd developed as protection in a world without his beloved wife had finally softened. His eyes twinkled as he watched Clare dance with her daughters Jill and Maggie and Erin's seven-year-old daughter Nina. "You seem really happy, Aid."

Aidan glanced over at his brother. "I'm going to marry her."

Colin's eyes widened. "Really?"

Aidan nodded. "If she'll have me."

"Why wouldn't she?"

"She's been through some tough stuff in the last couple of years. It's kind of a long story, but none of it matters to me. All I know is I'm happy again, and she's the reason—her and her girls. They're great kids. You should see them ski. They came up after Christmas and wore me out, man."

"How old are they?"

"Jill's nineteen and a sophomore at Brown. Maggie's thirteen, and there's a third one, Kate, who's eighteen. She's living in Nashville, chasing the music dream."

"Is she that good?"

"She really is. I didn't believe it myself until I heard her sing. She's got hugely talented."

"Wow. Well, I hope it all works out for you guys."

"Thanks. What about you? No ladies beating down your door?"

Colin snorted. "Hardly. I'm so busy at work, I don't have time for anything else."

"Da told me you agreed to take over the business."

"I heard you gave me a glowing recommendation."

"I just told him the truth."

Their father waved to them as he danced with his wife.

"He looks good," Aidan said. "Much better than the last time I saw him."

"He does," Colin agreed. "Anyway, I appreciate the endorsement."

"You know I'm just a phone call away if you ever need me, right?"

"I'll need all the support I can get, especially when Brandon hears about it."

Aidan's genial expression turned stormy. "He can bloody well deal with it. It's his own fault that he's in the boat he's in."

"Are you ever going to forgive him, Aid?"

Aidan's jaw clenched with tension. "I don't know." Colin watched Aidan seek out Clare on the dance floor. She was a petite blonde with dazzling blue eyes, and she'd had the family laughing over dinner with her jokes about being seven years older than Aidan—although she hardly looked it. She winked at him, and his expression softened. "After what he did to her, I don't know if I can forgive him. I see red whenever I think about it."

Colin nodded with understanding. He would feel the same way, but he couldn't help feeling for Brandon, too.

On Sunday evening, after he got home from Boston, Colin took the company truck to the gas station on Main Street to fill it up for the busy week ahead. If he allowed himself to think too hard about what he had to accomplish in the next six days, he'd never be able to sleep. He'd been working for his father's company for eighteen years and could remember when there used to be an off-season. These days, they stayed busy year round, and it took serious planning and coordination to ensure there was plenty of indoor work for the men during the cold weather. Most winters they also spent many long, dark nights plowing snow, but this year had been a rare exception to that rule.

Colin used his company credit card to pay for the gas and was zoning out watching the numbers click by on the pump when someone called to him. Looking up, he saw Meredith from Al-Anon using the pump across from him, looking adorable in a puffy pink hat over her shiny dark hair.

"Hi, there." He was delighted to see her and wondered what he should make of that.

"How are you? We missed you on Friday night. Did we scare you away last week?"

"Not at all. I was sorry to miss it this week, but I was in Boston for my brother's birthday. The big four-oh."

"Sounds like fun."

"It was, but the hotel will never be the same."

Her laughter was almost delicate. She finished pumping her gas and took her receipt from the printer.

"Do you have time for a cup of coffee?" he asked before she could get away.

She smiled. "Sure. Where do you want to go?"

"Is Priscilla's open this late?"

"I think so. Meet you there?"

"If this thing ever gets its fill of gas, I'll be there."

Colin arrived at Priscilla's fifteen minutes later to find that Meredith had already commandeered a booth.

"Sorry that took so long," he said when he slid in across from her. She wore a pink sweater, and her cheeks were flushed as if she'd spent most of the day outdoors. "That thing's a gas guzzler." He removed his "Chatham Townie" ball cap and put it on the seat next to him.

"Afraid to be mistaken for a tourist?" Meredith asked, amused by the hat.

"God forbid."

"I noticed the logo on your truck. A friend of mine worked for O'Malley Construction years ago. Paul Tobin. Do you know him?"

Colin realized two things in that moment—his cover was blown, and he didn't really care. "Sure, I know Paul. He worked for us three or four summers while he was in college. About ten years ago?"

"I think that's about right. You were his boss?"

"One of them." He extended a hand to her. "Colin O'Malley."

She seemed impressed as she shook his hand. "Meredith Chase. I see your company's trucks everywhere."

"I guess we're not anonymous anymore," Colin said, relieved there were no rings on her left hand and again wasn't sure why it mattered so much.

She shrugged. "That's okay. I've met some of my best friends through Al-Anon. It's important we never discuss what happens at the meetings or who we saw there, but there's no rule about being friends outside the Family Group."

"I can see how the anonymity helps with inhibitions."

The waitress came to take their order, and Colin ordered two slices of Priscilla's famous apple pie to go with their coffee.

"How's your brother doing?" Meredith asked.

"I'm not sure. He'll be home Tuesday, so I guess we'll see then. I wish I'd discovered Al-Anon sooner. I sure could've used it the last few years."

"Is this his first time in rehab?"

"Yes."

"It might not be his last time, though. You know that, right?"

"I'm cautiously optimistic. He hit a real low point right before he went into rehab, and I think it might've been enough to wake him up. At least I hope so."

"I hope so, too. Do you have a big family? You've mentioned two brothers."

"Three brothers and a sister, who finally became useful to her brothers when she had five kids in five years and took the pressure off us to produce grandchildren."

Meredith laughed as their coffee and pie was delivered. "I can't believe I let you talk me into this pie," she moaned a minute later. "I'll have to be on best behavior for a week."

Colin chuckled at her dismay. She was by no means heavy. Rather she seemed curvy in all the places that mattered. "So you know all about me, but I know nothing about you."

She shrugged. "There's not much to tell. I grew up in Orleans, and I teach fifth grade in Brewster. I have my parents, a sister, a nephew, a cat, and a lot of good friends. Pretty boring, really."

"That doesn't sound boring at all. Do you live here in Chatham now?"

She nodded. "Stepping Stones Road. What about you?"

"I have a house on Oyster Bay Lane off Cedar Street."

"Near the pond?"

He nodded.

"Did you grow up here?"

"Yep. My parents still live in the same house on Shore Road."

Her eyes lit up. "Oh, I love it out there. I walk on the beach at Chatham Light every chance I get."

"We always say the O'Malleys keep the neighborhood humble. My parents were there long before it became swanky. In fact, in a move that I'm sure made the neighbors cringe, my mother had the house painted Pepto-Bismol pink two years ago."

"I know that house! I love it!"

Colin groaned. "Tell me you're kidding."

"I'm not. It's so whimsical."

"If you ever meet my mother, you can't tell her that."

Meredith laughed. "I'm not making any promises." She reached for the check, but Colin swiped it away from her.

"This is on me."

"Thank you," she said with a faint blush to her cheeks that he found charming.

He paid the check and walked her to her car. The temperature had dropped during the hour they'd spent at Priscilla's.

"Is it supposed to snow?" she asked.

"Not that I've heard, but it sure smells like snow, doesn't it?"

She glanced up at him. "I was just thinking the same thing."

Colin found that he couldn't look away from her. "Can we do this again? Maybe dinner next time?"

She got busy finding her keys in her purse. "I don't think so, Colin. But thanks for asking and for the pie."

"Sure," he said, holding the car door for her.

"I'll see you at the meeting."

He stood there for a long time after she drove away, feeling more disappointed than he'd been in a long time.

Chapter 8, Day 30

Brandon felt the heat of all eyes on him. After several minutes of awkward silence, Steve, the group leader, zeroed in on him. "Brandon?"

Brandon nodded as a bead of sweat rolled down his back. *Is it hot in here, or is it me?* Finally, he cleared his throat, and without looking up, he said, "My name is Brandon, and…uh, I'm an alcoholic."

"Hi, Brandon," the group replied.

"I, um, I want to say that even though I haven't said anything before now, I've been listening, and you all have helped me a lot. So thank you for that." He released a long deep breath and looked over at Steve. "This is hard."

"Take your time."

After another long pause, Brandon continued. "I've learned a lot about myself and my drinking in the last month. I think I've always known I didn't drink the way other people did, but I never gave it much thought before now. My brothers and I would go out for a few beers, even when we were just old enough to drink, and they'd have two or three, but I'd down six in an hour. In the last couple of years, it would take me at least a twelve-pack to catch a buzz, so I started adding shots of whiskey to the mix. I was, uh, drinking so much I blacked out almost every day for the last few months before I came here. During those blackouts, I did a lot of shameful things—things I'll be dealing with for a long time."

Brandon took a drink from the cup of ice water he'd brought to the meeting and discovered his hand was trembling.

"Most of my life, I've kept some pretty big secrets that have festered into even larger resentments. All of that combined to bring me here, and I have a lot of amends to make when I get home."

Brandon looked up to find Alan leaning against the back wall.

He smiled and nodded with encouragement.

Fueled by his new friend's support, Brandon sat up a little straighter in his chair. "I've been told my attitude has changed a lot in the last thirty days, and I feel better physically than I have in years. So I just want to say I'm very determined to stay sober, and I'll be hoping all of you are successful, too. Thank you."

The group embarrassed him with their applause. "Thank you, Brandon," they said in unison.

"Keep going to meetings," Steve reminded him. "We recommend ninety meetings in the first ninety days. We've found that's how you set a pattern that lasts a lifetime."

"I will," Brandon promised.

When the meeting was over, Brandon went to talk to Alan. They shook hands.

"You did great, Brandon."

"I didn't say much."

"You said enough. How do you feel?"

"Relieved. I'd been kind of dreading that."

"It's always a big deal to say the words, 'I'm an alcoholic,' for the first time in a room full of people you hardly know."

"I do know them. Maybe not personally, in some cases, but I understand them better than most people would. After all, I'm one of them, right?"

Alan nodded with satisfaction. "I'm proud of you, Brandon. You've come so far from the day we first met, and it seems like you really get it now."

"That means a lot coming from you."

"How're you doing with the spiritual issues we discussed?"

"I've been doing a lot of reading and thinking about it."

"That's a good start. Remember, AA only encourages you to relate to a higher power as you define it." Alan reached for his wallet and withdrew his card. "Let's try this again, shall we?"

Brandon laughed as he accepted the card. "I won't throw it away this time."

"Call me—any time."

"I will." Brandon shook Alan's hand. "Thank you for everything."

"I'll pray for you."

"Thanks, Alan."

"So what do you think, Brandon?" Sondra asked at their final session. Brandon's father would be arriving soon to drive him home. "Ready to go back out and face the world?"

"I hope so. I feel good. Better than I have in a long time."

"How's the running going?"

"I'm up to five miles, and I've been lifting weights. I don't feel like I'm going to die from the effort anymore."

"You look much better than you did the first time we met."

"Yeah, well, my brother's fist hasn't been near my face in a month, so I should look better."

Sondra smiled. "How about inside? You know what you have to do?"

Brandon nodded. "Ninety meetings in ninety days, get a sponsor, read the *Big Book*, make my amends to the people I've hurt, and stay sober—not necessarily in that order."

"Yes, staying sober needs to be first on your list."

"I just worry about…"

"What?"

"Events where everyone's drinking—family dinners, weddings, parties… My family is forever celebrating something, and everyone drinks—not like I did— but alcohol is part of every gathering."

"It's very important that you not get too far ahead of yourself. Take each day and each event as they come. The only thing any of us really has is right now. Stay sober today. Worry about tomorrow tomorrow."

"I'll do my best."

"All you can do is keep your own side of the street clean. You'll hear that expression often in AA."

Brandon smiled. "I like it."

"I see clients in town on Wednesday and Friday afternoons if you'd like to continue your therapy. Call my service to make an appointment." She stood up and went to her desk. When she came back, she held a leather-bound book and a business card, which she handed to him. "My cell number's on there, too. Feel free to use it. I'm just a phone call away if you ever need me."

The lump in his throat surprised Brandon. The support he'd received here had been overwhelming, and he had no doubt they'd saved his life by teaching him how to live. The rest would be up to him.

"Before I let you go, I have a little tradition with all my patients," Sondra said. "There's always one thing that worries me more than anything else when it comes to my patients' future sobriety. My worries differ, and I give each of you the opportunity to decide whether or not you want to hear it."

"What do most people do?"

"Most choose to hear it, and they tend to be the ones who don't end up back here again."

"Okay, then, bring it on. I'm ready."

"With you, Brandon, my biggest worry is your resentment. You absolutely must work through your issues with Aidan and find a way to accept the hand that life dealt both of you. If you continue to harbor all these secrets and resentments, your ability to stay sober will be seriously impaired at some point. You must also tell your father how you feel about the business and his expectations for you."

"Yes, I know. I have to find a way to get through to my dad. As for Aidan, I doubt he's even speaking to me."

"Then write him a letter. Find a way to explain your feelings to him. It's going to be absolutely critical to your continued recovery that you let go of all the anger you've been hauling around with you for most of your life."

"I hear you."

"Call me if I can help."

"Um, I want to thank you. I don't know how you did it, but you got me to tell you things I've never told anyone."

She smiled. "My special gift."

"I'd say so," he said with a chuckle. "Thank you." He reached a hand out to her.

She squeezed his hand and handed him the leather book she'd retrieved from her desk.

"What's this?"

"A journal. I give one to all my graduates. Try to write something every day about the challenges and the temptations and how you feel about them. Sometimes putting it down on paper helps."

Brandon took the book and stood up. He wanted to hug her but thought it would be inappropriate.

She solved the problem for him when she took a step toward him with her arms out. "Good luck to you, Brandon. We'll all be praying for you."

"Thank you for everything," he said, returning her embrace.

"Be well."

After he signed discharge paperwork, Brandon returned to his room to finish packing. He zipped the book Sondra had given him into his bag, sat on the bed, and ran his hands through his hair. He was scared—truly frightened about his ability to stay sober once he left the safety net of the rehab facility. He felt as vulnerable as a newborn about to leave the womb. What if he couldn't do it? What if he fell back into old habits and routines once he returned to familiar surroundings? What if he disappointed everyone who had such high hopes for him?

Stop it. You can't fail at this. One by one, the faces of the people he'd let down flashed through his mind: his parents, siblings, nieces, nephews, Valerie, the men who worked for him, and the friends he'd abandoned on his spiral into alcoholism.

He reached over to unzip his bag and retrieved the journal. Rooting around in the bottom of the bag, he found a pen. On the first page of the book, he wrote the date. *"Today is my thirtieth day of sobriety. I promise myself I will stay sober. I vow to read this promise any time I'm tempted to solve my problems by drinking. I owe more to the people in my life than what they've gotten from me. I'm going to do better. I'm not going to forget what I learned at Laurel Lake."* He paused for a moment before he added, *"So help me, God."*

After he reread what he had written, Brandon returned the journal and pen to his bag and zipped it closed, releasing a long deep breath he hadn't known he was holding.

The intercom buzzed, and he got up to answer it. "Brandon, your father's here."

"Thank you."

He picked up his bag and took a last look at the sterile little room that had been his home for a month. "So help me, God," he whispered once more before he walked out the door to face what waited for him at home.

CHAPTER 9, DAY 30

On the forty-minute ride home to Chatham, Dennis kept up a steady stream of chatter about the goings-on at work, the latest funny stories about Erin's kids, and yet another project Colleen had embarked upon in the big, pink house.

Brandon turned his face into the chilly air coming in through the small crack he opened in the window. After being so removed from regular life, something as simple as fresh air rushing in through an open window seemed extraordinary. His senses, dulled for so long by alcohol, were on full alert to absorb the sights, sounds, and smells of life outside the walls of Laurel Lake.

"You look good," Dennis said, glancing at his son across the wide bench seat in his company truck as they traveled east along Route 6.

"I feel good." Everything they passed on the familiar road to home reminded Brandon of something from his past: the restaurant where he'd had his senior prom, the sports complex where he and his brothers had played baseball, the neighborhood where Valerie's parents lived, the parking lots he'd plowed after a hundred snow storms. On and on it went.

Brandon was surprised when his father went straight on Main Street rather than making a left to take Brandon to his house on Indian Hill Road, near the Chatham Municipal Airport. "Where're we going?"

"I thought we'd take a walk on the beach."

"Kind of cold for that, isn't it?"

Dennis cocked a blue eye at his son. "What've you gone soft on me in that place?"

"Hardly." Brandon snorted. "If you want to freeze your ass off, don't let me stop you."

Dennis pulled into the parking lot at Chatham Light and killed the engine. "Let's go."

Zipping his green company coat, Brandon wished for gloves.

Dennis flipped open the tool box in the truck bed and pulled out two pairs of work gloves, tossing a pair to Brandon.

"You read my mind."

"I don't want you to catch the sniffles," Dennis teased.

"Bite me," Brandon said with a laugh.

They walked down the long flight of stairs to the sweeping expanse of sand that made up the elbow of Cape Cod. Behind them was the huge white beacon at Coast Guard Station Chatham. Small-craft warning flags flew under the light, and the gusty wind gave the sand the appearance of having been swept by a broom. Since no one else was crazy enough to brave the elements that day, they had the beach to themselves.

"Should you be exerting yourself like this?" Brandon asked when they had walked into the wind for a few minutes.

"I'm fine." Dennis's warm breath came out like a cloud in the cold air.

"Is this some kind of character-building exercise we're undertaking here?"

Dennis laughed. "Something like that. I wanted to talk to you, actually."

"About?"

"Work."

"Listen, Da, I know you're mad about the thing with the gravel, and I'm going to apologize to Lewis and Simms."

"Good, but that's not was I was going to say." Dennis stopped walking.

Brandon came to a halt, turned his back to the wind, and as he waited for his father to continue, a chill went through him that he couldn't blame entirely on the cold.

"I've decided to retire."

Brandon smiled. "Yeah, right."

"I'm serious."

"But you always said we'd have to carry you out of there in a pine box," Brandon said, stunned.

"You almost got to."

"You're exaggerating, Da. You had a *mild* heart attack."

"It was a warning. Besides, it's time. Mum wants to do some traveling, and if I don't go with her, who'll keep her out of trouble?"

"That's a good point. So why'd you bring me out here to the tundra to tell me this?"

"Because I've put Colin in charge."

Raw fury streaked through Brandon, but he kept his expression neutral.

"I wanted you to hear it from me," Dennis continued. "I've made my decision, and I'm asking you to respect it."

Brandon rubbed a gloved hand against the stubble on his jaw. "Christ, I go away for a month, and now I'm working for my little brother?"

"You're going to have to find a way to deal with this, Brand. He's worked for the company the longest, and he's earned this opportunity."

"He's worked for the company the longest because he refused to go to college, something you made the rest of us do!" Brandon fumed. "How's that fair?"

"Do you honestly think you'd be able to run a business right now? With everything else you've got on your plate?"

"Maybe not right this minute, but hell, I would've liked the chance to try it."

"The men wouldn't work for you, Brandon. Not the way you've been the last couple of years. I had a lot of things to consider, and that was definitely one of them."

"I'm not taking orders from Colin, Da. No way."

"Then maybe you should think about getting another job," Dennis said with steel in his gentle blue eyes.

"*Are you serious?* I've given that company sixteen years of my life! There were other things I wanted to do, but I came back here and did exactly what you expected of me. You can't just push me aside!" The words were out of his mouth before Brandon could stop them. He hadn't planned on having this conversation today or pictured it coming out quite the way it had. The stricken look on his father's face told Brandon the words had cut him to the quick.

"What did you say?" Dennis asked in a voice that almost didn't register over the roar of the ocean.

Brandon's eyes burned. He looked away from his father. "I didn't want to work for the company," he mumbled. "I didn't even want to be an engineer." His stomach twisted with fear as one of his best-kept secrets came tumbling out.

Dennis stepped back as if Brandon had taken a swing at him. "You don't mean that."

"I'm not saying it to hurt you, Da, but it's true. O'Malley & Sons was never my dream, but I've devoted my entire life to that company. I deserve better than being pushed aside like I'm just another employee."

Dennis turned back to the stairs.

"Da," Brandon called. "Wait."

But Dennis kept walking.

Brandon jogged to catch up with him, grabbing the sleeve of his father's coat.

Dennis tugged his arm out of his son's grasp.

Back in the truck, Brandon removed the gloves and laid them on the seat between them. "I'm sorry, Da. I'd never want to hurt you or disappoint you. That's why I never told you this before. I tried to do what you wanted me to do, but that didn't work out so well for me."

"I just don't understand," Dennis said, shaking his head. His parents had been Irish immigrants, and even though Dennis was born in Boston, when he was tired or upset he tended to lapse into the brogue of his parents' homeland. More than anything, that told Brandon just how distressed his father was. "Why didn't you ever say anything?"

Brandon shrugged. "When Aidan went to medical school, I figured there was no way I could leave, too. I knew you were counting on the rest of us."

"What did you want? What would you have done if there'd been no family business?"

"It doesn't matter now."

"It *does* matter!" Dennis roared. "Tell me."

Brandon swallowed hard. "I wanted to be a Navy SEAL."

Dennis rested his big hands on the steering wheel and glanced over at his son with a look of astonishment on his face. "What kind of man does that make me?" he whispered. "What kind of father was I that you couldn't come to me and tell me that? Do you honestly think there was *anything* you could've wanted that I would've denied you? *Anything?*" His voice caught as he rested his head on his hands.

"Da," Brandon whispered. "I'm sorry."

Dennis's head whipped back up. "*You're sorry? You?* What do you have to be sorry about? I just don't see how…"

"What?"

"How did you keep this from me all these years? There was always a cloud of unhappiness and discontent about you, but I had no idea it was my fault."

"It wasn't your fault. It was mine. I should've said something. But you were so disappointed when Aidan decided to go to medical school—"

"What the hell are you talking about? *Disappointed?* I was over the moon! My father left school in the eighth grade, and my son was going to be a *doctor?* How could you think I was disappointed? It was one of the greatest thrills of my life."

"But you were so sad…" Brandon felt like he was standing on quick sand as everything he'd believed to be true turned out to be false. "You wanted us to come to work with you."

"I wanted you to be *happy*. And I didn't want any of you to have to struggle the way I did. The business was my legacy to you, son, but not if you didn't want it. That you didn't want it never occurred to me."

Brandon wanted to weep for lost dreams, for words unspoken, and for the awful pain he saw on his father's face. "I didn't want it when I was younger," Brandon admitted when he could finally bring himself to speak again. "But I've devoted my life to that business, and it's all I know, Da. You can't take it away from me. Especially not now."

"You're going to have to deal with Colin if you stay. I'm not changing my mind about that. And until you're back on your feet, we want you to take on a special project."

"What kind of special project?" Brandon asked with a wary glance at his father.

"I want you to manage the apartment building I bought on Old Queen Anne Road. The place needs some work, and I've got a pain-in-the-ass tenant over there bitching about the plumbing, the mice, and just about everything else. I want you to deal with it."

"You're not serious."

"It's the perfect thing for you right now. You'll have the time to go to your meetings and do what you need to do to stay sober without a lot of job stress to contend with."

"Was this Colin's idea?"

"It was my idea," Dennis said. "And there's, uh, one other thing."

"I can't wait to hear this."

"I want you to live there while you're doing the work. I want the tenants to feel like they have access to you."

Brandon snorted. "You've got it all figured out, don't you?"

"It's your call, Brand. But it's this or nothing. The men don't trust you after what happened with Lewis and Simms. You're going to have to ease your way back in, and this is a good first step."

Brandon thought about that for a moment. "Well, since I'm far too old to join the navy now, it looks like I'll be using my engineering degree from Notre Dame to be an apartment super."

"Very good, then," Dennis said as he started the truck.

"Let me ask you this, Da—what did Dec say when you told him Colin was going to be in charge?"

"I believe his exact words were 'better him than me.'"

Brandon tossed his head back and laughed. "I have no doubt." While he was not at all happy with the job he'd been given, it was a huge relief to have one less secret to carry around.

CHAPTER 10, DAY 31

Dennis O'Malley stared at the glowing embers of the fire in his study, but he was so lost in thought that he didn't pay much attention to the desperate bursts of flame or the sparks flying from the last remaining scrap of wood. He was still trying to process what Brandon had confessed that afternoon. "He sacrificed his own dreams for me," Dennis whispered as if saying it out loud might make it easier to believe.

He looked up when Colleen came into the room, tying the belt of her robe tightly around her. His bride was still so lovely, even at nearly sixty years old and after carrying his five children. Her bright red hair had faded to an attractive auburn, and her green eyes, usually so full of mirth, brimmed with concern.

"What are you doing up so late, love? It's after midnight."

Dennis held out a hand to bring her onto his lap. She had such a big, commanding personality that sometimes he forgot just how petite she was. Wrapping his arms around her, Dennis felt a surge of tenderness for the tiny dynamo who'd been the center of his life for more than forty years. "Couldn't sleep."

"Are you thinking about Brandon?"

"Yeah. I just can't see how this happened. Was I so unreasonable that my own son would be *afraid* to talk to me about something so important?"

"No, Denny." Colleen ran a soothing hand over his cheek. "You're a wonderful father. All the kids love you, and the boys worship you. You know they do."

"But are they working with me because they want to or because they felt they had to? All I wanted was for them to have the security we didn't have when we first started out. They'll never know that awful hand-to-mouth existence we had at first, remember?"

"Of course I do, love. We had a lot of lean years, but you've made the business into a great success."

"It wasn't really a success until the boys were old enough to work with me," Dennis admitted. "Do you think Colin and Declan feel the same way Brandon does?"

"Not Colin, that's for sure. He's doing exactly what he's wanted to do his whole life. And Dec certainly seems happy. There was always something different about Brandon, though, wasn't there?"

"Not always. He changed over that one summer when he was ten or eleven. Remember how we couldn't figure out why he was suddenly mad at the world? We said it was a phase."

"Except it never ended."

"I already blame myself for his alcoholism." Dennis sighed. "And now this."

Colleen lifted her head off his shoulder to look him in the eye. "Why in the world do you blame yourself for his alcoholism?"

"I drank every day of his life when he lived in this house. I set a terrible example for him and the others."

"If that were true, Dennis O'Malley, why aren't the other four alcoholics? Answer me that, now, will you, love?"

"Huh. I hadn't thought of it that way."

"That boy of ours is a complicated soul, but he's not an alcoholic because of you. Maybe he made some sacrifices by coming home to work with you, but he has a very comfortable life because of that business. We all do. It certainly hasn't been all bad for him."

"Back before the drinking got worse, he was so good at what he did. He helped us branch into areas we'd never been into before—septic systems, water supply, environmental stuff. It's so hard to believe he did all that but hated the job."

Colleen put both hands on her husband's face. "If he hated the job, truly hated it, he wouldn't have lasted sixteen years, Denny. He would've found a way out a long time ago."

"He found a way out, all right. He drank his way out."

"Well, that might be the case, but now that you know how he feels, you can love him enough to let him go if that's what he really wants."

"True enough." He leaned down to kiss her. "How did you get so wise, my love?"

"I was always wise. You, my friend, were just smart enough to marry me."

"As I recall, you didn't give me much choice," Dennis reminded her as he helped her up. Colleen's ultimatum in front of his drinking buddies outside a South Boston bar was the stuff of family legend. "It's them or me, Dennis O'Malley," she'd said. "Take your pick." Choosing her was, by far, the best thing he ever did.

She laughed. "Oh, you had a choice. Fortunately for you, you made the right one."

He stopped her at the doorway to the study. "I've never regretted it for one minute. You know that, don't you?"

"Of course I do, love. We've had our sorrows, but we've been so very blessed. And our Brandon will be just fine."

Dennis cocked an amused eyebrow at her. "How do you know?"

"Because I'm his mother," she said with supreme confidence, taking his hand to lead him to bed.

While his parents were talking about him, Brandon lay awake on the other side of town. He had come home to find his small house recently cleaned and his refrigerator stocked. His mother left fresh flowers in a vase on the counter along with a note that said, "Welcome home, love. I left some stew in the fridge for your dinner and some muffins for breakfast. I also changed the sheets on your bed. Colin says we have to let you do your own cleaning and shopping now, but you know you can always call on me if you need anything. We missed you. Come by and see me tomorrow. I love you. Mum."

Brandon couldn't remember the last time he'd spent an evening at home that didn't include at least a six-pack—or two—of beer. For the first time in several weeks, he was sorely tempted to drink, but he read and reread the passage he had written in his journal while somehow managing to overcome the crushing urge to seek out the release he could only find in a good strong drink. As the sleepless night wore on, Brandon realized that living at the apartment building for a while might have its benefits. In a new environment, he might be less likely to fall into old habits.

He turned on his side so he could look out the bedroom window where a half moon lit the night sky. He and Valerie had bought the house together after dating for a year. Brandon bought out her half when they broke up, but her touches remained in the furnishings, paint, and curtains. She had packed only her clothes and a few photos, leaving everything else behind when she moved out. Though it had been a long time coming, in the end Valerie's departure had been abrupt—and he hadn't even had the good grace to notice she was gone.

Brandon sighed, knowing there was no sense rehashing the past when the present required all his energy and attention. He planned to attend an AA meeting at eight the next morning, and then he was meeting his father at the apartment building to go over the work that needed to be done. He'd give that project a month, two at the most, biding his time until he could make a smooth return to his supervisory role at O'Malley & Sons.

In the meantime, he'd work twelve hours a day, if that's what it took, to plow through the repairs needed at the apartment building. He figured the busier he stayed, the less tempted he'd be to fall off the wagon. Working at the apartment building would also put some much-needed space between him and Colin. The last thing he wanted right now was to be taking orders from his younger brother. That would take some major getting used to.

Brandon must've finally dozed off, because the rain beating against his bedroom window awakened him at six thirty. For a moment, he lay perfectly still as he woke up in his own bed for the first time in more than a month. It was odd to greet a morning in this room, in this bed, without a dry mouth, a pounding headache, and a desperate need to puke.

Since he had time before his meeting, he got up to go for a run and stretched it to include a sixth mile for the first time since he began running again. Rain and sweat beaded together on his face, and he was breathing hard by the time he returned home to do fifty push-ups and one hundred sit-ups. His body was slowly returning to its former athletic form, and Brandon had noticed a boost in his energy level as well.

Peering into his closet was almost like finding a stranger's clothing in his house—shirts he didn't remember buying and jeans that would be too big for him now that he'd lost almost twenty of the thirty extra pounds he'd carried around for the last ten years. He grabbed one of the flannel shirts he wore to work and found a pair of faded jeans that still fit and then shaved, showered, and downed two of his mother's homemade blueberry muffins on his way out the door.

He chose a meeting in Harwich, hoping he wouldn't run into anyone he knew the first time out. It was enough to be a recovering alcoholic amid his family, coworkers, and friends without having to confront acquaintances from town at AA.

With the exception of a few school buses, Brandon had the road to himself as he drove his company truck north to the Harwich town line, passing the complex where Declan lived on his way. He reached the Harwich Community Center with five minutes to spare before the meeting. Hustling against the blustery cold and rain, Brandon ducked inside the door behind two women. He looked up and gasped when he saw his high school swim team coach among the group gathered for the meeting.

Mr. Coughlin seemed just as surprised to see Brandon and excused himself to come over and say hello. Since the last time Brandon had seen him five or six years ago, Mr. Coughlin's once dark hair had become shot full of silver, but his blue eyes were just as warm as Brandon remembered, even though there were more lines at the corners now. "How are you, Brandon?" he asked, extending a hand.

Brandon shook his hand, still trying to believe he'd found this larger-than-life figure from his youth at an AA meeting.

"I'm just Joe here," Mr. Coughlin added. "It's good to see you."

"Yes," Brandon stammered. "It's been a while."

"Too long. Is this your first meeting?"

"First one out of rehab. How about you?"

"I've been coming to this one for twenty-five years," Joe confessed.

"Even back when I was on your team?" Brandon asked, astounded.

Joe nodded. "Even then. How long have you been sober?"

"Thirty-one days." The low number embarrassed Brandon. "I just got out of Laurel Lake yesterday."

"Good for you. You're through the first month, and you're where you belong right now. Come on in, have a seat." Joe put an arm around Brandon's shoulders. "This is a great meeting. You'll like the people."

When the meeting was over, Brandon, who had chosen not to speak, was still trying to get his mind around the fact that the man who coached him to a full athletic scholarship at Notre Dame had been an alcoholic during all the years they'd spent big chunks of each day together. Brandon called his father to push their meeting at the apartment building back an hour and invited Joe to join him for a cup of coffee.

Since the rain had let up, they walked the two blocks from the community center to a small coffee shop in the center of town. Once they were seated in a booth, Joe said, "You look good. As fit as ever."

"You should've seen me a month ago. I've been running every day, trying to get back in shape. I really let myself go in more ways than one."

"What happened, Brandon?"

Brandon shrugged. "I stopped giving a shit about anything and drank myself into oblivion, basically. Then one night when I was in a blackout, I got rough with Aidan's new girlfriend, he got rough with me, and the next day I was at Laurel Lake. End of story."

Joe winced. "That's tough. I'm sorry. You landed in the right place, though. Laurel Lake has a great reputation."

"The people there were fantastic. They didn't let me get away with all my usual bullshit. They really called me on it, which was what I needed. What about you? I just never had any idea…"

"It wasn't something I broadcasted, especially back then when there would've been a lot of people frowning on an alcoholic teacher and coach at the high school. I was afraid if people found out, I'd lose my job. So I never told anyone. Ever. These days, I'm retired, and I don't really care who knows."

"That must be liberating," Brandon said as their coffee was served.

Joe added cream and sugar to his. "It is. But we live in a different world today. There isn't the same kind of stigma placed on our illness, because it's better understood than it was back then."

"I'm still not anxious to tell the world."

"You don't have to. Just work the program, live your life as best you can, make your amends. You know the drill by now."

"I sure do envy you."

Joe grunted out a chuckle. "Why in the hell would you envy me?"

"Because you've got twenty-five years of sobriety under your belt, and here I am just getting started."

"There's a story in the *Big Book* about a guy with thirty or so years in the program coming across a newly sober guy who says exactly what you just did. Old guy tells new guy he'd trade places with him in a minute if he could. Of course new guy can't believe that, but old guy knows something new guy never could—he'll find more joy than he can ever imagine on this journey, and if he could, old guy would go back to day one so he could experience it all again. If I could, Brandon, I'd trade places with *you* right now. Not only are you young and handsome," he joked, "but you're at the start of the most amazing journey you'll ever take in your life. *I* envy *you*."

Brandon sat back to absorb what Joe had said. "One of the first things on my to-do list is getting a sponsor. Would you, I mean—"

"I'd be honored. It'd be like old times, huh?"

Brandon laughed and raised his coffee cup in a mock toast. "Here's to old times."

"And new beginnings," Joe said, clicking his mug against Brandon's.

The smell of new wood and sawdust hung in the damp air as Colin inspected a restaurant the new construction division had just completed in Brewster. O'Malley & Sons had put up the frame and would be turning it over to other contractors to finish. Normally, Brandon would be the one to inspect and sign off on a job like this, but Colin knew what to look for and was pleased with what he saw. As he toured the building with the job foreman, Colin's phone beeped. He unclipped it from his belt to take the call from Lorraine, the office manager.

"Colin?" Lorraine had to be well into her sixties, and Colin had never seen her without her signature beehive hair-do and cat's eye glasses, which she owned in an amazing variety of colors and patterns. After nearly forty years of running the office, she was the glue that held the whole operation together.

"Yes, ma'am?" He lived in mortal fear that his father's retirement would spur Lorraine to make the same move, but so far she hadn't said anything, and he certainly wasn't asking.

"You wanted me to let you know when FedEx came."

"I'm waiting for a warranty part for one of the new trucks that's out of commission until it gets here."

"Nothing yet. Do you want me to track it?"

"That's all right. We'll give them until tomorrow. Anything else? Brandon hasn't been there, has he?" Colin was nervous about Brandon showing up to work at the yard rather than the apartment building.

"No sign of Brandon. You got a call from a Meredith Chase. Want the number or should I leave it on your desk?"

Colin's heart skipped a beat, and he reached for the pen sticking out from under his hard hat. "I'll take the number, please." He wrote it on his hand as Lorraine rattled it off.

"She said that's her cell number, and she's on a break until ten thirty."

Colin checked his watch. Ten fifteen. "Thanks, Lorraine." He returned his phone to his belt and turned to the employee he was with. "Excuse me for a minute, Ray. I need to make a phone call."

"Take your time."

Colin went out to his truck to make the call on his personal cell phone. While he waited for Meredith to answer, the phone beeped twice, but he ignored it. When he heard her voice, an image of her in the pink hat came rushing back to him. Despite his intention to forget about her and move on, he'd thought about her often in the days since she turned down his invitation to dinner.

"Hi, it's Colin O'Malley."

"Hi, Colin."

"I got your message."

"I hope it's okay I called your office."

"Of course it is. I was glad to hear from you. How are you?"

"I'm fine. I was just wondering if your brother got home and how you're doing."

Colin was disappointed to realize this was an Al-Anon call. "He's home. Our paths haven't crossed yet, but we're having dinner with him tonight. My dad spent some time with him yesterday and said he seems to be in good shape. We'll see."

"I'll pray for your family."

"Thank you. I'm actually in your school neighborhood right now."

"Really? Doing what?"

"We're the contractor on the new restaurant at the intersection of 28 and 6A."

"I know just where you mean." She paused. "Um, Colin, I feel bad about the way we left things the other night. I don't want you to think…"

"What?"

There was another long pause during which he wondered if she was still there. "That I didn't want to see you again," she said in a small voice. "It's not that."

"Then what is it?" he asked, relieved by her confession.

"It's nothing to do with you. I'd like to see you again. It's just that I don't, well, I don't date or anything."

"Why not?"

"Let's just say once burnt, twice shy."

A new level of understanding settled over him as he got his first clue as to what might've brought her to Al-Anon. "It doesn't have to be a date. We could just call it dinner and leave it at that. You do go out with friends, don't you?"

"Well, yes, I guess I do."

"I'd like to think we could be friends." Colin felt almost deceitful since he already knew he wanted to be much more than friends with this woman. There was something so sweet about her, and the clue she'd given him only fueled his desire to know more about her.

"I'd like that."

"So then would you like to have dinner with a friend on Saturday night?"

"That's date night."

He laughed. "How about Sunday, then?"

"That's a school night."

"I haven't heard that expression in twenty years," he said with a chuckle. "Which is worse? A date night or a school night?"

"Date night, definitely. Sunday it is."

"I'll call you," he promised.

"Okay. Are you coming to the meeting on Friday?"

"I'm planning to."

"I'll see you then. I've got to get back to class."

"See you Friday." Colin ended the call and let out a whoop. It wasn't a date, but it was a start. He looked up to find his employee, Ray, watching him from the door of the restaurant. His face heated with embarrassment as he got out of the truck.

"Everything all right, boss?" Ray asked with amusement. The men had called him that since Dennis announced his promotion at a meeting Monday morning.

"Let's get back to work," Colin grumbled as he put his hard hat back on.

Ray laughed. "After you, boss."

Brandon groaned when he pulled up to the house on Old Queen Anne Road. The rambling Victorian had been added on to over the years, and Dennis said it was structurally sound but needed some major aesthetic work to bring it into the twenty-first century. There were six apartments in all, five of which were rented.

As Brandon walked up the cracked front walk, he surveyed the overgrown landscaping and faded yellow paint peeling off the exterior. The wooden front steps sagged under his weight, and he found more peeling paint, gray this time, on the front porch where an ancient swing hung from the ceiling at the far end. "You'd be taking your life in your hands to sit on that thing," Brandon mumbled.

Dennis came out the front door. "Hey, there he is!" He clapped his son on the back. "The man of the hour!"

"More like the chump of the hour. Sorry I'm late. I ran into Coach Coughlin in Harwich this morning."

"How is he?"

"He's great. It was good to see him." He pushed a finger into the rotted frame around one of the front windows. "What the hell were you thinking buying this place, Da?"

"It's a great tax write off, *and* it has real potential. Come on, I'll show you."

An hour later, Brandon had been given a tour long on low points and short on highlights. The place needed everything. But while he grumbled to his father, inside, Brandon felt a spark of excitement at what he could do here. As he and his brothers had assumed more responsibility within the company, they'd gotten to do less of the actual work, and Brandon was surprised to discover he missed it. "So what's the budget?"

"I'd like to keep it under fifty thousand, not counting your time." Dennis handed his son a credit card he'd allocated to the project. "Do you think you can do it for that much?"

Brandon tucked the card into his back pocket, scratched his head, and took a good look around again at the downstairs apartment that would be his for the time being. The carpet had to go, the bathroom and kitchen would be torn out and replaced, everything needed paint, and this was just *one* of the six apartments. "I don't know. I can try. We'll get quantity discounts on a lot of it since there will be six of everything. If I'm getting close to fifty, I'll let you know. So where do the tenants live when I've got their places gutted?"

"Well," Dennis said, his eyes twinkling with amusement, "I was thinking you could do this place first so they could take turns staying here while you do theirs."

Brandon's eyes narrowed. "So I get to live in chaos to keep the tenants comfortable?"

"Something like that."

"I definitely have 'sucker' written all over me, don't I?"

Dennis became serious. "I thought you might enjoy this, but after what we talked about yesterday, I don't trust myself to make that decision for you anymore. If you really don't want to do it, you certainly don't have to. I can put it back on the market."

"I was just thinking that it's going to be fun," Brandon confessed as he realized he was committing to a project that would take much longer than a month or two. "It's the kind of stuff we used to do in the summers before we grew up and became important."

Dennis laughed. "Yes, and it's exactly what Aidan's doing in Vermont." His smile faded at the mention of his oldest son.

"What?"

"Something's up with him. Your Mum called him just to say hello this morning. She could tell something wasn't right, but he wouldn't tell her anything."

"Maybe she just caught him at a bad time."

"No, it was something more than that." Dennis looked up and went pale as a willowy blond walked past the window where they were standing. He grabbed his son's arm to pull him back from the window.

"What the hell is wrong with you, Da?" Brandon asked, tugging his arm free.

"Shhhh, she'll hear us. She already saw the trucks, so she's looking for us."

"Who is?" Brandon whispered, feeling like an idiot.

"The tenant from hell," Dennis whispered with a look of sincere fright on his face.

"Mr. O'Malley?" a woman's voice called from the hallway. "I know you're here somewhere, and you're hiding from me, but I can wait all day if I have to."

"Shit, shit, *shit*," Dennis whispered.

It was all Brandon could do not to dissolve into laughter. "Are you seriously hiding from a woman? After living with Mum for forty years?"

"That woman makes your mother look like a pushover," Dennis whispered.

"This I have to see." Brandon moved to the door.

"*Brandon!*" Dennis continued to press his huge frame against the wall between the windows. "Do *not* open that door!"

With a withering look for his father, Brandon opened the door to the most breathtaking woman he'd ever seen. And she was some kind of pissed off.

"Is Mr. O'Malley hiding in there?" she asked, hands on slender hips. Golden brown eyes narrowed with anger as she tried to look around Brandon into the apartment.

"I'm Mr. O'Malley." Brandon extended a hand to her. "What can I do for you?"

She ignored his outstretched hand and appeared briefly unnerved to be dealing with another O'Malley.

Brandon's mouth went dry when, in a gesture of anger, she tossed her long blonde hair over her shoulder, revealing high, full breasts under a form-fitting tank top.

"I've been trying to reach the *older* Mr. O'Malley for two weeks. There's a leak in the ceiling, my kitchen sink is backed up, and I'm *still* hearing the pitter-patter of little feet at night. You can tell him if he doesn't do something about it *today*, I'm calling the housing authority. I have a child living in that apartment."

"I'll be up after lunch. Will that do?"

Primed for a fight, she seemed unprepared for his easy capitulation. "Fine." She turned and stalked down the hallway to the stairs.

Brandon bent his head around the doorframe to watch her go. "Mmm, mmm, *mmm*, that is one saucy lady."

"That's one *cranky* lady," Dennis said from behind him.

Brandon turned to his father. "It's okay, Da. You can come out now. I took care of the scary girl for you."

"Shut up."

"Who is she?"

"I told you, the tenant from hell. Thank God she's your problem now."

"What's her *name?*"

"Daphne Van something. I have it written down at home next to the forty-six messages she's left me in the last two weeks."

"Why did you ignore her? She said she's got a kid. That's not like you."

"She yells at me."

That did it. Brandon threw his head back and roared with laughter.

"What the hell is so funny?" Dennis asked, insulted.

When Brandon finally caught his breath, he wiped the tears but not the smile off his face. Damn, it was good to be home. "Six-foot-four-inch Dennis O'Malley. Scared of a girl. I never thought I'd live to see the day."

"I was going to buy you lunch, but the hell with you," Dennis huffed, pushing past his son and out the door.

Brandon followed him. "I'll let you buy me lunch because you're getting my slave labor at this place, so it's the least you can do. And now that I know you're scared of one of the *girl* tenants, my price just went up."

"You have your laughs, sonny boy, but we'll see who's laughing when you've been dealing with that woman for a week or two. Yes, we'll just see who's laughing then."

CHAPTER 11, DAY 31

Brandon was tightening the final bolt under Daphne's sink when her keys jangled in the door. He heard her speaking in a low, controlled tone to a young child, and he decided to stay put until they discovered him. Lying flat on his back, he watched small, pudgy hands pull off bright red sneakers and drop them with a clunk onto the wood floor.

He'd been pleasantly surprised to find the third-floor apartment to be warm and inviting, in definite contrast to his first impression of the woman who lived here. The furniture wasn't expensive, but it was cozy. Lampshades with beaded fringe, colorful throw pillows, and bright yellow paint gave the living room a cheerful atmosphere. Candles sat on every surface along with a dozen framed photographs, but since he felt like an intruder, he hadn't stopped to study them. Toys were piled in one corner and an art easel occupied another. Clearly, the child who lived here was the center of his or her mother's life.

"Mike!" Daphne said. "Put those wet sneakers on the mat. You're making puddles on the floor."

Lighten up, Mom, Brandon thought. *Boys will be boys.* After the sneakers landed again—hopefully this time where they belonged—he heard little feet running in his direction, saw denim-clad legs come into the kitchen, and laughed when they came to a dead stop.

"*MOM!*" the child shrieked. "A man lost his legs in our kitchen!"

Daphne came running in. "Come out of there," she said in the same firm tone she'd used to handle the dripping sneakers. "Right now."

Brandon slid out from under the sink and sat up to find two furious, gorgeous, blonde females—one all grown up and the other just getting started—standing with their hands on their hips and their identical golden brown eyes narrowed in suspicion.

"What're you doing in my apartment?" they asked in stereo.

Brandon looked up at them from where he sat on the floor. "You said you wanted your sink fixed. Well, it's fixed."

"I didn't say you could come in here when I wasn't home," Daphne said.

"Actually, you did when you signed the lease." He got up, turned on the water, and tested his handiwork by washing his hands. "See? There you go. Good as new."

"Who are you?" miniature Daphne asked. She wore denim overalls, a long-sleeved red shirt that matched her rosy cheeks, and her blonde ringlets were contained in pigtails.

"Who are *you*?" Brandon retorted as he dried his hands on his jeans.

"I asked first."

He smiled. The kid had spunk like her mother. "Brandon O'Malley," he said, extending a hand to her.

She grinned with pleasure at being treated like a grown-up and shook his hand. "I'm Mike Van Der Meer, and I'm five years old."

He sized her up. "I would've guessed six, and I hate to tell you, short stuff, but Mike ain't a girl's name."

She crossed her arms over the bib of her overalls and narrowed her eyes again. "I'll be six in May, Mike *is* a girl's name, and ain't *ain't* a word."

Brandon laughed. "Well, I guess you told me."

"Mike, don't be fresh," Daphne admonished.

"Is that your artwork all over the fridge?" Brandon asked.

The girl nodded. "I'm a painter."

"So I see."

"I can do one for you if you want."

"My apartment downstairs could definitely use some color."

"I'll try to get one done for you."

Brandon smothered a chuckle at the serious pucker of her lips as she contemplated her busy schedule.

"Go on and play, Mike. I need to talk to Mr. O'Malley." Daphne scooted the girl to the living room and returned her attention to Brandon. "I really don't like you being in here when I'm not home. There's something very big brother about it."

"You said you were going to report us, and I had no way to know when you'd be back." He bent over to put his tools away in the red toolbox he'd picked up at home after lunch. "I found the source of the leak in the attic and plugged it. I'll try to get up here to fix the damage to your ceiling in the next week or so. I also set some mouse traps, and I'll come back tomorrow to check them."

Daphne's eyes darted around the room in search of the traps. "Where are they?"

"Nowhere that little hands can find them, don't worry. You said you had a kid, and I saw the toys. I'm not a total idiot."

"Just a partial?" she asked with the barest hint of a smile.

"A joke?" he asked, feigning shock. "Are you making a joke?"

"I'm not a total bitch."

"Just a partial?"

She laughed, and the sound of it shot through Brandon the way whiskey used to—hot and smooth.

"Touché," she said. "Thank you for doing the repairs so fast."

"You're welcome."

She leaned back against the counter and tilted her head as she studied him. "You're a lot more responsive than the *other* Mr. O'Malley."

"He's my father." Brandon's pointed look let her know that cracking on the other Mr. O'Malley wouldn't fly with him. "He's had a lot going on lately."

"Well, he should return his tenants' phone calls."

"I'll be around for the next couple of months doing some renovations on the place. I'll be living in the apartment downstairs, so if you need anything, let me know."

"The tenants are talking about the renovations. You should let them know what you have planned. The rest of them are elderly, and stuff like this makes them anxious." She followed him when he picked up the toolbox and walked into the living room.

"I'll talk to them. We're going to paint and do all the kitchens and bathrooms. We'll make my apartment available while we're working on your places. If any of you don't want it done, you don't have to."

"Great," she grumbled.

"We're trying to fix the place up some. What's the problem?"

"How long will it take you to jack up the rent to cover the cost?" She nibbled on her thumbnail nervously as she appeared to be doing the math in her head.

"We won't jack up the rent."

"Sure."

Since he knew he couldn't convince her, he didn't bother. "See you around, Mike."

"Bye, Mr. O'Malley," Mike said from the sofa where she was engrossed in an episode of *Dora the Explorer*.

"Is that really her name?" Brandon whispered.

"Michaela," Daphne said. "Call her that some time. See what happens."

"I'll bet you'd enjoy that."

"You have no idea," she said, again with a hint of smile that said there might be a softer side buried miles beneath her hard-as-a-rock exterior.

"Pleasure to meet you," he said with a phony smile as he crossed the threshold into the hallway.

"Oh, the pleasure was all mine. Stay out of my apartment."

Brandon laughed when she slammed the door behind him. *What a piece of work!*

He was still thinking about Daphne and Mike when he drove home to shower and change for dinner at Erin's house. The family was having a welcome-home party for him, but it had been billed as "just dinner." He planned to humor them for an hour or two before he came home to pack what he would take to the apartment the next day. Why his father was insisting he live there was anyone's guess, but Brandon wasn't going to fight it. He knew he needed to shake things up to keep from sliding into old habits.

The phone was ringing when he came in through the garage, and he lunged for the kitchen extension. "I'm coming!"

"Brandon? Hey, it's Alan."

"Oh, sorry, Alan. I figured this had to be either my mother or my sister confirming *again* that I'm coming to dinner."

Alan chuckled. "How's it going?"

"Today was a good day. I went to a meeting, found a sponsor, had lunch with my dad, got yelled at by a total babe, met a cute kid, and got some work done. Now I'm heading to dinner at my sister's."

"I'm impressed. Not a bad first day on the outside."

"Yeah, it was busy, but I think staying busy will help me."

"As long as you're not busy doing what you used to do. So you got a sponsor, huh?"

"Yeah, it was the weirdest thing. I walked into an AA meeting and ran into my high school swim coach. He's been in AA for twenty-five years. I never had a clue. Anyway, he agreed to be my sponsor."

"That's a really important step. Good for you. Well, I won't keep you. I just wanted to check on you."

"I'm glad you did. Let's, uh, have dinner or something. Christ, I was going to say grab a beer."

"Old habits die hard," Alan said. "But they *do* die. Why don't you come out to the house for dinner some night? I'd love for you to meet my wife and daughters."

"That'd be great, Alan. I'll give you a call next week."

As Brandon set down the phone, he tried to remember the last time he made a new friend who wasn't a drinking buddy. It felt good to know there were people out there who were wishing him well and who'd be there for him if he stumbled. Maybe that's what all this higher power stuff was about, he thought, as he sat on his bed to take off his work boots. He lay back on the bed and looked up at the ceiling.

"God, give me the strength to get through this night with my family," he whispered, expecting the earth to move or a bolt of lightning to come slashing through the window. But when half a minute passed without any sign of divine displeasure at his pathetic attempt at prayer, he got up to take a shower.

Every light was on in Erin's large Victorian home, which was located less than a mile from Brandon's parents' house on Shore Road. Erin and Tommy used a big chunk of the inheritance from Sarah that Aidan shared with his family for the down payment on a house and a neighborhood they otherwise could not have afforded. Tommy had done a ton of work to the place, and the result was a comfortable, chaotic environment.

The driveway looked like a used car lot, and Brandon groaned when he realized he was the last to arrive. His parents' silver Cadillac, Colin's company truck, and Declan's Mustang were in the driveway behind Tommy's company truck and Erin's minivan. Brandon parked his truck in front of the house, took a deep breath, and made his way up the walk.

Erin came bursting out of the door, ran down the stairs, and leaped into his arms.

"Jesus, you almost knocked the wind out of me, woman." Brandon planted a noisy kiss on the top of her strawberry blonde head as she clung to him.

"Good to see you," she whispered into his neck.

He held her for a long moment before he put her back down. "Tell me you're not crying."

She wiped her face. "Don't be ridiculous."

Despite the eight years between them, Brandon had shared a special bond with his baby sister until his drinking and her growing family took them in opposite directions.

Erin hooked her arm through his to lead him up the stairs. The family was gathered in the living room, and the first thing Brandon noticed was how stiff they all seemed as one by one they got up to greet him. He hugged and kissed his mother, who was also weepy. Dec enveloped him in a warm hug.

When Declan finally let him go, Brandon turned to Colin. "Hey, Col."

"You look good, Brand." Colin reached out to shake his brother's hand. "Really good."

"I feel good," Brandon replied as he shook hands with his brother-in-law Tommy. "Where're the kids?"

"Spending the night with Tommy's mother so we could have some grown-up time tonight," Erin said.

"Why's everyone acting so weird?" Brandon looked around and noticed none of them were drinking. "Oh, come on, you can have a beer or whatever. You're not going to knock me off the wagon."

"That's all right," Colleen said. "We don't need it."

"Mum, listen, you guys have to do your thing. I appreciate the consideration, but this isn't your problem. It's mine. Now, Erin, get these guys some beers and be normal, will you? Please?"

All eyes shifted to Colleen.

"Well, I guess it's all right, but if you change your mind, Brand, you just say something," Colleen said. "We don't want to make it any harder on you than it already is."

"I need normal, Mum." Brandon kissed her cheek. "Erin, get Da a beer before he starts drooling."

They all laughed at the scowl Dennis sent his son, and Brandon felt things slide back to normal, or what was passing for normal these days.

After they dined on barbequed chicken, baked potatoes, and salad, Colleen corralled her sons into the family room off Erin's kitchen.

The "boys" exchanged nervous glances. This felt an awful lot like the lineup they endured after they broke the window at Old Man Kuzminski's place and then lied about it, or the time they blew out all the tires in Jimmy Olsen's father's car when thirteen-year-old Jimmy took them on a joy ride that'd actually been Declan's idea.

"What's up, Mum?" Dec asked when Colleen closed the door. "What'd we do?"

"Don't be a dope. You didn't do anything. I talked to Aidan this morning, and he sounded odd. Have any of you talked to him?" Colleen was so dwarfed by her sons that she had to tilt her head at a dramatic angle to see their faces.

"Not since we got home from Boston on Sunday," Colin said.

"Why were you in Boston?" Brandon asked.

"Clare had us all to the city for Aidan's fortieth birthday," Colleen said.

Brandon felt a stab of remorse over missing what sounded like a fun time—a fun time that centered on Aidan. Interesting that he felt remorse and not anger, Brandon thought. Before he had a chance to chew on that revelation, his mother continued.

"I didn't like the way he sounded. Something's wrong with him, but he wouldn't tell me what it is."

"You don't know that, Mum," Colin said. "He could've just been tired or not feeling good."

"It's more than that. I could hear it in his voice the same way I'd hear it in yours if it were one of you. I want you boys to go up there this weekend to check on him."

"I've got plans," Declan protested.

"I've got a date," Colin said.

"He certainly doesn't want to see me," Brandon said.

Colleen held up her hand to shush them. "Something's wrong with your brother, and the three of you are going to Vermont on Friday to find out what it is." Her stern green eyes skipped from one of her grown sons to the other and then the third. They were as powerless against that particular look of hers in their late thirties as they'd been in their teens. "Do I make myself clear?"

They looked down at the floor and mumbled, "Yes, Mum," in three-part harmony.

"That's my boys," she said as she turned and left the room.

When she was gone, Colin spoke first. "How old do you think we're going to be before she can't pull that shit on us anymore?"

"Apparently, older than we are now," Declan said.

"She's only sixty," Brandon reminded them. "She could have thirty or more good years left in her."

They groaned.

"I have to be back by six on Sunday," Colin said.

"Jessica's going to be pissed," Dec said. "Her parents and sister are coming to town this weekend. I'd better go call her."

When they were alone, Colin turned to Brandon. "You look so good. I almost didn't recognize you."

"I've lost twenty pounds of bloat. Been running again, too."

"Is it hard? Not drinking?"

"Minute-by-minute struggle, but I'm handling it."

"Ah, Brand, about the work stuff—"

"Are you waiting for me to flip out?"

"Kind of," Colin admitted.

"I won't lie to you. I'm not thrilled about it, but I've learned that anger leads to some really bad shit for me. So I'm choosing not to be angry about it."

Colin opened his mouth to say something but closed it again as he studied his brother. "You surprise me."

"I surprise myself. Start getting bitchy with me at work, though, and I'll pound your ass into the ground—but not in anger, of course."

Colin cracked up. "Duly noted."

CHAPTER 12, DAY 33

Standing under the slow trickle of the shower in the super's apartment, Brandon made a mental note to address the piss-poor water pressure first thing on Monday. His muscles ached from two days of hard, physical labor, during which he'd replaced the sagging front stairs and torn out the carpet as well as the kitchen in his apartment. He also met the rest of the tenants, all of them older people who lived alone, and explained the renovation plans to each of them.

As he ran a razor over his face, Brandon remembered he needed to check the mousetraps in Daphne's apartment before he left for Vermont. Upon an earlier check, he'd discovered the little bastards had managed to swipe the bait without being caught. He felt like Wile E. Coyote trying to capture the Road Runner.

The frantic Road Runner music was still playing in his head as he ran a comb through his unruly hair and got dressed. *Time for a haircut*, he thought, studying his reflection in the mirror. His face had lost the bloated, unhealthy look he'd worn for years, and he was starting to recognize himself again.

At the AA meeting in Harwich that morning, he'd shared a small part of his story. Joe had encouraged him to take that step to get the first time behind him, and Brandon had to admit his sponsor was right—he felt better afterward. They also helped him locate a meeting he could attend while he was in Vermont.

Brandon checked his watch. He had fifteen minutes until Declan and Colin were picking him up in Dec's new Mustang. Taking the stairs two at a time,

Brandon made his way to Daphne's third-floor apartment and knocked on the door.

"Who is it?" Mike asked through the door.

"Brandon."

Mike opened the door and greeted him with a big smile. She'd been down to visit him a couple of times over the last two days, and while he wanted to be annoyed by her, he couldn't quite seem to get there. She was so damned cute.

"Hello, madame," he said with a low bow that made her giggle. "Is your mother home?"

"MOM!" Mike yelled.

"I could've done that." Brandon made her giggle again when he opened his mouth in a mock scream. He was relieved to discover he could still be playful with a child. Maybe there was hope for him with his nieces and nephews.

Daphne came out from the kitchen, and Brandon had to fight the urge to drool right there on her doorstep. She was wearing another of those tank tops—this time in a soft salmon color—and black yoga pants that left *nothing* to the imagination. Her blonde hair was piled on top of her head in a style that would've been messy on anyone else. On her it was perfection. She was a goddess—an unfriendly goddess—but a goddess nonetheless.

"You're staring," Mike whispered.

"What?" Brandon tore his eyes off the mother to gaze down at the equally fetching daughter.

"You're *staring*," she whispered again.

"Oh, um, I, ah, wanted to check the traps." He cursed the goddess for making him into a stammering fool.

"Come on in," Daphne said. "See, that's how it's done: you knock, I say come in. You're getting it."

"Yes, ma'am," Brandon said in a deliberately dense-sounding tone. "I might be a dumb man, but I can be trained."

Mike giggled.

Even Daphne cracked a reluctant grin.

Brandon went to check the traps and found that he'd been outfoxed again. "Damn it," he said under his breath.

"Ummm, you *sweared*."

Brandon almost jumped out of his skin. "Christ, you scared me," he muttered.

"You did it again!"

"I don't know what you're talking about," he said, amused by the scandalized expression on her cherubic face.

She plunked herself down next to him for a nice long chat. "Why's your hair all wet?"

"Ever heard of a shower?"

"Why would anyone take a shower when it's still daytime?" she asked, her nose crinkling with disgust.

He tossed his head back and laughed. "Because I needed it after working all day, and I'm going on a trip."

Her face fell with disappointment. "Where're you going?" she asked in a small voice that tugged at his heart. Yesterday he'd noticed her playing by herself in the fenced-in backyard. She was the only kid in the building, and there was an aura of loneliness about her that saddened him.

"I'm going to Vermont for the weekend to see my brother."

"You have a brother?"

"Three of them."

Her eyes widened with envy. "*Three brothers?* You must've had lots of fun when you were kids."

"We did." He smiled as he remembered the chaos of growing up with four siblings. "There was always something to do, that's for sure. I have a sister, too, and she has five kids, including three little girls just like you."

"You're so lucky. I just have my mom."

"Maybe you can play with my sister's kids sometime." The words were out of his mouth before he could stop them.

"*Can I?* Do you mean it?"

"Sure," he said, taking great pleasure in her delight.

"Mike, are you talking his ear off?" Daphne asked from the hallway.

"Of course not," Brandon answered with a wink at his friend. "She's keeping me company." He pulled out the baggie of cheese he'd brought with him to bait the traps. "Don't go near these things, Mike. Do you hear me?"

She nodded. "Uh-huh. Guess what, Mom? Brandon said I can play with his sister's kids sometime."

"Brandon said that, did he? Since when are you calling a grown-up by his first name?"

"Since he told me I could," she said with a conspiratorial glance at him.

"Mr. O'Malley is my father. I'm just Brandon." He tugged on one of the girl's pigtails. "My friends call me Brand."

"That's a nickname like Mike, right?"

He chuckled. "Exactly. Well, ladies, I have to run. My brothers will be here in a minute to pick me up. You guys have a nice weekend."

"When will you be back?" Mike's tiny lips twisted into a woman-sized pout.

"Sunday night. I'll come see you then, okay?" Again it seemed his mouth was working without backup from his brain as he made a promise to the child.

"Okay," she said and scampered off to her room.

"Sorry if she's being a pest," Daphne said.

"She's adorable. I like talking to her."

"I appreciate you being nice to her and everything, but…"

"But what?"

She bit her bottom lip, and Brandon found himself staring again, wondering if that lip tasted as sweet as it looked. "I don't want her getting attached."

"Why not? I'm not going anywhere."

"I don't know how long we'll be here, and the fewer attachments she forms, the easier it'll be when we move."

Disappointment spiraled through him. He'd have to wait until later to think about why. For now he wanted to enjoy being close enough to the goddess to smell her alluring fragrance. He was also close enough to touch her, even though he'd probably be risking a finger or two if he did. "Where're you going?"

"I don't know yet. It all depends."

"On?"

She shook her head. "Nothing," she said, shutting down so tightly he could almost hear the door slam in his face. "Thanks for checking the traps."

"No problem. Do you mind if I stop by to see Mike on Sunday? I sort of promised her I would."

"Fine," she said with a deep sigh, as if the weight of the whole world rested on her petite shoulders.

"I won't hurt her," he said with a fierce determination to mean it. For reasons he didn't quite understand, it mattered to him that he be someone the girl could count on, despite his horrendous track record in the reliability department.

"I won't let you," Daphne said with determination just as fierce.

Brandon held her gaze until the loud blare of a horn from the street jolted him out of his trance. "That's my ride. I'll see you."

She said nothing as he walked away.

The bickering began just south of Boston. Declan didn't like the smell of the salt-and-vinegar potato chips Colin bought at the gas station, so he forbade his brother to eat them in his new car. Colin opened them anyway, and when Declan made a grab for them, Brandon had to lunge from the backseat to rescue the chips before they went flying all over the car.

"For Christ's sake, you two. Knock it off." Brandon thrust the chips at Colin. "Open a window. They stink."

"That's why I don't want them in my car," Declan said.

"You're being such a *girl* about this car," Colin said.

"Screw you."

"Just because your girlfriend's pissed at you doesn't mean you have to be a jerk to us all weekend," Colin said.

"Quit busting his balls, Col." A headache had started behind Brandon's left eye that promised to only get worse in the next three hours if the two of them were going to keep up the uncharacteristic bitching. Brandon was nervous enough about how he would be received by Aidan without listening to the Bickersons go at it in the front seat.

He yearned for some peace and quiet so he could think about why Daphne made him want to drool and why the thought of them moving filled him with such sadness. He'd known them only a couple of days, but Mike was already working her way under his skin. He remembered something he'd heard at one of his meetings about the many blessings that came from living a sober life and wondered if Mike might turn out to be a blessing in his life.

Her prickly mother, on the other hand, had the potential to be more of a curse. He chuckled as he imagined her reaction to him drooling at the sight of her. It probably wouldn't be the first time a man made a fool of himself over her.

Colin and Declan had fallen into merciful silence.

"How pissed is Jessica, Dec?" Brandon asked.

"Royally."

"We could've gone without you," Brandon said. "Mum wouldn't have known."

Declan snorted. "As if. She'd find out, and I'd be even more screwed than I am with Jess."

Colin laughed. "Why do we still care so much about our mother being pissed with us? We probably need counseling or something."

They shared a laugh, and the fight over the chips was forgotten.

"Do you think if we ever have kids they'll fear us the way we fear her?" Colin asked.

"Hardly," Brandon said. "We'll be lucky if they don't end up in jail."

"How pissed do you think Aidan's gonna be that we're showing up there unannounced?" Dec asked.

"Depends on what's going on with him," Colin said.

"How was he when you saw him last weekend?" Brandon asked.

"On top of the world," Colin replied. "He said he was going to marry Clare."

"He did?" Dec turned to look at Colin. "When?"

"Friday night when the rest of you were dancing."

"Wow," Dec said. "That was fast. Didn't he just meet her?"

"A couple of months ago, but he said he loved her from the very beginning. She seems really good for him, and he loves her kids, too."

"She has kids?" Brandon asked.

"Three girls," Colin said. "Nineteen, eighteen, and thirteen. The oldest and youngest were there last weekend. They're nice kids."

"How do you guys think he'll feel about seeing me?" Brandon asked, expressing the worry that'd been on his mind since their mother issued her edict two nights earlier.

Colin turned in his seat to look at Brandon. "The two of you have to sort things out eventually."

"I have things I need to say to him," Brandon said. "To all of you, really."

"Like what?" Colin asked.

"Some of it I need to talk to Aidan about. Maybe not this weekend, if he's got other stuff going on, but sometime. It's crap that goes way back, but they helped me see in rehab what a big effect it's had on my life."

"You gotta give us something, Brand," Declan pleaded, glancing at his brother in the rear-view mirror.

Brandon stared out the window, watching the Boston city lights zip past as they crossed the Zakim Bridge on Interstate 93 North. He was going to have to do this at some point. Why not now? "Do you guys remember when Aidan got into medical school?"

"Sure," Colin said. "Before he and Sarah graduated from Yale, just before their wedding, right?"

"That's right. Well, I jumped to a huge conclusion at that time that I've only recently found out was wrong. Way wrong." When he took a deep breath to steady his nerves, he realized Dec had turned off the radio, and he had his brothers' full attention. "I assumed Da would expect the rest of us to come into the business."

"I think we all assumed that," Colin said.

"But I didn't want to," Brandon said so softly it was almost a whisper.

"What did you want to do?" Dec asked, making eye contact with Brandon in the mirror.

"I wanted to be a Navy SEAL. I wanted to go places. See things. I wanted out of the Cape."

"Why didn't you ever say anything?" Colin asked, incredulous.

"I figured Aidan had gotten the get-out-of-jail-free card, and there wouldn't be one for the rest of us."

"Why would you just assume that?" Colin asked.

Brandon shrugged. "When I talked to Da about it the other day, he made it clear I'd read the whole thing totally wrong. He was devastated, in fact. Made me feel like shit to upset him that way."

"So all these years, you've just been, like, hating life?" Declan asked.

"Not every minute, but a lot of it. Yeah."

Brandon gave his brothers a minute to process what he'd told them. "What about you guys? Wasn't there other stuff you wanted to do?"

"Not me," Colin said. "That's why Da couldn't get me to go to college. I was exactly where I wanted to be."

"Me either," Declan said. "I couldn't wait to get through school so I could come home and go to work."

"I guess it was just me." Brandon sighed. "And I blamed Aidan for the whole thing because he got to leave, and then when he gave up medicine—*even then*—he didn't come back home to work with us. I was really furious about that."

"Why?" Colin asked. "It wasn't his fault you hadn't gotten to do what you wanted to."

"I know that now. I know a lot of things now, but at the time, that's how I saw it. For many reasons, I blamed him."

"Is this tied into the, uh, other thing?" Declan asked.

"You can say the word alcoholism, Dec. It's not forbidden. And yes, it's all part of it. I've kept huge secrets and nursed even bigger resentments, both of which are very destructive to someone who has a natural inclination to drink too much. Together they're like gas and fire. I got so I couldn't deal with anything or anyone without alcohol to numb me first."

"So there's more?" Colin asked. "You said there were secrets, plural."

"Yeah, but the rest is stuff I need to work out with Aidan. Eventually." Brandon's stomach twisted. He couldn't imagine any scenario that would be conducive to saying to his older brother, *Your wife, the love of your life who died? Oh, by the way, I loved her, too.* A shudder rippled through him. *And I hated you because you had her and I didn't.* Yeah, this was going to be one hell of a weekend.

When they arrived just after ten at the A-frame house Aidan had built outside of Stowe, Vermont, they found him passed out on the sofa with a dozen empty beer bottles scattered around him.

"Shit," Colin said. "He's smashed."

"Aid." Declan poked at his brother. "Aidan."

"*What?*" Aidan grumbled. "What do you want?"

"Wake up," Dec said with a glance at Colin. They hadn't seen Aidan like this since Sarah died.

Brandon hung back at the door to Aidan's den, staying as far out of the way as he could.

"Aidan!" Declan said.

"What? I'm awake." His speech was slurred, and days had passed since his last shave. "What the hell are you guys doing here?"

"Your mother sent us," Colin said. "She wants to know what's wrong with you, and since you wouldn't tell her, here we are."

"There's nothing wrong, so go home." Aidan buried his face in his arm and appeared to be on his way back to sleep.

"Oh, no, you don't. We just drove four hours to get here, so you're gonna talk to us." Colin pulled his brother into an upright position.

That was when Aidan saw Brandon in the doorway.

"What the *fuck* is *he* doing here?" Aidan roared. "*Get him out of here!*"

"Mum made him come with us, so give him a break," Declan said. "Where's Clare?"

Aidan kept his eyes closed. "Gone," he muttered. "She's gone."

"Gone where?" Colin exchanged glances again with Declan.

"What does it matter?" he slurred. "She's not here, and she's not coming back."

"A week ago, you were going to marry her," Colin said. "What the hell happened?"

"She turned me down," Aidan said, his eyes filling.

"*No,*" Colin exhaled. "No way. She's wild about you."

"Yeah, well, apparently not as much as I thought."

"She loves you, Aidan," Declan said. "That was obvious to all of us last weekend. Tell us exactly what happened."

Aidan ran a weary hand over his face. "I asked her to marry me, and she said she wants to, but there's something else she wants, too."

"What?" Colin asked.

"She wants to adopt a kid."

"So what's the problem?" Declan asked.

Aidan shook his head. "I don't want a kid. Not now or ever. Her kids are fine, but I don't want one of my own."

They were all thinking in that moment of the son Sarah wanted so desperately she refused cancer treatment to give the baby a chance at life. His stillbirth had been almost as devastating to Aidan as Sarah's death two days later.

"So Clare didn't exactly say no, then, did she?" Colin asked.

"It doesn't matter. It's over, and she's gone."

The horrible pain etched into Aidan's face made Brandon ache for the brother he'd once wanted dead.

Colin and Declan managed to get Aidan up three winding flights of stairs to his bedroom on the top floor.

"What am I going to do now, Collie?" Aidan moaned as he dissolved into tears. "How am I supposed to live without her? Without her girls? I love them, too."

"I know you do." Colin tugged the blankets up over his brother. "You're going to get some sleep, and we'll figure this out tomorrow."

Declan came into the room with a glass of water and two Advils, which they got Aidan to take.

"I'll crash up here with him," Declan said when Aidan began to snore softly between sobs. "In case he pukes or something."

Colin rubbed the tension from the back of his neck. "Why couldn't things have worked out for him this time? Hasn't he had enough?"

"I know. Seeing him in tears is just so screwed up. That's not him."

"Really. I'm going to go check on the *other* one," Colin said with a dramatic roll of his eyes.

Declan chuckled. "When did we become the *older* brothers?"

"No shit. Give me a yell if the bear comes out of hibernation and you need a hand," Colin said as he left Declan with Aidan and went downstairs to find

Brandon dropping the empty beer bottles into a grocery bag. "Why don't you let me do that, Brand?"

"I can do it." Brandon bent to retrieve two bottles from the floor. "So this is what it looks like, huh?"

"What?"

"A big ugly drunk. This was me. How many times have you seen me like this?"

Colin shrugged. "A few."

"A lot," Brandon insisted. "Don't sugarcoat it, Col. It was ugly, and it went on for years. You even bailed me out of jail. Twice."

"It's in the past now. We don't need to dwell on it." Colin added a couple of logs to the woodstove in Aidan's cozy den, Colin's favorite room in the extraordinary house.

Brandon put the bag of bottles on the floor and sat on the sofa. "I had no memory of it, you know. Until I got your letter in rehab, I didn't even know. Everyone said some really tough shit to me in those letters, but yours was the one that finally got me to say the words."

Colin turned to look at Brandon. "What words?"

"The all-important words: my name is Brandon, and I'm an alcoholic—a very big moment in rehab. Your letter made me realize I could no longer deny what I was."

"I felt like an asshole for days after I wrote that letter," Colin confessed.

"You said things I needed to hear, stuff I didn't know. I honestly had no idea how out of control I had gotten."

"Well, we did a lot to make it easy for you. We were your quote-unquote enablers. As long as we were cleaning up after you, there was no need for you to take any responsibility."

"I've put you all through hell." Brandon dropped his head into his hands. "I'm truly sorry, Col. I really am."

"Hey." Colin waited for Brandon to look at him before he continued. "It's in the past. We'll figure out the rest. One day at a time, right?"

"How do you know about that?"

"Al-Anon."

"Really?"

Colin nodded. "I've only been once so far, but I plan to go back." He'd called Meredith to tell her why he wouldn't make the Friday night meeting and to confirm their plans for Sunday.

"That's cool. Thanks, Col, you know, for not giving up on me even when you were bailing me out of jail."

"I'll never give up on you—either one of you," Colin said with an upward glance to include Aidan.

Brandon snickered. "What a pair we are, huh?"

"No comment," Colin said with a smile as he flipped on the TV in search of sports.

CHAPTER 13, DAY 34

In the morning, Brandon borrowed the Mustang to go into Stowe for an AA meeting. Because he bore a striking resemblance to Aidan, who was well known in the small town, he kept quiet at the meeting, even though he was dying to talk for once. Seeing Aidan again had churned up a lot of feelings in Brandon, and the desire to drink on that cold winter morning was strong. He fought his way through it on the way back to Aidan's house, which was built into one of the foothills at the base of Mount Mansfield.

A winding road led to the house at the top of the hill, and Brandon noticed with relief that Aidan's truck was gone. The house really was a wonder. Brandon had to give Aidan credit for that. About a year after Sarah died, Aidan came up to Vermont, where they'd used a portion of the money she inherited from her grandmother to buy the lot for a future weekend home. Overwhelmed by grief and with his medical career abandoned, Aidan used the skills gathered over years of working summers with their father to throw himself into the building of the house. He'd planned to sell it, but by the time he finished it, he felt at home in the small mountain town, and his restoration business had taken off, thanks to word-of-mouth referrals.

Brandon walked into the kitchen and stopped short when he found Aidan sitting shirtless at the table, nursing a cup of coffee. Everything inside Brandon screamed at him to turn around and get out of there, but his feet wouldn't move. "Are you feeling okay?" he finally asked his brother.

"Yeah," Aidan grunted, his eyes bloodshot and his hair standing on end. "Never better."

"Do you mind if I have some of that?" Brandon asked with a nod at the coffee.

"I don't care."

A marvel of modern convenience, the kitchen featured artistic touches such as the tile backsplash and shining copper pots hanging over the center island. Aidan had always loved to cook, and the layout of the kitchen reflected the thought he'd put into it. Brandon brought his coffee over to sit at the table.

After several minutes of awkward silence, Brandon cleared his throat. "Um, I know you don't want me here, and I totally understand why, but you know how Mum can be when she gets something in her head."

Aidan's grunt might've been a chuckle if he'd been talking to someone else. "Held a gun to your heads, did she?"

"Something like that. Where're the boys?"

"Took my truck and went skiing."

Brandon wanted to groan. He'd be stuck here alone with Aidan for *hours*? "Do you want to go? I wouldn't mind skiing."

"Hell, no." Aidan ran a hand over his fragile head. "Not today. You go ahead."

Go! Brandon thought. *Run!* But despite the overwhelming urge to flee, he seemed frozen in place. "Can I say something?"

Aidan sighed and then winced when the movement was apparently more than his aching head could bear. "If you must."

"I know you've got other things on your mind, but I want you to know how very sorry I am about what happened that night at Mum's." He swallowed hard. "With Clare."

Aidan's eyes hardened at the mention of her name. "I'm not the one you attacked."

"You're right, and I'd like the chance to apologize to her, too."

"Why don't you just leave it alone?"

Oh, how I wish I could. "Because I can't. It's part of the program. Making amends."

"I heard she went back to Rhode Island. She couldn't wait to get away from me, I guess."

"You don't know that, Aid."

"You *certainly* don't know a thing about it," Aidan snapped.

Brandon raised his hands in defense. "You're absolutely right." He stood up to put his mug in the dishwasher. "If you have her address, I'll write her a letter."

"It's around here somewhere."

"Okay." Brandon moved toward the living room that had been built to show-case Sarah's baby grand piano.

"Brandon."

He turned around. "Yeah?"

"Can I ask *you* something?" Aidan looked more like himself as the coffee did battle with the hangover.

Brandon shrugged. "Sure."

"Why'd you turn into such a dick?"

"Don't hold back," Brandon said with a snort. "Tell me how you really feel."

"You used to be cool when we were kids, before you turned into a total asshole overnight. We were inseparable, and then all of a sudden you couldn't stand the sight of me. Why was that?"

Brandon's stomach clutched. "You don't want to talk about it, believe me. Not now."

"Do *not* tell me what I want to talk about." Aidan's dark green eyes shot daggers at his brother. "You lost that right when you started treating me like shit."

"It's not the time," Brandon said, feeling a bit desperate as Aidan dug in. "Seriously."

"I think it's the perfect time. It's just you and me, and this discussion is long overdue." Aidan reclined the kitchen chair onto its back legs. "Enlighten me."

Brandon shifted his weight from one leg to the other and crossed his arms over his chest. As a twitch began to throb in his cheek, he yearned for a drink in that moment more than any other in the last thirty-four days.

Aidan's steely gaze never wavered as Brandon worked up the nerve to proceed. *Okay*, he thought, *if there really is a higher power, now would be a good time to show up. Help me. Please, help me.*

"Before I say anything, you need to know this could be the last time we ever talk to each other. That's not how I want it, but you might."

Aidan released a bitter laugh. "It's not like we talk to each other now. What the hell difference will it make?"

Brandon leaned against the counter and kept his sweaty hands tucked into his folded arms. While he summoned the courage he needed, Dr. Walker-Smith's words echoed through his head. "You must deal with Aidan. Your recovery will depend on it."

A bead of sweat rolled down Brandon's back, and he knew he could be sick if he focused too much attention on his roiling stomach. Another minute of uncomfortable silence passed as he summoned the courage. "Do you remember the day we met Sarah?"

Aidan's eyes narrowed. "Of course I do."

"What do you remember about it?"

"We were playing football on the beach, and I threw the ball over your head. It landed right at her feet." Aidan's face lifted into a small smile as he recalled the long-ago day that changed his life in more ways than he knew.

"Right."

"You went to get the ball, and you were gone forever. So I went to get you."

"What happened when you came over to where we were?"

"She smiled at me, and nothing was ever the same. What's the point of this little trip down memory lane?"

Brandon's jaw shifted first to the left and then the right. "The same thing happened to me."

"What're you talking about?" Aidan asked, his face twisting with confusion.

"I was in love with her. From that very first day."

Aidan's chair dropped to the floor with a loud whack. "You have no right to say that." He sprang from the chair as if he'd been shot from a cannon.

Brandon didn't move when Aidan grabbed the front of his shirt.

"I'm giving you one chance to take that back," Aidan said, standing an inch from Brandon's face.

"Or what? You said you wanted to know. I'm telling you."

The battle of wills was fierce, but neither of them blinked for a long time. When Aidan finally released his brother's shirt, his hand curled into a fist.

"Go ahead and hit me if that'll make you feel better, but it won't change anything."

"You were right." Aidan appeared to be making a huge effort to contain his rage. "I don't want to hear this." He left the room, and a minute later, Brandon heard a door slam upstairs.

"Well," he said to the empty room. "That went well."

Declan and Colin returned from skiing early that evening with groceries for dinner. The house was dark when they came in to discover Brandon watching a Notre Dame basketball game in the den and Aidan upstairs in his bedroom.

"What happened around here today?" Colin asked.

Brandon shrugged. "The usual crap." He didn't mention that he'd spent hours working himself into a cold sweat as he tried to resist the urge to drink. In his desperation, he even called Joe to talk it out. His relief at seeing Colin and Declan was overwhelming, since he knew he'd never drink in front of them.

"Did you guys have a fight or something?" Declan asked.

"Or something," Brandon replied.

"Jeez, Brand, he's got enough going on without getting into it with you, too," Colin said.

"I know that," Brandon snapped.

The three of them drifted into stony silence as they started dinner. They were all proficient in the kitchen, thanks to their mother's relentless campaign to send self-sufficient men into the world, and they worked together like a well-choreographed team.

When dinner was ready, Colin went upstairs to get Aidan. He knocked on the door to Aidan's bedroom and opened the door to find his brother asleep. He nudged him awake.

"Hey." Aidan rubbed a hand over his eyes. "How was the skiing?"

"Great. Perfect conditions."

"I wish I could say the same about the goings on around here," Aidan said, his face set in an angry expression.

"What happened?"

"You wouldn't believe me if I told you. What're you guys cooking? Smells good."

"Dec made lasagna. Why don't you come have some?"

"I'll be down in a minute." Aidan got up to head for the large bathroom that adjoined his bedroom. "Hey, Col?"

"Yeah?"

"I'm glad you guys came up. I'm doing my best not to kill Brandon, but I'm glad you and Dec are here. This has been a horrendous week."

"I wish there was something we could do to help with the Clare situation."

Aidan sighed with resignation. "There's nothing anyone can do. It's just one of those things. We want different things out of life."

"Come down and eat," Colin said.

Aidan chuckled on his way into the bathroom. "You sound like Mum, throwing food at every problem."

"Yeah, okay, fuck you."

Aidan's laughter followed Colin downstairs.

When he got to the kitchen, Colin confronted Brandon. "What the hell did you say to him?"

Brandon shook his head and held up a hand to stop Colin before he got started. "I don't want to talk about it. Can we just eat, for Christ's sake?" *God, this weekend is sucking the big one! How many hours until I can get the hell out of here?*

Aidan came downstairs a few minutes later, and the four of them sat down to eat the lasagna, salad, and garlic bread. When ten minutes passed in unusual and awkward silence, Aidan looked up at Brandon. "So why don't you tell them what you told me today?"

Brandon's fork froze in midair. "That's between us."

Declan and Colin exchanged glances.

"I think your brothers need to hear about how you lusted after my wife for years."

"*What?*" Colin gasped.

Brandon got up so fast his chair toppled over. "That's *not* what I said, Aidan," he seethed. "Leave it to you to turn it into something ugly."

"You guys…" Declan said. "Take a breath."

"Come on, Brand, tell them *all about* how you fell for her the day we met her," Aidan goaded. "It's so sweet."

"Fuck you, Aidan. Fuck you straight to hell." Brandon spun around and grabbed his coat off a hook on the wall. He was out the door a second later to a blast of cold mountain air that smacked at his face. Tears stung his eyes and snow crunched under his boots as he made his way down Aidan's winding driveway.

"Brandon!" Declan called. "Wait!"

Brandon kept walking.

"Brand, stop!"

"Why?" Brandon asked over his shoulder. "So you can bust my balls, too? No thanks."

Declan finally caught up to Brandon. "I'm not going to bust your balls, but what the hell was that all about?"

"You heard him."

Declan's eyes widened. "Is it true? Did you have a thing for Sarah?"

Brandon sighed. "Yes."

"*For real?* And you *told* him this? Jesus, Brand, what've you got a death wish or something?"

"I'm trying to stay sober. Remember what I said about secrets and resentments?"

Declan shook his head as he tried to process it. "For how long? I mean…" he sputtered. "Shit."

"Always. From the day we met her, but she was all about him, as you know."

"So," Declan said with a knowing nod, "that's why."

"Why what?"

"Why you hate him."

Brandon stopped walking and turned to his brother. "I never said I hated him." At least he didn't think he'd ever said it out loud before he confessed it to Sondra in rehab.

Declan laughed but it had a bitter edge to it. "Do you honestly think you've done a good job of hiding it all these years?"

Brandon didn't realize he'd been so obvious. "I don't hate him, or I didn't until about five minutes ago." Brandon was still furious at Aidan for mocking him. "For a long time, I did, though. I won't deny that. I blamed him for everything that was wrong with my life. He got the girl; he got the career he wanted. He had it all, and I had nothing."

"But why in the world would you get into this with him right now? You're kind of kicking him when he's down, aren't you?"

"He flat out asked me why things had gotten so bad between us over the years. I told him it wasn't something we should talk about now, but you know how he can be. He wouldn't let it go."

"Damn." Dec exhaled a long deep breath that came out like a cloud in the cold air. After they walked for several minutes in silence, Declan stopped Brandon with a hand on his arm. "Let's go back."

"That's all right. I'll stay out here."

"Let's go back and deal with it. Let's put all this shit where it belongs—in the past."

Brandon shook his head. "I don't have it in me right now, Dec. I've had the worst time trying not to drink today. It's been harder than any other day since I quit. I'm not in a good place."

"I won't let you drink. I'll stay right with you all night if I have to, but I will *not* let you drink. Come back with me. Talk to him so you can put it behind you and get on with your life. Isn't it time, Brand? The cat's out of the bag, so let's deal with it."

Brandon had never before seen such fierce determination in his youngest brother's eyes, and without making a conscious decision to go, he let Declan lead him back to face Aidan once and for all.

CHAPTER 14, DAY 34

Colin and Aidan were cleaning up the kitchen when Declan and Brandon came in. When Brandon hesitated at the kitchen door, Declan nodded with encouragement and gave his brother a nudge.

"Aidan, Brandon wants to talk to you," Dec said. "Do you think we can try to be civil? Brandon needs to get past this. His recovery depends on it."

Declan's support and understanding of why this was so important overwhelmed Brandon.

Aidan kept his back to them as he finished washing the last pan. When he finally turned to his brothers, his expression was unreadable. He wiped his hands on a towel as he studied Brandon. "Talk."

All eyes shifted to Brandon. As the weight of their expectations settled heavily upon him, it was important to Brandon that he not run away anymore. He was so tired of them waiting for him to fuck up. Instead of fucking up, this time he would step up.

"I wasn't trying to hurt you before," Brandon said. "I was just trying to tell you the truth about something I've kept from you and everyone else for most of my life. I know the timing sucks because of what's happened between you and Clare, but you forced the issue earlier after I told you it wasn't a good time."

Watching their brothers circle each other, Colin and Declan were prepared to get between them if it came to that.

"I want to talk to you about this," Brandon continued. "I want to clear the air between us if we can, but not if you're going to make fun of how I felt about Sarah or make light of it. I won't put myself through that."

"What did you expect me to say?" Aidan asked. "This is just a little bit shocking."

"I know it is, and I expected you to be mad and surprised and maybe sad because we're talking about someone we all loved and lost. And I get that you lost a lot more than we did, than I did. But that loss wasn't all yours, Aidan. It didn't belong just to you."

Aidan's jaw clenched with tension as he studied the tiled kitchen floor.

"I was only eleven." Brandon forced himself to keep going. Where the will was coming from, he didn't know, but he couldn't stop now. "I had no idea what I felt for her was love, but I knew what I felt for you when she picked you over me was hate, pure and simple. I've come to see I wasn't fair to you. It wasn't your fault."

"Gee, thanks. It took you what? Twenty-seven years to come to that conclusion? And for all that time, you hated my guts and never even tried to hide it because she picked me over you?" Aidan shook his head with disbelief. "She wasn't a toy, for God's sake."

"I know that now, but I was just a kid. I had no idea how to handle what I felt, so I didn't handle it at all. I've paid a mighty price for that, if it's any consolation."

"It's not."

"Come on, Aidan," Declan said. "Give him a break. He's trying here."

"He's telling me he was *in love* with my wife!" Aidan roared. "How do you expect me to react?" Aidan suddenly went still as something else occurred to him. "Is this why you did what you did to Clare? To get back at me because I was happy again?"

"No!" Brandon said, horrified by the implication. "No. I was out of my mind that night. I have no memory of it, so how could I have done it on purpose? I'd never intentionally do something like that to a woman, no matter who she was with."

"This whole thing makes me sick," Aidan said, running a hand over the stubble on his cheek.

"There's more," Brandon said. If he was going to do this, he might as well go all the way. He told Aidan about the business and how much he resented him for getting the chance to leave. "And when you left medicine, *even then* you didn't come home to work with us. That made me so mad, because the way I saw it then, I'd given up everything so you could have what you wanted."

"Do you want to know why I didn't come home?" Aidan asked in a whisper.

"Yeah," Brandon said. "I guess I do." But there was something in the way his brother's face twisted with grief that made Brandon regret dredging up all these old hurts in Aidan, especially when a new one had just taken up residence.

"I didn't come home because it was so painful to be there that for years after she died, I had to *make* myself go home for holidays and stuff. There was no way I could've lived there then or even now. That's where we came to be, where it all began. To this day, it still takes my breath away to drive down Main Street in Chatham knowing I have to live the whole rest of my life without her."

"I'm sorry," Brandon said. "I didn't know that."

"You didn't know because you never asked. Instead, you just added it to the long list of grievances you had against me. What else have you got? Hell, you're on a roll. You may as well get it all out."

"Nothing. There's nothing else."

"That was more than enough."

"I was wrong about a lot of things. I realize that now. I've laid a lot of crap at your doorstep that didn't belong there. But I loved Sarah. I'm sorry if that hurts you, but it's true."

"She didn't even like you," Aidan said without malice. "She thought you were a jerk."

"I made sure you both thought I was a jerk. It was the only defense I had."

"I suppose you're going to tell me next that my wife and I made you into an alcoholic."

"No, I did that all on my own." Brandon glanced over to find Colin and Declan looking at him with something new in their eyes: respect. It felt good.

"Do you think maybe you guys can try to put this behind you now?" Colin asked.

Aidan never took his eyes off of Brandon when he replied, "I don't know. I need some time to process it. Just talking about Sarah and thinking about her and Colin…" He rested a hand on his chest, as if trying to contain the burst of grief brought on by the mention of the son he'd lost. "Sometimes it's like it all happened yesterday rather than ten years ago. The only time I've felt normal since then is when I was with Clare, and now she's gone, too."

"I'm sorry, Aidan," Brandon said, hesitating. "I'm probably the last person who should be saying this, but maybe you could do the kid thing, you know, if it meant you got to be with her." He braced himself for a blast of anger from Aidan that didn't materialize.

"I've thought about that," Aidan confessed. "But don't you think a kid deserves more than a father who's only there physically?"

"You'd be a great father," Declan insisted. "Erin's kids adore you."

Aidan shook his head. "I can't," he whispered. "I just can't take the chance something would happen again. I barely survived it the first time."

Since his brothers couldn't argue with that, they didn't try.

The brothers were quiet on the drive south through the Green Mountains on Sunday afternoon. Brandon watched the scenery pass from the front seat as Declan navigated the twisting mountain highway. As he relived the confrontation with Aidan, an array of emotions rioted through Brandon. A lifetime of secrets had come pouring out, freeing him from the enormous effort it took to keep them to himself. Relief mixed in with the regret and remorse for all the years he'd devoted to hating a brother who hadn't deserved it.

If only he'd reached out to someone to unload even a small portion of his pain. Either of his parents would have done what they could to help him. Teachers, coaches, friends, even his younger brothers or sister—any of them would've tried to help, if only he'd asked for it. How different his life might have turned out if he'd spoken up, but instead, he kept it all locked inside. And, like he'd said to Aidan, he had paid a mighty price for that.

"Hey, Col?" Brandon said.

"Mmm," the half-asleep Colin grunted.

"Do you know where Sarah's buried in Boston?"

"I do," Declan said.

"So do I," Colin said.

"Have you guys been there?"

"A couple of times with Mum and Da," Declan said. "Aidan told me he finally went for the first time recently with Clare." He sighed. "She was good for him. I wish they could work it out somehow."

"You never know," Brandon said. "Maybe they will."

"It sounds like they're at a pretty significant standoff," Colin said.

"So, um, do you guys think we could go to the cemetery on the way home?" Brandon asked.

"I don't mind," Declan said.

"I don't, either," Colin said. "As long as I'm home by six."

"Who's this chick you've got to get home for anyway?" Declan asked with a glance in the mirror at Colin.

"Just a friend I'm having dinner with tonight."

"A *friend*?" Declan asked.

"For now," Colin said.

"I have a date tonight, too," Brandon said.

"With who?" Declan asked with surprise.

"A five-year-old who's taken a shine to me in the apartment building. She's a cute kid."

"With crappy taste in men," Colin joked.

"Thanks a lot," Brandon said. "You ought to see the mother." He sucked in a breath and shook his head. "Total goddess."

"*Oh*," Declan chuckled. "I get it now."

"No, the kid's really cool," Brandon insisted. "I'll tell you what, I like her a lot more than the mother—the tenant from hell, as Da calls her."

"Maybe I should've volunteered for the apartment job," Colin said. "Sounds like you're running Melrose Place over there."

"Yeah, right!" Brandon hooted. "Funny, I don't recall *volunteering* for the apartment job. The rest of the tenants are senior citizens. They're probably more interested in bingo than hot-tub parties."

"There's a visual," Colin said dryly.

"So you guys," Declan said. "Since we're having true confession weekend, I wanted to tell you…"

"What?" Brandon asked, turning to Dec.

"I'm thinking about asking Jess to marry me. That is if she's still speaking to me after this weekend."

"Get out of here!" Colin said. "You've only known her a couple of months."

Declan shrugged. "There's something different about her. I realized it almost right away."

"I can't imagine you married," Brandon said.

"I know, but I'm ready. I want a family, and let's face it, we're not getting any younger."

"Ain't that the truth?" Colin said. "I've been thinking about that myself lately. I never imagined I'd still be single at thirty-six."

"That's funny, because I've never imagined myself married," Brandon said.

"Because you were hung up on a girl you couldn't have," Declan reminded him.

"Maybe. When she died, I think I just shut down on that front. That's why Valerie never stood a chance with me."

"Poor Valerie," Colin said. "She had it so bad for you."

Brandon winced. "She was better than I deserved. That's for sure."

"So while we're in Boston, how would you guys feel about helping me buy a ring?" Declan asked.

"You're serious," Brandon said. "You're really going to do this."

"I think I am."

"Six o'clock," Colin reminded them. "I can't be late."

"There's more to this story than he's letting on," Brandon said to Declan.

Dec nodded in agreement. "No doubt."

"Six o'clock," Colin said again.

"Shouldn't we get flowers or something?" Brandon asked as they drove through the stone gates at the cemetery.

"We don't have to," Dec said. "It's enough to pay our respects."

"I appreciate you guys understanding that I need to do this."

"I gotta say, this whole thing with Sarah sure does explain a lot," Colin said. "I can't believe no one ever figured it out."

"I worked very hard to keep it a secret. I was ashamed of it sometimes, especially after they were married."

"There it is." Colin pointed as Declan parked the car.

They got out of the car and pulled on their matching O'Malley & Sons coats to walk up the small hill to where Sarah was buried with her son Colin and her grandmother.

The brothers studied the stone marker for several quiet minutes before Colin and Declan left Brandon alone at the grave.

He ran a hand over the smooth granite headstone. "I'm sorry I was such a jerk, Sarah," he whispered. "I wish you'd known how much I loved you. I would've done anything for you. I've never stopped thinking about you, and I just hope you've found peace wherever you are now." His eyes burned with tears. "Aidan's hanging in there, so you don't need to worry about him. I think he and I will be better now. At least I hope so." He swiped at a warm tear that rolled down his cold cheek. "Well, I'd better go. Colin's got a date that's not really a date, and he's anxious to get home. I'm sorry it took me so long to get here. We all love you and miss you and baby Colin." Brandon stood hunched against the cold for another long moment before he returned to the car.

"You okay, Brand?" Declan asked.

"Yeah," Brandon said, his voice heavy and raw. "Let's go find that ring you need."

CHAPTER 15, DAY 35

They arrived in Chatham at five thirty with a two-carat diamond ring locked in the glove compartment of Declan's car.

"Don't do anything rash, Dec," Colin said as he got out of the car at his house. "Just because you have the ring doesn't mean you have to pop the question to get out of the dog house."

Declan laughed. "I'll try to control myself. Have fun on your date or whatever it is."

"You'll go by and see Mum?" Colin asked Brandon.

Brandon nodded. "I'll take care of it."

"She's gonna be bummed," Colin said. "She loved Clare."

"I know," Brandon said.

"Well, it's been real." Colin grabbed his backpack from the trunk. "I'll talk to you guys tomorrow."

When Declan dropped him off at the apartment building, Brandon tossed his bag into the back of his truck and drove to his parents' house. He wanted to check in with them before he kept his promise to Mike.

"Hello," he called as he walked into the pink house. "Anyone home?"

"In here, love," his mother called from the family room.

His parents were in their side-by-side easy chairs watching the news.

"Hey," Dennis said. "You guys are back. How was the trip?"

Brandon kissed his mother and sat down on the footstool in front of her. "It was, ah…eventful."

"So what's wrong with your brother?" Colleen asked, cutting right to the chase.

Brandon took her hand. "He and Clare broke up."

"*What?*" Colleen gasped as tears filled her eyes. "No…"

"I'm sorry, Mum. I know how much you liked her."

"What happened? They're madly in love! That was so obvious."

"I think they still are, but she wants to adopt a child."

"And he doesn't want that," Colleen said, nodding with understanding.

"No."

"But why?" Dennis asked. "He'd be such a great father."

"We tried to tell him that, but he said he just couldn't do it, you know, after what happened with baby Colin and everything."

Colleen wiped at a tear. "I really thought he was going to marry her."

"I guess this all came up when he proposed."

Colleen winced.

"Poor Aidan," Dennis said with a grim set to his mouth. "He must be heartbroken."

"He is, but he's going back to work tomorrow, and I think he'll be okay. He doesn't want you guys worrying about him."

"Fat chance of that," Colleen said. "How about you? Did you work things out with him?"

"Well, we cleared the air a little." Brandon hesitated before he added, "Listen, ah, some stuff came up this weekend that I should probably tell you about before you hear it through the grapevine."

"What kind of stuff?" Dennis asked.

For the second time in as many days, Brandon confessed to his feelings for Sarah and how they'd colored his relationship with Aidan.

"She was your brother's wife," Colleen said in a scandalized whisper, her hand over her heart.

"She wasn't my brother's wife when I fell for her, Mum."

"But still," Colleen stammered. "Mother of God."

"What did he say when you told him this?" Dennis asked with shock showing on his face, too.

"Needless to say, he was quite upset, but we talked about it, and I hope maybe we understand each other better. It was quite a weekend."

"Sounds like it," Dennis said.

"I just can't see how you kept this to yourself all this time," Colleen said.

"Remember when you were so mad that I didn't go to her funeral? I didn't go because I couldn't. I was so devastated, Mum, and I didn't even have a right to that much. Do you understand what that did to me?"

"You've kept so much locked inside of you, love. It's no wonder you turned to alcohol."

"It was the only way I could get any relief. But I'm discovering there's a lot of relief in honesty."

"I was right to send you up there," Colleen said. "I knew there was something wrong with him, and I wanted you two to work things out."

Brandon smiled. "Killed two birds, did you, Mum?"

"I did what needed to be done," she said with a shrug.

Brandon shot an amused glance at his father. "She really plays us, doesn't she, Da?"

"It's better for me to stay out of it. Self-preservation."

"Oh, hush, Denny." Colleen ran a soothing hand over her son's hair. "Do you need something to eat?"

"No, thanks." Brandon stood up. "I've got to run." He leaned over to kiss his mother. "Try not to worry, Mum. Aidan will get through this. He's a survivor."

"So are you, love. I'm proud of you for taking responsibility and for working so hard to stay sober."

He squeezed her hand. "I'll give you a call tomorrow."

"Take care, son," Dennis said.

Colin brought flowers. He knew he probably shouldn't have, but after looking forward to seeing her all weekend, he'd turned this into a date in his mind. Meredith's house on Stepping Stones Road was a traditional two-story shingled cape. Colin followed the path created by lantern lights lining the walk to the front door.

Before he could ring the bell, she came to the door wearing a white sweater that might've been cashmere, with black pants and high-heeled boots. Her sleek dark hair cascaded past her shoulders.

"Hi," she said, opening the storm door for him.

Colin kept the flowers behind his back as he was hit with an unexpected burst of nerves. He should've skipped them. "You look great." Since he couldn't very well keep them hidden all night, he handed her the flowers. "For you."

"Oh," she said, her cheeks flushing with color.

"From a friend," he clarified.

"They're beautiful. Thank you. Come in."

He followed her through the cozy house to the kitchen, where she found a vase for the flowers.

"I see you're into antiques."

"My mother says I bought the house when my antiques overtook my apartment."

"Something smells good."

"I hope you don't mind, but I was just hanging out today, so I cooked. Is that okay?"

When her cheeks flushed to a rosy pink, his tongue tied itself in knots. "Of course, that's fine. Let me call to cancel the reservation."

"I'm sorry. I messed up the plans."

"It's fine. I'd much rather stay here."

"You're sure?"

"Positive." He pulled his cell phone from his coat pocket and handed the coat to Meredith. After a quick call to the restaurant to cancel the reservation, he turned off the phone.

"Do you want some wine? Or I have beer, too. I wasn't sure what you'd like."

"What're you having?"

"One glass of merlot."

"That sounds good." He took the bottle from her to open it. When he'd poured them each a glass, he handed one of them to her. "Cheers."

She touched her glass to his. "Cheers."

"Are you nervous, Meredith?" he asked, looking at her over the rim of the wineglass.

"Does it show?"

"You don't need to be afraid of me."

Her eyes never wavered. "I think I do."

"Why do you say that?" Colin asked, making a huge effort to sound casual when his heart was thumping.

"Because I couldn't wait to see you tonight."

He wanted to jump up and down but kept his expression neutral. "Maybe I should be afraid of you, then."

"How come?"

"Because I couldn't wait to see you, either."

Her smile was shy, and Colin had to resist the urge to find out if her rosy cheeks were as soft as they looked.

"How was the trip with your brothers?"

Colin rolled his eyes. "Interesting." He gave her a brief summary of the high- and lowlights.

"Sounds like a lot of drama. Brandon seems to be really working the program."

"He's very determined. I continue to be cautiously optimistic."

Meredith took a sip of her wine. "How did you feel when Brandon confessed to being in love with Aidan's wife? It must've been so…"

"Shocking?"

She nodded.

"It was, but in some ways, I can understand it. She was so beautiful, and we all loved her. Her death was devastating."

"How long ago did she die?"

"Ten years. Aidan's been kind of a lost soul since then, so we were hopeful he'd make a go of it with Clare. It's such a bummer that it didn't work out for them."

"You're really close to them, aren't you? Your brothers?"

Colin nodded. "They're my best friends. Maybe it's because we've also worked together all these years, but my parents were big on reminding us that we'd always have each other. I guess we took it to heart."

"Brandon's lucky to have you guys on his side right now. That's what will get him through this."

Colin leaned back against the counter and studied her as she stirred something on the stove. She was so easy to talk to, and the empathy he'd seen in her at Al-Anon seemed to be a big part of who she was away from the program, too.

"Are you hungry? I didn't know what you liked, so I made some of everything." Her face flushed again with embarrassment.

This time, Colin didn't try to resist the urge to run a finger over one of her pink cheeks. As her breath caught, he watched the pulse in her throat flutter in response. He leaned in to brush his lips against hers and lingered when her hands landed on his chest. Drawing her closer, he discovered the sweater was indeed cashmere. He kept the kiss undemanding, but the taste of wine on her lips was intoxicating.

Opening his eyes, he found hers closed in acquiescence. Encouraged, he ran his tongue lightly along her bottom lip, which caused her to draw a sharp deep breath. Moving to plant soft kisses along her jaw, he worked his way to her neck.

The scent of her skin and the feel of her silky hair against his face fueled his desire, but still he went slowly in fear of scaring her away.

Colin kept waiting for her to stop him, and when she didn't, he captured her mouth again, this time holding nothing back. Several passionate minutes passed before Colin forced himself to slow down. "Meredith," he whispered against her ear. "You're making me crazy."

She shuddered. "I think something's burning."

"It might be me," Colin said as he trailed more kisses along her jaw.

"On the stove," she said with a giggle.

After she adjusted the temperature on the burner, Colin drew her back into his arms.

"I don't do this kind of thing," she said.

"What? Make out over a hot stove?"

"Make out anywhere."

"Why not? You're good at it."

She laughed. "Stop."

"Do I have to?" he asked, kissing her again.

"*Colin.*"

"What?" he asked, his lips pressed to her neck.

"Stop."

Something about the way she said the single word stopped him cold.

"I'm sorry."

"Don't be. I'm just not very good at this."

"I thought we'd already covered that. You're very good at it." He kissed her cheek. "Why don't we eat some of this feast you cooked? It smells wonderful."

"I hope you're really hungry."

"I'm starving."

She'd made roast beef, seafood casserole, new potatoes, asparagus, salad, and fresh-baked bread.

Colin ate until he couldn't move. "That was fabulous. Thank you."

"I made too much," she said, continuing to sip from her first glass of wine.

"My mother still cooks for seven, even though it's just the two of them now."

"She must've had to cook for an army when she had four boys at home."

"She did. We ate like horses, but she made us all learn how to cook so we wouldn't be helpless."

Meredith smiled. "She sounds like quite a character."

Colin reached across the table for her hand. "She would like you."

Meredith looked away from him.

He slid his chair closer to hers while keeping a firm grip on her hand. "So what are we going to do about this no-dating rule of yours?"

Alarm marked her expression when her gaze whipped up to meet his.

"Because I want to see you again." He laced his fingers through hers. "Soon."

"I'm a bad risk, Colin."

The sadness he heard in her tone tugged at him. "I don't think so."

She shook her head.

"Do you like me, Meredith?" He pressed his lips to the inside of her wrist, where he could gauge her response by the flutter of her pulse.

She nodded.

"Then maybe we could see what happens?" When she didn't answer, he continued. "I won't hurt you. I'd never hurt you."

"I'm afraid I'll hurt you."

"Oh, I'm tough. I'll take my chances."

He was startled when her eyes went shiny with tears. "You don't understand," she whispered.

"Help me," he pleaded. "Help me to understand why a beautiful, sweet, thoughtful young woman would have a no-dating rule, especially a woman who's so passionate."

"I'm not passionate."

"Do I need to refresh your memory?" he asked, kissing her softly.

She pulled away from him and stood up. "I can't do this, Colin. I just can't."

"You can't or you won't?"

"Both."

Colin sighed and got up to retrieve his coat. "Dinner was great. Thank you."

"Colin…"

He zipped his coat.

"I'm sorry."

Running a hand over her soft hair, he kissed her cheek. "Not as sorry as I am. I think we could have something great here. You know where to find me if you change your mind."

She nodded.

He left her standing in the kitchen and let himself out the front door. On the short drive home, he realized with dismay that he now understood what'd been missing with his ex-fiancée Nicole.

She wasn't Meredith.

CHAPTER 16, DAY 35

Brandon resisted the temptation to run upstairs the minute he arrived at the apartment building. He unpacked, showered, and shaved. When he splashed on a bit of cologne, he told himself he was being an idiot for primping for a five-year-old.

Grabbing the bag he'd dropped on the sofa, he headed out the door and up the stairs. Reaching the third floor, he took a deep breath and knocked on the door.

Daphne seemed surprised to see him when she answered the door. "Hey," she said. "Come in."

"How was your weekend?"

"Fine. Nothing special. Mike's in the tub."

"I was going to ask if I could take her out for ice cream or something."

Daphne's eyes widened. "By yourself?"

"Of course not. You're invited, too."

Daphne bit her fingernail as she thought it over. "Well, she has school tomorrow, and she's already in the tub."

"Maybe another time."

"Have a seat." Daphne gestured to the sofa. "I'll go get her."

Brandon sat to wait and used the time to finally study the framed photos of Mike that sat on the end table. Next to a picture of her blowing bubbles as a toddler was one of Daphne, baby Mike, and a sandy-haired man who Brandon assumed was Mike's father.

She came flying into the room in a pink flannel nightgown, her blonde ringlets still wet from her bath. "You came," she said, breathless with excitement.

Touched by how pleased she was to see him, Brandon grinned. "I told you I would."

She placed a tiny hand on each side of his face. "Thank you for not forgetting."

He held out his arms to her, and when she came to him as if she'd been doing it all her life, he fell flat on his face in love. He closed his eyes and breathed in the sweet scent of baby shampoo. When he opened his eyes, he found Daphne leaning against the doorframe, watching them with a mixture of fear and suspicion in her eyes.

"Hey." Brandon lifted Mike onto his lap. "I brought you something."

Her smile lit up her face. "You did?"

He handed her the bag.

She squealed with delight when she pulled a teddy bear from the bag. He was light brown and wore a green sweater that said VERMONT in white block letters. "Oh, I love him," she said, kissing Brandon's cheek. "Thank you."

Her pleasure at such a small gift tugged at his heart. "What will you name him?"

"Brandon," she said without hesitation. "Brandon the Bear."

"That's a very good name."

Mike giggled. "You smell good."

"You think so?"

"Uh-huh." She rested her head on his shoulder as she cuddled the bear. He felt his shirt grow damp under her wet hair, but he didn't move her.

"Mike, it's time for bed," Daphne said.

"Not yet, Mom. Brandon just got here."

"If you want a story, it's now or never."

Mike turned to Brandon. "Will you read to me?"

"Sure, if it's okay with your mom. Go get a book."

She grabbed the bear and took off for her room.

"It was nice of you to bring her something," Daphne said almost grudgingly.

He shrugged. "It was nothing."

"Not to her."

Mike returned with a book about zoo animals plotting their escape and reclaimed her place on his lap.

Brandon surprised himself when he managed to create a different voice for each animal, which thrilled Mike.

"All right, Mike," Daphne said. "Say good-night."

"Can I come see you tomorrow?" Mike asked Brandon.

"I'll be doing some painting in my apartment. Why don't you come help me when you get home from school?"

"Can I really?"

"Sure you can. Just wear something old."

Mike hugged him again and whispered in his ear, "I love you." She kissed his cheek and was gone before he could respond.

"I'll be right back," Daphne said as she followed her daughter.

Brandon sat back against the sofa and released a contented sigh. He remembered Alan saying there was nothing like loving someone and having that love returned. Finally, he understood exactly what his friend had meant.

Daphne came back a few minutes later. "Do you want something to drink? Some wine or a beer?"

Brandon swallowed hard. "Um, no, I'm good. Thanks."

"Do you mind if I have a glass of wine? It's my reward for getting through the day."

"I don't mind."

"Thank you for being so nice to her. She can be a bit much sometimes, but you're very patient with her."

"She's a great kid."

Daphne brought her glass of wine with her when she sat down next to him. "She always has been. Ever since she was a baby, she's just had this way of connecting with people that I've never had. She gets that from her father."

"Can I ask you something that's none of my business?"

Daphne's glance was wary. "I guess so."

"Where is he? Her father?"

"He died five years ago."

"I'm sorry."

"I'm sorry for Mike that she never knew him."

"What happened to him?" Brandon worried that he was pushing his luck. He kept waiting for her prickly side to reemerge.

"He had a lot of problems." She gazed into her wineglass as she remembered back in time. "It was almost like the simple act of living was too much for him."

"How do you mean?"

"Randy came from a powerful family. They were big into politics, and he hated the way they were forced to live in the public eye. He was a gifted artist, but that wasn't good enough for them. He could never live up to their expectations."

"I'm almost afraid to ask…"

"I found him in the garage with the car running. They said he'd been dead for an hour. Mike was just a year old then."

"Jesus, Daphne. I'm so sorry." He reached out to her and was almost startled when her fingers curled around his.

"It was horrible. I knew he was depressed, but I had no idea he was that despondent."

"He was probably afraid to let it show to anyone, even you," Brandon said, speaking with some authority on keeping secrets.

She shrugged. "Maybe. Anyway, Mike and I have been a team ever since, and we're doing just fine."

"You've done a wonderful job with her."

"Thanks."

"Do you have any help? Any family nearby?"

She shook her head. "No, it's just us."

Brandon couldn't imagine being so alone in the world and felt his heart go out to Daphne, too. These two were getting him all twisted up inside, but for some reason, he didn't mind. It felt good to care about someone other than himself for a change. He rested his head against the back of the sofa. "You don't have to be all alone, you know."

Daphne glanced down at their joined hands. "Why are you?"

He hesitated for a second before he decided to be honest with her. "Because for most of my life I was in love with a woman I couldn't have, and I made a lot of bad choices as a result."

"That's as good a reason as any, I suppose. Are you still in love with her?"

"She died ten years ago."

"I guess we have more in common than I thought."

"I didn't have a child with her. In fact, I never had anything with her, so it's not the same as what happened to you."

"It's still a loss."

"What did you mean the other day when you said you might be leaving soon?"

"We move around a lot."

"Why?"

The door slammed shut as she extricated her hand from his. "It's getting late."

Brandon stood up, regretting that he'd pushed her one step too far. "Send Mike down to paint when she gets home tomorrow."

"Are you sure you don't mind?"

"I don't mind. I'm right downstairs if you ever need anything."

"Thank you," Daphne said, but the warmth he'd seen in her earlier was gone.

"Good night." Brandon went back downstairs with the odd feeling that he'd once again lost something he'd never really had.

CHAPTER 17, DAY 70

Over the next month, Brandon's days fell into a manageable routine. He began each morning with a long run and an AA meeting in Harwich, followed by coffee with Joe. Then it was back to the apartment building, where he worked until exhaustion forced him into bed. He'd finished his apartment and one other and was now hard at work on Mrs. Oczkowski's place.

When he helped move her essentials into his apartment so he could work on hers, Mrs. Oczkowski urged him to "do it well, and do it fast." She was what his mother would call a hot ticket.

Mike came to find him the minute she got home from morning kindergarten every day. Brandon usually had something to keep her busy for a couple of hours, and he marveled at her ability to fill that much time with nonstop chatter. She never, ever ran out of things she needed to tell him. He knew about all her friends at school, every detail of the morning kindergarten routine, and most of the tenants' personal business.

Brandon checked his watch. Mike would be home any minute, and she'd be more excited than usual today since they were finally going to his sister's house so she could play with Erin's kids. He was aware that Daphne had major reservations about letting him take Mike out by himself, but she'd reluctantly agreed to it when Mike wore her down with her relentless begging.

From Mrs. Oczkowski's second-floor window, he saw Daphne's red SUV pull into the parking area. He grinned when Mike shot out of the car on her way to the porch. Daphne called her back, and with great protest, Mike turned around to get her backpack.

Brandon went out to the hallway to watch for her.

She came flying up the stairs and shrieked when she saw him.

He scooped her up with one arm. "What's the hurry, squirt?"

Her annoyed expression was so sophisticated she might've been thirty instead of five going on thirty. "You *know*," she said with exasperation.

"What? Is today something special?"

She punched his shoulder. "I'll be ready in ten minutes," she said, squirming out of his arms as Daphne caught up to them.

"I hope you know what you're getting into," Daphne said when Mike had gone upstairs.

While his friendship with Mike continued to flourish, Daphne had been friendly but cool to Brandon in the weeks since they'd talked about Mike's father.

"It'll be fine. She'll have a good time with the kids, and I'll bring her back tired."

"For that, I shall be eternally grateful."

Brandon chuckled. "How grateful?"

Her saucy smile almost stopped his heart. "*Very.*"

"Really," he stammered. "Well, uh…"

She laughed at his befuddled expression. "Smooth. Very smooth."

"I used to be. Until I met you."

"Sure, blame me."

It was her turn to be speechless when he twisted a lock of her blonde hair around his finger. "You're so beautiful," he whispered. "You make me into a tongue-tied fool."

She reached for his hand. "Brandon…"

"I'm ready," Mike yelled as she came bounding down the stairs.

Daphne dropped his hand, and the moment was lost. "Be careful with my baby," she said softly so Mike wouldn't hear her.

"She's safe with me. You both are."

Daphne squatted down to zip Mike's coat. "Brandon's in charge. You mind him, do you hear me?"

"Yes, Mom."

"And be good at his sister's house. No getting wild."

"Okay." Mike patted her mother's cheek. "Don't worry. Brandon will take good care of me."

Her utter faith in him made Brandon want to weep. He just hoped he could be worthy of it for as long as she was in his life. It was nearly enough on its own to keep him sober.

"Come on, squirt." Brandon held out a hand to her. "Let's go." To Daphne, he added, "You have my cell number if you need to reach us, right?" He'd given the number to all the tenants.

She nodded.

Brandon ran a finger over her soft cheek. "Don't worry."

"I won't."

Brandon's smile told her he didn't believe her.

"Grab her booster seat out of my car," Daphne called as Brandon and Mike went down the stairs together.

He waved to let her know he'd heard her.

"Whew," Mike said when they were outside. "I didn't think she was going to let us go."

"It's hard for her. She doesn't know me that well, and she's letting me drive away with the most precious thing in her world."

Mike's eyes were wise beyond her years when she looked up at him. "I'm all she has."

"That's why it's so hard for her to let you go." He buckled her into the booster in the front seat of his company truck and reached under the dashboard to turn off the passenger-side airbag.

"But we can trust you."

Curious, Brandon studied her. "How do you know that?"

"Because I know you." She put her hand over his heart. "I know you in here."

Staggered by her, Brandon was rendered momentarily speechless. He reached up to retrieve her hand from his chest and squeezed it before he closed the door and walked around to the driver's side. If he hadn't already been head-over-heels in love with her, he would be now.

On the short ride to Erin's house, she asked him to tell her again about his nieces and nephews. He'd answered this question a hundred times in the last week, but he indulged her. "I already told you, and you know it by heart, so you can't fool me. Josh is eight, Nina is seven, Cecelia is six, Ben is five, and Amanda is four."

"Do you think they'll like me?" she asked in a small voice.

Surprised by her unusual lack of confidence, he reached for her hand. "Of course, they will. I told you, they can't wait to meet you."

She nodded but kept a firm grip on his hand until they arrived at Erin's big Victorian house. Mike gasped. *"That's where they live?* It's like a princess castle!"

Seeing the house through her eyes was like seeing it for the first time. "I guess it is."

Erin waited for them at the front door with Amanda in her arms. "Hey, come on in." She swung open the storm door and put Amanda down in one smooth move.

Brandon never got over how easy his sister made motherhood look.

"You must be Mike," Erin said, reaching out to shake Mike's hand.

"Yes, ma'am. Are you Brandon's sister? You don't look like him."

Erin laughed. "I'm his sister, all right, but he looks like our dad, and I look like our mom."

"You have pretty hair."

"Thank you, so do you. This is Amanda."

Brandon squatted down to Amanda's level and held out a finger to her.

She wrapped her pudgy fingers around his and squeezed.

"Can Uncle Brandon have a smooch?" he asked, making a pathetic face that made both girls giggle.

Amanda studied him for a long moment, during which Brandon prayed the child wouldn't run away in fear of him.

Mike broke the tension when she kissed his cheek.

Not wanting to be left out, Amanda kissed the other side of his face.

"Thank you, ladies," Brandon said, touched by what Mike had done for him. He was amazed at her ability to understand things that should've been far beyond her.

"Amanda, take Mike up to the playroom and introduce her to the kids, okay?" Erin said.

"K," Amanda said, and the two girls scampered off.

"What a beautiful child," Erin said as she led her brother into the kitchen.

"Isn't she?"

"I can't believe you—making friends with a five-year-old."

"It's the new me."

"I like it."

"So do I."

She poured them each a cup of coffee, and they sat at the big kitchen table. The house was filled with the clutter created by five young children, but Erin managed to make it appear somewhat organized.

"So how are you, Brand, really?"

"I'm doing okay. At least I think I am. Seventy days of sobriety today."

"That's a great accomplishment. Congratulations. Do you still, you know—"

"Have the urge to drink?"

She nodded.

"Every day. But so far I seem to have a stronger desire to not go back to the way I was living before."

"You look wonderful. You're all trimmed down."

"I run every day. Plus the manual labor Da's got me doing at the apartments helps, too."

"Do you hate having to work over there?"

"Not as much as I thought I would."

Erin's eyes suddenly flooded with tears.

"What's with the waterworks?" he asked, perplexed.

"I'm sorry." She brushed at a tear. "I'm just so glad to have you back. I missed you so much."

He reached out to hug her. "Thanks for not giving up on me."

"I'd never give up on you."

"Have you heard about what happened in Vermont?"

Her eyes lit up with mirth as she sipped from her mug. "What do you think?"

"That you knew about it five minutes after Mum did."

"More like three minutes," Erin confessed with a smile. "It took a lot of courage for you to tell Aidan the truth. I can't imagine what that must've been like for you."

"It was the scariest thing I've ever done."

"You must've felt so much better once it was off your chest."

"I did, but I felt bad because the timing stunk for him. He had just broken up with Clare."

"I talked to him last night. He seems to be doing better. He's working a lot, and he finished the job he was doing on Clare's brother's house in Stowe."

"I wish they could work things out. Everyone thought she was so good for him."

"She was. Mum really liked her."

He laughed. "And we all know that's half the battle."

Erin snorted in agreement. "No shit."

"Were you shocked by it? The thing about Sarah?"

"Yeah, but it sure did explain why you seemed so mad at the world for all those years."

"I can see now that I wasted a lot of time being mad at the world—and at Aidan. I wasn't fair to him."

"I'm proud of you, Brand. You're really getting your life together, and I know it can't be easy for you."

"Thanks. Having all you guys in my corner certainly helps." When they heard the kids go running through the second floor, Brandon glanced up. "Do I need to check on her?"

"Nah, she's fine," Erin said, amused by his nervousness.

"I'm new at this. I'm not sure what I'm supposed to do."

"You really care about her, don't you?"

"I do. She's managed to worm her way under my skin. Thanks for letting me bring her over to play with the kids. She's pretty lonely at the apartments."

"Bring her over any time. It's amazing how one extra kid can entertain my five for a whole afternoon. In fact, Valerie brought her daughter over to play last week."

"I didn't know you still kept in touch with her."

"I see her all the time."

"How is she?"

"She seems happy. Content with her life. Her daughter Chelsea is adorable."

"That's good. I'm glad to hear that. I'd like to see her—to apologize for the way I treated her if nothing else."

"That might not be a good idea. It took her a long time to get over you, and she's really got her life together now."

"I'd never do anything to mess with that, but... Would you ask her? I need five minutes, and I wouldn't ask if it wasn't important."

Erin nodded. "Sure. I'll ask, but don't be hurt if she says no."

"I'd totally understand. She certainly doesn't owe me anything."

A wail from upstairs had Brandon shooting out of his chair and flying up the stairs. He found Mike in a ball on the playroom floor holding her head and crying her eyes out. His nephew Josh was in the same condition. Erin scooped up Josh while Brandon went to Mike. The other children looked on with big eyes.

"What happened, baby?" Brandon smoothed Mike's hair back to find a red lump on her forehead. He'd never seen her cry before, and her tears unnerved him.

"Josh and I bumped heads," she said between sobs. "It was an accident." She slurred the word so it came out like ass-ident.

"Let's go downstairs and get some ice on those bumps." Erin handled the situation with the calm of someone who'd cared for many a boo-boo.

Brandon, on the other hand, was certain he was having a heart attack as he carried Mike downstairs. Her arms were wrapped tightly around his neck, and his shirt was damp from her tears. He kept her on his lap while he held an ice pack on her bump. Eventually, her sobs became more like hiccups, but still he held her close to him.

"I think I'm okay now," she said.

"Are you sure?"

"Uh-huh."

"Do you want to go home?"

"No! We were having fun 'til we bumped heads."

"Sorry, Uncle Brandon," Josh mumbled with a wary glance at Brandon as he got down from his mother's lap.

"It's okay, buddy." Brandon reached out to ruffle his nephew's blond hair. "It wasn't anyone's fault."

"Come on, Mike." Josh sprinted for the stairs as if nothing had happened. "I want to show you my remote control truck."

Mike was right behind him.

When they were gone, Erin turned to her brother. "It's okay, Brand," she said, laughing at him. "You can breathe now. She's fine."

"Jesus," he said, still trying to recover. "That scared the crap out of me."

"You've got it bad, man." Erin shook her head with delight. "What's her mother like?"

"Picture Mike, only twenty-five years older."

"Wow."

"You said it."

"So you've got it bad for both of them, huh?"

"It's starting to seem that way."

"Is that a good idea so soon after rehab?"

"Probably not, but what am I supposed to do? She's the greatest kid, and they're here all alone. No family nearby."

"Why don't you bring them to Easter?"

"I don't know. The O'Malleys might be too overwhelming for Daphne. She's kind of a loner."

"We'd behave. Ask her."

"We'll see."

CHAPTER 18, DAY 70

"Did you have fun?" Brandon asked when Mike's uncharacteristic quiet started to get to him on the way home.

"Oh yeah, a lot of fun."

"Then why so quiet?"

"I was just thinking that they're so lucky to always have someone to play with."

"That's true, but from what I hear, they always have someone to fight with, too."

"Why aren't you close to them?" She looked over at him. "The kids, I mean."

Once again she floored him. "I, uh, well… That's kind of a long story, but I'm working on it. Maybe you can help me with that."

"Sure. I'll think about it."

He laughed at her serious tone. "Thanks."

They arrived at the apartment building, and after Brandon returned Mike's booster seat to Daphne's car, he followed her upstairs.

"Mom!" she yelled, bursting through the door. "I'm home!"

"Hi, Pooh."

Brandon caught the flash of relief that crossed Daphne's face when they walked in.

"Hey, what happened to your head?" Daphne asked her daughter.

Brandon winced. He should've known she'd zero right in on the bump.

"Oh, it's nothing. Josh and I bumped heads when we were reaching for the same toy."

Daphne kissed the bump. "Did you have fun?"

"It was awesome! They have the coolest house. It looks just like Cinderella's castle."

Daphne smiled. "I'm glad you had a good time. Now go get washed up for dinner."

"Okay," Mike said, but she rushed over to hug Brandon first. "Thanks for taking me."

"It was my pleasure."

"Did she cry?" Daphne asked after Mike left the room.

"Like crazy."

"Freaked you out, did it?"

"Just a bit."

Daphne laughed. "Kids are made of super elastic bubble plastic. Didn't you know that?"

"Hell, no," he said with a scowl, playing along with her. "You could've told me that before."

"It's more fun to imagine you all frazzled."

He smiled, enjoying a rare glimpse at her playful side. "I'm glad I'm available to entertain you."

Her expression turned serious, and she studied him for a long moment.

Squirming under her scrutiny, he said, "What?"

"You're very..." She looked away, embarrassed.

He closed the distance between them. "I'm very what?"

She turned her gaze up to meet his. "Handsome," she whispered.

He seized the moment with a kiss that turned hot so fast, it left him light-headed.

"Don't," she said a minute later when she pulled back from him. "Mike..."

"What time does she go to bed?"

"She's asleep by nine thirty."

"I'll be back." He waited for her to object, but she didn't.

Brandon forced himself to wait until nine forty-five. He'd gotten in a few hours of work in Mrs. Oczkowski's apartment, eaten a sandwich for dinner, and at nine o'clock, he took a shower and shaved. He would've loved a drink to take the edge off his nerves. Instead, he flipped on an early season Red Sox game and sat down to wait.

His heart was in his throat by the time he walked upstairs and knocked softly. He wondered if she would let him kiss her again, or if the distrust and suspicion that seemed to be so much a part of who she was would've returned in the hours they'd spent apart.

She opened the door, wearing a pale blue tank top and the drool-inducing black yoga pants.

Their eyes met in the instant before they both took a step forward.

Brandon lifted her to him, and their lips met with frantic urgency. He kicked the door shut behind him and carried her to the sofa where they landed without breaking the kiss. When he felt her fingers weave into his hair to tug him closer, it was all he could do not to groan out loud. So this was what he'd been missing during all the years he spent pining for a woman he couldn't have, not to mention the years he spent with a woman he didn't want—not like this anyway.

He slid his hand under her shirt and cupped her breast.

She gasped and arched into him. "Brandon," she whispered against his ear.

He ran his thumb over her nipple, and it hardened instantly.

She whimpered and pulled him close enough to kiss again.

This time, though, he went easy, running his tongue over her lip with a slow patience that made her moan. He gave her ear the same attention as he tried to catch his breath from that first, explosive burst of passion. If he didn't slow things down, this was going to get out of hand. Fast.

She wasn't cooperating with the slow-it-down plan, however. Her hands were all over him. He shivered when she dragged her fingernail along his spine and then pushed a hand into the back of his jeans.

"Brandon, take me to bed," she whispered.

He was thinking of his recovery and all the warnings about too much too soon when he said, "I can't."

She moved her hand around to the front of his jeans and pushed it against his rigid length. "It seems to me like you can."

Reaching down to stop her while he still could, he withdrew her hand, brought it up to his mouth, and left a lingering kiss on her palm. "I'm not looking for a one-time thing."

"I might be up for twice."

He laughed. "You're not taking me seriously."

"I haven't had sex in five years. Believe me, I'm taking you *very* seriously."

"Five *years*?"

She rolled his earlobe between her teeth. "Five years, Brandon," she whispered.

"You're officially killing me. I'm trying to be a good guy here."

"You *are* a good guy. That's why I want you in my bed." She kissed him again and pulled out all the stops to entice him.

Telling himself he was an idiot to resist her, he was on the verge of giving in when Mike called for her mother. He lifted his arm to free Daphne to go to her.

Brandon sat up, ran a hand through his hair, and tried to catch his breath. He'd never been more turned on in his life.

Daphne came back a few minutes later. Her cheeks were flushed, her lips swollen from kissing him. "She knows you're here. Do you mind going in to see her?"

"Of course not." Brandon got up to follow her down the hallway. A nightlight on Mike's bedside table cast a faint glow upon the room. As he sat on the bed, he was touched to see Brandon the Bear tucked in next to her. "Hey, what're you doing awake?"

Daphne sat on the other side.

"I had a bad dream," Mike said, her lip quivering.

"Want to tell me about it?" Brandon asked.

She shook her head. "Will you stay here with me until I fall asleep?"

Brandon looked over at Daphne.

She nodded.

"Sure." Brandon stretched out next to Mike while Daphne did the same on her side of the bed.

Mike sighed and closed her eyes. "Thanks."

Brandon kissed her cheek.

Daphne put her arm around Mike and reached for Brandon's hand.

As Daphne's fingers linked with his, he was filled with contentment. He drifted off to sleep next to them, saying a silent prayer of thanks to whatever higher power had brought them into his life.

Chapter 18, Day 71

The Mickey Mouse clock on the bedside table told Brandon it was just after four. Mike was using him as a pillow. Daphne had her arm around both of them, and a leg tossed over him. Brandon lay perfectly still to listen to the soft cadence of their breathing. The nightlight allowed him to watch them sleep, and the intimacy of it was almost spiritual.

When he realized he wouldn't be able to go back to sleep, he moved slowly to extricate himself. He eased Mike's head back onto her pillow, brushed her hair off her face, and left a light kiss on her forehead.

When he sat up, Daphne's eyes opened.

"Did you sleep at all?" she whispered.

"Yeah, but I'm awake, so I'm going to go." He leaned over to kiss her.

"Thanks for this," she said with a glance at Mike.

How could he tell her that nothing had ever given him more pleasure than sleeping with the two of them snuggled around him? "Sure. I'll see you later?"

She nodded but couldn't seem to look away from him.

What passed between them in that endless second was the understanding that this could be the start of something important—for all of them.

He went around to her side of the bed to kiss her again. When her hand curled around the back of his neck, he lingered longer than he'd planned to.

"Go back to sleep for a while," he whispered with one last kiss.

***

Brandon's thoughts were full of Daphne on his early morning run. He could remember feeling this way only once before, and he'd already had more with Daphne than he'd ever had with Sarah. This had the potential to be a healthy relationship, which was a novel idea to him. He needed to take it slow and not get ahead of himself, though. No matter how strong his feelings were for Daphne and Mike, his recovery had to come first right now.

At that morning's AA meeting, Brandon raised his hand when the leader asked who wanted to start the discussion.

"I'm Brandon, and I'm an alcoholic."

"Hi, Brandon," the group replied.

"I've been sober for seventy-one days, and so far I think I'm doing pretty well. I still get the urge for a drink, but I'm getting better at controlling those urges. I've also been trying to make my amends to the people I hurt when I was drinking."

The others nodded with approval.

"When I was in rehab and first learning about the program, the part I had the biggest problem with was the spiritual aspect. Since I've been out, though, I've begun to experience some of the blessings that come from living a sober life." Brandon took a sip of his coffee before he continued. "One of those blessings is an adorable five-year-old girl who's come into my life and shown me what it's like to love someone so much I'd do anything for her. I'm also becoming involved with her mother. I know this isn't the ideal time for me to be starting new relationships, but I've decided that as long as I stay focused on my recovery, there may be room in my life for other things, too. Well, that's what I wanted to say. Thank you."

"Thank you, Brandon."

After the meeting, Brandon walked with Joe to the coffee shop where they were now daily regulars.

"So the girl you mentioned at the meeting is the one who lives in the apartments where you're working, right?" Joe asked.

"That's right. Her name is Mike, which is short for Michaela, and she has me wrapped firmly around her little finger."

Joe grinned. "I have three daughters. I feel the pain, believe me. What's the story with her mother? What's her name?"

"Daphne," Brandon said with a smile. "She's…" He found himself at a loss for words. "She's very courageous. She's raising Mike completely on her own, but she doesn't ever seem overwhelmed by the responsibility the way most people would be. And she's stunning. I mean drop-dead gorgeous."

"You seem smitten."

"They're becoming very important to me."

"I was glad to hear you say at the meeting that you're keeping your recovery front and center in your life. But I wouldn't be doing my job as your sponsor if I didn't caution you to be vigilant. You're feeling stronger than you have in years—physically and emotionally—which is a big accomplishment. However, if this relationship doesn't work out, you could be seriously jeopardizing all your hard work. Many a relapse is caused by disappointment."

"I know. Believe me, I wish it'd happened a year from now when I'd be better equipped to handle it. But this could be my first opportunity for a real relationship with a woman. I can't miss out on it just because the timing isn't ideal."

"Be careful, Brandon. Not just for your sake but for theirs, too. The more they come to care for you and depend upon you the greater the potential becomes for you to disappoint them should you suffer a relapse."

Joe's words sent a jolt of fear through Brandon. "I won't let that happen."

When he returned to Chatham, Brandon stopped at his house to pick up his mail, which included a letter from Aidan's ex-girlfriend, Clare.

Dear Brandon,

Thank you for your lovely letter. I appreciate you taking the time to write to apologize for what happened at your parents' home. I understand you were in the throes of your illness that night, and I forgive you. I was also pleased to hear you're making such positive strides in your recovery.

I, too, am sorry things did not work out between Aidan and me. He's a wonderful person, and I feel blessed to have known him and the rest of the O'Malleys. You're fortunate to have the support of such a strong and loving family at this time in your life. Please give your parents my best regards. Thank you again for your letter.

All the best,

Clare Harrington

Brandon sighed with relief. It was good of her to forgive him, but he was again swamped with remorse—and shame—over what he'd done to her.

Dennis was waiting for Brandon when he arrived at the apartments.

"Hey, have you been waiting long?"

"Just got here," Dennis replied.

"Thanks for the help today."

"No problem. A man can't hang cabinets by himself. Besides, I appreciate the excuse to get out of the house. Your Mum's driving me nuts planning this trip to Ireland."

"When are you leaving?"

"Not until September, but I swear it's all she talks about. Five more months of this before we even go!"

Brandon laughed at his father's distress. "Why don't you throw her a ringer and take her to New York for a weekend to change the subject?" he asked as they climbed the stairs to Mrs. Oczkowski's apartment. The new kitchen cabinets were scattered about on the floor of her living room.

"That's not a bad idea." Dennis ducked around the corner to inspect Brandon's work in the bathroom. "Nice job, son." He nodded with approval at the gleaming new vanity, freshly painted walls, and tiled floor. "It looks great."

"Thanks. That's your training paying off."

"What pleases me most is I haven't gotten a single call from a tenant since you've been here."

"They're nice people. Did you know Mr. Pauley in 2C was a Flying Tiger in World War II? He was telling me all about it the other day."

"I didn't know that." Dennis helped Brandon carry the first of the cabinets into the kitchen. "Hey, have you talked to Colin?"

Brandon had to stop to think. "You know, now that you mention it, not in a week or so. I've left him a couple of messages, but he hasn't called me back, which isn't like him. Why do you ask?"

"I hear he's been kind of cranky at work. I had lunch with Dec yesterday, and he says Colin's been a bear."

"That's odd. I wonder what's up."

"I hope he's not overwhelmed by the new job. I worry that I dumped it all on him and walked away."

"You didn't dump it on him, Da. He's been preparing for this his whole life. He should be in his element running the show. I'll stop by in the next day or two and check on him."

As Brandon prepared the wall for the first of the cabinets, he noticed his father watching him. "What?"

"It's nice to have you back," Dennis said softly. "From wherever it was you were the last couple of years."

Brandon smiled. "It's good to be back."

Brandon and his father were hanging the last of the cabinets when Mike came bursting through the open door to Mrs. Oczkowski's apartment. She stopped short when she saw that Brandon wasn't alone.

"Hey, squirt, how was school?"

"It was great. We got to finger paint today."

"Did you get any on the paper?" Brandon asked with a grin. Her shirt was covered with paint.

She gave him her now-familiar withering look. "Very funny. I'm Mike," she said, reaching out a hand to Dennis.

"Are you now? I'm Dennis O'Malley. Pleased to meet you."

"He's my dad," Brandon said.

"You're lucky. I don't have a dad."

Brandon put down the caulking gun and turned to her. "No, you don't. But you have friends like me, right?"

"Uh-huh."

"Mike!" Daphne called from the hallway.

"In here!" Mike yelled.

Dennis gasped when Daphne came through the door.

"Oh, hello, Mr. O'Malley."

"Hello, there, how are you?" Dennis managed to say.

Brandon hid his amusement at his father's fumbling reaction to Daphne.

Daphne's cheeks flushed when she glanced at Brandon. "Mike, you need to go finish your lunch."

"Can I come back after?" Mike asked Brandon.

Brandon squatted down to talk to her. "Today I have to say no because my dad and I are cutting out Mrs. Oczkowski's new countertop, and we have to use some really dangerous tools."

Her face fell with disappointment.

"How about I come see you after I'm done at work? Would that be okay?"

That seemed to be all she needed to hear. "Okay," she said, skipping out the door to go finish her lunch.

"Um, could I talk to you for a minute?" Daphne asked Brandon.

"Sure. I'll be right back, Da."

Brandon ignored his father's raised eyebrow when he put a hand on Daphne's back to guide her from the apartment.

"What's up?" he asked when they were in the hallway. He wanted to pull her into his arms and show her how much he'd missed her since he saw her last.

"I'm, ah, I'm mortified by the way I acted last night."

"What do you mean?" Brandon asked, confused. "There wasn't anything to be mortified about."

"I was like a sex-starved maniac," she whispered as her cheeks flushed with color that he found adorable—and arousing.

Brandon laughed and put his arms around her. "And here I've spent all day hoping you might jump my bones again tonight."

"*Stop*," she moaned, burying her face in his denim work shirt. "It's embarrassing."

Tilting her chin up, he kissed her lightly. "There's nothing embarrassing about it." He backed her up against the wall and pressed his erection against her. "You think you're embarrassed? Look at the condition you've got me in just being near you."

"*Brandon*," she gasped.

Laughing at her scandalized expression, he kissed her nose and then her lips. "No more talk about being embarrassed, okay?"

"Okay."

"Can I take you and Mike out to dinner tonight?"

"She'd love that."

Brandon pressed his lips to her neck. "How about you?"

"Yes," she said breathlessly. "Me, too."

Brandon gave himself a good five minutes to settle down after Daphne left him to go upstairs to Mike. When he finally returned to Mrs. Oczkowski's apartment, Dennis pounced.

"Are you *canoodling* with the tenant from hell?" Dennis asked in a loud whisper.

Brandon laughed. "What the hell does canoodling mean?"

"You know what it means. Are you?"

"Maybe."

"But she's…"

"What?"

"Awful," Dennis said with characteristic bluntness. "Don't be fooled by how she looks."

"That's not fair, Da. You don't even know her. She's raising that little girl all by herself. She hasn't had it easy."

"The kid sure is a cutie," Dennis said. "I couldn't believe the way she introduced herself."

"She's an amazing kid."

"Go easy with the mother, son. There's something about her that bothers me. She's lucky I let her stay here when I bought the place. She pays her rent in cash, she would only sign a month-to-month lease, and she refused to give me her last address. That's odd, wouldn't you say?"

Brandon kept his expression neutral so his father wouldn't see just how odd he found it. "I guess, but that doesn't mean it's shady. She could have a perfectly good reason for all we know."

"I don't like it, and I don't want to see you hurt by her. You've been through enough."

"Don't worry about me, Da. I can take care of myself."

After Dennis left, Brandon went looking for Mike. He had missed her incessant chatter that afternoon. From the second-floor hallway, he saw her bouncing a ball on the sidewalk that ran along the back of the building.

He went down the back stairs and out the door into the warm mid-April day. The yellow forsythia bushes in the backyard were in bloom, and the air was filled with the fragrant smell of spring. Brandon couldn't remember the last time he'd noticed a change of season.

Mike was concentrating on dribbling the ball and didn't see him coming.

"What's up, squirt?"

Surprised, she looked up at him. "Are you done working?"

"For now. What're you up to?"

"Nothing."

"What's the matter?"

She shrugged.

"Want to walk down to the park?"

"I guess."

"Go tell your mom."

She went into the house without her usual exuberance and was still listless when she returned wearing a sweater.

Brandon lifted her to his shoulders to carry her the short distance to the park. "So how come you never play on the swing set in the yard?"

"My mom won't let me. She says I'd need a tetchis shot to play on that rusty old thing."

Brandon laughed. "You mean tetanus? I guess it is kind of rusty."

As Brandon pushed her on the swing, he studied the playground equipment and was struck with an idea that took shape over the next few minutes. He was startled out of his thoughts when she suddenly asked him to stop pushing her.

"What's wrong, honey?" He eased the swing to a stop. "You're not yourself today."

"My stomach hurts," she said, clutching her middle.

He ran a hand over her face and discovered she was burning up. "You've got a fever. Come on, let's get you home."

"Wait," she said when he tried to pick her up. "I think I'm going to throw up."

Brandon moved fast to carry her over to the big open garbage can and held her as her little body convulsed with wave after wave of nausea. He'd never felt so helpless.

When it was finally over, tears spilled down her cheeks. "Sorry," she whispered.

Her embarrassment broke his heart. "Don't be sorry, baby. You couldn't help it." He tugged a bandanna from his back pocket and wiped her face and mouth before he hoisted her gently into his arms.

She rested her head on his shoulder and was asleep before he made it through the gate at the park.

Brandon got her home as fast as he could and tapped on Daphne's door.

She was alarmed to find Brandon carrying a sleeping Mike. "What happened?"

"She said her stomach hurt, and then she threw up. She's really hot, too." He followed Daphne to Mike's room and settled the child on the bed.

Daphne untied Mike's red sneakers and pulled them off. "She seemed fine when she came up to tell me she was going with you."

"She was kind of blah." Brandon smoothed the hair off Mike's hot forehead. "Definitely not herself."

"I'm going to go grab the thermometer. I'll be right back." She returned a minute later and gasped when the thermometer reached 102 degrees. "God, that came out of nowhere. She was fine earlier."

"What do we do?" Brandon asked, gripped with worry for his little friend. He glanced up to find Daphne looking at him with an odd expression on her face. "What is it? Are you scared?"

"No. It's just a fever, and she'll be fine, but that's the first time anyone's ever asked me, 'What do we do.'"

Touched, he reached for her hand. "So what do *we* do?"

"*We* give her some Tylenol and hope she isn't sick all night."

Brandon helped her rouse Mike long enough to get her to swallow the liquid Tylenol. Then they changed her into pajamas and flipped on the nightlight. Daphne tucked a barf bucket and Brandon the Bear into bed next to Mike.

Daphne tugged on Brandon's hand to get him to leave Mike to sleep. "She'll be okay."

"Promise?" Brandon leaned over to kiss Mike's warm cheek one last time. "Remember what I said about super elastic bubble plastic?"

He finally let her lead him to the living room, where she held out her arms to him.

"You've had a trial by fire the last two days—a bump on the head and a puking incident. You're going to run for your life away from us."

"No, I'm not," he said in a husky voice as he buried his face in her fragrant blonde hair.

"Sorry about dinner."

"We can do it another time. Why don't I go get us some takeout?"

She pulled back to look at him. "You don't have to do that. You've probably got better things to do than sit at home with a sick child."

"Is it okay to say there's nothing I'd rather do than sit at home with that particular sick child?"

"It's okay," she said, smiling as she reached up to kiss him.

"What do you feel like eating?"

"Whatever you want. Surprise me."

He kissed her. "I'll be right back."

Brandon called his sister's house from the truck.

"Maloney residence," Josh answered.

"Hey, Josh, it's Uncle Brandon. How's your head?"

"I've got a cool bruise. It's all purple and yellow. Mike's got a hard head."

Brandon laughed. "Sounds like you ended up worse off than her. I could hardly see hers today."

"Can she come play again sometime? She's cool."

"Sure, buddy." Brandon was ridiculously pleased by his nephew's approval of Mike. "We'll do it again soon. Is your dad around?"

"Hang on, I'll get him."

Brandon chuckled when Josh yelled for his father right into the phone. He also heard Tommy's quiet reprimand of the boy's phone manners before picking up.

"Hey, Brand, what's up? How's it going in Siberia?"

Brandon laughed. "Very funny. I'll be back busting balls in the yard soon enough."

"Good. Maybe you can do something about Colin while you're at it. He's been in a hell of a mood lately."

"So I've heard. I told my dad I'd talk to him, but I'm not sure how much good it'll do. Listen, the reason I called is I'm wondering where I can get one of those backyard playground thingies. A good one."

"We got ours down at Foster's. Is your dad putting one in at the building?"

"No, I'm doing it on my own."

Tommy released a dry chuckle. "Ya ever put one together before?"

"No, but how hard can it be?"

This time Tommy laughed out loud. "Building a house is easier. I can help you after work on Saturday afternoon if you want. I'll mention it to Col and Dec, too. You'll need all of us."

"No way."

"I'm not kidding. Do you know how much they cost?"

"I'm almost afraid to ask."

"About three grand for a good one."

"Get the hell outta here!"

Tommy howled.

"You're enjoying this, aren't you?"

"Oh, yeah. I'll be over on Saturday, and I'll bring a load of the mulch you'll need for padding underneath it. Just make sure you have plenty of beer." Tommy paused when he realized what he'd said. "Jesus, Brandon, I'm sorry. I wasn't thinking."

"Don't be sorry. Of course I'll have beer for you guys if you're helping me out."

"You don't have to. We don't need it."

"Don't sweat it, Tom."

"Well, your sister is dancing around trying to get my attention. I'm getting the feeling she wants to talk to you."

Brandon got to listen to the wrestling match for the phone between his sister and her husband.

"Sheesh," Erin said when she finally succeeded in getting the phone away from Tommy. "What a pain in the *ass* he is."

"You love him."

"Whatever. So I talked to Valerie today. She said you can come by any afternoon between two and four when her daughter naps. I left you a message with her number."

"Thanks, Erin."

"Did you ask Daphne about Easter?"

"Not yet, but I will. So Mike has the stomach bug."

"Oh, no! I hope she didn't get it from one of my kids."

"No sign of it there?"

"Nope. Let's hope it stays that way with Easter this weekend. Is the playground for Mike?"

"Yeah."

"That's really nice of you, Brandon."

"She's a nice kid. I'll talk to you soon."

Next he tried to call Colin but got voice mail at home and on his cell phone, so he left his brother another message. On an impulse, Brandon made a U-turn and went to the office, hoping to find Colin still at work.

He drove through the gates of O'Malley & Sons for the first time in nearly three months. Since it was after seven, the yard was deserted, and the trucks were silent after a long day. But in the upstairs office, Brandon saw a light burning. He pulled in next to Colin's company truck and went upstairs, passing his own dark office on the way to what used to be their father's office, where he found Colin bent over the computer.

"Hey," Brandon said, startling Colin. "Burning the midnight oil?"

"Hardly. Just trying to figure out Da's inventory system. I'm beginning to think it makes sense only to him."

Brandon sat down in the chair next to the desk. "How's everything else going?"

"Crazy busy. You know how this time of year is. The minute the ground thaws, we're going full tilt."

"How are *you* doing?"

"Fine, I guess. A few transition issues here and there, but nothing I can't handle."

"I've left you a couple of messages."

Colin ran a hand through his hair, his every gesture filled with weariness that was not like him. "I know. I'm sorry. I haven't had time to call anyone."

"What's wrong, Colin?"

"Nothing. Like I said, I'm just really busy."

"You're sure that's all it is?"

"Yeah, well…"

"What? Tell me."

"There's this girl," Colin said tentatively.

"Ah-*ha*! I knew there was something going on. What's the deal?"

"No deal. That's the problem. I really like her, but she's not interested in pursuing it, even though we have a really good time together."

"Why isn't she interested?"

"That's the bitch of it. I don't know, but I know she likes me, too." Colin sighed. "This is so high school, isn't it?"

Brandon laughed. "Nah, it's just proof that it doesn't get any easier even when you're old goats like us. Is this the one you were in a big rush to get home to see when we went to Vermont?"

"Yeah. I can't stop thinking about her, you know? It's driving me crazy that she won't even give it a chance."

Brandon thought about that for a minute. "Is there some way you could see her without pressuring her? Just make it so your path crosses hers?"

"I suppose I could do that. I'll think about it."

"Good." Brandon got up to leave. "In the meantime, maybe you could sweeten up around here. I've heard a few grumbles about the new boss's foul mood."

Colin looked stunned. "For real?"

"Yep."

"Shit. Thanks for cueing me in. How're you? Everything going okay?"

"Better than okay, but I can't get into it now. I'm organizing a work party at the apartments on Saturday afternoon. Can you make it?"

"Sure. What's the job?"

"Oh, you'll see," Brandon said with a smile and a wave as he left Colin's office.

Chapter 20, Day 71

Brandon returned to Daphne's apartment with Chinese food. When he found her rocking Mike in the living room, he stashed the food in the kitchen.

"What happened?" he whispered, running a hand over Mike's damp hair.

"Sick all over the place," Daphne whispered. "Poor thing. She was so upset about making a mess. I just got her out of the tub."

"What can I do?"

"Want to take over here so I can deal with her bed?"

"I can do the bed if you'd rather stay with her."

"That's okay." Daphne got up slowly and transferred Mike into Brandon's arms.

She whimpered when Brandon sat down with her.

"It's okay, baby," he said, brushing his lips over her hair.

"Sick," Mike whispered.

He held her close to him as he rocked her. "I know. I hate that bad bug."

Her giggle turned into a grimace. "Don't go."

"I'm not going anywhere."

"Love you, Brandon."

He was powerless against the tears that filled his eyes. "Love you, too, squirt. We've got to hurry up and get you better before the Easter bunny comes."

She nodded and was back to sleep a minute later.

He could feel the heat of her fever through his shirt.

"Okay," Daphne said when she returned. "I changed the bed and threw the sheets in the wash. Want to put her back to bed?"

"Do I have to?"

She smiled as she rested a hand on Mike's forehead to check her fever. "She's completely and utterly in love with you. You realize that, don't you?"

"She'd better be, because the feeling is completely and utterly mutual."

Daphne bent to kiss his cheek. "Let's put her to bed so you can eat."

Brandon rocked Mike for another minute before he got up to carry her to bed. Her room held the faint odor of vomit, and again he felt sorry for Mike as he settled her into bed. "Where's Brandon the Bear?"

"In the washer," Daphne said.

Brandon winced. "Poor guy. Took one for the team, huh?"

She chuckled. "Big time."

They got Mike settled and went back to the living room. "Are you okay?" he asked, massaging her shoulders.

"*Oh*, that feels good."

He turned her around and gave her back the full treatment while dropping soft kisses on her neck. "Hungry?"

"I don't know if I could eat after cleaning that up. You go ahead. I'll just have a glass of wine."

"Don't," he whispered against her neck.

She turned to him, perplexed. "Why?"

He hadn't planned on getting into this tonight, but he knew he needed to tell her sooner rather than later. "All I've thought about today is kissing you again, but if you drink the wine, I can't."

"Why?"

He kept his arms looped around her as he gazed into her golden eyes. "Because I'm an alcoholic, and I want to taste you, not alcohol." His heart stopped while he waited for her to say something.

She worked herself free of his embrace. "How long have you been sober?"

"Seventy-one days."

She blinked. "That's not even three months."

He put his hands on her shoulders. "Daphne, please, listen to me. I'm sober, and I'm going to stay sober. I swear to God, nothing could make me go back to living the way I was—if for no other reason than I adore you and Mike. I'd never do anything to hurt either of you."

She ran her fingers through her hair. "I don't know what to say. I've let my daughter become so attached to you. I can't risk her."

"I love her. You know I do. Don't take her away from me because of mistakes I've made in the past. I'm not the same person I was then. Everything's different now."

"Can you tell me you'll never drink again? Can you promise me that?"

Brandon shifted from one foot to the other. "No. I can't make that promise. I'm doing the best I can every day to keep my side of the street clean. That's the best I can do—that's the best any of us can do."

Daphne blinked back tears. "I don't know what to say. My job is to protect Mike."

"Do you honestly think you'll ever have to protect her from me?" he asked, feeling as if his very life was on the line.

Daphne studied him for a long time. "No."

"Then give me a chance. That's all I'm asking for."

She rested her head against his chest. "I want to hear more about it."

"And I'll tell you—anything you want to know, but not tonight, okay?" He hugged her to him, feeling weak with relief. At least she hadn't kicked him out of their lives. "All you need to know right now is I won't let you down, and I won't let Mike down, either. That much I *can* promise you."

She looked up at him, and he wiped the tears off her face before he leaned in for a kiss that turned hot when she clung to him.

"I'm so afraid, Brandon," she whispered. "Mike isn't the only one who loves you."

His heart lurched. "No?"

She shook her head. "You've been so good to her, to both of us. I can't remember what we ever did before we had you in our lives."

He held her gaze for a long moment before he lifted her off her feet to kiss her again. He wanted to tell her he loved her, too. But he'd never said those words to a woman, and after waiting thirty-eight years for this—for her—it wasn't something he wanted to just blurt out. No, he needed to do this right.

"I want you so much," she whispered. "It's all I think about."

"Me, too," he said against her ear, sending a shiver through her. "But not with Mike sick in the next room. The first time will be just for us."

"When? How?"

"Leave that to me, okay?"

She nodded. "Aren't you hungry?"

"Not for food."

Her laughter filled the room. "Put me down and go eat."

"Do I have to?" he asked for the second time that night.

"Yes, you have to, or I'll jump you right here despite your strong ethical code."

"The longer I have your sexy self wrapped around me, the less I'm able to hear my conscience speaking."

She tugged herself free, dragged him into the kitchen, and pushed him into a chair. "Eat," she ordered, handing him a plate and silverware.

He dove into the Chinese food while she poured them each a Coke.

"My sister wants you and Mike to come to Easter dinner at her house."

Daphne turned to look at him. "I don't know…"

"Come on, it'll be fun. Mike will have a blast. Erin does a big Easter egg hunt for the kids."

Her expression was filled with yearning.

STARTING OVER 195

"What?"

"I can't remember the last time I spent a holiday with anyone but Mike."

"Why are you so alone in the world, Daph?"

"Because I choose to be, or at least I did until my daughter decided you were essential to her."

He smiled. "She's a girl who knows what she wants."

"Yes, she is. God help us all."

"That doesn't tell me why you two are so alone."

She leaned against the counter and studied him over the rim of her glass. "It's how I keep her safe."

"From?" he asked, putting down his fork.

"From people who'd take her away from me if they got the chance."

Brandon suddenly felt sick himself as he got up to face her. "Who would take her away from you?"

Daphne shook her head, as if she regretted saying so much.

"You can't drop that on me and not finish it." Brandon rested his hands on her shoulders. "Tell me."

"Randy's parents," she whispered. "They're looking for her."

"What do you mean 'looking for her'?"

She sighed. "I told you his family was politically powerful, right?"

He nodded, and his jaw clenched with tension as he realized he wasn't going to like this.

"His father is the senior US senator from California."

Brandon gasped. "Jesus. You weren't kidding."

"Randy was their only child, and they went to great lengths to cover up how he died. The rest of the world thinks he died in a car accident. Crazy, huh? No one knows the truth but the three of us and a handful of people they pay to make these kinds of things go away. After his funeral, I found Randy's mother in Mike's room, leaning over her crib. She was saying she couldn't lose her, too, and Grandma would take care of everything. I saw what they did to Randy, what they drove him to. I knew if I didn't get Mike out of there, they'd do the same thing to her. So that night, I took her and the few things we couldn't live without, and I left. I've been running from them ever since."

Brandon stared at her, incredulous. "But you have rights. You're her mother."

Daphne snickered. "I'm no one. I wouldn't stand a chance against them."

"That's why you move around so much."

She nodded. "Whenever I feel them getting close, we move. It takes them a while to find us, but they always do. This is the longest we've ever been anywhere—almost two years."

Brandon stared at her in disbelief. "How long can you keep this up?"

"For the rest of my life, if that's what it takes to protect my child."

"I want to help. Let me get you some help."

She shook her head. "They have power and money and people who do whatever they tell them to. I have nothing to fight them with, and I won't take the chance that they'd win."

"I can get you money, lawyers, whatever you need." He'd have to go to Aidan for the money, but for Mike, he'd do it in a heartbeat.

She reached for his hand. "Thank you for wanting to help, but I'm handling it."

"You're not handling it, you're running from it. That's no way for Mike to grow up."

"Do you think I don't know that?" Her golden eyes heated with anger. "But the alternative is unimaginable. Just ask Randy."

He wanted to weep as he took her into his arms. "Daphne, please, there has to be something we can do to free you from having to live like this."

She rested against his chest and put her arms around him. "You're helping me just by being here. Can't that be enough for now?"

Brandon was all churned up inside as he pulled back to look at her. "I have so many questions."

"Such as?"

"How do you hide in plain sight?"

"By not leaving a paper trail."

"But how do you support the two of you?"

"I find people who're willing to pay cash for what I do for them."

"Am I going to like this?"

She laughed. "It's nothing seedy. In my old life, I was a CPA, but that requires a license, and licenses create paper. So now I'm a glorified bookkeeper. I got really lucky here. The guy who owns the nightclub where I work has a bunch of other businesses, so he's my only client. He lets me work from home most of the time, and I only have to go into the club two or three afternoons a week for a couple of hours to do the deposits and the payroll. He doesn't mind if I bring Mike with me."

"Do you make enough money doing that?"

She nodded. "We don't need much."

Brandon ran a hand through his hair. "What about health insurance?"

"I've gotten lucky there, too. We haven't needed it, and it's cheaper to pay as we go."

"Do I even know your real names?" he asked, pacing the small kitchen.

"Our first names. Van Der Meer was my grandmother's maiden name."

"What's your real last name?"

"Monroe."

Stricken, Brandon stared at her. "Harrison Monroe was your father-in-law?"

She nodded.

"Not just any senator—the Senate majority leader."

"I told you he was powerful."

Brandon took an unsteady deep breath. "How much does Mike know?"

"All of it. I told her as soon as I felt she was old enough to understand the basic facts. I didn't want her to be afraid, but I needed her to be aware of what we were dealing with so she could be vigilant."

"No wonder why she's so mature."

"I hate that she has to live like this, but I think she's a happy kid for the most part."

"She seems to be, but there's definitely an old soul living in that tiny body."

"I know." Daphne sighed. "I always say if I had to go it alone with her, I got the right kid. She's the best thing that's ever happened to me. That's why I can't lose her."

"I'll tell you something right now," Brandon said fiercely. "They'll take her away from you over my cold, dead body, you got me?"

Her laughter was soft and delicate, just like her. "Where have you *been* all my life, Brandon O'Malley?"

He ran his thumbs over her jaw and buried his hands in her hair. Tugging her to him, he kissed her with the same fierce determination. "I've been right here waiting for you."

"Now that you have me, what will you do with me?" she asked with a saucy grin that shot heat straight through him.

"Oh, no. Don't start that again. I thought you were mortified. What happened to 'I was a sex-starved lunatic'?"

"It was maniac—there's a difference—and I got over it," she said, pressing her hips against him.

Brandon closed his eyes and tried to count to ten as her hands dipped under his shirt. He made it to two. "Big brain under attack from little brain," he chanted. "Little brain winning the battle."

Daphne laughed. "I like the way little brain thinks."

"I want it to be special, Daph." He captured her wandering hands in his and wondered where all this self-control was coming from. "I don't want it to be just another roll in the hay."

She raised an eyebrow. "Do you really think it will be?"

"I know it won't be. That's why I want to wait until we're alone." He kissed her cheek. "Really alone."

"Okay. You're right."

"I'd better go while I still can. Can I check on Mike first?"

"Of course." She followed him into Mike's room.

Brandon felt the sleeping child's face. "She's cooler than she was."

"She threw up most of the Tylenol that second time, so I'm glad some of it stayed down."

"What if she wakes up again? I told her I wouldn't leave."

"Then don't. Sleep with me. We don't have to do anything."

He snorted. "Yeah, right."

She came up behind him and wrapped her arms around him. "I'll behave, I promise. I want you to stay."

He put his hands over hers as his better judgment waged war with everything he felt for her. "Let me run downstairs and get changed."

"You'll start a scandal in the building if anyone sees you coming back."

"The senior set is probably long asleep by now. I'll be right back."

He was back ten minutes later wearing sweats, a T-shirt, and a look of amazement on his face. "You aren't going to believe it."

"Believe what?"

"I heard voices on the first floor, so I peeked down the stairs and saw Mr. Pauley and Mrs. Oczkowski making out in the hallway."

"Shut up! They were *not*!"

"I swear to God! They're both, like, what? Eighty-five?"

Daphne giggled. "And here I thought we'd be the scandal."

"My brother Colin said I'm running Melrose Place over here. It's starting to look like he might be right."

She laughed. "Yeah, Melrose: the Senior Years."

"Is that, um, what you wear to bed?"

She had changed into satin pajama bottoms and a form-fitting camisole. Looking down at what she was wearing, she said, "Yeah, why? What's wrong with it?"

"Nothing." He gulped. "Nothing at all. This might not be such a good idea."

Snickering at the expression on his face, she took his hand to lead him to her room. "I promised to behave."

"I didn't."

"You will. You're Mr. Ethical High Ground, remember?"

"Little brain is Mr. Degenerate, though. He's the problem."

Daphne laughed as she turned on the bedside lamp. A tangerine-colored scarf covering the lamp cast an amber glow over the pretty, feminine room.

"I like your room," he said as a hint of her fragrance in the air caught Mr. Degenerate's attention.

"It's my garden," she said, referring to the flowers on her comforter and wall-paper. "We move too much to have a real one, so I take this one with me wherever I go." She turned down the bed and held out a hand to him.

"What will Mike say if she finds me here?" he asked as he lay down next to her and drew her into his arms.

She rested her head on his chest. "I asked her today if she minded if you were my boyfriend."

"What'd she say?"

"She said, 'Why would I mind? I picked him for us.'"

Brandon laughed. "She's too much. Fixed up by a five-year-old. I love it."

"She did pick you, you know." Daphne turned to face him. "She's never taken to anyone the way she took to you from the first minute she met you."

"I haven't, either. I can still picture her little feet coming into the kitchen when I was under your sink. I thought she was a boy because I heard you call her Mike."

Daphne laughed.

"I don't know how I could've *ever* thought she was a boy. She's *all* girl. Just like her mama," he said, running a hand up Daphne's back. He leaned in to kiss her and was lost in her the second his lips touched hers. It was still a revelation to be doing this with someone he loved and to discover that love made all the difference. The kiss was unlike any other, even with her.

By the time they came up for air, he was on top of her, and her hands were massaging his back under his shirt. He gazed down at her and kissed her again. Somehow, his shirt ended up on the floor. Hers landed next to it a minute later. He caressed her breasts as his lips coasted over her smooth skin.

"I told you we couldn't be in bed together and behave," he whispered as he ran his tongue around her nipple.

"Brandon," she gasped, burying her hands in his hair to keep him there.

When he heard Mike whimper in the next room, he stopped to listen before he reached for Daphne's shirt and helped her put it back on.

She went to check on Mike.

Brandon fell against the pillow and willed his body to settle down. *God, what that woman does to me!* Just being near her was enough to send him into the most painful state of arousal. He couldn't begin to imagine what it would be like to make love with her. "Is she okay?" he asked when Daphne returned.

"Yeah, she's dreaming."

When she got back in bed, he put his arm around her. "Saved by the bell," he said.

She giggled. "Go to sleep."

"Yeah, right. My head feels like it's going to blow off my neck."

"One, two, three, sleep." She pressed her lips to his chest and sighed with contentment.

He felt her drift off to sleep, but he was awake for a long time, thinking about everything she'd told him and trying to figure out how he could fix it for her.

CHAPTER 21, DAY 72

Brandon was suspended somewhere between sleep and consciousness when he felt a hand moving on his chest. He was aware enough to remember he'd slept with Daphne, and reached for her hand. Her tiny hand… His eyes flew open to find Mike standing beside the bed. Cursing himself for forgetting to put his shirt back on, he held his breath and waited for her to say something.

"You have hair on your chest," she whispered, scandalized by the discovery.

"Uh, yeah." He was not at all sure how to handle this. Since Daphne was curled up to his back sound asleep, she was of no help to him at the moment. "Do you feel better?"

"A little."

He lifted the sheet to invite her to lie down with them.

She looked at him for a long, endless moment, as if she was making up her mind about something before she got in next to him.

He pulled the covers up around them and rested his hand on her face. "You still have a bit of a fever," he whispered. "Does your belly feel better?"

"Yeah."

"Do you mind that I'm here?"

"No. I asked you to stay, remember?"

He nodded.

"Do you love my mom?"

He was touched by the question and her serious expression. This was important stuff. "Both of you," he whispered.

"I don't want to move anymore. I want to stay here with you."

He tugged her closer to him and kissed the top of her head. "We're going to figure something out, squirt. Don't worry about it, okay?"

"Okay."

He sacrificed his morning run to have breakfast with Mike. They let Daphne sleep while he made Mike toast and brewed a pot of coffee. She told him where everything was and bombarded him with orders—cut off the crusts, put the cinnamon on first, *then* the sugar.

"Don't eat it too fast," he warned her. "You don't want to upset your stomach again."

She licked the butter and cinnamon off her fingers. "I hate throwing up. It's so gross."

"But you felt better afterward." He caught her studying him. "What?"

"You look different in the morning," she said with a giggle.

He sat down at the table with her. "Different how?"

"Your hair's all messy, and you have scratchy stuff on your face."

"Well, excuse me, madam, but no one told me this was a dress-up breakfast." He feigned offense as he ran a self-conscious hand through his hair and then over his face. "Most girls like the scruffy look."

She made a face that told him she wasn't one of them.

"Are you bummed about missing school today?"

"There's no school today, silly. It's Good Friday."

"Ah, so it is. I forgot."

"We're on vacation all next week, too."

"Great way to start your vacation—being sick."

"I know, but my mom will let me have all the ice cream I want later," she said with a mischievous grin.

He was relieved that she was feeling better and acting more like herself this morning. "What's your favorite kind?"

"Chocolate chip."

"Mine, too!"

Her smile was full of love for him, and he could've burst from the simple joy she'd brought to his life.

Daphne came into the kitchen and made a beeline for the coffee.

"She's not a morning person," Mike whispered to Brandon.

"Good to know," he whispered.

"I can hear you two," Daphne grumbled as she poured herself a cup of coffee.

Mike giggled.

"Are you better today, Pooh?" Daphne asked.

"She's planning an ice-cream party for later, if that's any sign," Brandon offered, feasting his eyes on Daphne's sleep-rumpled hair and rosy cheeks.

She met his glance and held it as a hundred thoughts and feelings passed between them. "Thanks for letting me sleep in. I can't remember the last time I got to sleep past seven."

"I had a lesson on how to make cinnamon toast Mike-style," Brandon said as he got up to leave.

Daphne rolled her eyes. "The pampered princess will only eat it *without* the crusts."

"So I discovered." He kissed the top of Mike's head. "I'll be out for a while today, but I'll check on you when I get back, okay, squirt?"

"Okay."

He held out a hand to Daphne, and she walked him to the door.

"Not a morning person, huh?" he whispered in her ear as he put his arms around her.

She snuggled into his embrace. "Not usually, but I could get used to this."

He tilted her chin and kissed her. "That would be fine with me."

She ran a lazy finger over the stubble that had fascinated her daughter. "I'll see you later?"

"I can't wait."

After his AA meeting and coffee with Joe, Brandon called Alan. They'd spoken a few times by phone but hadn't seen each other since Brandon's last day of rehab.

"Hey, Brandon, nice to hear from you. What's going on?"

"I was wondering if you might have a few minutes free today. I need some legal advice."

"You're not in any trouble, are you?"

"No, nothing like that."

"Well, that's a relief. Since it's Good Friday, my office is closed, so I'm just catching up on some paperwork. Come on over." He gave Brandon directions to his office in Dennis on Cape Cod's north shore.

"I'm in Harwich, so I'll be there in about twenty minutes," Brandon said.

Arriving at the office, he saw a sign for Alan St. John, attorney at law, and realized his days of anonymity with Alan were over.

Alan waited for him in the reception area.

"You're looking well, Brandon," Alan said as they shook hands.

"Thanks. How're you?"

"Busy as hell, but it keeps me out of trouble." He led Brandon into his spacious office and gestured for him to have a seat on the sofa. "Coffee?"

"No, thanks."

Alan poured himself a cup and sat down across from Brandon. "What can I do for you?"

"If I tell you something when I'm not technically your client, it's still confidential, right?"

"Of course. You have my word, Brandon. Nothing we talk about will leave this room unless it's something I'm legally required to report."

"I have this friend. She's a single mom with an adorable five-year-old daughter."

Alan raised an eyebrow. "New friends?"

"Yes." Brandon knew what Alan was thinking in terms of his recovery. Joe had lectured him again on the subject that morning over coffee. Without naming names, Brandon outlined Daphne's situation to Alan.

"Hmm." Alan scratched his chin as he pondered it. "So she's had no contact with the grandparents in five years?"

"No," Brandon said. "Tell me she has rights, Alan. They can't just take her kid away from her, no matter who they are, can they?"

"They'd be hard-pressed to find a judge who'd give them custody. They'd have to prove she was unfit, and it sounds as if they'd have a hard time doing that. But these days, the courts are recognizing that grandparents have rights, too. The fact that she's denied them access to the child for all these years might be a problem."

"What kind of problem?"

"They'd probably get visitation, at the very least."

"She doesn't want them in her daughter's life at all."

"Then she'll have to decide if it's worth it to continue living the way she is now."

"She'd say it's worth it," Brandon said with dejection. "She blames them for her husband's suicide and fears her daughter would get sucked into their world if she gives them an inch. She didn't come right out and say this, but I also got the sense the father-in-law is crooked and pays people off to get what he wants."

"I hate to say it, but it does happen—not often, fortunately. Let me run this by a family court judge I know and get his handle on it. Why don't you bring them out to the house for dinner one night this week? Her daughter can play with my girls, and we can hash it out."

"That'd be great, Alan. I appreciate your help. Send me the bill for your time."

"Don't be ridiculous. I'm happy to help. Why don't we see what we can do to get your friend out of this mess?"

Brandon sighed with relief. He'd come to the right place. "Thank you."

"So she's just a friend, huh? The mom?"

"Um, well…"

Alan laughed at Brandon's befuddlement. "I'm sure you've already been read the riot act by your sponsor for getting involved with someone so soon, so I won't add to the chorus. But I hope you're being careful."

"Don't worry," Brandon said. "I know what's at stake—for all of us."

"I'll talk to the judge, and I'll call you to set something up for next week."

"Thanks again, Alan."

Brandon left Alan's office and drove to Foster's in Harwich where he spent half an hour trying to decide which of the fifty different playground setups would be best for Mike. Since she wasn't even six yet, he rejected the one with the rock-climbing wall in favor of a tree house, two slides, three swings, and monkey bars. Thirty-five hundred dollars later, there were four huge boxes stacked in the back of his truck. For an additional five hundred dollars, Foster's would've sent some guys over to put it together for him. Brandon scoffed at that. He had a civil engineering degree from Notre Dame, for Christ's sake. If he couldn't do it himself, who could?

He hit a bump, and the million pieces inside the boxes rattled and clanked in the truck bed. "Gives new meaning to the phrase 'some assembly required,'" he mumbled to himself on the way back to Chatham. "Maybe I should've coughed up the five hundred extra bucks."

He'd spent several hours one night recently going over his financial situation, and when he was done, one thing was clear—he'd blown through a shitload of money in the last few years, most of it on booze. The two hundred fifty thousand dollars Aidan had given to his parents and each of his siblings after Sarah died was long gone—the first half of Brandon's share went toward buying and renovating the house he bought with Valerie. Most of the second half was used to buy her out when they broke up. Brandon hadn't wanted the money from Aidan in the first place and relented only when Aidan insisted that Sarah would've wanted them all to have some of it.

Brandon reimbursed his father almost eight thousand dollars for the payments he made on the small mortgage Brandon still had on the house and sent Colin a check for four grand, hoping it was enough to pay his brother back for bailing him out of jail—twice—and for the bar tabs Colin had paid for him over the years. As far as he knew, Brandon didn't owe money to anyone else. He figured he'd eventually hear about it if he did.

Dennis used a complicated formula to determine their annual salaries, and what they made depended on how the business did in any given year. Brandon, Colin, Declan, and Tommy were equal partners with Dennis, and in recent years, none of them had made less than one hundred fifty thousand in a year.

Brandon's night of financial reckoning revealed that after all his debts were paid, he had just over twenty grand left in the bank, and the boxes rattling around in the back of the truck had just put a sizeable dent in that. He was ashamed to have pissed away more than a hundred thousand dollars over the last few years on bars, booze, and God only knew what else.

He would throw every dime he had left at lawyers, if that was what it took to keep Mike with Daphne and to end this crazy cat-and-mouse game she was playing with her former in-laws. His gut clenched when he thought about how expensive a protracted court battle could get. If it came to that, he'd take a second mortgage on his house to pay for it. And if he had any doubt about how hard he'd fallen for Daphne and Mike, he wouldn't hesitate to swallow his pride and go to Aidan, who still had several of Sarah's millions squirreled away. No matter what it took, Brandon would find a way out of this for Daphne.

Before he went back to the apartments to check on Mike, Brandon had one more thing he needed to take care of. This had been weighing on him, and it wasn't going to get any easier if he continued to put it off. So he reached for his cell phone and called the number he'd gotten from Erin.

"Hi, Val, it's Brandon," he said when his ex-girlfriend answered.

"Oh, hi," she said, sounding tentative. "Erin said you might call."

"Am I catching you at a bad time?"

"Um, no. Not at all."

"Do you mind if I come by for a few minutes?"

"Sure. That would be fine." She gave him directions to her house.

Brandon recognized the address as a new development in North Chatham. "I'll be there in about fifteen minutes."

Driving into the neighborhood, Brandon let out a low whistle at the rows of swanky new houses his father called "McMansions." Valerie's was a brick colonial with black shutters, a sweeping front porch, and an ornate two-story window over the front door. A stone wall lined the property. *She sure has come up in the world since her days with me,* Brandon thought as he pulled into the circular driveway.

Valerie waited for him on a wicker sofa on the front porch, and when she stood up to greet him, he saw that she was well into her second pregnancy. The sun brought out the red highlights in her brown hair, and Brandon thought she'd never been lovelier.

Her eyes widened as he came up the stairs to the porch. "Look at you." She shook her head, as if she couldn't believe what she was seeing. "You look wonderful! You couldn't have had the decency to look like crap?"

His laughter broke the ice. "You're gorgeous, Val. Pregnancy certainly agrees with you." He kissed her cheek and sat next to her on the sofa.

"God, I can't get over you. Erin told me you were doing really well, but you look ten years younger than you did the last time I saw you."

"I've been working out again. Feels good to be back in shape. In fact, it feels good to be back in life, to be honest with you."

She rested a hand on top of his, and the sunlight reflected off a big diamond ring. "I'm proud of you, Brand. You're really doing it, aren't you?"

"I'm trying. You've got a beautiful place here."

"Thanks."

"When's the baby due?"

"Mid-June, if I make it that far. I was early with Chelsea." She ran a hand over the baby. "This one's a boy, and he's a kicker."

"I hear Chelsea's a cutie."

"She's a sweetheart. We got really lucky with her."

"Are you happy, Val?"

Blinking back tears, she looked away from him. "Yeah. My husband, Pete, is a wonderful father."

"What does he do?"

"He's in sales for a software company."

"Are you working at all?" She'd been the executive assistant to the CEO of a local bank when they were together.

She shook her head. "I'm a stay-at-home mom these days."

"Erin said your husband's a good guy."

Valerie swiped at her eyes. "He loves me, you know? Really loves me."

"You deserve that."

"I know you never loved me, Brandon, but I thought if I loved you enough for both of us that one day you'd fall in love with me, too."

His heart aching, he kept a firm grip on her hand. "I couldn't be more sorry for the way I treated you. You were so good to me, and you stayed with me a lot longer than most women would have. I certainly didn't give you much reason to stay."

"I loved you so desperately. I don't think you ever had any idea how much."

Her softly spoken words brought tears to his eyes. "I'm so sorry," he whispered. "It wasn't anything you did or didn't do. I want you to know that."

"Then what was it?"

Brandon wiped his face and took a deep breath. "I was in love with Sarah. Aidan's wife."

Valerie gasped. "But she'd been dead for two years when we met. I don't understand…"

"I'd been in love with her since I was a kid, but she was always my brother's girlfriend and then his wife. When she died…" He shook his head when he was unable to continue.

"Does Aidan know?"

"He does now."

"Oh, my God," she whispered. "What did he say?"

"He was shocked, to put it mildly."

"It certainly explains some things."

"None of what happened between us was your fault, Val. I hope you see that. I didn't think I could love anyone after she died. It was like that part of me died, too, or at least I thought it had. I was wrong to become so involved with you when I knew I had nothing to give you."

"Thank you for telling me this. It helps to know there wasn't anything else I could've done. I spent a lot of time after I left you asking myself that."

"There wasn't. You were up against the ghost of a girl who was never even mine. I let it screw up my life and yours."

"It wasn't all bad, though, was it?" she asked softly. "We had some good times, didn't we?"

"We had some great times."

A cry from the baby monitor on the table startled them out of their memories.

"I guess that's my cue." Brandon stood up. He wanted to ask if he could meet her daughter but knew he didn't belong inside the home she shared with her husband. He suspected she knew it, too, which was why she'd met him on the porch.

"I'm glad you came," she said, taking the hand he offered to help her up.

"So am I." He drew her into a hug. "Can I ask you one thing?"

She pulled back from him. "Sure."

"You didn't say you love him—your husband. You do, don't you?"

"I love him as much as I'm able to, but it's different. It's not the all-consuming love I felt for you. That only comes along once in a lifetime. Everything else just pales in comparison."

Brandon nodded to show he understood, but he was sorry he'd asked. "Thanks for seeing me. Good luck with the baby."

"Good luck with your recovery."

"Thanks." He kissed her cheek and went down the stairs.

She was still standing on the porch when he drove away.

CHAPTER 22, DAY 73

Brandon snuggled with Daphne on the sofa in her living room. They'd been out to dinner with Mike, who was almost fully recovered from her bug, but she fell asleep early.

Daphne ran her fingers through his hair. "Everything okay? You've been quiet tonight."

He shrugged.

"What is it?"

"I saw my ex-girlfriend today."

"Oh."

"It's not what you think, hon, so don't go there. I'm not still hung up on her. I needed to see her as part of my recovery. I owed her a big apology."

"For what?"

"I wasn't very nice to her, and I caused her a lot of pain."

"I can't imagine that."

"You didn't know me when I was drinking, thank God. I was an awful person, and I hurt a lot of people, including Valerie, my ex."

"Those days are behind you now."

"I'm still tempted to drink, but then I think about how far I've come and what I have in my life now, and I see it's not worth it."

"So it was hard? To see her?"

"Actually, it was nice to see her. We were together for five years, and it ended badly, so it was good to have the chance to fix that. But she said some stuff that was hard to hear."

"What kind of stuff?"

"I just have a better idea now of how much I hurt her. I'm still getting used to dealing with things like that without the anesthesia I used to get from booze."

"I get this pain, right here in my stomach, when we talk about this."

He winced. "I'm sorry."

"That doesn't mean I don't want to talk about it, because I do. So why did you guys break up?"

"I never loved her, and she got sick of putting up with my shit while she was waiting for me to come around."

"You were with a woman you didn't love for five years?" Daphne asked with amazement.

"It's just one of many things I'm ashamed of, believe me. I'm going to have to tell you this stuff in small doses if I want to keep you around."

She framed his face with her hands. "I didn't know you then, but I know you now, and I love the man you are today. I love you, Brandon."

"I love you, too," he said, unable to keep the words inside for another minute. He leaned in to kiss her softly. "I've never said that to a woman before. I used to think that was so pathetic, but now I'm glad I saved it for you."

"Brandon," she sighed as she pressed her lips to his.

The kiss was hot and deep, but Brandon pulled back before they ended up making love on the sofa. He had plans, and that wasn't one of them. "Will you do something for me?"

"Sure."

"Come with me to my sister's on Sunday, and bring overnight bags for you and Mike?"

"Easter dinner with the O'Malleys is a sleepover?" she asked with a saucy smile.

"Very funny." He kissed the end of her nose. "Will you just do it and not ask questions?"

"What needs to be in these hypothetical overnight bags?"

"Well, Mike needs PJs, a toothbrush, a change of clothes, and Brandon the Bear." He was amazed to realize he could pack the child's bag himself if he had to. "And you just need a toothbrush in yours."

She laughed. "That's it?"

He pretended to give it significant thought. "Yeah, that's about it."

"What're you up to, Brandon O'Malley?"

"Nothing you need to know about now. Will you do it? Come to Erin's and bring the overnight stuff?"

"Are you sure your family won't mind us being there? I don't think your father likes me very much."

"Oh, he's a big blow-hard. Don't let him scare you off. They'd love to have you, and Mike will have so much fun with the kids."

Daphne bit her lip as she gave it some thought. "Okay. We'll go, but on one condition."

"I can't wait to hear this."

"Come to church with us on Easter morning?"

Brandon's smile faded. "I don't really do the church thing anymore."

"I do it for Mike. Well, that's not entirely true. I do it for me, too. With all the moving around, it's the one thing that's familiar no matter where we are. There's comfort in that, you know?"

Strangely enough, he did. "I can see what you're saying, but it's not my scene."

"Do it for me?"

"Don't make that face," he groaned. "I can't say no to that face."

"I'll have to remember that."

Brandon smiled. "Okay, you win. I'll go—but just this once. Now, there's one other thing I need you to do for me."

"You're becoming very high maintenance," she joked.

"I'm just getting started, baby." He gave her a sloppy, wet kiss. "Will you keep Mike out of the yard tomorrow afternoon?"

Daphne raised an eyebrow. "Why?"

"The Easter bunny left her an early present, and I don't want her to see it until it's ready for her."

"What did you do, Brandon?" Daphne asked, all signs of kidding around gone.

"It's nothing." He squirmed under the heat of her glare. "Just a little surprise. I can buy her something if I want to, can't I?"

Daphne sat up. "I don't want you to spoil her. It'll just make it harder when we..."

"When you what?" he asked, sitting up next to her.

"When we have to go," she said softly.

Her words struck fear in his heart. "You're not going anywhere, Daphne."

"I won't want to, but I will if I have to."

Slipping an arm around her, he guided her head onto his shoulder. "While I was out today, I went to see a friend of mine who's a lawyer." He'd planned to wait to tell her until he had more information from Alan.

She gasped and looked up at him, her face white with fear. "You didn't tell him..."

"I didn't use any names. I'd never do anything to endanger you or Mike. You have to know that." When he saw that he'd succeeded in reassuring her, he continued. "My friend, Alan, is doing some research on our behalf. He's going to call me this week and wants us to come to his house for dinner. He has two girls Mike can play with while we figure this out with him."

"I can't afford lawyers, Brandon."

"I can. I'll spend every dime I have if that's what it takes to work this out."

"I can't ask you to do that."

"You didn't ask me, so don't worry about it. You can't expect me to sit idly by and wait for them to turn your lives—and mine—upside down when they find you again. I can't do that, Daph. I promised Mike I'd find a way out of this, and I'm going to do it."

"When did you talk to Mike about it?"

"She told me this morning she doesn't want to move anymore, and I promised her I'd fix it. Let me fix it, please?"

"I'm almost more afraid of stirring things up than I am of them finding us," she confessed.

"We'll be very, very careful. I promise you. I won't let anyone separate you and Mike. Trust me?"

The look she gave him was the same one he'd gotten that morning from Mike when they discovered they liked the same ice cream. It was full of love and trust. "Of course I do."

"I need you to promise me you won't ever leave without telling me. I'd go out of my freaking mind if I didn't know where you two were."

"There've been times when I've had to leave within hours. That's how fast it can happen. If that happens here, I'll call you as soon as it's safe. That's all I can promise."

Brandon's jaw clenched with tension. "This has to stop. It's going to stop."

"Thank you for trying to help. Even if it doesn't work, I've never had anyone to share this burden with."

"You do now, and it's *going* to work." He couldn't imagine the alternative.

The next afternoon, Brandon walked into a liquor store for the first time in seventy-three days. The sweet smell of the place made his mouth water, but he stayed focused on what he was there to do. "A case of Sam Adams, please," he said to the kid working at the desk. "Cold. Two bags of ice, too."

By the time Brandon paid for the beer and ice and stashed it in the cooler in the back of his truck, he was in a cold sweat. Not that long ago, he could've downed this much beer on his own. How he longed for just one of them now. Maybe this wasn't the brightest thing he'd ever done, but he'd just proven he could walk into a liquor store and buy something he had no intention of drinking. He made a mental note to discuss the transaction with Joe after the next meeting.

He returned to the apartment building and dragged the cooler into the backyard. His brothers and Tommy were due soon, so Brandon dismantled the old swing set and then decided to get started on the new one. By the time the others arrived, he was ready to shoot himself.

"Are you already making a mess of it?" Tommy asked. He was tall and blond with blue eyes and a big smile. Erin had set her heart on him the day she met him, and the poor guy never stood a chance against her.

"Shut up and help me, will you?"

Tommy laughed as he grabbed the instructions and turned the page around. "This end up. That's your first problem, jackass."

Brandon fell back onto the grass laughing. "I should've paid the five hundred frickin' bucks to get them to do this for me."

"Bad time to be cheap, Brand," Declan agreed as he came into the yard with Colin trailing behind him. They surveyed the pile of parts, pieces, wood, bolts, and tools, and turned around to leave.

"Get back here," Brandon bellowed. "No one is leaving until this is done." When his brothers reluctantly came back, Brandon added, "There's beer, but only if you help."

All eyes fell on Brandon.

"You bought beer?" Colin asked.

"It's no big deal, so don't make it into one. Let's get busy. We don't have much time." Daphne had taken Mike to lunch and the park, but she couldn't keep her away forever, and Brandon knew Mike would come looking for him the minute she got home.

They'd made only a small dent two hours later when Dennis strolled into the yard with Aidan, who was home for Easter.

"We heard you all were up to something over here," Dennis said. "What the hell are you doing? I didn't authorize a playground, Brand."

"Relax. I paid for it."

"Looks like you're paying, all right," Aidan remarked with a smile as he took in the chaotic scene.

"Either help or shut up," Brandon said.

With a glance at Aidan, Dennis shrugged and rolled up his sleeves.

"Why don't they have a class on how to do this in college?" Declan asked. "All future fathers should have to be trained in this."

"I tried to tell him," Tommy said.

"Do you girls always talk this much when you're working?" Brandon asked. "It's a wonder the company isn't bankrupt."

Aidan snickered, and Brandon caught his eye to share the joke. The resentment and anger were gone. What remained was maybe the start of something new.

Another hour and a half passed, and the playground was taking shape, thanks in large part to Aidan, who'd done the job many times before for clients in Vermont.

Mike ran into the yard and shrieked when she saw what they were doing.

"Oh!" Brandon scooped her up to turn her away from the action. "You're not supposed to see it until it's done."

"Is it for *me*?" she asked with wide eyes as she bent her head around him so she could see it.

"Sure is. Do you like it?"

"It's *awesome*." She wrapped her little arms around his neck in a fierce hug. "Thank you." She kissed his cheek and turned up her nose with distaste. "You're all sweaty."

He rubbed his sweaty face over hers, making her squeal with laughter.

When Brandon looked up, the others were watching him with interest. "This is Mike. You know my dad, that's my brother, Aidan, my brother-in-law, Tommy—he's Josh's dad—and my other brothers, Declan and Colin."

Declan whistled under his breath. "And *who* is *that*?"

"Oh, it's the goddess," Colin whispered.

Brandon turned in time to see Daphne come into the yard. He shifted Mike to his hip and held out a hand to her mother. "This is Daphne," he said, repeating the introductions.

"This is your *little* surprise, Brandon?" Daphne surveyed the playground with a mixture of amazement and dismay on her face. "I can't believe you did this."

The others went back to work, leaving Brandon to fend for himself with Daphne.

"It *is* a little surprise," Brandon insisted.

"It's a *big* surprise," Mike said.

"Thanks a lot, squirt," Brandon grumbled as Mike scampered out of his arms to go supervise the workers. Brandon turned to Daphne, who had her hands on her hips and her mouth set in that thing she did when she was annoyed. He hadn't seen that in a while. "She needed a place to play, and you told her she'd have to have a 'tetchis' shot to play on the other one, so…"

Daphne smiled.

"What?"

"You're a good guy," she said, going up on tiptoes to kiss him.

Tuning out the catcalls from his brothers, Brandon surprised her by hooking an arm around her waist and taking the kiss to the next level.

"Get a room!" Declan hollered.

Brandon didn't let her go until he was good and ready to.

By the time she finally managed to break free of him, Daphne's cheeks were rosy with embarrassment. She ran a self-conscious hand over her mouth. "Well, I'll let you get back to work. Do you want me to take Mike?"

"Nah, she can stay."

After Daphne went inside, Brandon turned to find the others staring at him. "What?"

"I told you he was canoodling with her," Dennis said to no one in particular.

"Let's finish this damned thing," Brandon said, annoyed with the lot of them.

"*Ummm*, you *sweared*, Brandon," Mike said, scandalized.

He gritted his teeth and pretended not to hear the others laughing at him, as he realized it would've been a whole lot less painful to pay the extra five hundred bucks.

Chapter 22, Day 73

Most of the beer was gone and the playground almost finished by six when Dec said he had to leave for a date with Jessica. After he was gone, Colin whispered to Brandon, "I think tonight's the night." They were working together to install the second slide on the far end of the playground.

"Why do you say that?" Brandon asked.

"Just a hunch. He's been acting weird all week."

"It's still hard to imagine him married."

Colin grinned. "I know."

"Hey, squirt, that's high enough," Brandon called to Mike, who was climbing up the side of the tree house. "You're supposed to play *in* it, not *on* it." While Mike climbed down with assistance from Aidan, Brandon turned back to Colin. "How about you? Any progress with your lady?"

Colin's expression changed abruptly from amused to dejected. "No. I'm ashamed to say I went to an Al-Anon meeting last night hoping to see her—that's where I met her, but don't repeat that to anyone. Anyhow, she wasn't there. No one seemed to know where she was."

"Can you think of anywhere else you might run into her?"

"She said she walks on the beach at the Light, but I can't very well camp out there and wait for her. That has 'stalker' written all over it."

Brandon smiled. "True. Why don't you just call her?"

"Because if there's a next move, it has to be hers. She made it pretty clear she wasn't interested."

"I'm sorry, Col. That sucks."

"It does. There was like a loud click with her, you know what I mean?"

"Yeah, I think I do."

"Speaking of chicks and clicks, you've been keeping some secrets over here at Melrose Place. Looks like you and Daphne are pretty hot and heavy."

"I'm in love with her."

"Seriously? That was fast."

Brandon shrugged. "It's like you said, I heard the click."

"She sure is easy on the eyes."

"Keep your eyes and everything else off her," Brandon said, but he was kidding and Colin knew it.

"What does she think of you?"

"She loves me, too," he said with a touch of awe. "It's amazing how much better it is when it works both ways."

"Good for you, Brand. You deserve something like this after all you've been through. Does she know about…everything?"

"Most of it. I just hope…"

"What?"

Brandon looked over at Mike, who had cajoled Dennis into pushing her on one of the swings. "I love them both. I'm terrified I'm going to screw it up somehow."

"Just keep thinking about what it would feel like to lose them, and you won't."

Brandon smiled when Mike's giggles filled the air. "I can't even think about losing them. That's *not* an option."

Long after everyone left, Brandon continued to push Mike on the swing. Except for a brief pause for dinner, they'd played on the new playground all evening.

"Time to go in, squirt," he said when he noticed her finally starting to tire.

"Not yet. It's still early."

"It's time." He brought the swing to a stop and tossed her up over his shoulders.

"This was the best day ever," she said as he carried her inside.

"I'm glad you had fun. Did your mom tell you that you guys are coming with me to Josh's house tomorrow?"

"Yep. I can't wait."

"Special delivery," Brandon called when they reached Daphne's apartment. He stopped short when he found her sitting on the sofa with a pile of paper on her lap, a pencil tucked into her ponytail, and wire-rimmed glasses perched on the end of her nose.

"You're staring again," Mike said.

"I can't help it. Your mother is so gorgeous, she makes me want to drool."

Mike giggled.

Daphne smiled and reached for her glasses.

"No," he said. "Leave them on." He flopped down on the sofa with Mike still in his arms and leaned over to kiss Daphne. "You look very smart."

"I *am* very smart."

"She's an accountant," Mike said, making them laugh when she tripped over the word.

"Time for a bath," Daphne said, reaching out to tweak Mike's nose.

"I need to leave you ladies for a bit to run over to my house and get some clothes for tomorrow," Brandon said.

"You have a house?" Mike asked. "Where is it?"

"Just a mile from here."

"Can we go there sometime?"

"Sure."

"What should I put out for the Easter bunny?" Mike asked.

Brandon had gotten used to how fast the subject changed when she was involved in the conversation.

"He's probably sick of carrots, don't you think?" Mike asked.

Her face was so serious that Brandon fought the urge to smile. "How about some chips? That's what I'd want if I were the Easter bunny."

"Not cookies?"

"No, definitely chips."

"Okay, I'll go get some," Mike said, springing off Brandon's lap.

"Do you plan to come back and eat all the chips she's going to put out?" Daphne whispered.

"Will you keep those glasses on until I get back?"

She leaned over to kiss him. "We might be able to work something out."

"I hope the Easter bunny is *really* hungry," Mike said when she returned with a huge bowl of chips.

Daphne looked at Brandon with amusement. "I'm sure he'll be starving. Go on in and get ready for your bath. I'll be right there."

"See you in the morning, squirt."

Mike put down the bowl and hugged him. "Thanks again for the playground."

"You're welcome."

She clung to him for a long moment and then sprinted from the room.

"That's about the fifth time she's thanked me. She's such a sweetheart."

"I still can't believe what you did. It must've cost a fortune, Brandon."

"Don't sweat it." He kissed her and got up. "I'll be right back."

"Hurry. You have a lot of chips to eat."

At his house, Brandon went straight to the closet in his bedroom and rifled through his clothes until he found his khaki suit in a dry-cleaning bag way in the back. He hadn't worn the suit in years, so he assumed Valerie had taken it to the cleaners for him. He sure as hell hadn't done it.

Valerie's words kept running around in his mind. "It's not the all-consuming love I felt for you. Everything else pales in comparison." It made Brandon sick to think about how careless he'd been with her feelings. He wished there was something he could do to make it up to her, but he knew he had to leave her alone and let her live her life. All he could do now was make sure he never hurt anyone else like that.

He grabbed a royal blue dress shirt and a yellow tie and draped the dry-cleaning bag over the clothes. Unearthing a pair of wing-tipped shoes he'd forgotten he owned, he threw them into a bag and went into the bathroom to take a quick shower.

After he'd changed into jeans and a shirt that hadn't fit him in years, he returned to the bathroom in search of condoms. When he reached into the cabinet under the sink, his hand closed around a fifth of Jack Daniels.

He slowly brought the half-empty bottle out from under the sink and sat down on the floor, wondering what in the hell he'd been thinking when he stashed a bottle of whiskey in his bathroom. Balancing the bottle between his hands, he watched the amber liquid slosh from side to side.

It would be so easy to take one sip. To unscrew the lid, tip the bottle up, and take one long drag. He could feel the heat of the whiskey burn through him just imagining it. *No one would ever have to know.* But then he thought of Daphne and Mike at home waiting for him. This wasn't his home anymore and sitting on the floor with a bottle in his hand wasn't his life anymore. No, his home and his life were with them now.

Getting up from the floor, he opened the bottle and poured the whiskey down the sink with the water running to get rid of it before he could smell it. In an urgent rush to get out of that house, he dropped the bottle into the trash, grabbed the box of condoms from the cabinet, tossed it into his bag, and ran out the door a minute later.

He stopped at the grocery store on his way back to the apartments to buy orchid corsages for his girls. His father had always done that on Easter for Colleen and Erin, and Brandon thought it was a nice tradition to continue. When he got back to the building, he hung the clothes on a door frame in Mrs. Oczkowski's apartment and stashed the flowers in her new refrigerator.

Before he went upstairs, he called Erin.

"Hey, Brand."

"Did I catch you in the middle of bedtime?"

"Nope, Tommy's doing it. I'm trying to finish the Easter baskets. What's up? Daphne and Mike are still coming, right?"

"Yeah, they're looking forward to it. I was wondering if you can do me a favor tomorrow."

"Sure, what do you need?"

"Can you invite Mike to spend the night at your house?"

Erin snorted with laughter. "What're you up to?"

"None of your business. Will you do it? Please?"

"I wish I was mean enough to make you beg, but lucky for you I'm feeling generous. I'd love to be in on your scheme."

"It's not a scheme. Exactly."

Erin laughed. "No problem. I'll think of some way you can pay me back. In fact, we have a couple of weddings coming up. You can babysit for one of them."

"You'd trust me to do that?" he asked, touched.

"Of course, I would."

"That's kind of a crooked deal—I'm asking you to watch one kid, and I'm getting five in return?"

"How bad do you want to get laid?"

"Pretty bad," he confessed.

"Then I'd say it's fair."

Brandon cracked up. "You should've been a litigator."

"I try to use my gifts for good rather than evil, but every so often, it's fun to be evil."

"I like your evil side better when it's directed at other people."

"I'm sure you do."

"Um, listen, there's something you need to know if you're going to have Mike. I want you to tell Tommy, too, but no one else, okay?"

"Okay. What is it?"

Brandon told her about Mike's grandparents.

Erin gasped. "Oh, my God! What're we going to do?"

Brandon appreciated that his sister made his problem her problem. He expected nothing less from her. "I'm handling it, but I wanted you to know about it because that's the only way Daphne would ever leave her."

"She'll be safe here. You know that."

"That's why I asked you. Thanks, Erin."

"I'll see you tomorrow."

Brandon flew up the stairs. Forty-five minutes away from her felt like forever. He tapped on her door.

She answered wearing a short floral satin bathrobe over a nightgown that ended at mid-thigh. The delicate glasses were perched on her nose, and her hair was in a high ponytail. "You don't have to knock," she said with a shy smile that stopped his heart.

He was struck dumb by the fragile sweep of her neck, the rosy glow of her skin, the sexy glasses, and the satin robe.

"Brandon? What's wrong?"

"Nothing," he whispered as he removed her glasses and put them on the table by the door. He ran his hands slowly down her back and lifted her. Wrapping her legs around his waist, he turned and pressed her against the door to close it.

Seeming breathless, she waited for him to kiss her.

He dodged her lips and ran his tongue along her jaw and ear.

Her fingers clutched his shoulders as he rolled her earlobe between his teeth. When he moved on from her ear, she brushed her lips against his and moaned with frustration when he turned his attention to her other ear.

His mouth went dry when he discovered she was naked under the nightgown. Carrying her to the sofa, he laid her down and knelt on the floor. "Is Mike asleep?" he whispered against the soft skin of her inner thigh.

"Out like a light," she managed to say as his lips moved on her leg. She arched her back in encouragement.

He slid a finger through her damp heat to the place that throbbed with desire. Making lazy circles with his finger, he watched her eyes flutter closed, and her breathing become ragged. He could tell she wasn't expecting him to replace his finger with his tongue or to push two fingers into her. Her eyes flew open, and she gasped as the combination of fingers and tongue sent her into orbit.

"Oh, God, *Brandon*," she gasped as she came apart under him.

He stayed with her as she trembled and shook, and without giving her time to recover, he took her up and over once more. Then he stretched out next to her on the sofa. That was when he noticed the tears on her face. "What, baby?" Alarmed, he kissed away the tears. "Did I hurt you?"

"No." She shook her head and held her arms out to him. "No."

"Then what is it? Why are you crying?"

"I love you, Brandon."

He could feel her heart beating fast as he rested against her chest. "And I love you. I want you so much. I've never wanted anything the way I want you."

She combed her fingers through his hair. When he felt her other hand on his chest, he discovered she had unbuttoned his shirt. Raising herself over him, she tugged her hair free from the ponytail and kissed her way down his chest.

Brandon ran his fingers through her long, soft hair and sucked in a deep breath when her tongue left a damp path on his stomach. He clutched her hair. "Daph," he said, strangled with desire. "Stop."

She fixed her eyes on his, pulled at the button to his jeans, and unzipped him.

He reached for her hand. "Daphne, come on…"

"What?" she whispered, pulling her hand free and pressing it against his erection. "You can make me crazy, but I can't return the favor?"

"You don't have to. Come up here."

"I know I don't have to." She slid her hand into his pants and wrapped it around him. "I want to."

Brandon closed his eyes and fought for control as she stroked him. He was winning the war until she replaced her hand with her mouth. "Jesus... *Daphne...*"

"What?" she whispered as she went back for more.

Surrendering, he whispered, "Don't stop."

"Wasn't planning to." The heat of her mouth, the drag of her tongue, the tug of her hand... The combination was overwhelming. Then she sucked hard on him and took him somewhere he'd never been before, somewhere he'd never expected to go. If this was love, he finally understood, right in that moment, why people went to such enormous lengths to get it and keep it. Now that he had it, there was no way he'd ever let it go.

"I hope you know CPR," he muttered when he'd recovered the ability to speak. "I think you stopped my heart."

Resting on top of him, she giggled. "Let's go to bed."

"I can't."

"You can," she insisted. "Come on, I'll take you."

"No, I mean I really can't. I can't sleep with you tonight and not make love to you. Tomorrow night."

"What about it?" she asked, running her fingers through his chest hair.

"Tomorrow night, I'm going to make love to you." He slid his hand up and down her back. "At least twice—maybe even three times. And then I'm going to sleep with you in my arms. But tonight I can't."

She shivered. "Thanks for the warning."

He would've laughed, but it required too much effort.

"Where will Mike be in this scenario of yours?"

"I've got it covered, don't worry. What time is church?"

"Eleven thirty at Holy Redeemer."

Brandon groaned.

"What?"

"That's the mass my parents go to. My mother will see me there and declare an Easter miracle."

"We can go somewhere else if you want."

"No, that's okay. Not that you'll need them, but you'll score a thousand easy points with my mother for getting me there."

"Free points are good. I'll take 'em."

Brandon summoned the small bit of energy he had left to sit them both up. "I'm going to go." He hooked his arm around her neck and captured her mouth in a deep, sensual kiss. His tongue tangled with hers in a dance that left him breathless. "I love you, and I have no idea how I'll get through tomorrow when all I can think about is getting you naked."

Smiling, she buttoned his shirt. "Try not to think about that while we're in church."

"I'll be thinking of nothing else."

"Neither will I," she confessed.

He stood, zipped his jeans, and offered her a hand up. Running his thumbs along her jaw, he dipped his head to kiss her once more. "Tomorrow night," he whispered in her ear. "One more night." He kissed her cheek and left.

When he was stretched out on Mrs. Oczkowski's sofa, he realized he'd forgotten about the Easter bunny's chips.

CHAPTER 23, DAY 74

By the time Brandon arrived on the third floor at eleven the next morning, he'd been to a meeting and then rushed home to get changed for church. The door to Daphne's apartment was open, so he stopped to listen.

"Hold still, Pooh. I'm almost done."

"Hurry up. You've already brushed it six times."

"Don't you want to look pretty for Easter?"

"I *do* look pretty for Easter. Brushing my hair *again* isn't going to make me any prettier. When is Brandon getting here?"

"Any minute."

"Good."

He peeked around the corner. *Oh, look at them.* They wore matching yellow cardigan sweaters over pale yellow sundresses with tiny blue flowers all over them. Mike's hair shone from all the brushing, and it fell to her shoulders. Used to seeing her in red high tops, Brandon thought her tiny white shoes and lacy socks were adorable. Daphne adjusted Mike's small straw hat before the girl squirmed out of reach.

Daphne stood up, and Brandon muffled a gasp watching the silky dress cling to every curve.

"I think someone's spying on us, Pooh," Daphne said without so much as a glance at the door. "Why don't you go see who's out there?"

Mike scampered into the hallway and laughed when she found Brandon leaning against the wall like he belonged there. "You're busted," she said. "Hey! You match us!"

Brandon looked down at his blue shirt and yellow tie. "So I do."

"We look like we go together," she said, pleased by the coincidence.

"We *do* go together." He twirled a lock of her hair around his finger. "I almost didn't recognize you without your pigtails and overalls."

She rolled her eyes. "You can't wear *overalls* on Easter. Everyone knows that."

"I love your dress."

"Mom made our dresses. She makes them every year."

"Does she now?"

"Yep. It's our tradition. What're you hiding behind your back?"

"How do you know I'm hiding something?"

"What is it?" she demanded, trying to scoot around him to see what he had.

"Mike, ladies in dresses do not wrestle with men in suits," Daphne said as she came to the door. Her eyes traveled over him with admiration. "Even very, very handsome men in suits."

"You're beautiful." He kissed Daphne's cheek. "Both of you."

She slid her fingers over his tie. "You're not too shabby yourself."

"As stunning as my two best girls are, though, it seems there's something missing."

Daphne and Mike exchanged glances. "What?" Mike asked.

"These," he said, bringing the orchids from behind his back.

"Oh," Daphne said. "They're gorgeous!"

"Can I smell?" Mike asked.

Brandon held the flower for her to smell and then bent to pin it on her sweater.

"Thank you, Brandon," Mike said, kissing his cheek.

"Go brush your teeth, Mike," Daphne said. "We have to leave in a few minutes."

After Mike went into the apartment, Brandon turned to Daphne with the orchid. "Your turn." He slipped his hand under Daphne's sweater to pin on the flower. His fingers brushed against her warm skin, and he lingered there much longer than he needed to. With the flower in place, he drew her into his arms and dropped soft kisses on her neck.

"The flowers are beautiful. Thank you." She reached up to cup the back of his neck and tugged him down for a proper kiss.

"Do I have time for one more cold shower before church?" he asked, his lips still pressed to hers.

"Nope. Time to go."

"This is going to be a *very* long day," he groaned as he reluctantly released her.

When they arrived at the church, they created the stir he'd predicted. They sat several rows behind his parents and Erin's family. His mother turned in her seat to stare at him, Erin's mouth hung open, and Dennis shook his head in amazement. Colin scooted in next to Brandon a few minutes after mass began. He saw no sign of Declan or Aidan, but Brandon knew his older brother hadn't set foot in a church since Sarah died, and his younger brother was probably still celebrating his engagement.

He watched his mother and Erin whisper to each other while trying not to be obvious as they stared at Daphne.

"Let me guess," Daphne whispered with a smile. "Your mother and sister?"

"What's the give-away? The staring or the gawking?"

She laced her fingers around his and squeezed.

An unexpected surge of love for her left him breathless. He was taken aback when his eyes flooded with tears. Joy, like sorrow, often struck without warning in the midst of his sober life, leaving him raw and exposed to emotions that were all new to him. He'd be hard pressed to describe the feeling to anyone who hadn't experienced the highs and lows of finally discovering life almost halfway through it.

Not much had changed in the more than twenty years since he'd been in the church—the pungent smell of incense, the music, and the pageantry were all as he remembered. Mike crawled into Brandon's lap and rested her head on his shoulder during the priest's homily. He noticed Colin staring at someone on the other side of the church and nudged his brother to ask who he was looking at.

"That's her," Colin whispered. "Meredith."

Brandon stretched his neck to get a better look at the woman with long, dark hair but couldn't see her face. "How do you know?" he whispered.

"I'd know that hair anywhere," Colin said without taking his eyes off her, as if he was afraid she'd slip away when he wasn't looking.

Brandon returned his attention to the mass, easing back into the routine of it like he'd never been away. He was impressed by how well behaved Mike was during the hour-long service. Obviously, she was used to being there.

Colin bolted after communion, hoping to see Meredith.

Outside the church, Brandon held hands with Mike and Daphne while he waited for his parents and the Maloneys to catch up to them.

"Mum, Erin, this is Daphne."

Colleen shook hands with Daphne. "So nice to meet you, love. And who is this adorable girl? Could this be the little Mike I've been hearing all about?" She held out her arms to Mike who walked into them as if she'd been waiting all her life for this grandmother to find her.

Accustomed to being annoyed by his mother's antics, Brandon felt his heart swell with love for her as she embraced the child he'd come to think of as his.

"Hey, Mike," Josh said when Colleen finally released the girl. "How's your head?"

"All better. How about yours?"

He smiled and lifted his blond hair to show off a still-colorful bruise before he led Mike over to where Erin's children waited for their parents.

Brandon looked around but didn't see Colin anywhere. He hoped his brother had managed to track down the elusive Meredith.

Erin hooked her arm through Daphne's. "Let's get going," Erin said.

Daphne glanced over her shoulder in search of Brandon.

"I'm coming," he said.

Erin's driveway was full of cars when Brandon parked Daphne's SUV at the curb.

Mike ran for the house when she saw Josh on the front porch, but Daphne stopped Brandon as he reached for the door.

"What, hon?"

"I'm nervous," she confessed, clutching the bright bouquet of tulips she'd brought for Erin.

He leaned over to kiss her cheek. "Don't be."

"There're so many of them."

He laughed. "I'll be right there with you."

"Promise?"

"I promise. Kiss me."

Daphne glanced at the porch full of O'Malleys. "Not here."

"Right here," Brandon said, pointing to his mouth.

She resisted for a second before she gave him what he wanted—and then some.

Groaning, he pulled away from her. "That was mean!"

"You asked for it."

"We're attracting an audience," Brandon said, nodding to the porch where his parents, Erin, Tommy, and Aidan acted like they weren't watching them. Brandon got out and walked around to open her door. "Come on." He tugged her from the car. "I love you. I'll be right there with you."

The O'Malleys went out of their way to make Daphne feel welcome. Even Dennis was especially friendly, which Brandon appreciated. He and Daphne chose virgin Bloody Marys from the drinks Erin offered.

Colin came in a few minutes later and went straight to the bar. When Brandon caught his eye, Colin shook his head.

"I need to talk to Colin for a sec," Brandon whispered to Daphne. "I'll be right over there."

"Okay."

"What happened?" he asked Colin, who was twisting the cap off a beer.

"She was with her family, so I didn't get a chance to talk to her."

"Did she see you?"

He nodded. "She looked so sad. She might've talked to me if she hadn't been surrounded by people."

"I still think you should call her."

Colin shrugged.

Brandon glanced over to where Daphne was being grilled by Colleen and Erin. "I need to go rescue her. Are you okay?"

"Yeah, go ahead. Daphne and Mike look beautiful."

"Don't they?"

"You're a lucky man."

"I feel lucky lately. You'll get your turn, Col. I know it."

"Yeah, sure. Any day now."

Declan and Jessica arrived a short time later.

Noticing how they were glowing, Brandon exchanged glances with Colin.

After they greeted everyone and introduced Daphne to Jessica, Declan put his arm around Jessica. "So listen, everyone, we have news." He looked down at Jess. "We're engaged!"

The room erupted with congratulations, hugs, and kisses.

"Tommy!" Erin called as she reached for Jessica's hand to see the ring. "Bust out the champagne!"

Brandon watched Aidan congratulate Declan and Jessica and then go out the front door to the porch.

Caught up in the excitement of looking at Jessica's ring and hearing the story of how Declan popped the question, Daphne didn't notice when Brandon slipped away.

He found Aidan hunched over the railing, studying the garden below.

"Who'd a thunk it, huh?" Brandon said, joining his brother at the rail.

"I know. It's hard to imagine *him* as the only married O'Malley brother."

"No kidding. Thanks for all the help yesterday. We'd still be there if you hadn't shown up."

"It was no problem. You've got yourself a beautiful lady there, Brand. Two of them, in fact."

"Thanks. I'm doing my best not to screw it up."

Aidan laughed.

"I, uh, I got a really nice note from Clare," Brandon said, not sure if he should mention it.

Aidan's eyes sparked with interest. "Really? What did she say?"

"She thanked me for my letter and apology and wished me well with my recovery."

"Anything else?"

"Just that she was sorry things didn't work out with you."

Aidan's jaw clenched as if he was absorbing a punch.

"Have you talked to her at all?"

Aidan shook his head. "What would be the point?"

"I'll bet she misses you, too."

"Maybe."

Declan joined them on the porch. "Erin's looking for you, Aidan."

"I'm supposed to be helping her in the kitchen," Aidan said on his way inside.

"How's he doing?" Declan asked.

"Suffering in silence."

"Sucks. I felt bad coming in here with my news after what happened when he proposed to Clare."

"He's happy for you. You know that. Although none of us can believe you're going down first."

"I know," Declan said with a grin and a shrug. "But it's the right time and the right girl."

"When's the big day?"

"Fourth of July. Neither of us wants the big white wedding, so we're going to have a clambake in Mum's backyard and let the town provide the fireworks."

"That sounds perfect."

Declan turned to him. "I need a best man. Are you interested?"

Brandon stared at his brother. "*Me?*"

"Yes, you," Dec said with a chuckle. "What do you say?"

"I'd be honored." Brandon hugged his brother and made a mighty attempt not to bawl his head off.

The door opened, and Daphne came out. Brandon extended his hand to her. "Hey, baby, I'm sorry. I was just coming back in."

She took his hand. "I was fine, don't worry. Jessica's ring is beautiful, Declan."

"This guy helped me pick it out." Dec squeezed Brandon's shoulders. "I'd better go back in with Jess before Mum takes over the wedding plans."

When they were alone, Brandon drew Daphne into his arms.

"So you knew about this?" she asked.

"I didn't know when it was going to happen, but Colin and I helped him buy the ring on the way home from Vermont."

"It must be nice to be so close to your brothers."

"He asked me to be his best man."

"That's wonderful, Brandon!"

"Just a couple of months ago, none of this would've been possible for me. I wasn't close to my brothers when I was drinking. I wasn't close to anyone but the bottle. That's why I'm so astounded Dec asked me to be his best man. I mean, why me?"

"Because he knows he can count on you now." She reached up to caress his face. "Do you miss it? Drinking?"

"I miss a cold beer at the end of a long day. I miss the guys I used to drink with. It would be a stretch to call them my friends, but we had some good times. I don't miss feeling like shit every day or waking up somewhere and not knowing how I got there. I don't miss that at all."

Daphne winced. "What am I going to do if you go back to that? I know it's possible things won't work out between us, but if I lose you to that—"

"You won't. And don't even talk about it not working out between us. It'll work out because I have something now that's so much better than a cold beer ever was."

She smiled. "Oh, yeah?"

"Oh, *yeah*," he said, losing himself in a hot, deep kiss.

"For God's sake, will you two cut it out?" Erin said when she came outside a minute later.

Daphne's face flushed to a bright pink.

Brandon resisted her efforts to escape. "Buzz off, Erin."

"I was just going to tell you it's time to eat, if you can come up for air long enough."

"Don't listen to her," he said to Daphne. "How do you think she ended up with five kids in five years?"

"Shut up and come eat," Erin said, laughing as she went back inside.

When Brandon tried to pick up where they left off, Daphne pushed him away. "Let's go. There'll be time for that later."

"I'm not going to make it to later."

She sent him a coy smile that was full of promises. "Be strong and *behave*."

"I don't like your attitude," he grumbled as he followed her inside.

CHAPTER 24, DAY 74

Brandon reached his limit at six o'clock. He had followed Mike around with her Easter basket while she searched for eggs, played a competitive game of Wiffle ball with his brothers, Tommy, and the kids, and put in his time with the family. Now he wanted to take his lady and get the hell out of there. He went looking for Erin and found her loading the dishwasher for the second time.

"Time for Operation Mike," Brandon told her. "Be subtle, okay?"

"I know what to do. Don't worry."

"What's our curfew in the morning?"

"You don't have one. We're taking it easy tomorrow because the kids are on vacation, and everyone will be tired after today—especially me."

Brandon kissed his sister's cheek. "Thank you."

"I'm happy to have her, Brand. She's such a cute kid. She and Josh are like two peas in a pod, aren't they?"

"Totally. Mike followed him around all day, but he doesn't seem to mind."

Erin took off the apron she'd put on over her lavender silk dress. "Leave Daphne to me."

Brandon hung back to watch as Erin went outside to join Colleen and Daphne on the deck. They looked over to where the kids were playing on the swings. He saw the exact moment when Erin asked if Mike could stay.

Daphne's expression became closed and guarded as she shook her head to say no.

Brandon's stomach fell with disappointment.

Erin reached for Daphne's hand and spoke quietly to her.

Brandon held his breath while he waited to see what Daphne would do.

She looked over at Mike and then back at Erin. This time she said yes.

Brandon wanted to whoop with relief when he joined them on the deck. The morning's bright sunshine had given way to clouds, and rain threatened as he sat next to Daphne and put his arm around her.

"Erin invited Mike to spend the night," Daphne said.

"What a great idea," he said, feigning surprise.

Daphne rolled her eyes to let him know she wasn't buying his act and called Mike over to them.

Mike's yellow dress had held up well despite the busy day, but her cheek was smudged with dirt, and the white shoes and socks had been abandoned.

"What'd you want, Mom?" she asked, annoyed when Daphne tried to brush the dirt off her face.

"Mr. and Mrs. Maloney invited you to spend the night with the kids. Would you like to do that?"

Again Brandon held his breath.

Mike's face lit up for a brief second and then fell just as fast. "Not if you don't want me to."

"I think it'll be okay."

"You do? Really?"

Daphne nodded. "We even have a bag for you in the car. What a coincidence, huh?" she asked with an amused glance at Brandon.

He shrugged with innocence.

"Did you bring Brandon the Bear?" Mike asked.

"Sure did," Daphne said.

Mike bit her fingernail, her eyes shifting from her mother to Brandon. "But what if, you know…"

Brandon held out his arms to Mike and brought her close enough to whisper in her ear that Erin and Tommy knew everything and she would be safe with them. "I'd never let you be anywhere that wasn't safe."

"Can I call you and Mom if I get scared?"

"Of course, you can," Brandon said. "I'll write down my cell phone number for you, okay?"

"Okay."

The solemn expression on her little face tugged at his heart. He nodded to encourage her.

"Thank you, Mrs. Maloney," she said to Erin. "I'd like to stay."

"We'll have a great time," Erin assured her. "But Mrs. Maloney is my mother-in-law. You have to call me Erin, deal?"

Mike grinned when she achieved first-name status with yet another adult and shook Erin's outstretched hand. "Deal." She hugged and kissed Daphne and Brandon and took off to rejoin the kids.

Brandon waited on the deck while Erin went with Daphne to get Mike's bag.

"You have a way with that child," Colleen said.

"She's my buddy."

"You love her."

Brandon nodded.

"Both of them."

"Right again."

Colleen studied him. "Good. That's exactly what you need."

Brandon laughed. "Says who?"

"Says your mother." She squeezed his hand. "Cherish it, love. Be careful with it."

He leaned down to kiss her good-bye. "I will."

***

Daphne was quiet as they drove away from Erin's.

Brandon reached for her hand. "Are you okay?"

"Yeah." She cradled his hand between hers.

"Are you worried about Mike?"

"I'm sure she'll be fine. She was so excited."

"Has she ever done anything like this before?"

Daphne shook her head. "Another first."

Brandon stopped the car and turned to her. "Why don't we go back and get her? She's not ready. I shouldn't have done this."

"She'll have so much fun she won't give us a thought."

"How about you?" He kissed the palm of her hand. "This'll be the first night you've spent away from her, won't it?"

She nodded. "Do you know who was the first person to ever put her in a car and drive her away from me?"

"No, who?"

"You. The day you took her to play at Erin's."

Brandon sighed. "You must've been freaking out the whole time we were gone."

"No, I wasn't. I knew she'd be safe with you, just like I know she'll be safe with Erin and Tommy. If I wasn't sure of that, I wouldn't have left her."

"I hope you don't mind that I told them, but I knew you'd never go for it if they weren't in the loop."

"You handled it perfectly. Thank you for arranging all of this and for sharing your wonderful family with us. This was the nicest day I've had in a long time."

"I'm glad you enjoyed it. I was hoping they weren't overwhelming you."

"They were lovely. It was so sweet of your mother to bring an Easter basket for Mike, too."

He shifted the car back into drive. "Let me tell you what—if she likes you, you're home free with the O'Malleys, and you scored a grand slam with her."

"I take it that's good?"

"Clearly, we need to work on your baseball knowledge. Just don't tell me you've never heard of the Red Sox. That could be a deal breaker."

"We're still talking baseball, right?"

"*Oh, come on*," he groaned. "Tell me you're kidding me!"

"I'm kidding you."

He smiled. "Good thing. I'd hate to have to dump you off at home after all I did to get you alone."

"And where exactly are you taking me?" she asked as they left Chatham behind.

"Away."

Thirty minutes later, Brandon pulled into a gravel parking lot at the end of Rock Harbor Road in Orleans, on Cape Cod's north shore.

"Where are we?" Daphne asked.

"The Rock Harbor Inn. A friend from my high school swim team owns it."

Daphne's eyes were shiny with tears.

"What?" he asked, alarmed. "Do you not want to do this? We don't have to—"

She silenced him with a kiss that made him want to beg first for mercy and then for more.

"Why the tears?" he whispered, brushing them away with his lips.

"I can't believe you went to all this trouble."

"It was no trouble. I told you I wanted our first night together to be special, and I didn't want to be too far from Mike, just in case…"

"It's perfect."

"How about a walk in the rain? The beach is just down that path over there. Do you mind getting wet?"

"Not at all."

They walked arm in arm across the inn's expansive front lawn. At the top of the stairs, Brandon stopped her. "Do you smell that?" He tilted his face into the light rain and took a deep breath.

"What?"

"That earthy smell that comes with the rain. I used to love that smell when I was a kid. I can't remember the last time I noticed it."

"I love the smell of the beach."

"Did you grow up near one?" he asked, helping her down the small flight of stairs to the beach. They kicked off their shoes at the foot of the stairs.

"Stinson. North of San Francisco."

"I've been to San Fran but not Stinson. Is that where you lived?"

"No, we lived in Sausalito, just over the Golden Gate from San Fran. My parents owned an art gallery in town. They carried Randy's work. That's how I met him."

"Where are they now? Your parents?"

"Still living in Sausalito, but they're retired. They sold the gallery a few years ago. They're both painters, and I picture them whiling away their days in front of their easels."

"Did you get any of their artistic ability?"

"No, but Mike did. I can already see it in her painting. I got all the left-brain stuff—math and logic—and none of the creative genes the rest of my family has."

Brandon walked her to a lifeguard chair and helped her up the ladder. He climbed up behind her and drew her onto his lap.

"What was your name then? Before you were married?"

"Flemming."

"Daphne Flemming," he said, trying it on for size. "When was the last time you saw your parents?"

"Two days before Randy died. Their house was the first place Monroe's thugs went after we left."

"Oh, Daph." Brandon hugged her to him. "You must miss them so much."

"I do. I have two brothers and a sister, and nieces and nephews I've never met. Being with your family today made me sad for what Mike and I are missing with mine."

"Do you have any contact with them?"

"I get word to them once or twice a year, so they know we're safe, but that's it. I have no idea how far the Monroes would go to find us, so the less my family knows, the better."

"Alan will find a way out of this for us." Brandon prayed it was true. "This week, we'll figure something out."

She brushed away the raindrops that had gathered on his face. "I hope you know how much I appreciate your help, but if all I ever had was you and Mike, that would be enough for me. I could hide out with you forever."

He kissed her then the way he'd been longing to all day. Finally, no one was watching, no one needed them for anything, no one would interrupt. He could take his time to savor every feeling and satisfy every desire. "Do you know what I've never done?" He kissed her cheeks, the end of her nose, and her forehead.

"What?" she asked, breathless.

"I've never in my life made love."

Confused, she said, "But, surely you've, you know…"

"I've had plenty of sex, but never with someone I loved. Will you come with me and show me what I've been missing?"

She got up from his lap and offered her hand.

They climbed down from the lifeguard chair, and when Daphne surprised him by dashing for the stairs, Brandon laughed and raced after her.

CHAPTER 25, DAY 74

Colin got home from Erin's house and changed into jeans and a T-shirt. He'd tried to talk Aidan into going out for a beer, but his brother declined, saying he had a headache and was going to bed. Colin suspected Declan's engagement and Brandon's obvious love for Daphne had pushed Aidan into an even deeper depression over losing Clare. Colin could sympathize. Watching his brothers enter into relationships that had "forever" stamped all over them made him feel more alone than ever, too.

He sat down to watch Sports Center but couldn't bring himself to care about the latest scores or controversies. The restlessness that had plagued him since his last time with Meredith had gotten worse after seeing her in church. *If only I could've talked to her. Even for just a minute.*

Sitting alone in the dark, quiet house was suddenly unbearable. He grabbed a jacket, went out to the garage, and pulled the cover off his motorcycle. When the Harley roared to life, Colin secured the helmet, rode the bike out of the garage, and closed the door. He took a month's worth of impotent frustration out on the bike when he hit a straightaway on Route 28 and opened it up. With the tourist season about to begin, there wouldn't be many more opportunities to let the big bike loose on the Cape's crowded highways. On that Easter evening, he had the four-lane highway to himself and took full advantage of the solitude to push the bike past eighty-five miles per hour for the first time ever.

Colin knew he was being reckless and that his parents would have a joint heart attack if they could see him right then, but he was so sick and tired of being cautious, of doing the right thing, and of being the guy everyone could count on. *What the hell good has it done me? I'm thirty-six years old, and I'm alone.* Right then he could see why people turned to alcohol the way Brandon had. *It must be nice to have something to make it all go away.*

The road narrowed, and Colin downshifted to slow the bike. All at once, he felt like an idiot for behaving so foolishly. He was in charge of a business that provided a living for more than forty people. His responsibilities to them and their families kept him from throttling back up on the next stretch of flat, empty road. This wasn't helping anyway. The only thing that would help was the one thing he couldn't have.

At the next opportunity, Colin made a U-turn to head back to Chatham. Since he had the cover of his helmet and facemask to hide behind, he decided to drive by Meredith's house when he got back to town. He took a slow turn on to Stepping Stones Road and kept the bike in second gear as he crept along the quiet street. His stomach fluttered with nerves as he approached her house—this definitely felt like stalking, but he'd gone beyond caring about that earlier in the day when he'd been unable to talk to her. The porch light was on, and Colin almost fell off his bike when he saw her sitting on the front stairs. Crying. Even with just the faintest of lights shining on her, there was no doubt about it. She was crying.

He drove past the house and the cemetery across the street to a stop sign at the end of the block. The bike idled loudly while he tried to decide what to do. *If you go back, she'll know you were cruising by her house like a lovesick teenager. Aw, screw it. Who cares?* He turned the bike around.

When he slowed to a stop in front of her house, Meredith stood up and reached for the handle to the storm door. *What the hell?*

"Hey, it's only me." He propped his helmet on the seat. "What's the matter?"

"Oh, Colin," she said, her hand over her heart. "You scared me."

"Who did you think I was?" he asked, sitting next to her on the top step.

"Um, no one. But you're about the last person I'd expect to see on a motorcycle."

"Am I that much of a nerd?"

She laughed, a delicate sound that reminded him of crystal glasses and champagne toasts. "That's not what I meant. Although I *am* wondering how your motorcycle found its way to my street."

"Why are you crying on Easter?"

"I asked first."

"I missed you." He turned so he could see her big brown eyes. "Your turn."

"I missed *you*," she confessed, her cheeks blushing to that fetching shade of pink he'd first fallen in love with. Any doubt that he was in love with her had vanished the moment he saw her crying.

He took her hand and kissed it. "Why didn't you call me?"

She shrugged. "I thought you wouldn't want to hear from me after the last time."

"You thought wrong." He held her hand against his lips. "I've been a grumpy, cranky, pain in the ass. My employees have had it with me, and it's all your fault."

"How's it my fault?" she asked, amused.

"Because all I could think about for the last month was the girl I couldn't have." He used their joined hands to tug her closer and kissed her ever so softly. When he pulled back, he said, "Want to go for a ride?"

Her eyes widened. "On that?"

He nodded, breathless with longing.

She studied the bike for a moment. "Yes. Take me for a ride, Colin."

His heart soared with hope. "Grab a jacket."

"I need to get changed," she said, gesturing to her skirt. "Give me five minutes?"

"Take your time. I'm not going anywhere."

After she went inside, Colin turned his face into the light rain that had begun a few minutes earlier. He said a silent prayer of thanks to whatever god might've put her on the front porch at the same time he was riding by. Maybe this time...

"Ready?" she asked when she came back wearing form-fitting jeans and a denim jacket.

Colin whistled as he stood up. "You're one *hot* biker chick."

"Yeah, right," she snorted. "That's me. A real biker chick."

She followed him to the curb.

He put his helmet on her, secured it under her chin, and helped her onto the back of the bike.

"What about a helmet for you?"

"We'll swing by my house to get another one." He got on in front of her and reached back for her hands. "Feel free to hold on as tight as you can."

She giggled. "This is all a ploy, isn't it?"

"Hey, whatever works." As he started the bike, the pressure of her thighs clutching his backside made him rock hard. When her full breasts pressed against his back, he was thankful that the roar of the bike drowned out his groan.

"Ready?"

He felt her nod and gave the bike some gas.

She held on tight for the short ride to his house, where he grabbed a second helmet from the garage.

"Now that you know where I live, you can drive down my street anytime you want," he said.

"I'll keep that in mind."

When he got back on the bike, she resumed the position. Having her wrapped around him was the closest thing to heaven he'd ever known, and Colin wondered how long he could reasonably keep her there. He went back out to Route 28, but this time he stayed under fifty miles per hour in deference to the rain and his precious cargo. At the Brewster town line, he turned around and went back to Chatham. They cruised down Main Street to Shore Road.

Colin parked at Chatham Light and turned off the bike, removed his helmet, and helped Meredith with hers.

"That was great." She used her fingers to straighten her hair. "I loved it."

He sat facing her on the small seat, and ran his hands over her denim-clad thighs. "You're all wet from the rain."

"I don't care."

They gazed at each other with hungry eyes for a long, breathless moment before Colin hooked a hand around the back of her neck to bring her to him. The kiss was full of tender restraint, but it packed a powerful punch to the gut. He kept the kiss chaste until her tongue sought out his. That was when he angled his head to go deeper.

She moaned.

Lifting her legs over his, Colin pulled her onto his lap.

She wrapped her arms around him, and when he cupped her bottom to keep her anchored to him, she rewarded him with a provocative tilt of her hips.

The kiss was broken when Colin groaned and swore softly. He kept one hand firmly on her bottom while his other hand ventured under her shirt in search of warm soft skin. Nudging her silky dark hair aside, he trailed his tongue lightly over her neck. "Are you going to take a chance on me, Meredith? On us?"

She shivered from the attention he was paying to her neck. "Oh, Colin, I want to, I really do, but nothing's changed."

"One thing *has* changed," he whispered.

"What?"

"I'm in love with you."

"Colin…" She pulled back from him. "You aren't. You can't be."

"I am and I can. I've thought of nothing but you since I saw you last." She looked down, and he rested his hand on her face to bring her gaze back to his. "Tell me what it is—what's standing in our way. Tell me who you thought I was earlier and why you were afraid."

She gripped his wrists and dissolved into tears.

"Oh, honey, don't." He hugged her tightly. "I'm sorry. You don't have to tell me. I don't want you to cry." He held her for a long time, until her sobs finally subsided.

"When you pulled up on the motorcycle," she said, brushing the tears off her face, "I thought you were the man who almost killed me when I was nineteen."

Colin gasped.

"He's out of jail, and he wants to see me."

CHAPTER 26, DAY 74

Brandon carried their bags from the car and led Daphne to a guesthouse behind the inn. "You were only supposed to bring a toothbrush," he said, pretending to be burdened by the weight of her bag.

"I snuck in a few other necessities," she said with a sexy grin that made his blood boil with lust.

"That sounds interesting."

"Where'd you get the key?"

"I came over to get it yesterday. I wanted to get all the 'how've you been for the last twenty years' small talk with my friend out of the way, so I wouldn't have to waste half an hour of my night with you on that."

Daphne's giggle was tinged with nerves. "You've put a lot of thought into this. I hope I don't disappoint you."

He dropped his shoes and their bags inside the door and turned to her. "It's not possible for you to disappoint me." Running his fingers through her long blonde hair, he dipped his head to kiss her. "I love you so much, Daph," he whispered. "So much." He kissed her again. "And I love this dress. I can't believe you made it yourself."

"I make them every year."

"Even when it was only the two of you who'd see them."

"We had our own celebrations." She gave him a quick kiss and reached for her bag. "I need ten minutes in the bathroom."

"It's right there," Brandon said, pointing to a door off the sitting area.

"This is a beautiful room."

It was decorated in bold floral patterns and white lace. An antique cherry sleigh bed with a lace canopy was the room's focal point.

"Your friend left us a note," Daphne said. "Dear Brandon and Daphne, Welcome to Rock Harbor! The champagne is on me. Breakfast is served in the main house beginning at nine, or we can bring it to your room, if you'd prefer. Stay as long as you'd like tomorrow. Good to see you yesterday, Brandon. Enjoy!"

"That's nice," he said. "Do you want some champagne? It won't bother me if you have some."

"But then you won't be able to kiss me, and we can't have that, now can we?"

Riveted by her softly spoken words, Brandon shook his head.

"I'll be right back," she said.

Brandon removed his suit coat, unbuttoned his shirt, and tugged it free of his pants. Using a book of matches on the mantel, he lit the fire that had been laid for them in the fireplace and then the candles that were scattered about the room. In the kitchenette, he ran cold water over his face, brushed his teeth, and splashed on a touch of cologne.

He turned on the radio and traced a finger over the condensation on the bottle of champagne floating in the ice bucket. In his old life, he would've needed a shot or two of Jack Daniels right about now to calm his nerves. In his new life, he didn't want anything to take away from the exquisite pleasure of this moment with the love of his life.

"Brandon."

He turned to her.

She leaned against the doorway, wearing a long silk nightgown in the palest shade of peach. The firelight cast a warm glow upon her face and hair.

Brandon couldn't take his eyes off her as she moved toward him like a dream come true.

She pushed his unbuttoned shirt off his shoulders, and it fluttered to the floor behind him.

He brought her into his arms. "After I first met you," he said gruffly, "I thought of you as 'the goddess.' But now I'm in need of a better word, because that one doesn't do you justice."

She laughed softly as she nuzzled his chest hair.

With a finger on her chin, he lifted her mouth to his. Calling on patience he didn't know he had, Brandon kept the kiss light. "Dance with me," he said, raising her arms to loop them around his neck.

His hands never stopped moving over the silk gown as they moved together.

"Oh, this is the song Declan sang to Jessica when he proposed," she said after they'd danced to several songs.

"Who is it?"

"Keith Urban." She sang along in a quiet voice about love and making memories.

"I like it. I'll bet Dec's version was awesome. He can really sing. Aidan can, too. And you ought to hear him play the piano. He's amazing."

"What about you?"

"I got none of it."

"Come on," she cajoled.

Waggling his eyebrows, he said, "I have other skills."

"Such as?" she asked with a coy smile.

A groan rumbled through him as he leaned down to mold his mouth to hers, this time exploring every corner of her sweet warmth. When her tongue mated with his, Brandon tightened his arms around her and lifted her. He walked them to the bed and gently laid her down, stretched out next to her, and picked up the kiss where he'd left off.

She rolled into his arms, her hand cruising over his back and then clutching his biceps as he caressed her breast through the silk gown. Her fingers in his hair urged him to replace his hand with his mouth.

He suckled her through the silk barrier before he slid the fragile straps off her shoulders and nudged the gown to her waist. "God, you're so beautiful," he whispered against her breast.

"Brandon," she gasped, tugging at his pants. "I want you."

He took her hand to stop her. "Wait, baby. This time's for you."

But she had other ideas. Smiling, she sat up and pushed him onto his back. "No, my love, this time's for *you*." She kissed her way to the waistband of his pants.

The soft drag of her hair over his chest and stomach had him gasping for air. "Daphne, honey…" He groaned as she quickly removed the rest of his clothes and let her nightgown drop to the floor.

A fine sheen of sweat covered his skin as she stretched out naked on top of him.

"There's a condom in my pocket," he managed to say.

"We'll get to that." She skimmed her tongue over his ear. "Eventually."

Brandon had no choice but to lie there and take it as she set out to drive him wild. Her lips and hands were everywhere—on his face, his neck, his chest. When the tip of her tongue teased his nipple, he buried his fingers in her hair and fought the urge to flip her over and take what he wanted so desperately. But since he could see how much she was enjoying her power play, he resisted the urge and let her have her way with him.

She cupped his pectorals. "You're so strong, Brandon. I always feel safe when I'm with you."

As he exhaled a long deep breath that was one part emotion, two parts desire, a tremble rippled through him. "You won't be safe for much longer if you keep that up."

She dragged her tongue over his belly. "Keep what up?" Stroking him with her hand, she looked up at him. "This?"

"*Daph...*"

"What?"

At the exact moment her tongue swirled over the head of his penis, he reached his limit. Wrapping his arms around her, he turned them over.

"Hey," she protested. "I wasn't done."

"I was." He leaned in to kiss her, his tongue thrusting deep, his arms tight around her. When he finally came up for air, he kept his lips close to hers. "I've never felt anything even close to this. My heart feels like it's going to burst through my chest."

Her eyes were bright with emotion as she reached up to lay her hand on his chest to feel for herself. "I've never felt like this before either, Brandon."

Her confession fueled his already rampant desire, but since he was anxious to regain some semblance of control, he started all over again at her lips. He nipped, sucked, and teased.

She moaned, and when her hand closed again around his erection, Brandon went blind with lust. All thoughts of slowing things down were abandoned. "Let me get the condom," he said, his voice hoarse.

"Hurry."

A minute later, he returned to her.

She held out her arms to him.

He sank into her embrace, overwhelmed by emotions that were all new to him. "I love you, Daphne. It took me so long to find you and to say those words. Now it's like I can't say them enough."

"I'll never get tired of hearing them."

He bent his head for a kiss that was more about love than desire.

"Brandon?"

"Hmm?"

"Turn over."

Startled, he looked down at her.

With her hands on his shoulders, she urged him onto his back.

"Daphne..."

"Shh." She straddled him and took him in. Tilting her head back, she sighed with contentment.

The effort to hold back, to wait for her, had him trembling as he gripped her thighs. Her skin was so silky smooth, her scent so intoxicating, and the wet, hot sound of their loving so enticing, Brandon had to bite his lip—hard—to keep from exploding.

Her sighs drifted into moans. The sway of her hips became more urgent. Her nails scored his chest.

"*God*," he groaned. "Daphne..."

Suddenly, she stopped. Her eyes closed, and her lips parted, she climaxed with a mighty shudder.

Feeling her clutch him hard from within, he gripped her hips and finally let himself go.

Brandon couldn't have moved even if the place was on fire. So much for his big talk about two or three times—he'd be lucky to ever recover from this first time with her. "I found a new word."

"For what?"

"To replace goddess."

Since she was still stretched out on top of him, her laughter echoed through him. "What've you got?"

"Witch. You've cast a spell over me and left me paralyzed."

She nibbled on his lip. "That way I can have my way with you over and over again, and you can't stop me."

The one part of him that wasn't paralyzed came back to life. "Stopping you isn't in my plans, don't worry."

Laughing, she kissed him lightly. "Was it different, Brandon?"

"I've never been rendered paralyzed before, if that's any indication."

"It seems not *all* of you is paralyzed."

Brandon rolled them over so he was on top of her. "Everything about you is different from anyone I've ever known." He gazed down at her. "I think I knew that the first day when you yelled at me—twice."

Daphne laughed and hid her face in embarrassment. "Your father had driven me to it. You were just the one who answered the door."

"Best thing I've ever done," he said, reclaiming her lips, "was answer that door."

"*Brandon,*" she gasped when he moved in her.

"What?" he whispered.

"I thought you were paralyzed."

"Looks like it was temporary."

Colin ignored his ringing cell phone as he tried to process what Meredith had said. *Someone tried to kill her?* When the phone rang again a minute later, he pulled it from his pocket with impatience to check the caller ID. "I'm sorry, I have to take this. It's work." He flipped open the phone. "O'Malley."

"Hey, Colin, it's Jesse," said Chatham's director of public works. "We've got a break in the sewer main. We need someone right away. Can you guys do it?"

Pulled in two directions at once, Colin's head spun. It was a big job, and the town had called them first, so it wouldn't be a good idea to refuse. "I'll see what I can do and get right back to you." He ended the call and clutched Meredith's hand. "I'm sorry, honey. Give me one minute to deal with this, okay?"

She nodded, still wiping tears from her face.

Colin wanted to toss the phone onto the beach, but instead he called Declan. "What?" Dec growled.

"I need a favor. Can you round up a crew and get in touch with Jesse Silvia? They've got a broken sewer main."

Declan groaned. "I'm in bed, Col. Come on…"

"It's eight thirty."

"I didn't say I was sleeping."

Colin took a deep breath to summon patience. "I wouldn't ask for help if I didn't really need it. I'll explain tomorrow. Will you do it?"

"All right," Dec grumbled. "But this had better be good."

"It is. Thanks." He turned off his phone and put it back in his pocket. "I'm sorry."

"Don't be," Meredith said. "You're running a business."

"This is much more important—you're much more important."

She swiped at the tears that spilled down her cheeks.

"Tell me."

Hesitating, she seemed to be making a decision. After a long pause, she took a deep, rattling breath. "He was my high school boyfriend. Kevin was quarterback of the football team, everyone's best friend, a great student, you know, the whole package. I had the biggest crush on him, but I didn't want to be like the girls who were always throwing themselves at him. Maybe that's why he picked me over all of them."

Colin tucked a strand of long dark hair behind her ear. "I'll bet you were the prettiest girl in school."

"I wouldn't say that. But anyway, we dated our whole senior year and all that summer before we went to college."

"Where'd you go?"

"Boston College. He went to MIT, so we stayed together while we were in Boston. The only thing about him I didn't like was the way he drank. It was never a social thing. The goal was always to get drunk, and when he was drunk, he could be mean."

Colin held her hands and waited for her to go on.

"I finally broke up with him at the end of our sophomore year of college. By then, he was drinking every day, and one time he got rough with me when we were…" A tear rolled over a cheek that had turned red with embarrassment.

"What?" He brushed away the tear as his stomach clutched because he already sensed what she was going to say.

"In bed," she whispered. "He hurt me, and I told him it was over between us. I gave him a choice—he could either drink or he could have me. He said some really awful things to me that night, and it was clear he wasn't going to pick me."

Colin pulled her back against him. "He was a fool."

"He was an alcoholic, but he didn't know it yet. After we broke up, a friend told me about Al-Anon. I went to my first meeting that summer, and I've been involved ever since." She took a deep breath to calm her emotions. "Anyway, I didn't see him again for about three weeks, and then he turned up at a party one of our mutual friends was having. He begged me to talk to him, and for once he didn't seem drunk, so I did. I know I was so naïve, but I hoped we could be friends after spending three years together."

"Anyone would want that."

"We went for a ride in his car, and I didn't realize he had beer with him until it was too late. He was drinking in the car, so I asked him to take me home." She started to cry again, her face resting against Colin's chest. "But he said we were going to talk first, and he drove to the beach. He kept telling me how sorry he was and how much he loved me. Then he started to cry and said he couldn't live without me. He made me cry, too, and one thing led to another… I was so mad at myself after. I'd made a clean break with him, and it took him all of five minutes to get me back."

"You loved him."

"I really did." She took a deep breath. "I insisted he let me drive to my house, and when we got there, I took the keys and got out of the car. I was going to talk him into sleeping on the sofa in the basement. My parents liked him, but they had no idea how much he drank. They were always lecturing my sister and me about drinking and driving, so I knew they wouldn't care if he stayed. We went through the gate to the backyard, and he started wrestling with me for the keys. The whole thing escalated into a screaming match, because I knew if I gave them to him, he'd go meet his buddies and get even drunker. More than anything, I was afraid he'd kill himself in a car accident. So I threw the keys into the pool."

She began to tremble in Colin's arms. He wanted to tell her to stop, but he knew if she didn't finish this, there'd be no chance for them.

"He went crazy," she said in a small voice. "He was screaming and swearing, calling me every name you can think of. He grabbed me by the hair to drag me into the pool and held me under the water, screaming, 'Get those keys, you fucking bitch!' He just kept saying it over and over again and was so loud I could hear him underwater. I was struggling to get away from him, but he was so strong. I started to see spots in front of my eyes and knew I was going to drown if he didn't let me go soon."

Listening to her, Colin had tears running down his face, too.

"That's the last thing I remember. I woke up in the hospital a week later. Apparently, my sister, Melanie, heard us fighting, but by the time she came outside to see what was going on, he was gone, and I was floating facedown in the pool. We had air-conditioners in our bedrooms, but she hadn't turned hers on that night, so she was able to hear us. That's the only reason I'm alive today. She pulled me out of the pool and did mouth-to-mouth to get me breathing again. When I came to and told them what happened, Kevin was arrested and charged with attempted murder."

"Jesus," Colin whispered.

"I had to testify against him—the first boy I ever loved, the only boy I'd ever made love with. I put him in jail for ten years, Colin."

"But you got a life sentence, didn't you? This is why you don't date. It's why you won't let yourself take a chance on another relationship. He took so much more from you. Ten years was the least he could do."

"He was released four months ago. He got sober in prison, and he's working the program, making his amends. That's why he wants to see me, but I can't see him. I just can't."

"You thought I was him tonight when I pulled up on the bike."

"Yes."

"I'm sorry," he said, brushing his lips over her hair.

"I was so glad it was you—and not just because you weren't him."

"I'm not him." Colin tilted her face to receive his kiss. "I'd never, ever hurt you."

"I'm starting to believe that."

"You *can* believe it."

"This last month, knowing you were out there somewhere, it was just…"

"Torture?" he asked, using his own word for it.

She nodded.

"I'm right here, Meredith, and I love you." He kissed her with a new sense of urgency, knowing if she sent him away this time he'd never survive it. "Has there been anyone else? Anyone since him?"

She shook her head.

"Let me show you how it's supposed to be. Let me show you what it's like to have someone love you the way you deserve to be loved. We can take it slow…" His breath got caught in his throat when she dragged a fingertip lightly over his bottom lip.

After a long pause filled with hope and possibility, she said, "Show me, Colin."

CHAPTER 27, DAY 75

The patter of raindrops on the roof would forever remind Brandon of this night with Daphne. He'd devoted himself entirely to her pleasure the second time, and her breathless moans had driven him wild with love and a burning passion he hadn't known he was capable of. In the quiet after the storm of their loving, his heart beat in rapid time with the rain falling on the tin roof.

Her hand blazed a lazy trail over his chest. "Who was she, Brandon? The woman you loved but couldn't have?"

He sighed. "She's on that list of shameful things I told you about. I'm afraid if I tell you, it'll change—"

She stopped him with her fingers on his lips. "I love you. Nothing you tell me will change that."

The unexpected rush of emotion filled him so completely it was almost painful. He turned on his side to face her. "I don't know what I ever did to deserve you."

"To begin with, you loved my child like no one but me ever has."

"Loving her—loving both of you—is the easiest thing I've ever done." All at once he wanted her to know his shameful secrets so he could put them behind him and focus on the life he wanted so desperately with her and Mike. "She was Aidan's wife, Sarah." If Daphne was shocked, she did a good job of hiding it. "But she wasn't his wife when I fell for her." Swallowing his fear, he told her the whole story—from that first day on the beach to confessing it all to Aidan in Vermont.

Tears glistened in her eyes when he was done.

"You're appalled, aren't you?"

"No." She wiped the grim expression from his face with the gentle caress of her fingers. "It's so sad. No wonder you turned to alcohol."

That she understood, that she was on his side, told him more about how much she loved him than anything else ever could. "Alcohol wasn't the answer. I found that out the hard way." Since he was on a roll, he told her about what he had done in a drunken blackout to Aidan's girlfriend and how he'd landed in rehab the next day. "At the time, I thought my brothers were out to get me, but now I know they saved me by getting me into rehab when they did. I don't know how much longer I could've survived living the way I was."

"I can't believe that you're still so sweet and generous after everything you've been through. It didn't make you bitter."

"Oh, I was bitter for a long time, believe me. I felt like I'd been roped into a career I didn't want, my brother got the girl I was supposed to have, my complaints went on and on. I was so resentful, and I can see now how stupid that was—and how destructive. I think I'm becoming what's known as a 'grateful alcoholic.'"

"What do you mean?"

"Well, if I hadn't been through all that crap, I'd never appreciate what I have now. With you." He smoothed the hair back from her forehead. "I'm in this for keeps, Daphne. I hope you know that."

"I'd be terribly disappointed if you weren't and so would Mike."

"We're going to have it all—a nice big house where you can have your garden and a brother or sister for Mike. Hell, maybe even both."

She smiled at the picture he painted, but her eyes were far away from him.

"Hey, where'd you go?"

"You make it sound so easy, like we can really have a normal life together."

"We can. We will."

"But not if—"

"Don't." He silenced her with a kiss. "Not tonight. Tonight's for us, okay? Soon enough, you won't have to worry about that anymore."

She surrendered to his kiss and sighed when he rolled on top of her.

"I promised you a trifecta," he said with a smile.

"And do you always keep your promises?"

"I do now."

Colin watched Meredith sleep and knew he would do whatever it took to wake up to that face forever. Her bedroom was done in tasteful shades of what he now knew was her favorite color. His memories of discovering the pink bra and panties she'd worn under tight jeans made him want her all over again.

He reached for her, and when she sighed in her sleep, he couldn't resist taking yet another taste of her soft skin. Trailing his lips over her shoulder, he nudged the sheet down to draw her nipple into his mouth.

She awoke with a shudder and a moan. "Again?" she whispered.

"Again."

"I have to go to work," Colin said much later when his yearning for her had been satisfied—for now.

"Lucky me, I'm on vacation this week."

"Vacation," he said with a sigh. "What's that?"

"You work too hard."

"We were careless, Meredith. What if you're pregnant?"

She shrugged. "Then we'll have a baby whose mommy and daddy love each other and who'll love him or her."

"And does Mommy love Daddy?" he asked, his heart hammering.

She nodded. "I do love you, Colin. I realized that about five minutes after you left the night we had dinner here."

He hugged her tightly. "Thank you," he said, his voice gruff with emotion, "for taking a chance on us, and for the most amazing night of my life. This is just the beginning. I hope you know that."

"What color hair do you think our baby would have?" She played with a lock of his strawberry blond hair. "Your hair is so fair, and mine's so dark."

"I want a little person who looks just like his or her mother." He captured her lips in what he had intended to be a quick kiss. "I need to call the office," he said when he finally resurfaced. "I think I'm going to be late."

She laughed and let him up to go find his cell phone. "Where was it?" she asked when he came back.

"In my coat pocket on the kitchen floor next to your jeans." He brought his hand from behind his back and dangled the pink bra and panties from his finger. "This," he said, smiling as he held up the bra, "was decorating the banister. And these very sexy pink panties were halfway up the stairs."

Her cheeks burned with embarrassment.

"God, I love that." He sat on the bed to trace a finger over her blush.

"I hate it."

"You can't hate it. It totally turns me on. Speaking of turning things on…" He made a face and powered up his cell phone. It went crazy beeping with messages. "Shit," he groaned as he listened to one irate message after another from Declan. When the last one ended with, *"Where the fuck are you?"* Colin groaned. "I'm sorry. I have to handle this. Why don't you go back to sleep for a while?"

"Do you have to go?"

"Not yet," he said, pulling the covers up around her and kissing her.

He found his jeans in the hallway outside her room and tugged them on before he went downstairs to call Declan.

"Jesus Christ, Colin, *where the hell have you been*? I've been trying to reach you all night."

"What's wrong?"

"This sewer main thing is *huge*. I had to call everyone in."

"Shit," Colin muttered.

"You said it. Shit everywhere. I could use some help here."

Looking up the stairs to where Meredith slept naked in the bed where they'd made love all night long, Colin made a decision. For once, just this once, it was going to be all about him—and her. "I'm taking this week off. I need a vacation."

"*Are you out of your fucking mind?* Did you hear what I just said? We've got a crisis going on here. You can't just dump it on me."

"Here's what I want you to do—call Da and Brandon and get them over there to help you and Tommy. Sewer stuff is Brandon's forte anyway."

"He's off somewhere with Daphne. He won't want to come in."

"They have to pick up Mike at Erin's at some point today, so he'll be around. It's time to get him back in the fold. He's done his sentence in Siberia."

"What the hell's gotten into you, man? It isn't like you to blow off work."

"Tell Brandon things clicked for me. He'll know what I mean, and he can fill you in. In the meantime, you're in charge for the next week. If you hit a bump, call Da. I haven't taken a vacation in six years. I need a break, Dec."

"Yeah, well, your timing sucks."

"I'm sorry, but you'll be fine. I've got to go."

Declan was still grumbling when Colin ended the call. He wanted to jump around with delight. A whole week to spend with Meredith! Scrolling through his phone numbers, he found his friend Tony Peluzo.

"Hey, Colin," Tony said when he answered the phone at Tony's Travel. "Nice to hear from you. What's up?"

"I need a favor." Colin knew he didn't have to remind Tony of the deal he'd given him on the driveway O'Malley & Sons put in at his house last year. "I want to be somewhere warm by tonight. Two people, first class all the way. What can you do?"

"That's a tall order. It's April vacation week, and things are pretty well sold out."

"Come on, there's got to be something."

"Let me see what I can do, and I'll call you back."

"Thanks, Tony." Colin sprinted up the stairs and got back in bed with Meredith.

"I thought you had to go to work," she mumbled when he snuggled up to her.

"I took the week off."

One big brown eye opened and then the other. "You did?"

"Yep, and my brother's rip-shit pissed at me," Colin said with a big giddy grin.

"A whole week," she sighed.

"Is that okay?" he asked, suddenly worried that he was rushing things.

"It's more than okay." She drew him into a wanton, carnal kiss that made his head spin.

"I need a whole week to recover from last night. I'm glad we're taking it slow."

Blushing, she laughed, and his heart skipped a crazy beat.

His phone rang, and he tugged it out of his pants pocket. "Hi, Tony. What's the verdict?" Colin listened for a minute. "Hang on a sec." He held the phone to the side and looked at Meredith. "What's your pleasure? Jamaica or Grand Cayman?"

Her eyes widened, and then she gasped.

"Well, what's it going to be?"

"Grand Cayman." She threw her arms around him. "Definitely Grand Cayman."

CHAPTER 28, DAY 79

The crews from O'Malley & Sons spent five full days repairing the broken sewer main and fixing the weaknesses Brandon discovered when he inspected the area around the break. His coworkers warmly welcomed him back, even Simms and Lewis, who accepted his apology for the near miss with the gravel. Brandon had been delighted to hear from Declan that things had clicked for Colin. When he connected the dots for Dec, his younger brother's attitude toward Colin softened but only a little. Brandon agreed that Colin had picked a hell of a time to finally click with Meredith.

At some point during that long week in the trenches, Brandon came to a decision—he didn't want to do this anymore. As challenging as it had been to put his education and experience to work to fix the sewer main, he could no longer pretend the job was satisfying or rewarding. He had something else in mind, but he wanted to talk it over with Daphne before he did anything about it. If she agreed with his plan, he'd also have to run it by his partners. He was prepared to leave the company if it came to that, but he hoped it wouldn't.

He came home Friday night filthy and exhausted, but he rushed upstairs because he couldn't wait to see his girls. He'd all but moved in with them over the last week.

Mike came running to him the way she did every night, but Brandon held her at arm's length. "I'm gross, squirt. Let me take a shower, okay?"

She waved a hand in front of her face. "You stink."

He laughed and lunged at her.

She squealed, darting out of his reach.

Daphne was on the phone, so he blew her a kiss on the way to the shower.

Long after he scrubbed off the day's filth, he stood under the heat of the shower to work out the kinks in his back and shoulders. The bathroom door opened and then closed. He pulled the curtain aside and smiled at Daphne. "What are you doing in here?"

She reached for him. "Just saying a proper hello," she said, kissing him senseless. "Bad day?"

"Hideous until right now. Want to join me?"

Her eyes traveled over him. "Mmm, more than anything, but…" She gestured to indicate Mike in the next room.

"I know." He leaned in for one more kiss. "Are you guys ready to go?"

"Whenever you are."

"I'll be quick. Alan said to come anytime after six."

She bit her bottom lip, her face twisting with worry.

"What's the matter, hon?"

"Are you sure we're doing the right thing, Brandon? What if they manage to get her away from us? What'll we do then?"

He turned off the water, took the towel she handed him, and wrapped it around his waist. "We have to do this so we can live without threats and worries hanging over our heads. We have to do this for Mike."

Reassured, she nodded and rested her face against his damp chest hair. "You're right."

He hugged her tightly. "It's going to be okay."

Alan's contemporary house in Dennis faced Cape Cod Bay. After dinner, he ushered Brandon and Daphne into his study while his wife Janice got dessert for Mike and their daughters, Haley and Kendall.

"I love this house, Alan," Brandon said with profound respect for the life his friend had built after hitting rock bottom as an alcoholic. "And you've got such a beautiful family."

"Thank you. Now that you know where we are, you'll have to come out to the beach this summer."

"We'd love to." Brandon reached for Daphne's hand as they sat together on a sofa. Tuning into the nervous tension radiating from her, he squeezed her hand.

Alan sat across from them, attuned to Daphne's sudden nervousness. "I want to help you, Daphne. I hope you can trust me and let me help you."

With a glance at Brandon, she nodded. "Thank you—both of you. I can't tell you what it means to me to have your help."

Alan reached for a legal-size yellow pad and a pen. "Tell me the whole story—names, dates, places. Don't leave anything out, even if you think it's trivial, okay?"

Daphne's story began on the day she met Randy and ended with the aftermath of his suicide, the conversation she overheard his mother having with Mike, and their five years on the run.

"Was Randy abused by his parents?" Alan asked.

"Not physically—at least not that I know of. They abused him in every other possible way by forcing him to abandon his art and go to law school. He hated that and the years he spent working in his father's firm. It was all for show, so they could say their son was successful. A starving artist wasn't conducive to his father's political career. He embarrassed them, and they made sure he knew it. I think his spirit died long before he took his life." Daphne's eyes welled with tears. "Despite the way they'd treated him, though, his suicide was a terrible shock to them—to all of us. But rather than mourn their son the way normal people would, they went into cover-up mode. They told the world he'd died in a car accident.

"Do you know how many people in positions of authority have to be involved to kill off a high-profile person in an accident that didn't happen? I saw first-hand that week after he died how far-reaching their power was. Between that and what his mother said to Mike, I knew I had to get her out of there or she'd be sucked into their world the way Randy had been. He was gentle and sweet, certainly no match for them. I didn't know then how strong Mike would turn out to be. I'm fairly certain now that she could've fought them better than her father did, but I couldn't take that chance with a one-year-old whose personality had only begun to emerge."

Brandon, who was hearing some of this for the first time, struggled to stay calm.

Alan took copious notes about the Monroe's efforts to find her. "Why do you suppose they haven't made any attempt to grab her?"

"They did. Once."

Brandon gasped. "When?"

"The last time they found us, in Raleigh, North Carolina. I'd been asking myself that same question, and I'd decided they didn't want the bother of a baby. She was almost four when they made their move."

"What happened in Raleigh?" Alan asked.

"I enrolled her in a preschool two mornings a week so she could be with other kids for a few hours. One of Monroe's guys went to the school and tried to sign her out, saying he was her grandfather. He even had an ID with the last name we were using at the time. They refused him because no one but me was authorized to pick her up."

"That seems kind of bush league for someone like Monroe," Alan said.

"It was his only chance to get at her when she wasn't with me. That told me how desperate they were. We left Raleigh that day, and after zigzagging the East Coast for a few weeks, we ended up here."

Brandon sat back against the sofa and exhaled a long deep breath.

Daphne laced her fingers through his, offering comfort as much as taking it.

Satisfied he had all the facts, Alan set the notebook aside and put down his pen. "I want to get an investigator to do some digging around. If Monroe's got dirty laundry, it'll give us some leverage if it comes to that."

"Let's do it," Brandon said.

"It'll cost you," Alan warned.

"How much?" Daphne asked.

"Depends on how long it takes, but it could be as much as ten or fifteen grand."

Daphne gasped.

"I know a guy who specializes in this kind of thing," Alan added. "He's discreet but thorough. If there's something to find, he will."

"Do it," Brandon said without hesitation. "Have him bill me. What else can we do?"

"I have a friend from law school who practices in Nebraska. I'll draft a letter to feel them out and have him send it for me so we won't blow your cover until we know more about what they're after."

"I know what they're after—they want full custody," Daphne said.

"They won't get that, Daphne. I talked to my colleague, the family court judge, and he'll hear your case in his courtroom if it comes to that. He makes no promises to either side, but he's not for sale at any price. I can guarantee you that. The best thing we can do if it goes to court is keep it on our turf, which puts Monroe at a significant disadvantage. He may have cronies in California, but I doubt he has any here."

"How do you see this resolving itself, Alan?" Brandon asked.

"If it goes to court, you'll probably have to let them see Mike. Since you'll be hard pressed to prove what they've done to you for the last five years, the court would be sympathetic to grandparents who've lost their only child and want a relationship with their only grandchild."

Daphne panicked. "I can't let them near her. They'll take her, and I'll never see her again. I know how they operate."

"When we reach the negotiation stage, we'll offer supervised visitation only. A social worker would have to accompany Mike at all times."

"What if they push for unsupervised visitation?" Brandon asked, his arm wrapped tightly around Daphne.

"We'll fight it with everything we have." Alan gestured toward the pages of notes he'd taken. "Our ace in this situation is that a seasoned politician like Monroe won't want the publicity of an ugly, protracted custody battle, during which his former daughter-in-law will testify that he drove his only child to suicide and then covered it up. The media would go crazy, and he doesn't need that, especially right now. Have you heard the latest rumblings?"

Daphne shook her head. "No, what?"

"He's on the short list to be Tucker's vice president." Alan referred to the Democratic Party's presumptive presidential nominee. "With the convention just over two months away, the last thing he needs is a boatload of negative publicity. This could be the perfect time to work something out with them."

Full of optimism and hope, Brandon and Daphne exchanged glances.

"Let's get that letter written," she said with a smile.

Later that night, long after they tucked Mike in, Brandon held Daphne close to him in what had become their bed. They'd made love with complete abandon, buoyed by the meeting with Alan and filled with hope for a future without the worry and fear she had carried with her for five long years.

"What are you thinking about?" she asked.

"That I can't believe how, even after nearly a week of long, hot nights with you, I want you more now than I did the first time."

"I know. My itch for you seems to be getting worse rather than better."

He smiled. "I hope it's never fully scratched and you keep coming back for more."

She rewarded him with a deep, wet kiss that guaranteed she'd be back for more.

He reluctantly tore himself away from her. "Listen, before you get me all revved up again, there's something I want to talk to you about."

"Something bad?"

"No, baby, nothing bad," he said, touched by her concern. "After we work this thing out with Mike, I don't want to see that fearful look on your beautiful face ever again. Do you hear me?"

She smiled and nodded.

"That's better," he said, but her smile faded. "What now? Why is the worried face back?"

"It's just..."

"What, hon?"

"I hate that this is going to cost so much—"

He silenced her with a kiss. "I don't want to hear another word about that. Not one word. She's my little girl now, too, and there's *nothing* I wouldn't do for her. Or you. I don't want you to give it another thought." He sighed when she closed her eyes against a rush of emotion. "No tears."

"I love you," she whispered.

"Lucky, lucky me."

"No, lucky me." She caressed his face and gazed into his eyes. "What did you want to talk to me about?"

"I've been doing some thinking about my work situation." He'd already told her about his mixed feelings about his career at O'Malley & Sons. "This week has really shown me I need a change."

"Spending a week up to your eyeballs in crap would make anyone take stock," she joked for the hundredth time since Declan called in a panic on Monday morning, forcing them to cut short their stay at the Rock Harbor Inn.

"While I'm sure you have a few more shit jokes in your inventory, I'm actually trying to be serious here."

She smothered her grin and kissed him. "I'm sorry, baby. I'll try to behave."

"I'm thinking about going into the restoration business. Bringing this place back to life has been the most interesting thing I've done in years." He had only the building's exterior and Daphne's apartment left to renovate. They'd be moving to his house while he did the work in her apartment. If everything went according to his plan, they wouldn't be coming back to the apartment. "Aidan has built a booming business in Vermont refurbishing old houses, and I think there's a market for it here, too."

"What would it entail?"

"I'm hoping I can do it under the auspices of O'Malley & Sons, but if they're not into it, I'll leave the company. If that happens, things would be tight for a while until I get established. But over time we should be okay."

"I'm used to tight, so don't worry about me. If we resolve this situation with the Monroes, I can renew my CPA license and make a lot more money than I do now."

"I don't want you to have to work at all if you'd rather be at home with Mike and any other little O'Malleys who might come along."

Her eyes went liquid with love and hope. "I'll probably always want to do something." She raised herself up to kiss him. "But you're so sweet to want to give me choices."

"I want to give you everything. That's my only hesitation with making this change. I make damned good money now—well over a hundred and fifty a year. This doesn't seem like a good time to be giving that up."

"You have to do what fulfills you, Brandon. The rest will fall into place. I can't imagine us being any happier than we are right now in this tiny apartment. We don't need anything else."

"We're going to have it all, even if I have to work twenty hours a day to get it."

She kissed her way from his chest to his belly. "If you work twenty hours a day, you won't have time for this."

He sighed when she stroked him to arousal. "Baby, I'll *always* have time for that."

CHAPTER 29, DAY 80

The ceiling fan mesmerized Colin as it moved the light breeze drifting in through the open French doors. From their bed, they had a perfect view of the sugar-white sand on Grand Cayman's famous Seven Mile Beach and the azure Caribbean in the distance.

"What will we do for a honeymoon after this?"

Meredith giggled. "Still taking it slow, are we?"

"A turtle's pace," he said with a smile.

"*No more turtle jokes.* I can't believe I let you trick me into eating turtle."

"You can't come to the Caymans and not try the turtle."

"I would've survived without it."

"I wouldn't have survived without you." He traced a finger along the tan line above her milky white breasts. "I would've missed you for the rest of my life."

"Colin…"

Reaching under the pillow and then for her hand, he said, "Marry me." He slid a square-cut diamond ring onto her finger.

"Oh! Colin, but when…" she sputtered. "You've been with me every minute for almost a week!"

"Except for half an hour when we were shopping in Georgetown," he reminded her.

"You said you had to call work."

"I lied."

Holding up her hand for a better look at the extraordinary ring, tears leaked from her eyes.

"I'm sorry I lied." He wiped away her tears. "I'll never do it again."

"Oh, shut up," she cried, throwing her arms around him.

"Is that a yes?"

"Yes," she said, choking on a sob. "That's a yes."

On the flight from Miami to Boston the next day, Colin took her hand to admire the way the ring sparkled on her finger. His ring. His fiancée. He still wanted to pinch himself to make sure he wasn't dreaming.

"It's the most beautiful ring I've ever seen."

"I'm glad you like it. I was hoping you weren't one of those girls who always dreamed of picking out her own ring."

"I didn't have dreams. I never saw any of this happening to me."

"Well, start dreaming because it's become my sole purpose in life to make you happy."

She pressed her lips to his neck, whispering, "You're doing a very good job so far."

"Meredith, honey, there's something I want you to do for me and for us, but mostly for you."

Her eyebrows knit with curiosity. "What is it?"

"I want you to see Kevin." He stopped her protest with a finger to her lips. "I want you to see him and hear him out so you can put it behind you once and for all. I'd be right there with you."

"I don't know, Colin. Just the thought of it makes me sick."

"So let's do it and get it over with. I don't want you worried all the time about running into him somewhere. Let's do it on your terms."

"You'd really go with me?"

"Of course I would."

"I'm afraid..."

"Of what, sweetheart?"

"That it'll cause a setback. I feel so good now, and it took me such a long time to get here."

"I wish I'd met you years ago." He hated the idea of all the time she'd spent alone and afraid.

"I wouldn't have been ready for you then."

"No matter what happens, I'll be there for you. We'll get through it together."

She mulled it over for another moment. "Okay," she finally said. "I'll do it for you."

He wanted her to do it for herself, but he'd take what he could get. Tugging her closer to him in the wide first-class seat, he hoped he was doing the right thing by encouraging her to see Kevin. "So what kind of wedding do you want?"

"I want the fairy tale."

He raised an eyebrow in surprise. "Didn't you just say you hadn't given it any thought?"

"I've had almost twenty-four hours to think of nothing else."

He groaned. "My mother's going to love you."

"Sweet Mary, Mother of God," was Colleen's reaction to learning that another of her sons was engaged. "Are you boys trying to put me in an early grave?"

Colin laughed. "I swear it's not a conspiracy, Mum."

"She's a beautiful girl," Colleen said, glancing across the room to where Dennis was doing his best to charm Meredith.

"I know."

"It's kind of fast, though, isn't it, love? You're sure?"

"Do you remember how upset I was when Nicole called off our wedding?"

"Of course I do. That was an awful time for you, for all of us."

"All I can think about now is how grateful I am to Nicole for not marrying me. I don't know what I would've done if I'd met Meredith when I was married to someone else. She's the one for me. I knew it right away."

She hugged him. "I'm happy for you, love. I just can't believe my boys are finally settling down—all at once."

"Except for Aidan."

She shook her head with dismay. "I don't know what we're going to do about that poor boy."

Colin smiled at her description of his forty-year-old brother. "He'll land on his feet."

"I hope you're right. What's her family like?"

"I'm meeting them tomorrow night."

"You brought her here first," Colleen said with a satisfied smirk.

"I told her we had to come here first because if my Mum didn't like her, I couldn't marry her."

Colleen swatted him. "Don't give me that malarkey, Colin O'Malley! You didn't say any such thing."

"Um, okay. If you say so."

Chapter 30, Day 100

Brandon marked his one-hundredth day of sobriety in mid-May by presiding with Daphne over Mike's sixth birthday party in the backyard at his house where they were living during the renovations to the apartment. It took a crane, a flatbed truck, and six men, but Brandon managed to move the playground from the apartment building to his yard. Between the O'Malley clan, Alan's family, and Mike's friends from school, almost thirty kids had taken the place over for the afternoon.

That night Brandon tucked Mike into bed and read her two of the books she'd gotten for her birthday while Daphne cleaned up.

"So what was your favorite part of the party?"

"When you almost dropped my cake," she said, choking on a giggle.

"It was my first time! A rookie mistake." He pushed his lip into a pout that sent her into hysterics. "Good thing Meredith was able to grab it before I lost it, huh?" The save had earned his future sister-in-law a permanent place in Brandon's heart.

Mike nodded, still convulsed with laughter. Just when he thought she couldn't get any cuter, she'd lost her two front teeth in time for her birthday.

"Are you done laughing at me yet?"

She wiped the tears from her eyes. "Almost."

"Brat," he muttered, poking her ribs and sending her into a new fit of giggles.

When she finally settled down, she reached for his hand. "Thanks again for the party and the bike."

"You're welcome. What's the rule?"

"Always wear the helmet," she mimicked.

"Are you sure you want to be making fun of me again?" he asked, threatening to tickle her.

She tugged playfully on his hair. "Brandon, what's a coholic?"

"Huh? A what?"

"A coholic."

"Oh." He felt like he'd been sucker punched when he realized what she was asking. "Do you mean an alcoholic?"

She nodded.

His stomach twisted with anxiety. "Where did you hear that word?"

"Josh told me you were a coholic, but he said I don't need to be worried about it because you're not mean anymore."

All the air left Brandon's lungs in one big exhale as he said a quick, silent prayer for guidance. "An alcoholic is someone who can't drink things like beer and wine the way other people do because they can't stop once they start. It's a disease."

"Can you die from it?" she asked with big solemn eyes.

"People who don't stop drinking can die from it, yes."

"But you're not going to die, are you?"

Overwhelmed by her concern, he fought the urge to weep. "No, baby. I don't drink alcohol anymore. Do you know those meetings I go to in the mornings?"

She nodded.

"The people I see there are alcoholics, too, and they remind me of all the good things I have in my life now—like you and your mommy—so I won't drink anymore."

"Can I come with you sometime?"

"When you're a little older, I'd be happy to take you." He waited, giving her a chance to process it all.

"So if you stopped drinking, then you aren't an alcoholic anymore, right?"

"I'll be an alcoholic for the rest of my life. It's not something that goes away. You just learn to live with it."

"You aren't going to drink again, are you?"

"I don't plan to, and I hope I never will."

"Were you mean like Josh said?"

"Sometimes. I didn't want to be mean, though, because I love Josh and his brother and sisters, but the disease made me do a lot of things I'm not proud of. I'll never be mean to you, though. I promise. Do you believe me?"

She reached for him. "I believe you."

"Good." She hugged him for a long time before he kissed her good-night. "I love you, squirt."

"Love you, too."

He turned off the light and found Daphne waiting for him in the hallway.

She held out her arms to him. "Are you okay?" she whispered.

"Yeah." He let her wrap him in her love. "She kind of knocked the wind out of me for a minute there."

"When I heard what you were talking about, I didn't know what to do. You handled it so well, Brandon."

"Do you think so? I was freaking out."

"You did great. Between birthday cakes and life lessons at bedtime, we might just be making a daddy out of you."

"Don't forget the hazardous duty points for the head bump and the puking."

She laughed softly so they wouldn't disturb Mike and reached up to bury her hands in his hair. "I love you," she said, bringing him down to her.

"Mmm," he said against her lips. "Me, too."

***

After they restored order to the house, Daphne said she had some work to do for her client, so Brandon took his cell phone to the back deck and called Aidan.

"Hi, Brand. How's it going?"

"Well, I survived a six-year-old's birthday party today." Brandon hated the flutter of anxiety he still felt at the sound of his older brother's voice. He hoped it would fade in time.

"Sorry I missed it."

Brandon chuckled. "No, you're not. So how are you?"

"Hanging in there."

"How about Colin, huh? The two of them in one week! Can you believe it?"

"Must be something in the water down there. You guys are falling like dominoes."

"I won't be far behind them."

"Really?" Aidan asked, laughing. "Mum will have a total meltdown."

"Hey, she's been after us to get married for years."

"I don't think she meant all at the same time."

They shared a laugh, and Brandon relaxed a bit. "Listen, the reason I called is I'm looking for some advice."

"Sure, shoot."

Brandon outlined his idea for a restoration and renovation arm of O'Malley & Sons. "I'm wondering if you think the market would be as good here as it's been for you in Vermont."

"Definitely. New England is full of old homes in need of updating."

"How did you get the ball rolling once you decided to do it?"

"I never really decided. I did a house for a friend, and he told someone, and the next thing I knew, I had a business. Once you do a couple of houses, I'm sure it would be the same for you."

"Do you think the others will go for it as part of O'Malley & Sons?"

"They'd be foolish not to. It's a gold mine if you do it right, and I'm sure you will."

"I'm meeting with them in the morning to pitch it to them. Would you be willing to be on the phone during the meeting? Just in case they have questions I can't answer."

"I'd be happy to."

"Thanks, Aidan."

Brandon was nervous, even though he knew he shouldn't be. After all, it was just his father, his brothers, and his brother-in-law in the room. But they'd be determining his future in the next hour or so, and he hoped it would include O'Malley & Sons. With a potential custody battle looming, it wasn't the time for Brandon to be quitting his job. However, if he'd learned anything in his one hundred and one days of sobriety, it was that he couldn't fake it anymore. This was what he wanted to do, and one way or the other, he'd find a way to do it.

"I've asked Aidan to join us by phone," Brandon said, dialing Aidan in on the conference room phone.

"Why?" Colin asked.

Aidan had signed over his shares in the company to his siblings years ago and had no say in its operation.

"I'll explain in a minute," Brandon said.

When Aidan answered and they'd had a chance to say hello, Brandon cleared his throat. "The reason I asked you all to meet with me today is I want to propose a new branch of O'Malley & Sons, focused on the restoration of old houses, like what I did at Da's apartment building, and the renovation of newer homes that need updating."

When no one raised an immediate objection, he continued. He'd done his homework and had statistics on the number of homes built on the mid and lower Cape before and after 1960, and a list of the services he planned to offer. "Aidan agrees there's a market for it here, and he thinks that once we get a few under our belts, we'll benefit from referrals."

"Let me add one more thing," Aidan said. "I've been seeing a real trend up here of people buying their second or third homes. They've got more money than they had the first time around, and they want to tear out the old kitchens and bathrooms. They're willing to pay, and Brandon knows what he's doing. Plus you'd have the added benefit of name recognition."

"Do you plan to go it alone or would you want a crew?" Declan asked.

"By myself until I'm turning a profit," Brandon said. "If I stay with the company to do this, my salary would be enough of a drain until it's profitable. I wouldn't expect you guys to take a further hit by paying a crew."

"Wouldn't you make money faster if you had help?" Tommy asked.

"I guess so," Brandon said. "I hadn't really given that much thought. I figured I'd do it on my own."

"What did you mean when you said 'if I stay with the company'?" Colin asked.

"I'm prepared to leave—with no hard feelings—if you guys aren't into it. I'm going to do this, with or without the company, but I'm hoping it'll be *with* the company."

"What do you think, Da?" Declan asked.

"You boys are in charge now, so it's your decision," Dennis said.

"But you still have a financial stake," Brandon reminded him.

"I'm in no danger of starving to death any time soon." Dennis patted his round belly. "So I leave it in your capable hands."

"How about you, Col?" Brandon asked, knowing Colin's opinion was the one that mattered most.

"It's interesting you should have this idea right now, because I've been doing some thinking about how we could reorganize to be more efficient," Colin said.

"How do you mean?" Tommy asked.

"I want to have a life away from this place, so I've been trying to figure out how I can free myself up some. In light of Brandon's idea, I picture three divisions—excavation, new construction, and renovation/restoration."

With those words from Colin, Brandon knew he wouldn't be leaving the company.

"Tommy would head up excavation, Dec would oversee new construction, and Brand would have renovation," Colin said. "Each of you would be entirely independent to make any and all decisions in your areas, bringing me in as needed. I'd oversee estimating, equipment, maintenance, the office, inventory, etc. What do you think?"

"How would we divide the guys?" Dec asked.

"We'd let them pick where they want to work based on seniority," Colin said.

"Sounds good to me," Tommy said.

"It might take a year or two to make my end profitable," Brandon warned them.

"I don't think it'll take that long, Brandon," Aidan said. "Especially if you have help."

"I appreciate the vote of confidence," Brandon said, touched by his older brother's support.

"I'd like to say something," Dennis said, and all eyes turned to him. "Three months ago, I asked Colin to take the helm and work with the rest of you to make this business your own. I'm very pleased by the way you all have supported him and the steps you're taking to position the company for the future. It's your legacy to your children—that is *if* they want it," he added with a wink for Brandon.

Brandon smiled at him, and for the first time in his life, the business felt like a blessing rather than a burden.

"We'll announce the plan at a staff meeting in the morning," Colin said, pushing back from the table.

"Before you all run away, there's something else I want to talk to you about." Brandon asked Aidan to stay on the phone while he filled them in on the situation with Mike's grandparents. "Needless to say, we could be looking at quite a battle."

"It's an outrage!" Dennis said, his face reddening. "No wonder Daphne was so secretive. I feel terrible for what I said about her, son."

"You didn't know, Da, and from your point of view, her behavior was odd. I told Tommy and Erin about it when Mike spent the night with them, but no one else knew."

"They can't just snatch her child away from her," Declan said. "We can't let that happen."

"I'm not going to let it," Brandon said. "But they've tried to grab her once before, and we believe they'd do it again if they knew where she was. Daphne's convinced it's only a matter of time before they find her, so we're hoping to work something out before that happens."

"What did Alan suggest you do?" Colin asked.

Brandon told them about the private investigator and the letter Alan sent to the Monroe's attorneys.

"Do you need money?" Aidan asked.

"I might," Brandon said. "I'm good for now, but this could get long and ugly."

"Whatever you need. Just let me know."

"Thank you, Aidan," Brandon said in a hushed tone. "Thank you all for your support and for standing by me while I got my life together."

"Just let us know what we can do to help you and Daphne," Dec said.

"I will."

Chapter 31, Day 108

Brandon was applying yellow paint to the exterior of the apartment building the following week when Colleen's silver Cadillac skidded to a stop at the curb. She bounded out of the car and came rushing through the front gate.

He put down the paintbrush. "What's gotten into you?" he asked, kissing her cheek.

"You won't believe it!" Her eyes sparkled with tears of joy.

"Believe what?"

"Aidan and Clare are back together, and they're *engaged*!"

"No way! What happened?"

She tucked her hand into the crook of his arm and led him to the new porch swing. "This place looks wonderful, love."

"Forget about that. Tell me what happened."

"Well, Clare's youngest daughter, Maggie, the thirteen-year-old, had a terrible accident yesterday. She fell backward off the ladder to the attic at her father's house and broke both her arms and a rib. It's so awful. She's such a love. We had the best time with her at Aidan's birthday in Boston."

"How did he hear about it?"

"Clare's oldest daughter, Jill, called him while they were waiting for Maggie to wake up. She has a severe concussion, too, so it was touch and go yesterday. Anyway, Jill thought Aidan would want to know, so she called him."

"Is Maggie okay now?"

"Yes, she's conscious and out of the woods. Of course, she's got a long road ahead of her with the broken arms."

"Well, that's a relief. So Aidan went to Rhode Island?"

She nodded. "He drove for hours not knowing if the little girl would be alive when he got there, and he said he had a bit of an epiphany during that long ride."

"How do you mean?"

"He realized he's already a father—a stepfather, but a father nonetheless—and he was terrified they would lose their dear, sweet Maggie. He told Clare he'd been a fool to let her go, and if she wants more kids it's fine with him." Colleen wiped a tear from her cheek. "I'm so happy you were here. Da's playing golf, and I needed to tell someone. After everything he's been through, no one deserves this more than Aidan."

"I couldn't agree with you more," Brandon said sincerely as he hugged his mother. "I'm thrilled for him. He was so heartbroken over losing her."

"He told me Clare's middle daughter, Kate, the one who lives in Nashville, has the number one song on the country music charts this week. Can you believe that?"

"Sounds like he's marrying into quite a family."

"*Three boys engaged*," Colleen marveled. "My friends have been teasing me mercilessly about two. This'll send them into a tizzy."

"What do you think they'll say about four?"

Colleen's mouth dropped open in shock.

He howled with laughter. "I've finally found a way to render you speechless. Wait 'til I tell the boys about this!"

When Colleen recovered, she managed to say, "Have you asked her?"

"Not yet but soon."

"Da told me about what's going on with Mike's grandparents. Don't you let them get their hands on that child, Brandon."

"They'd have to kill me first."

Sighing, she rested her head on his shoulder. "That would kill *me*, so don't let it happen."

"Don't worry, Mum. We're handling it."

They enjoyed the gentle sway of the swing and the warm spring breeze for several quiet minutes.

"You know I love all my children, right?"

"Yes, and we all know Aidan's your favorite."

She smacked him. "Hush. That's not true. He was my *first*. You should understand now that you have your Mike."

"Hmm, I hadn't thought about that, but you're right. Even if I have five more, there'll never be another quite like her."

"Exactly. Now, what I was *going* to say..." she said with exasperation that made him smile, "is that nothing has ever made me prouder than watching you reclaim your life over these last few months. I'm so very, very proud of you, Brandon."

"Thanks, Mum," was all he could say.

"You and Daphne make such a beautiful couple. You should see yourselves together. You're breathtaking, both of you."

"Now you're embarrassing me."

"The two of you are going to make me some very pretty grandbabies."

"I think it's safe to say there's about to be a huge baby boom in this family."

"Six grandchildren and holding—for now."

Realizing her count included Mike, Brandon's heart swelled to overflowing. "Love you, Mum."

"I love you more."

Alan called the next day with an update. "There's good news and bad news. Which do you want first?"

"Bad," Brandon said, bracing himself.

"I just heard from my friend in Nebraska. A virtual army has descended upon his town looking for Daphne and Mike. They even got into his office somehow and tossed the place upside down."

"Jesus," Brandon muttered.

"He also got a certified letter from Monroe, demanding we produce the child immediately and stating their plans to sue for full custody."

Brandon swallowed hard. "What's the good news?"

"If they're tearing up a town in Nebraska, they have no idea where she is."

"That's true."

"I also got a call from Scott," Alan said, referring to the private investigator. "He's on to something, and he hopes to get back to me soon with an update."

"Call me when you hear anything."

"I will."

"You know, the fact they're all over that town in Nebraska also means they aren't going away. Everything I've been reading says Tucker's going with Monroe for vice president. I was hoping that would pull his attention away from Mike, but they're not letting it go, are they?"

"It doesn't look that way," Alan said. "Just stay calm, and let's see what Scott can find out."

"Okay."

"On another note, we've got a guy at Laurel Lake who reminds me a lot of you when you first arrived. A real tough case. I was wondering if you might come with me one afternoon this week to have a chat with him."

"You really think I'm ready for step twelve?" Brandon asked.

"Your story is exactly what this guy needs to hear."

"Sure, I'd be happy to try if you think it'll help."

"Great, thanks. I'll be in touch."

When he hung up with Alan, Brandon went home to update Daphne.

After he told her the latest she paced back and forth across the living room with her glasses perched on the end of her nose and a pencil shot through her ponytail.

"What are you thinking, babe?" he asked when he couldn't bear the silence any longer.

"I hope the PI you're paying all that money to comes through with something we can use to blackmail Monroe—and soon."

"Alan said he's getting close." Brandon put his arms around her. "We just have to be patient for a little while longer."

"My stomach hurts all the time," she confessed.

"Since when?" he asked, alarmed.

"The last week or so. I'm wondering if I've finally worked myself into an ulcer."

"Let's get you to a doctor. That's nothing to mess around with."

"I'll call this afternoon."

"Promise?" He ran his thumbs over her fragile jaw, noticing for the first time the dark circles under her eyes. The stress was getting to her.

"I promise."

He scooped her up into his arms and carried her to their bedroom.

"What're you doing?"

"Putting my baby down for a nap." He removed her glasses and the pencil from her hair. "You're going take a break from worrying and have a nice long rest. I'm picking up Mike today since I'm now *officially* on the list."

She smiled. "You're so proud of that, aren't you?"

"You bet your ass I am."

"Just bring her home."

"No way. We have plans. We're going out to lunch, and then she's coming over to do some painting for me this afternoon. You, my love, have the afternoon off. No work, no Mike, no worrying, no nothing, you hear me?"

"Yes, sir."

"Oh, I like that," he said with a satisfied grin as he leaned in for a kiss. "Say it again."

"Never. It was a one-time lapse."

He discovered right then that laughing and kissing make for an interesting combination. "When you get up I want you to take the longest, bubble bath ever and then get dressed up. I'm taking my girls out to dinner tonight."

She sighed with contentment.

He kissed her eyes closed. "Sleep, baby. I'll take care of everything."

"Love you," she whispered as she nodded off.

Brandon watched her sleep for a long time before he left to pick up Mike.

Brandon and Mike arrived at home just before five to find Daphne still asleep. He sent Mike to wash up and sat on the bed to trail kisses up and down Daphne's neck.

Still half asleep, she put her arms around him and pulled him down with her.

Brandon could have stayed there all night, but he knew Mike would be back in a few minutes. "Wake up," he said, kissing her neck again.

"Don't want to."

"Have you been asleep all this time?"

"Uh-huh." She yawned. "What time is it?"

"Almost five."

Her eyes flew open. "For real?"

He studied her. "What's going on, hon? Maybe we should get you to a doctor tonight."

"I'm okay." She started to get up but sat right back down.

"Daph, you're scaring me."

"I got up too fast, that's all. I thought we were going out tonight."

"Why don't we just stay in?"

"Would you be terribly disappointed if we did?"

He brushed the hair off her face. "Of course not. Mike and I will cook. I want you to take it easy."

"You and Mike are going to cook?" she asked with an eyebrow raised in amusement. "That ought to be interesting."

"We have many skills you don't know about. Go soak in the tub and relax." He kissed her and sent her on her way, but all he could think about was how pale she was. Reaching for the bedside phone, he called Erin.

"What's going on?" she asked.

He told her about Daphne not feeling well and asked for the name of a doctor. "She thinks this whole thing with Mike might be giving her an ulcer."

"I can't believe she hasn't had one for years. I know just the guy. She'll love him."

Brandon called the doctor and made an appointment for nine o'clock the next morning. He also made a mental note to ask Lorraine in the office about getting Daphne and Mike added to his health insurance. Daphne was soaking in the big tub when he went into the bathroom. "I got you in with Erin's doctor at nine in the morning."

"I told you I would call," she said, her brows furrowed with unusual annoyance.

He bent to kiss away her scowl. "I'm worried about you. You're pale as a ghost and sleeping half the day. That's not like you."

"I'm sorry." She seemed startled when her eyes flooded with tears. "I don't know what's wrong with me lately."

"Then let's find out, okay?"

She nodded.

After a dinner of spaghetti and salad that Daphne had to admit was surprisingly good, they snuggled on the sofa with Mike to watch *The Lion King*.

"How many times have you seen this, squirt?" he asked.

"I think like a hundred," she said, fixated on Simba.

"It's got to be more like two hundred," Brandon said. "Even I know the words to the songs, and that's saying something."

Daphne giggled and squeezed his hand.

Brandon couldn't remember ever being more content, with Daphne resting her head on his shoulder and Mike using his leg for a pillow. "Do you think we could pause the movie for a minute?" he asked once he had the lump in his throat under control.

Mike sat up and reached for the remote.

"I'll be right back." He got up, went into the bedroom, and came back with a big bag.

"What is that?" Mike asked.

"It's a present for you and your mom."

Mike's eyes lit up. "Is it for my birthday?"

"Nope. This is for something different." Brandon sat between them. "In my family, we have a tradition. You've seen my green coat with the O'Malley & Sons company name on it, right?"

Mike nodded. "It has all the yellow shamrocks, and it says 'Brandon O'Malley.'"

"That's the one. Well, every member of our family has one. Because there are O'Malleys and Maloneys, we have our full names on them. And since you guys are my family now..." He pulled a small green jacket out of the bag and handed it to Mike. "This one's for you, and this one's for your mom."

"Mine says Mike O'Malley on it," she said, looking at Brandon with confusion.

"Yes, it does."

Daphne had tears in her eyes as she skimmed her fingers over the gold embroidery that spelled Daphne O'Malley.

"I don't get it," Mike said.

"I do," Daphne whispered, kissing Brandon's cheek.

"Try it on, squirt," he said, making an effort to stay focused on Mike.

Still looking perplexed, Mike stood up and slid it on.

"Does it fit?"

"Yep."

He adjusted the coat and zipped it up.

She put her hands in the pockets. "What's this?" she asked, pulling out a small box wrapped in gold paper.

"Why don't you open it and find out?"

Mike tore the paper off the box and found a velvet jeweler's box. Inside was a diamond solitaire on a delicate gold chain. She gasped. "Is that *real*?"

"Yes, it's *real*," Brandon said, grinning at her reaction. He took the necklace from the box and put it on her. "I love you, Mike. I want to adopt you and give you my name. How does Mike O'Malley sound?"

"Do you mean it?"

He nodded. "Will you be my daughter?"

Her golden eyes sparkled with tears. "I'd like that, Brandon."

"Good." He hugged her. "I was thinking we could use Monroe as your middle name so your first daddy would always be with you, too. Would that be okay?"

"What do you think, Mom?"

Dealing with her own flood of tears, Daphne nodded. "That'd be perfect, Pooh."

He settled Mike on his lap. "Mommy's turn," he said, reaching for the box in the pocket of Daphne's jacket.

Her hands trembled as she removed the gold paper. When she stopped to wipe away tears, Brandon took the box from her.

"All my brothers are getting married." His face twisted into a pout that made Daphne laugh even as new tears spilled from her eyes. "I don't want to be left out."

"We can't have that," she said, caressing away his pout.

"I never imagined I'd have a home and a family of my own. The two of you have given me that and so many other things I didn't even know I wanted. I love you—both of you—with everything I have, everything I'll ever have. Will you ladies marry me?"

Daphne glanced at Mike. "Yes," they said in unison.

Brandon hugged them for a long time.

"What did you get for Mom?" Mike asked, toying with her new necklace.

"Ah, yes, how could I forget that?" He opened the box. A cushion-cut diamond was surrounded by topaz.

"Oh, I love it!" Daphne said. "Topaz is my favorite. How did you know?"

"I didn't. The color reminded me of your eyes and Mike's. Calling them brown doesn't do them justice, so when I saw a topaz in the window of Chatham Jewelers, I said, 'That's it, that's the color.'" He put the ring on her finger, hooked his free arm around her neck, and kissed her.

Mike squirmed off his lap. "Eww, gross, if you're going to start that, let me down," she said, making them laugh.

When Brandon heard the movie go back on, he took advantage of the opportunity to kiss Daphne properly. "We're getting married," he whispered.

"Your mother will freak."

"Nah, I warned her. I was going to do this a week ago, but then Aidan got engaged. I decided to give him a week before I knocked him off the front page."

"Did I mess up your plans by not wanting to go out tonight?"

"Not at all. This was much better."

"This was perfect," she whispered. "Thank you for including Mike the way you did."

"It wouldn't have been right without her."

"No," she said, kissing him. "It wouldn't, especially since you fell for her first—after she chose you for us."

"I can't deny that, so I won't even try. When do you want to tie the knot? We've got Dec's wedding at the beginning of July, Aidan's in mid-July, and Colin's in August. That leaves September. My parents are going to Ireland for the first two weeks of September, so how's late September?"

Her smile faded, and the worried look was back.

"What's wrong? Is it your stomach?"

"No."

"Then what?"

"I want to wait to get married until we resolve this thing with the Monroes. I don't want to start our life together with that hanging over our heads."

"I don't care about that. If we wait then we're letting them run our lives even more than they are already. Let's set a date, and if it's not resolved by then, so be it."

"Can we wait a few weeks to see what happens before we make any plans?"

"I suppose we could do that, but we will be married before the end of the year, even if it's not resolved, you got me? You can just say 'yes, sir' again. That works for me."

"No way. You caught me in a moment of extreme exhaustion. You'll never get that out of me again."

"I've got a *lot* of years to work on you."

With a sly sideways glance that made his mouth go dry, she ran her hand up his leg. "Give it your best shot."

He tore his eyes off hers long enough to find Mike on the floor watching the movie. "Time for bed, squirt."

When Mike insisted on wearing her new necklace to school the next morning, Daphne protested. "You're not wearing a diamond necklace to kindergarten. Your teacher will think I've lost my mind."

"I want to show it to everyone and tell them we're engaged," Mike said.

"It's insured," Brandon whispered to Daphne.

"It is?"

"I was giving a diamond to a six-year-old. I'm not a total idiot."

"Just a partial?" she asked with a smile.

He laughed at the reminder of the day they met. "Let her wear it today, and then we'll put it away for special occasions."

"All right, Mike. Your new daddy has gone to bat for you once again. You can wear it today, but that's it. And I expect you to be very careful with it."

With a grateful grin for Brandon, Mike said, "I'd never let anything happen to it, Mom. Don't worry."

"I'll drop her off on the way to my meeting," he said.

"Thanks."

"Call me the minute you leave the doctor. I want to know what he says."

"I will."

Brandon spent the morning rehanging shutters on the freshly painted apartment building. Soon he'd be finished at the apartments and would be moving on to his new venture. When he told his sponsor about his plans for the renovation business, Joe asked to be his first client. "My wife has been after me for a new kitchen for years. And my daughter just bought an old place in Brewster. You'll probably be hearing from her, too." It was a start, and Brandon was excited about the future. He had so much to look forward to these days.

He was on a ladder hanging a shutter on one of the second-floor windows when Daphne pulled up in front of the building. Moving quickly to turn the last of the screws, he scurried down the ladder to meet her as she came through the gate.

"What did he say?" Brandon put his arm around her and sat with her on the stairs. "Is it an ulcer?"

Her eyes seemed even bigger than usual against the backdrop of her pale face as she shook her head.

"Then what? Come on, you're taking years off my life here."

"I'm pregnant."

Brandon stared at her. "What? But, how..."

Amused by his astounded expression, she patted his face. "The usual way, I suspect."

"But we've been so careful."

"Not always," she reminded him. "Remember that day you came back home after you took Mike to school?"

"That's all it takes?"

"Apparently."

"Pregnant." He dropped his head onto her shoulder and for once gave in to the need to weep.

"What?" she asked, alarmed. "Are you mad?"

He shook his head. "I was just thinking about how much I have to look forward to. That there could be even more..."

She wiped the tears from his face and kissed him.

He wrapped his arms around her.

The kiss went on for several minutes until he took her hand to pull her up. He scooped her into his arms and carried her inside to his apartment.

"Where are we going?" she asked as he kicked the door closed.

"To celebrate."

Chapter 32, Day 132

Colin left work early on the June day that he and Meredith were scheduled to meet with Kevin.

"What're you doing home already?" she asked when he arrived at her house at two. She had taken a personal day from school, knowing she'd never be able to concentrate on her students that day. "We don't have to leave until four thirty."

"I know." When he leaned down to kiss her, she put her arms around him to encourage him to join her on the sofa.

"I came right from a job site, so I'm filthy. Let me grab a shower."

"I don't care."

"I do. Hold that thought for five minutes."

He emerged from the shower with a towel wrapped around his waist to find her lying on the bed waiting for him.

She patted his side of the bed, and he stretched out next to her.

"That AC feels good," he said, bringing her closer to him.

Her hand traveled over his chest and stomach. "You feel good."

"Why don't you take a nap before we have to go? You were up half the night."

"How do you know that? You were sleeping."

"I always know when you're not with me."

"You say the sweetest things, Colin. Did you come home to babysit me?"

"Maybe."

She tugged at the towel. "I'm glad you did."

"What're you up to?"

"We don't have to leave for more than two hours."

"I want you to sleep."

"I don't want to sleep." She pulled the towel free and wrapped her hand around his erection.

"*Meredith.*"

"Take my mind off of it, Colin. Please?"

Since that's what he'd come home to do, he happily obliged.

They pulled up to a ranch house in Eastham right at five o'clock. Meredith didn't want Kevin anywhere near her house, and she hadn't wanted to see him in public, so they were meeting at his sister Joanie's house where he'd been living since his release from prison. Meredith had sent a letter to his parole officer indicating her willingness to see him so the meeting wouldn't violate his parole.

"Will you be able to do this?" Colin asked, concerned about her suddenly pale face and the iron grip she had on his hand.

She nodded. "Just don't let go."

"Never." He raised their joined hands to kiss hers. "Let's go hear what he has to say and get it over with, okay?"

She took a deep breath. "Okay."

Colin let go of her hand only long enough to help her out of his truck.

Joanie waited for them at the front door. Colin wasn't surprised when Meredith greeted her with a hug since he knew Kevin's sister used to be one of her closest friends.

"This is my fiancé, Colin O'Malley."

Colin would never get tired of hearing her refer to him as her fiancé.

"Come on in," Joanie said, leading them into a spacious living room.

Colin and Meredith sat together on the sofa and declined Joanie's offer of drinks. "Are those your kids?" Meredith asked, pointing to framed photos on the wall.

Joanie nodded. "Phillip's twelve, and Matt's seven. They're with their dad this week. We're divorced."

"I'm sorry," Meredith said.

The death grip on his hand told Colin, who was looking at the photographs, that Kevin had joined them.

"Hello, Meredith," Kevin said. "Thank you so much for coming."

Tall with thinning blond hair, Kevin was still built like a football player. But his broken blue eyes told the story of his life since the golden days of high school.

"This is my fiancé, Colin O'Malley," Meredith said in a small voice.

Since shaking Kevin's hand would have required letting go of Meredith's, Colin just nodded.

"Nice to meet you," Kevin said, sitting down across from them next to Joanie.

A long, pregnant pause ensued while they waited for Kevin to say what they had come to hear.

"You look great," Kevin said to Meredith.

"Thank you."

Colin knew how much she must've hated the blush that flamed her cheeks.

"I, um, I know it's such an insignificant thing in light of what I did to you, but I wanted the chance to tell you how sorry I am, Meredith. That I could've hurt you the way I did, it just…" He blinked back tears and shook his head. "When you ended it between us, I went nuts, and I was drinking more than ever. I know what I did to you is unforgivable, but it was important to me that you know how very sorry I am."

Joanie wiped away a tear and reached for her brother's hand.

"I forgive you." Meredith surprised Colin and apparently herself, too. "You have a disease."

"That's no excuse. You'd be dead if Melanie hadn't found you."

"Well, fortunately for both of us, she did. It's time for us to put it behind us and get on with our lives. I appreciate your apology, but we don't have anything else to say to each other." She glanced at Colin, and they stood up. "It was good to see you, Joanie."

"You, too, Meredith. Good luck with your marriage."

"Thank you."

When they reached the front door, Kevin said, "Meredith."

She turned around.

"I loved you. No matter what else you remember about me, I hope you'll remember that, too."

She nodded, and Colin put his arm around her to lead her from the house.

"Are you okay?" he asked when they were in the truck.

"Yeah. Let's get out of here, and then I need a very big hug."

"Coming right up." He drove to the Eastham Town Beach, parked, and reached for her. "I'm so proud of you, sweetheart."

She clung to him. "I'm just glad it's over."

"You were so brave in there."

"My knees were knocking."

"I couldn't tell."

She caressed his face. "Thank you for encouraging me to do that. You were right. I would've always been worried about running into him somewhere. Now if we do it won't be such a big deal."

"He can't hurt you anymore. I won't let him."

"I love you, Colin O'Malley."

"I love you, too."

Spring slipped into summer on Cape Cod, and the O'Malleys were consumed with the planning of four weddings. When the private investigator failed to immediately uncover anything they could use against Monroe, Brandon convinced Daphne to set a late September date for their wedding.

"Maybe by then we'll have it worked out," he said.

She tired easily but otherwise felt better as her pregnancy progressed. They'd decided to keep the news about the baby to themselves until she began to show.

Despite their ongoing worries about Mike's grandparents, it was the best summer of Brandon's life. He dug two gardens in the backyard—one for vegetables and the other for flowers—and Daphne and Mike worked for hours on them. They also planted flowers all over the front yard and began to make some changes inside the house. Daphne's beaded lampshades replaced the ones Valerie had bought years earlier. They painted Mike's room a pale lilac, bought her a new canopy bed, and began to quietly gather baby items in a spare bedroom that Mike never ventured into.

They spent a weekend on Nantucket with Erin's family, went sailing on Colin's boat, and lounged on the beach every chance they got. Mike slept over at least once a week with Erin's kids at "Grandma" Colleen's house and seemed to spend as much time at Erin's house—usually trailing behind Josh—as she did at home.

The wedding frenzy began on the Fourth of July with Declan and Jessica's clambake in Dennis and Colleen's backyard and continued two weeks later when the family trekked to Vermont for Aidan and Clare's wedding.

In late July, Brandon and Daphne watched the Democratic National Convention on television, during which Harrison Monroe officially became John Tucker's vice presidential nominee.

"With California's fifty-five electoral votes up for grabs, the popular senior senator brings an almost certain win for Tucker in the Golden State," one of the commentators said after Monroe addressed the convention.

Daphne moved closer to the television to get a better look at Monroe and his wife Eleanor as they stood next to Tucker and his wife on the big stage. "She looks different," Daphne said.

"All that stuff the media's been saying about her being a virtual recluse since her son's death has probably taken a toll on her," Brandon said.

"There's something about her eyes."

The day after the convention ended, Alan called. "We've got him."

"What do you mean?"

"Monroe's got a mistress."

Brandon gasped.

"He's got her set up in a townhouse in Georgetown. Scott's got pictures. This is what we've been hoping for."

"I think it's time I paid Senator Monroe a visit."

"You read my mind."

Two days later, Brandon flew to St. Louis. Scott had managed to get his hands on the senator's schedule for the first week of the campaign. After a series of appearances in the morning, Monroe had a strategy session planned for his hotel suite in St. Louis that afternoon.

Brandon wore a suit, hoping it would make him look like he belonged in the midst of a presidential campaign, and carried with him only the envelope full of damning photos. He took a cab from the airport to the Omni Majestic Hotel on Pine Street and rode the elevator to the top-floor suite Scott had identified as Monroe's.

A Secret Service agent stopped Brandon as he came off the elevator. "This is a secure floor."

"I need to see Senator Monroe."

"Do you have an appointment?"

"No, but he'll want to hear what I have to say. You can tell him he can hear it from me or on the news within the hour."

"I need to see some identification," the agent said.

Brandon produced his Massachusetts driver's license.

The agent studied it for a moment and gave it back to Brandon. "Wait right here." The agent signaled to one of the aides in the hallway.

Brandon watched the agent talk to the aide, who looked over at Brandon and shrugged.

The aide disappeared down the long hallway. When he came back, he signaled to Brandon. "The senator will give you two minutes."

The Secret Service agent patted Brandon down. "What's in the envelope?"

"Photographs."

"I need to see them."

Brandon handed him the envelope.

The agent flipped through the photos and then handed the envelope to Brandon with a nod to proceed.

Brandon followed the aide to a suite at the end of the hallway. Once inside, he found Monroe in a luxurious sitting area surrounded by aides, all of them with legal-size pads on their laps.

"State your business," Monroe barked. "I'm in a meeting."

"It's personal. You'll hear what I have to say, or the media will. Your choice."

Maybe it was the expression on Brandon's face or perhaps it was the envelope he held in his hand, but either way, he had Monroe's attention.

"Give us the room."

Monroe's aides got up and filed out.

Brandon was thrown for a loop when Eleanor Monroe came into the room.

"What's going on, Harrison?"

"Nothing, Ellie." He spoke gently to her like he would to a precious child. "Go on into the bedroom. I'll be there in a minute."

"That's okay, I think I'll stay."

Shit, Brandon thought. *She wasn't part of the plan.* Daphne was right, though. Something was off about the dignified older woman. If he were being unkind, he would say there was a crazy look in her eyes.

"Who are you, and what do you want?" Harrison Monroe demanded.

"My name is Brandon O'Malley." He knew the Secret Service agent would give them his name if he didn't. "Daphne Flemming is my fiancée, and I'm about to adopt your granddaughter."

Eleanor gasped.

"So here's the deal. Call off your thugs, and leave us alone. Any chance you had at having a relationship with that child ended the day you tried to snatch her away from her mother. Am I clear?"

"I don't know what you're talking about," Monroe said, looking baffled. "We've never tried to take her from her mother. All we've ever wanted was to see her. Our son is dead, and your fiancée has denied us his child for five years."

"Don't give me that crap. You know why your son is dead—and how he really died. You want to take that child and use her like you did your son for your own political gain. So you can save the poor deprived grandfather act. Call off the dogs, or the contents of this envelope will be sent by overnight mail to every media outlet in the country. Your political career will be over." Brandon put the envelope on the table in front of Monroe and turned to leave.

"What's she like?" Eleanor asked. "Michaela."

Turning back to her, Brandon bit back the urge to tell her off. "She's the best person I've ever known. Stay away from her, or I'll make you both very sorry."

He was on a flight back to Boston two hours later.

The first thing Brandon did after he returned home from St. Louis was buy three airline tickets to San Francisco for the following weekend so Daphne could see her family for the first time in five years. They had a joyous four-day reunion with her parents, her sister, her brothers, and their families. Relieved of her terrible burden, Daphne met her nieces and nephews for the first time, and Mike discovered a whole new group of aunts, uncles, cousins, and grandparents who were thrilled to see her—and spoil her.

On Brandon's first day back to work after the trip to California, the restoration arm of O'Malley & Sons went into business by tearing out Joe Coughlin's kitchen. Brandon was pleased with the group of veteran employees who'd chosen to work with him. Included among them was Bob Simms, one of the two men Brandon had nearly dropped the gravel on when he was drinking.

Brandon was in high spirits when he drove home from the most satisfying day he'd had in nearly seventeen years with the company. His new crew, infused with the enthusiasm that came from having a say in where they worked, had gelled exactly the way Brandon had hoped they would.

He pulled in next to Daphne's car and dodged the sprinkler when he picked up Mike's bike from the driveway and leaned it against the garage door.

The smell of something burning hit Brandon the minute he went in through the open front door.

"Daph? Mike? I'm home." He went into the kitchen to turn off the heat under chicken that had burned in the pan. Daphne's purse and cell phone were sitting on the table next to her car keys. "Daphne?" he called again before he went out to the backyard to see if they were in the garden, but there was no sign of them.

He went back inside and called for them again. One of Daphne's ceramic lamps had toppled off a table in the living room and smashed to pieces on the wood floor. As Brandon studied the broken lamp, a cold, hard blast of fear struck his heart.

"Daphne!" He ran into his bedroom, but they weren't there. Finding Brandon the Bear on the floor at the door to Mike's room, Brandon somehow knew his worst nightmare had come true. Monroe had found them, and they were gone.

CHAPTER 33, DAY 170

"Nine one one, please state your emergency."

"I need to report an abduction."

"Please verify your name, address, and phone number."

Brandon rattled off the information robotically.

"Who's been abducted, sir?"

"My fiancée and her daughter."

"What are their names?"

"Daphne and Michaela Van Der Meer. Michaela goes by Mike."

"How old are they?"

"My fiancée is thirty-one, and her daughter's six."

"How can you tell they were abducted?"

"Because they were! Send some cops over here right now!" As he hung up the phone, helpless rage and overwhelming fear flooded through him like a tidal wave.

When he'd recovered the ability to breathe, he picked up the phone again.

"Colin," he said when his brother answered.

"Brand? What's the matter?"

"They're gone."

"Who's gone?"

"Daphne and Mike. Monroe's got them."

Colin gasped. "I'm on my way."

"Col," he said before his brother could hang up. "Don't tell Mum. I told her he'd have to kill me to get to them." He finally broke down. "I didn't keep them safe. I left them here alone, and he took them."

"I'm coming, Brandon. I'll be right there."

The cops arrived first.

"I'm Detective Russell. This is my partner Officer Hargraves. You reported an abduction?"

Brandon stepped aside to let them in. He quickly filled them in and showed them the burnt pan, the broken lamp, Daphne's purse and keys, and the bear Mike never would've left behind. "They were taken from here under duress."

"You expect us to believe that Harrison Monroe, the candidate for vice president of the United States, orchestrated the abduction of your fiancée and her daughter?" Russell asked, his expression rife with skepticism.

"That's exactly what I expect you to believe. Contact my attorney, Alan St. John in Dennis. He's been handling our efforts to get rid of the Monroes. He'll confirm everything I've told you." Brandon gave them Alan's number, and the younger officer went outside to call him. "While you're dicking around thinking I'm lying, they're getting farther away with my family."

"Give us a minute to confirm what you've told us. Put yourself in our shoes, Mr. O'Malley. It sounds pretty far-fetched."

"It's not," Colin said as he arrived with Meredith. "If they're not here with my brother, the only other place they'd be is with Harrison Monroe and his wife—and they're with them against their will."

The younger officer came back in and nodded to his partner.

"I told you," Brandon said.

"We'll issue an alert for the child, but we can't do anything about your fiancée until she's been missing for twenty-four hours." Detective Russell gestured for his partner to go ahead and put out the alert.

"By then she could be dead." Brandon ached at the very thought of it. "They aren't interested in Daphne. They want Mike."

Colin put his hands on Brandon's shoulders. "Don't think that way, Brandon."

"*Why shouldn't I?*" Brandon cried. "She's kept their grandchild from them for *five years*. They hate her. It would be nothing to them to have her killed to get her out of their way. For Christ's sake, they turned their son's suicide into a car accident. What would stop them from disposing of his uncooperative wife?"

Declan, Jessica, Erin, and Tommy came rushing through the front door. Erin, who was in tears, threw herself into Brandon's arms. "We're going to find them, Brand."

Brandon sank into the warm comfort of his sister's embrace.

"Did you and Daphne ever discuss what she would do if this happened?" Declan asked.

Brandon nodded. "She promised she'd call me the minute it was safe."

"Do you have a recent photograph of the child?" Detective Russell asked.

Brandon went into Mike's room and brought back the photo album from what she referred to as "the summer of fun." He flipped it open to the first page and withdrew a photo from Mike's birthday. She had her arms around him and Daphne, and her toothless grin hit him like a shot to the heart. He sat down hard with his head in his hands as sobs rattled through him.

Erin wrapped her arms around him and held him. She took the photo and handed it to the detective.

"Find them," Brandon whispered. "Please find them."

The cops asked them to wait outside for two long hours while crime scene experts scoured the house for evidence, but they found nothing they could use to locate Daphne and Mike.

Alan arrived as the cops were leaving. "They've called in the FBI, which is routine in child abduction cases." He shook hands with Brandon's brothers, whom he'd met at Mike's birthday party.

"Monroe has an alibi," Brandon said. "But that's no surprise. It's not like he'd come here and snatch them himself." He stood up. "I'm going to San Francisco. They'll take them there."

"They're getting a warrant to search the Monroe's house in San Francisco," Alan said. "There's nothing you can do out there that's not already being done."

"Where's the wife?" Brandon asked. "Eleanor?"

"Campaigning with him in Texas," Alan said.

"Alan's right, Brand," Colin said. "The best thing you can do is sit tight and let the cops do their jobs. You need to be here if Daphne calls."

"She'd call my cell," Brandon argued. "Mike would, too. I made a game out of getting her to memorize the number, just in case."

"What if they call you from somewhere other than California?" Dec said. "Then you'd have to waste time flying all over the place."

"So I'm supposed to just sit here and do nothing?"

"For right now," Alan said. "They're Mike's grandparents. They're not going to harm her."

"What about Daphne?" Brandon asked. "What'll they do with her?"

The question hung in the air because no one had the answer.

Brandon spent most of that long night pacing. When he wasn't pacing, he stared at his home and cell phones, willing one of them to ring.

The others insisted on staying, and Meredith and Jessica got busy in the kitchen. Despite their encouragement, Brandon couldn't eat anything. What he really wanted was a drink—a good strong shot of whiskey to take the edge off the gnawing, sickening panic.

"Why don't you try to get some rest, Brandon?" Alan asked just after three. The others were sacked out on sofas and chairs. "You won't be any good to them if you're exhausted."

"I couldn't sleep, but you should go home."

"I'm not going anywhere."

"You've been a good friend. Thank you."

"You need to be very careful this doesn't cause a crisis in your recovery," Alan said.

"I was just thinking about how much I'd like a shot of whiskey."

"Do you remember the story I told you about the night my son got sick with meningitis?"

Brandon nodded.

"And do you remember what I did instead of drinking?"

"Yes."

"Would you like to pray, Brandon?"

"If you think it'll help."

"The only thing I know for sure is the whiskey won't help."

Brandon took the phones and followed Alan outside to the deck.

They sat together at the table, and Alan bowed his head. "Dear God, we ask you to watch over Daphne and Mike and keep them safe."

Brandon swiped at the tears that rolled down his face as he listened to Alan's quiet words and added his own silent plea that someone up there would hear their prayers.

By five in the morning, Brandon was dead on his feet, but still he paced. His cell phone rang at five fifteen, and he lunged for it.

"Brandon!" Mike said frantically.

"I'm here, baby. Where are you?"

"*Brandon!*" she cried again.

A fierce struggle ensued, and he heard a man yelling in the background. Mike was crying when the connection went dead.

"*Mike,*" he wailed, dropping to his knees and dissolving into tears.

Awakened by the phone, Erin, Colin, and Declan surrounded him on the floor.

"What did she say?" Colin asked.

"Just my name. Twice. But she was crying and someone was yelling in the background."

"Oh, my God," Erin whispered.

Declan reached for the phone to check the caller ID. "Crap, it's a private line, and the call was too short to trace."

"What am I going to do?" Brandon cried. "I have to do *something*."

His brothers each put an arm around him and helped him to his feet. "You need to lie down for a bit, Brand," Colin said. "You've got to get some sleep."

Brandon had no choice but to let them lead him into his bedroom where they urged him to lie down. He hadn't imagined it possible that he could sleep, but he drifted off and was beset by dreams that Mike and Daphne were just out of his reach. He would catch up to them only to have them drift away before he could get to them.

He awoke with a start at eight when he heard Mike calling him, but it was another dream. When he remembered Mike and Daphne were gone, he rolled onto his side and moaned into the pillow that held Daphne's scent.

Aidan and Clare arrived at nine, fresh off their honeymoon. "We just got home to Rhode Island last night and got your message," Aidan said to Colin. "What can we do?"

Colin shook his head. "We're just waiting, hoping Daphne will call. The cops have a nationwide alert out for Mike, but so far there's been no sign of her."

"What about the Monroes?" Aidan asked.

"Both have airtight alibis," Declan said.

"If they want Mike, won't one of them eventually lead us to her?" Clare asked.

Dec nodded. "That's the hope. The cops are all over them."

"Monroe must be loving that in the midst of the campaign," Aidan said.

"Who gives a shit about him or his campaign?" Brandon said when he came into the room. "It's time to blow him out of the water. Let's get those pictures of him and his mistress out to the media."

"You don't want to do that, Brandon," Alan said. "If he's at all unstable and you anger him, you could be putting them in danger."

"Don't you mean *more* danger?" Brandon asked as he fell into a chair.

Aidan squatted down in front of him. "You have to hang in there, Brand. We're going to find them."

Brandon could barely speak over the panic that gripped him. "What if we don't? What if I never see them again?"

Aidan squeezed his brother's arm. "That's not going to happen." He turned to Alan. "What's the story with that PI who was working for Daphne and Brandon? Is there anything he can do?"

"He's already on it," Alan replied.

"Can we get him some help? Whatever it costs, I'll pay. And I want to offer a half-million-dollar reward for any tips that lead to their safe return."

Alan nodded. "I'll make some calls."

"What about the media?" Aidan asked. "Let's get this on TV and name some names. It might make Monroe mad, but he's not going to do anything to them if the whole world is watching."

"Someone needs to tell Mum and Da before we do that," Colin said.

"I'll go over there," Dec offered.

"Don't let her come here." Brandon had no doubt his mother would be hysterical. "I can't deal with that right now."

"I'll take care of it," Dec said. "Don't worry."

"I have a college friend who's a TV reporter in Boston," Meredith said.

"Call her," Aidan said.

"Thank you," Brandon whispered to his brother.

"We won't rest until we find them," Aidan said. "I promise you that."

By noon, every media outlet in the country was reporting that vice presidential candidate Harrison Monroe's estranged daughter-in-law and granddaughter were missing, and a Massachusetts man was accusing Monroe of abducting them.

"I had absolutely nothing to do with this," a clearly rattled Monroe declared when reporters surrounded him after a campaign stop in Houston. "Mr. O'Malley is hysterical and looking for someone to blame for the disappearance of his fiancée and her daughter. Perhaps the police should be focusing their attention on him rather than me. Eleanor and I are praying for the safety of our daughter-in-law and granddaughter, and that's all I'm going to say."

"You son of bitch!" Brandon screamed at the television. *"You know exactly where they are!* Screw this." He grabbed his cell phone. "I've got to get out of here." He flew out the front door and through the crush of reporters gathered on the front lawn. Mike's bicycle, still leaning against the garage door, stopped him in his tracks, reminding him of her birthday, of chasing her down the street as she learned to ride without training wheels and picking her up when she crashed on the neighbor's lawn. Oblivious to the photographers capturing his every emotion, he stared at the bike with tears running down his face.

"Come on, Brandon." Aidan led him away from the bike and urged him into the cab of his truck as reporters yelled at them for a statement. With reporters chasing them down the street, Aidan floored the accelerator and got them out of there. They drove around for a while and eventually ended up on Main Street.

"Can we go to the Light?" Brandon asked.

"Wherever you want."

At Chatham Light, Brandon got out of the truck and sat on the guardrail facing the beach and ocean. "Mike loves it here. We flew a kite on the beach just last weekend."

"You can bring her again when she gets home," Aidan said, sitting next to his brother.

"I didn't really understand until just now when we drove through town what you meant when you said you couldn't come back here after Sarah died," Brandon said. "I couldn't live here anymore without them. Everywhere I look, I see something that reminds me of them."

"I know it's really hard, but try not to think the worst. Monroe might be a control freak and a crooked politician, but he's not a murderer."

"This is what it was like for you when Sarah refused treatment, wasn't it?"

Aidan nodded. "There's nothing worse than feeling completely helpless."

"And you'd been with her for almost twenty years by then. I've had five months with them. I can't imagine what you must've gone through when she was sick."

"If someone you love is in danger and you can't help them, the feeling is exactly the same whether you've loved them for five months or twenty years."

"Only one thing could keep Daphne from calling me for this long." Brandon looked out at the endless ocean. "She must be dead."

"Brandon, don't…"

"She's pregnant."

Aidan gasped. "Oh, God."

"No one knows, not even Mike," he said as new tears fell from eyes already raw from crying and lack of sleep.

Aidan put his arm around his brother. "You have to stay positive for them. They need you to keep it together."

"Thank you for all you're doing to help, Aid. For posting the reward and everything."

"It would've broken Sarah's heart to know how you felt about her and to think she'd been cavalier with your feelings. I have no doubt she'd approve of me using her money to help you."

Overcome, Brandon could only nod.

CHAPTER 34, DAY 171

Brandon passed most of the second long night lying on Mike's bed with the summer of fun photo album. He flipped through it over and over again and stopped each time to study the photo taken on Nantucket of Josh and Mike with their arms around each other. They were like two blond angels with dark tans and big smiles. They'd gotten used to seeing each other almost every day, and Erin was struggling with what to tell Josh about where his best buddy had gone.

The next three pages were from Declan's wedding. Brandon's favorite among them was one Daphne took of him and Mike, their faces alight with color from the Fourth of July fireworks. Included was a shot of the O'Malley family, which had grown from thirteen to eighteen this year—twenty-one if they counted Clare's daughters, who were included in the family picture taken at Aidan and Clare's wedding. He paused to study a great shot of Aidan and his best man, Colin, sharing a laugh before the ceremony.

Brandon ran a finger over the photo of a beaming Aidan surrounded by the women who made up his new family—Clare and Jill to his left, Kate and Maggie, still wearing a cast on one of her arms, to his right.

On the next page was a picture of Aidan at the piano, serenading Clare with the song "Beautiful in My Eyes." Everyone in the room had been in tears by the time Aidan, accompanied by Declan and Kate singing backup, had played the last notes of the song. His family hadn't heard Aidan play since before Sarah got sick, and it was an unforgettable moment for all of them.

A star-struck Mike had taken several photos of Clare's daughter Kate, who showed them why her song "I Thought I Knew" was number one on the country charts when she sang it for her mother and new stepfather. The following week, Brandon heard Mike telling someone at the beach that her Uncle Aidan was Kate Harrington's stepfather, and Kate was going to be a *big* star.

Brandon flipped to the photo of Clare surrounded by the O'Malley brothers. She had acted like nothing ever happened between her and Brandon when she put her arm around him for the photo. On the facing page was a shot of him with Daphne on Aidan's deck. They'd been captured in an unguarded moment with Mount Mansfield in the background. Anyone could see how deeply in love they were just by looking at that photo.

He choked on a sob. "I miss you, Daph." Rolling his face into Mike's pillow, he breathed in the scent of her baby shampoo.

It settled in on him during another long night that Daphne might really be dead. "If you're gone, baby," he whispered, "I swear to God I'll spend every ounce of energy I have getting our girl back from them. I'll raise her myself if I have to, but they aren't going to."

In all the chaos of the last few days, Brandon hadn't spent much time thinking about how Monroe found them. However, once he took the time to ponder the question, it didn't take long to figure out how it happened.

With a sick feeling in his stomach, he got up and went into their bedroom, touched the space bar on Daphne's computer, and waited for it to boot up. He opened the browser and typed "Brandon O'Malley" into the search engine.

The list of results was long, but the item at the top was all it had taken.

Swallowing hard he clicked on the link to the company Web site. The caption under his photo said, "Brandon O'Malley, Professional Engineer and Principal, O'Malley & Sons Construction, Inc. Headquartered in scenic Chatham, Massa chusetts, O'Malley & Sons is one of Cape Cod's largest family-owned and operated businesses."

"Oh, God," he whispered. In trying to rid them of the Monroes, he'd led them right to Mike and Daphne.

His mind raced. *Daphne was right. I should've just left it alone. Instead, I stirred things up, and now they're gone.* He'd been so confident that the photos would scare off Monroe, especially in the midst of the campaign. Clearly, Brandon had underestimated the senator's obsession with his granddaughter. As he sat on the bed, he yearned for something to dull the awful ache that had been with him every minute since he came home to find them gone—the ache that sharpened into unbearable pain when he realized he had only himself to blame for leading Monroe right to their doorstep.

Thinking back to when he was drinking, he tried to recall all the places he'd hidden booze in the house. Surely there was one bottle left that no one had found. And then he remembered—the garage, in the cabinet over the basement stairs. Walking quietly through the living room where his brothers were sleeping, he went out to the garage through the kitchen door.

Using a step stool, he reached for the cabinet where Valerie had kept the Christmas decorations, opened the door, and found not one but two bottles of Jack Daniels. He reached for the unopened bottle and brought it down from the cabinet.

He sat on the garage floor and leaned against the wall, cradling the bottle. Tears rolled down his face as he worked up the nerve to toss away one hundred and seventy-one days of sobriety. He'd honestly thought he would never drink again. But nothing could've prepared him for how it would feel to discover he had endangered the two people he loved the most.

The cap resisted his fumbling attempts to break it open, almost like it knew what was at stake.

When he finally managed to open the bottle, the smell hit him first, promising the sweet relief he couldn't get anywhere else.

Blinded by tears, he held the open bottle up to his nose.

"What're you doing?"

Colin's voice startled him.

"Go away, Col." The disappointment he saw on his brother's face was excruciating.

"Where did you get that?" Colin asked, grabbing for the bottle.

Brandon held it out of his reach. *"Get the fuck out of here!"*

"You don't want to do this, Brand. It won't help anything."

"What the hell do you know about it?"

"You've worked so hard for almost *six months*. Come on, give it to me."

"Leave me alone, Colin. I mean it."

"Don't you want them to be proud of you?" Colin pleaded, squatting so he was at eye level with Brandon. "Think about Daphne and Mike coming home to find you drunk. Don't let them down like this. They're counting on you."

Deep, gulping sobs seized Brandon. He didn't resist when Colin took the bottle from him, set it aside, and dropped to his knees to console him. Brandon fell against his brother's chest and cried until there was nothing left. "It's all my fault, Col."

"What do you mean?"

"When I confronted Monroe, I gave him my name. I'm all over the Internet because of the company. That's how Monroe found them."

"They've found them before without any help from you, and they would've found them again. They weren't going to give up. You can't do this to yourself. We all thought those pictures of him with his mistress would put an end to this whole thing."

Brandon wiped his face. "How will I ever live without them if we don't get them back?"

"You won't have to."

The open bottle of whiskey sitting on the garage floor was a stark reminder of what Brandon's life without them might be like.

***

At Colin's urging, Brandon finally went to bed and slept until ten the next morning. While he knew he needed the sleep, waking up and remembering they were gone was agonizing, as was realizing how close he'd come to chucking his hard-earned sobriety. He was amazed by how easily he'd tossed aside all the resolve he'd built up over the last six months. Of course, he knew alcoholism was a lifelong disease, but he'd thought he had it beat. The events of the previous night had shown him otherwise.

He could also no longer ignore the fact that he was starving. The smell of bacon got him up and into the shower where he stood under the pulsing water without feeling a thing. Everything he did was by rote and out of necessity—wash, shave, comb, brush, dress.

In the kitchen, his mother stood guard over the bacon. She turned and held out her arms to him.

As he stepped into her embrace, Brandon could see that she'd been crying.

"I couldn't stay away any longer."

"I'm sorry, I just knew you'd be disappointed…"

"What're you talking about?"

"I promised I'd keep them safe."

"You couldn't be with them every minute of the day. You did everything you could, Brand."

"I did a little too much," he said, filling her in on how Monroe found Mike and Daphne.

"You can't blame yourself. You were trying to help them." She held him for a long time. "Are you hungry, love?" She reached up to smooth the damp hair off his forehead.

He nodded. "Where is everyone?"

"Da, Dec, Aidan, and Clare are outside. Colin and Tommy had to go to work for a while. Meredith and Jessica went home to get changed, and Erin's at Tommy's mother's house checking on the kids. Is that everyone?"

"I think so." Everyone was accounted for except the two people he needed most.

Colleen put a steaming plate of bacon and eggs down in front of him. "Coffee?"

He nodded. "Thanks." The food tasted good, but it was a struggle to get it past the lump that had taken up residence in his throat at the sight of his face on the Internet. I may as well have given them directions to my house, he thought, wishing there was something he could smash.

When his cell phone rang, Brandon lunged from his seat to grab it off the counter.

"Brandon." She was weak, and her voice was strained, but it was Daphne.

He sat down hard in the kitchen chair. "Oh, God, Daph, are you all right?"

"*They have her!* They took my baby."

"Honey, where are you?" He was so weak with relief he could barely speak.

"In a motel in Topeka," she whispered. "They gave me something that knocked me out. They took her and left me here."

Each word seemed to sap her energy.

"I kept trying to wake up, but they'd give me another shot, and I couldn't…" Her sobs stole her voice. "I tried, Brandon. I tried to fight them, but they had guns."

He swallowed hard and swiped at the tears on his face. "It's okay, honey. Can you tell me exactly where you are? I'll get you some help right away, and I'll be on a plane as fast as I can."

"Hold on. The address is on the phone." She gave him the name and address of the motel. "It was her, Brandon. Eleanor's the one who's been chasing me for years, not him."

Brandon gasped as he walked outside to pass along her location to the cops. "How do you know?"

She took a deep breath to summon the energy to continue. "I heard them when they thought I was knocked out. They were talking about the old lady this, the old lady that. We don't want to piss off the old lady."

"That's why the pictures didn't work. I couldn't figure out why he'd risk the campaign by pulling this now."

"He probably never showed them to her. But she's the one behind this whole thing. She has been from the beginning."

"That's good information, baby. That'll help the FBI find Mike."

"What if we don't find her?" she asked, weeping again. "What'll we do?"

"We'll find her. I was so afraid when you didn't call…"

"How long has it been? I have no idea how long I've been here."

"Almost two days. I was terrified they'd killed you to get you out of their way."

"I think I lost the baby," she said, hiccupping with sobs.

"*No,*" he wailed. "No."

"There's blood all over me, and I had terrible pain."

The loss hurt all the way down to his bones, but Brandon struggled to stay focused on what she needed. "They're sending an ambulance to you, honey. Aidan's had a plane and crew on alert in case you called, so I'll be there in a couple of hours. I love you so much."

"I love you, too. Hurry, Brandon. I need you."

Chapter 35, Day 172

His brothers insisted on coming with him to Kansas, and they piled into Daphne's SUV for the ride to Hyannis, where Aidan had leased the plane. They picked up Colin at the office and hit the road.

"Are we going to be able to fly in this?" Colin asked, casting an eye at the pea-soup fog that was a staple of Cape Cod summers.

"Worst case, it should burn off in an hour or two," Declan said from the driver's seat.

Brandon groaned at the thought of a delay. Since it wasn't a beach day, they were sharing the busy road with cyclists, runners, and couples pushing baby strollers. Declan sped around a rotary and cut off two angry motorists in his haste.

What should have been a forty-five-minute ride took nearly ninety minutes as they fought the summertime congestion.

Distressed to discover the fog was worse in Hyannis than it had been in Chatham, Brandon moaned.

At the airport, Aidan walked across the terminal to consult with the pilot he'd hired.

Watching the pilot shake his head, Brandon's stomach fell.

"The airport's closed," Aidan said when he came back to where his brothers were waiting. "They had some sort of incident on the runway. It'll be an hour or two."

"Can we go to Boston?" Brandon asked desperately.

"In this traffic, by the time we get there, this airport will be open," Colin said.

"This is *unfuckingbelievable*," Brandon moaned.

Five interminable hours later, a cab deposited them at St. Francis Hospital in Topeka.

Brandon raced inside and up to the fourth floor, where he'd been told Daphne was after having been admitted. He burst into her room and suppressed a gasp when he found her asleep, pale as a ghost, and dwarfed by the big hospital bed. It didn't matter how pale she was, though. She was alive, and that was all that mattered.

Wiping away tears, he reached for the hand that wasn't attached to a monitor. When he pressed his lips to the palm of her hand, she stirred. "Brandon?"

"I'm here, baby," he whispered. "I'm sorry it took so long."

She held out her arms to him, and he crawled onto the bed to hold her.

"God, I thought I'd never see you again." Blinded by tears, he buried his face in her hair. "I've never been more afraid in my life."

"Have they found Mike?"

"Not yet. They've searched the Monroe's house twice but didn't find her. I talked to the agent in charge an hour ago, and based on what you overheard, they're bringing Eleanor in for questioning. They want to talk to you, too, when you're up to it."

"I'll do it now. Today. Whatever I have to do to get Mike back."

"Let me just hold you for another minute, and then I'll call him."

"You look so tired, hon." She caressed his face. "You didn't drink, did you?"

"No. I wanted to, though. I came close last night, but Colin stopped me, thank God."

She combed her fingers through his hair. "Oh, Brandon."

"It's all my fault, Daph. I should've listened to you and left it alone. I led them right to you."

"Shhh," she said with her fingers to his lips. "This would've happened eventually. She wouldn't have rested until she got her hands on Mike."

"Are you okay? What did the doctors say?"

"I lost the baby," she whispered. "Whatever they gave me killed our baby."

Red-hot rage blasted through him, but he showed her none of it. Rather he just held her closer. "She won't get away with this. I don't care who she is."

"I wanted it so much," she said, weeping into his shirt.

"So did I, honey. But we'll have others—lots and lots of them. We're going to find Mike, go home, get married, and have a ton of kids."

"Promise?"

"I promise, and you know I always keep my promises." He leaned in to kiss her and was surprised by the burst of passion that hit them the moment their lips met. "I love you so much. I couldn't have lived without you."

"I won't be able to live without Mike. We have to find her."

"We will. I promise."

After two days of intense searching by law enforcement officials they were no closer to finding her. When Daphne was released from the hospital, Brandon flew her to her parents' home in California since the FBI was certain Mike would be found somewhere in the Monroe's home state. He tried to send his brothers home, especially Colin, whose wedding was just a week away, but they refused to leave until Mike was located. They holed up in a Sausalito hotel to be close to Brandon and Daphne.

She was able to give detailed descriptions of her abductors, but the snippets of their conversation she recalled weren't enough for the FBI to arrest Eleanor, who was questioned and released without giving any useful information.

Brandon finally convinced his brothers to go home when it appeared there wasn't going to be a quick end to the case. They stopped by Daphne's parents' house to say good-bye before they left on a commercial flight to Boston. Aidan insisted on leaving the chartered plane in case Brandon needed it.

"We'll be home with Mike in time for the wedding," Brandon said to Colin with more confidence than he felt. "But if we're not, I want you to focus on Meredith and your big day, do you hear me?"

Colin looked away from his brother as he nodded. "I wish there was something we could do."

"I know, but there isn't. So go home and get ready for your wedding. I'll be okay."

"Are you sure?"

"I'm positive. Thank you for what you did for me that night. I don't know what the hell I was thinking…"

"You weren't thinking. You were terrified."

"I'm so glad you were there to stop me, Col."

"So am I."

Brandon hugged him. "Don't let this ruin your wedding, please? Mike would hate that."

Colin blinked back tears and nodded.

"Where's the best man?" Brandon called.

"Right here," Declan said.

"He's all yours." Brandon shook hands with both of them. "Thanks for everything, you guys."

"We'll be praying for you, Brand, and for Mike," Dec said, hugging his brother. The two of them walked away and left Aidan to say good-bye.

"You know how to reach me—day or night—if you need anything, right?" Aidan asked.

"I'll never be able to thank you for everything you've done. You came in and took charge, which was exactly what I needed. After everything that's happened

between us that you could be so totally *there* for me..." Brandon stopped and shook his head when emotion overtook him.

"That's all in the past." Aidan rested his hands on his brother's shoulders. "What matters now is the future. There's nothing I wouldn't do for you, Brand."

"Including being my best man in September?"

Aidan smiled. "Yeah?"

"Yeah."

"I'd love to."

"I'll see you next week at Colin's wedding. Mike would never miss a wedding."

"That's right." Aidan hugged him. "Hang in there, man."

"I'm trying."

They got a break the next day when the three men who abducted Daphne and Mike were arrested in San Francisco's Chinatown. All of them pointed to Eleanor as the mastermind, and the large recent deposits to their bank accounts were all the proof the FBI needed to arrest her. She was taken from her home in Pacific Heights, fingerprinted, booked, and charged with kidnapping, kidnapping a child, attempted murder, and kidnapping for hire.

Later that morning, a drawn and subdued Harrison Monroe held a press conference at which he resigned from the campaign and the Senate. He claimed to have no knowledge of his granddaughter's whereabouts and pledged to stand by his wife until the "baseless" charges against her were dropped.

The media went wild, broadcasting the images of Eleanor being led from her mansion in handcuffs over and over again. Daphne was bombarded with requests for interviews and finally agreed to talk to the NBC affiliate, hoping it would generate some leads. She and Brandon watched the broadcast that night on the sofa in her parents' family room.

"You did great, baby," he said, kissing her hand.

"I look like death."

"You look beautiful."

"You have to say that."

"Was it hard to talk about Randy?"

"Not really. It was such a long time ago, and it's time people knew how he died and why."

"Hopefully, someone will see it and help us find Mike," Brandon said, his heart hurting when he pictured her alone and scared. The image was almost more than he could bear, and it sent a shudder through him.

"What is it?" Daphne asked.

"I miss my little girl."

"I can't stand to think about what she must be going through, wondering why we haven't come to get her."

Brandon buried his face in his hands so she wouldn't see his tears.

She put her arm around him and rested her face against his back.

When he felt warm wetness through his shirt, he realized she was crying, too.

He reached for her, and they fell together, sobbing.

"You don't have to hide it from me."

"I'm so scared," he confessed.

She kissed away his tears.

He captured her mouth in a deep, soulful kiss that chased it all away for a brief moment.

The phone rang, startling them. Brandon reached for it.

"We've got a lead," Agent Jackson said without preamble. "A maid in the house heard about the reward and came forward claiming there's a secret room on the third floor that Eleanor had built for her granddaughter. Mr. Monroe says he has no knowledge of it, and Eleanor's not talking. We're sending in a team now."

"We'll be right there," Brandon said.

"No, stay put. It's going to happen fast. I'll call you the minute I know anything."

Brandon hung up and relayed the information to Daphne.

"Oh, God," she whispered. "What do we do? We have to do something."

He reached for her hand. "Pray with me."

Twenty of the longest minutes of their lives later, the phone rang again.

"We've got her, and she's fine," Agent Jackson said. "She said her grand-mother was nice to her."

Brandon whispered the news to Daphne and kept his arm around her as she dissolved into tears. "Can we talk to her?"

"The paramedics are taking a quick look at her, and then we'll bring her home. You should've seen this room, man. It was hidden behind a panel in the wall, and it looked like FAO Schwartz exploded in there. There were clothes hanging in the closet from infant size up to teen. Eleanor built the room when Harrison was in Washington and paid off everyone to keep quiet about it. Without that maid having a burst of conscience—and a thirst for half a million bucks—I don't know if we would've ever found her."

Brandon's heart skipped a crazy beat at how close they'd come to losing her forever.

"We'll have her home within the hour," Agent Jackson said.

Brandon, Daphne, and her parents were on the front porch waiting when a police cruiser pulled up forty minutes later. Still weak from her ordeal, Daphne was wrapped in a blanket Brandon insisted on.

He walked down the stairs as the back door of the cruiser flew open.

Mike bolted from the car wearing a frilly dress that was all wrong on her.

Tears streaming down his face, Brandon held out his arms to her.

She flew into his embrace. "I missed you," she said, sobbing and clinging to him.

"It's okay, baby." He wept into her soft hair as he carried her to Daphne. "You're okay now. Daddy's got you."

EPILOGUE

Brandon faced the mirror to adjust his bow tie and brush some lint off the shoulder of his black tuxedo. He ran a trembling hand through hair streaked with the strands of silver that began appearing after the kidnapping.

The butterflies that had stormed around in his stomach for days had grown into bats overnight. He reached for the roll of antacids in his pocket. *How will I ever do this?*

"Dear God," he said to his reflection in the mirror, comfortable now with the daily requests he made to his higher power. "Please help me get through this day without embarrassing myself."

He made one last unsuccessful attempt to straighten his bow tie and left the men's room in the back of Holy Redeemer Church.

His mother came out of the room reserved for brides, wiping a tear from the corner of her eye. "She looks beautiful, love."

"So do you, Mum."

"Thank you," she said. "She's making us all cry in there."

He smiled. "She's holding up okay?"

"Cool as a cucumber. Just what you'd expect of her. How're you?"

He popped another antacid into his mouth. "I'm kind of a wreck, to be honest."

Colleen patted his face. "You can do it, love. I'll be pulling for you."

"Thanks, Mum." He kissed her. "I'll see you in there."

The door to the bride's room opened again. Seventeen-year-old Isabel and fifteen-year-old Emily emerged in strapless dark green gowns. Isabel's chestnut curls were swept up into a glamorous style that left him breathless. *When had she become a woman?* Emily's light blonde hair, so much like her mother's and Mike's, was twisted into the same elegant style as her sister's.

"Daddy, she's asking for you," Isabel said, kissing Brandon's cheek and adjusting the wayward bow tie yet again. "You look dashing."

"And you, my ladies, are stunning. The maids of honor are not supposed to outshine the bride."

They giggled.

Daphne, exquisite in a dusty rose silk gown, emerged from the bride's room wiping her eyes.

"Hey." Brandon kissed her. "Are you okay?"

Daphne nodded. "She's ready for you."

Brandon glanced at the closed door and then at his wife. "Am I ready for her?"

She laughed. "I doubt it."

"You're still a goddess," he whispered in her ear, curling a lock of her now shoulder-length hair around his finger. "Love you."

She went up on tiptoes to kiss him. "Love you, too."

"Well, here goes nothing." He knocked on the door and went in.

Her back was to him, so the first thing he noticed was the six-foot embroidered train and her bare shoulders under the light film of her veil.

She looked up then, and their eyes met in the full-length mirror.

"Oh, God, look at you, baby," he whispered, staggered by her. "You're gorgeous."

She turned to him, all grown up at twenty-five—his little girl, his Mike—or Michaela as she was known these days, but still and always Mike to him.

He moved toward her, wanting to hold her, wanting to stop time and go back to when she was learning to ride a two-wheeler, scraping her knee, flying a kite with him on the beach, skiing on Mount Mansfield, learning to drive… But she was so perfect, he didn't dare touch her.

"Have you seen Josh? How's he doing?"

"He's just fine and waiting for you. In fact, he's been waiting for you since you bumped heads at five and eight."

"Was I terrible to make him wait until we established our careers?"

"You were right to wait until you were ready, even if it took twenty years."

She laughed. "Do you suppose people think it's weird? I mean we all know Josh and I aren't technically cousins, but others…"

"You've never thought of yourselves as cousins. Even when you were kids, there was something special between you. Anyone who knows either of you knows that."

"I love him, Daddy. I love him the same way you love Mom."

Brandon's throat closed with emotion. "How am I supposed to give away the most precious thing in the world to me?"

Her eyes swam with tears. "Don't make me cry. You'll ruin my makeup."

The diamond necklace he'd given her so many years ago sparkled around her neck on a new, longer chain.

She reached up to touch it. "My something old."

"You look so much like your mother did when I first met her." He shook his head. "It's unbelievable."

"I remember it all, you know, everything about our first months together—finding you under the sink, Brandon the Bear, the playground you built for me, all the weddings. Remember when you almost dropped my birthday cake? Was I six or seven?"

"Six," he said with a grin. "It was your first birthday after I met you."

"It was the best birthday of my life because you were there. You were the first man I ever loved. You know that, don't you?"

"Now you're going to make me cry."

"I have no idea what my life would've been like if I hadn't found you under my sink."

Brandon laughed even as tears spilled down his face.

"The way we were living then…" She shook her head. "You saved me from a life on the run. You and all the O'Malleys… You saved me."

He took her hand and raised it to his lips. "Oh, no, my love, it was quite the other way around. *You* saved *me*."

"What day is today?" It was a question she asked often.

"Seventy-three hundred and six." He was a longtime leader in AA, and others regularly turned to him for help, which still struck him as ironic at times. "Twenty years and six days."

"That's just about how long we've been together."

"It's no coincidence, you know. You and your mother gave me the will to stay sober. The two of you, your sisters, and the boys *kept* me sober."

"Six kids would be enough to keep anyone sober," she said with a smile.

"Yes, indeed. You all are the reason I keep my side of the street clean."

The door opened behind them, and Isabel poked her head in. "Whenever you guys are ready."

Brandon offered an arm to his daughter. "Shall we?"

The wedding party included all of Colleen's nineteen grandchildren. Mike and Josh went round and round for weeks trying to trim the size of their wedding party until Josh finally said, "The heck with it. Let's have them all." Josh's sisters Nina, Cecelia, and Amanda, and Declan's four daughters preceded Isabel and Emily up the aisle. Josh's brother Ben was his best man. Joining him at the altar were Brandon's sons Jake, Sam, and Dennis, Colin's sons Nate and Will, and Aidan's sons, Max and Nick.

When the girls reached the front of the church, the organist launched into the wedding march.

Brandon glanced down at Mike. "Ready?"

She squeezed his hand and nodded.

All eyes were on them as they moved slowly down the aisle, past Colin and Meredith, Declan and Jessica, Aidan, Clare, Maggie, Jill, Kate, and their families. Mike, still one of Kate's biggest fans, had asked her to sing at the reception.

We've been so very blessed, Brandon thought. *But we've had our share of sorrows, too.* He and Daphne had mourned the baby they lost for a long time, even after all the others arrived. And they still missed Dennis, who had succumbed to a heart attack four years earlier, leaving a gaping hole in the lives of his wife, children, and grandchildren.

The business Dennis had built continued to thrive under the care of his children and now several of his grandchildren. Josh was Brandon's right-hand man in the restoration business, which the year before eclipsed new construction as the most profitable arm of the company. Mike recently earned her master's degree in architecture, and when she returned from her honeymoon, she would join Declan in the new construction branch, bringing yet another facet to O'Malley & Sons Construction. After Brandon and Daphne's youngest son Dennis started first grade three years earlier, Daphne became the company's chief financial officer and whipped them all into shape.

Tall, blond, and handsome, Josh never took his eyes off his bride as she made her way toward him on the arm of her father.

In the second row on the left side of the aisle, Harrison Monroe sat next to Colleen and Daphne's parents. Mike never held Harrison responsible for his wife's actions and made an effort over the years to maintain a relationship with him. After pleading guilty by reason of insanity, Eleanor died in a state psychiatric hospital nine years after the kidnapping.

In the front row on the right side, Erin and Tommy watched their son's bride come down the aisle. Like Daphne across from her, Erin was wiping away tears by the time Brandon and Mike reached the front of the church.

Brandon raised the blusher from over Mike's face and kissed her cheek. "I love you," he whispered.

"I love you, too. First and always."

He held her gaze for a long moment before he joined her hand with Josh's. Watching them climb the steps to the altar, Brandon remembered a long-ago photo of two blond children with their arms around each other. They never had let go.

"Who gives this woman to be married?" the priest asked.

Brandon cleared the lump from his throat. "Her mother and I do." He turned then to take his place next to Daphne.

She linked her fingers with his and held on tight as they watched their girl marry the boy she had loved all her life.

Brandon had given her away, but he'd never let her go.

Keep Reading for a preview of Coming Home, book 4 in the Treading Water Series, which reununites Kate Harrington and Reid Matthews ten years after Marking Time.

THE HOUSE THAT JACK BUILT

The first character to take up occupancy in my mind as a living, breathing human being, was a handsome, successful architect named Jack Harrington. Jack and I ran around together for a long time before I ever put fingers to keyboard to tell his story. I wanted to write about a man who has it all—a wife he still adores after twenty years of marriage, three beautiful daughters he'd do anything for, and a life most people would envy. That life is turned upside down when his wife is hit by a car and plunged into a coma. I wanted to show Jack's struggles to rebuild his life as he becomes the custodial parent for his daughters—two of them teenagers with all the accompanying issues—and I wanted to show his conflict when he finds a new love. These issues make up the core of the first book I wrote, *Treading Water*, which led to three sequels, *Marking Time, Starting Over* and *Coming Home*. It's *Treading Water*, however, that is the book of my heart.

Since I finished *Treading Water*, I've thought of my writing as "The House That Jack Built," tying into his career as an architect and the unexpected building blocks that came from *Treading Water*. As I was finishing *Starting Over* in July 2006, I decided to drive out to Chatham, Massachusetts, so I could finish it in the town where it was set. Yes, this was a huge indulgence, but it coincided with the halfway point of summer vacation, and my kids were driving me nuts.

The first thing I did when I got to Chatham was drive around to check out the four streets I had chosen from hundreds on a map to place the O'Malley family's homes. I figured if there was, say, a cement factory on both sides of the street, the good people of Chatham would know I hadn't bothered to come out there and check. I am pleased to report there were houses on all four streets, but on the corner of the fourth street, there was something else—a red house with a sign on the side that said, "The House That Jack Built." No, I am not kidding, and yes, I sat there and cried. If ever there was a "sign" that I was on the path I was meant to be on, there it was. It was without a doubt, one of the most amazing moments of my life, and I will never, ever forget it. (View a photo of the house at *marieforce.com/marie/about-writing/24-the-house-that-jack-built.*)

That same week, after I got home and told my sister-in-law this story, she approached me at a family party to say, "You won't believe this! I was having trouble sleeping at my friend's house the other night and got up to see if she had a magazine or something I could look at." She found an old copy of *Architectural Digest*, and there was a spread with the headline "The House That Jack Built." She had torn it out for me and that page is framed over my desk to remind me that this is a marathon, not a sprint, and it's about the journey, not the destination.

Thanks for taking the journey with me. I hope you enjoyed the series that began with *Treading Water,* continued in *Marking Time, Starting Over* and *Coming Home.* And I hope now you know why these books are my favorites! I'm thankful every day for my wonderful readers, and I love to hear from you. Write to me any time at *marie@marieforce.com.*

COMING HOME
CHAPTER 1

The darkness came faster this time, too fast to prepare before it was upon her. Bright lights, the roar of the crowd, the band behind her... One minute, Kate Harrington was in the middle of a show. The next minute, she was in an ambulance being rushed—again—to the emergency room. This was the third time she'd passed out since a bout of pneumonia had weakened her, but it was the first time she'd done it on a stage in front of twenty thousand screaming fans.

As the paramedics started an IV and put an oxygen mask over her face, her sister Jill watched the proceedings with big, frightened eyes.

Kate couldn't remember where they were. There'd been so many cities, so many hotels, so many venues, so many crowds over the last ten years that they'd begun to blend together into a panoramic muddle of images. When she thought about the media coverage this incident would garner, she held back a groan.

The paparazzi followed her every move like a band of rabid dogs. Passing out in the middle of a concert would make for a big story.

She pushed the mask aside. "Call Mom and Dad so they don't hear it on the news," she said to her sister, who doubled as her manager and attorney.

"Okay," Jill said, pulling out the phone they called her Siamese twin because she was permanently attached to it.

As the ambulance sped through the night in the city she couldn't remember, Kate could only imagine what they'd say this time. She'd been accused of everything under the sun, from cocaine addiction to secret pregnancies to mistreating her staff. Nothing was off-limits. No lie was too big or too preposterous. Such was life in the celebrity fishbowl.

Though she'd gone looking for a career in country music, her "cross-over" appeal had made her a huge star—much bigger than she'd ever hoped or wanted to be. She'd sold more records in the last decade than any other female performer in the world, and along with that success came rabid interest in her every move.

The speculation about her personal life had been worse than ever since pneumonia forced her to cancel two weeks of shows, which was why she'd resumed the tour so soon, hoping to put an end to the vicious rumors. They'd said she was back in rehab, drying out from years of drug abuse. Her plan to go back to work and shut down the rumors had been working well until she passed out on stage. Now the gossip would be worse than ever.

If it hadn't been such a nuisance to deal with, the buzz would've amused her. She was, without a doubt, the most boring celebrity in the history of celebrities. She never went anywhere that didn't involve work. After a few spectacularly public romances fizzled, she'd sworn off men, especially well-known men. When she wasn't working, she holed up at her farm in Tennessee with her horses, her family and her close friends—few as they were.

Of course, boring didn't sell magazines, so they made up most of what they said about her. To the outside world, she was just another pill-popping, dope-snorting, pampered princess who'd had too much success far too soon. The people closest to her knew the truth, but sometimes she suspected even her own family wondered if any of the rumors were true.

They arrived at the hospital, and as they whisked her inside, she heard someone mention Oklahoma City and remembered arriving at the hotel suite with Jill and the sound check at the Chesapeake Energy Arena. She recalled asking Jill if they could tour the memorial at the Murrah building, and Jill saying they didn't have time to arrange the security she'd require for such an outing. Kate had been to every major city in America and countless others overseas, but she'd rarely gotten to see anything while she was there. She was always too busy working—or too insulated by the security required to go anywhere.

This late-fall tour had been the idea of her mentor, friend, producer and fellow superstar, Buddy Longstreet. He and his record company, Long Road Records, had made her a star, and there wasn't much she wouldn't do for Buddy when he asked for a favor. That was how she found herself coming off a summer tour and heading right into a second tour that was due to wrap up on New Year's Eve at Carnegie Hall.

Since she could barely lift her head at the moment, the idea of performing at Carnegie Hall in a few weeks seemed as daunting as climbing Mount Everest. Her chest hurt, her eyes were so heavy she could barely keep them open, and she felt like she could sleep for a year.

The piercing pain of another needle being jammed into her hand forced her eyes open as a team of doctors and nurses swooped in on her. Outside the cubicle, she saw Jill on the phone, pacing back and forth in the sky-high heels and power suit that was her uniform. As she rarely saw her sister dressed in anything else, Kate liked to tease her about sleeping in a suit.

Truth be told, she didn't know what she'd do without Jill to manage all the details, to hammer out the contracts, to fight the battles and manage the team that made it happen. Thanks to Jill, all Kate had to do was show up and sing. Worries that her sister was sacrificing her own life to run hers was something that nagged at Kate more often than she'd care to admit. But since existing without Jill at her right hand was unimaginable, Kate stayed mum on the subject, and Jill certainly never complained.

She worked like a dog and collected the big salary Kate paid her, but Kate wondered if she ever spent a dime on anything other than suits and heels and the latest and greatest in smartphone technology. The sisters were never home long enough to spend any of the money they'd made over the years.

As she watched her beloved older sister swipe at a tear, Kate reached her breaking point. Jill didn't cry. Ever. Jill was a pillar of strength and fortitude. The pressure was getting to them both, and it was time to step off the treadmill for a while.

The medication they were pumping into her made Kate's tongue feel too big for her mouth, but her thoughts were clear. Enough was enough. Images of the huge log-cabin-style house she'd built five years ago on her sprawling estate in Hendersonville, Tennessee drifted through her mind, making her yearn for home.

Kate must've dozed off, because when she awoke, she was in a darkened room. She blinked a few times to clear her vision and saw Jill standing at the window, staring out into the darkness.

"Hey," Kate said.

Jill spun around to face her. "You're awake."

"How long have I been asleep?"

"A couple of hours. They admitted you because you're dehydrated. That's why you passed out."

"I'm really thirsty."

Jill helped her to take a few sips from a cup of ice water on the table.

"Where are we?"

"St. Anthony's Hospital."

"Is the press going crazy?"

Jill shrugged. "I haven't looked."

"Yes, you have," Kate said with a small smile. "Don't lie to me."

"They're flipping out, as usual where you're concerned. This time they're saying it was a combination of pills and booze."

"I wish I had half as much fun as they think I do."

"I wish both of us did."

"It's probably high time we had some fun, don't you think? Let's stop the madness and go home."

Jill's eyes widened, and her mouth fell open. "What're you saying?"

"I've had enough, Jill. We've been everywhere, done everything, made a fortune. Now it's time to live a little. How many nights have you spent in your place since it was finished?" Kate had given Jill three acres of property and a "gift certificate" good for the house of her choice. After her initial reluctance to accept such an extravagant gift, the house had been built to Jill's exacting specifications.

"I don't know. A month, maybe two?"

"And it's been done for a year. That's ridiculous. What're we trying to prove? Who're we trying to prove it to?"

"You have contracts, Kate. Obligations. Buddy will freak if you bail on the tour."

"I can get a note from my doctor," she said with a playful smile.

"You're apt to be sued. It's no joke."

"I'm not joking. Let them sue me. I need a break. A real break. I want months at home. I want the family in Tennessee for Christmas. I want to see Mom, Dad, Andi, Aidan, the boys and Maggie and spend *real* time with them, not twenty-four rushed hours between tour stops. Don't you want that, too?"

"You know I do, but it's not feasible right now. We've got thirty dates left on the calendar before we're done." She didn't mention that they'd get only a few days off before they were due in the studio to record Kate's sixth album. After that, it was back on the road for another tour. "How am I supposed to get you out of all those obligations?"

"If anyone can do it, you can. I should've done this after I was sick. Instead, I went back too soon and collapsed in front of an arena full of people, giving the press enough fodder to last for weeks. I'm done, Jill."

"For now or forever?"

"I don't know yet. For now, definitely. I'll let you know about forever after I've had a break."

"There could be big trouble over this, bad press..."

Kate released a harsh laugh. "What other kind is there where I'm concerned?" She reached for her sister's hand and held on tight. "We're twenty-eight and twenty-nine years old, and we've spent the last five years working ourselves into early graves. We have millions in the bank, gorgeous homes that we pay people to keep clean for us, nice cars sitting unused in the garage, horses we pay people to ride for us, and five little brothers who are growing up far too fast and barely know us."

Jill nibbled on her bottom lip, seeming stressed as she listened to Kate.

"You haven't had a real vacation since you graduated from law school and came to work for me. I haven't had one in so long, I think the last one was Christmas break of my senior year of high school. It's time to *live* a little. What good is all the money in the world if we never do anything fun? Don't you want to have *fun*, Jill?"

And there was something else Kate wanted to do, something she should've done a long time ago, but that was her secret and hers alone. It wasn't something she could share with anyone, even her sister and closest friend.

"Our work *is* fun," Jill said. "I enjoy it, and you do, too, when you're feeling well."

"I haven't enjoyed it in a long time—long before I got sick." Saying the words out loud was somehow freeing. "I feel like I'm on a treadmill with every day exactly the same as the last. The only thing that changes is the city and the venue."

"What about the band and the roadies and all the people your show employs?"

"We'll give the roadies and the tour people a nice severance package and pay the band to give us six months before they sign on with anyone else. You think they won't welcome some time at home with their families? Some of them have kids who barely recognize them on the rare occasion they're actually home."

Jill nibbled on her thumbnail as she mulled it over. Her mind worked a mile a minute, which made her such an asset to Kate. After several minutes of mulling and nail biting, Jill glanced at her sister. "Let me see what I can do."

Damn, it was good to be home, Kate thought as she took her horse, Thunder, on a slow gallop through the woods that abutted her home twenty minutes outside Nashville. At thirteen, Thunder was showing no signs of slowing down and hadn't lost his enthusiasm for outings with Kate.

"We'll be spending a lot more time together for the next little while, boy," she said, stroking his neck as his hooves clomped along the well-worn path.

He nickered in response to her, as he always did, drawing a smile. She swore he was a human stuck in a horse's body, and the comfort of being with him filled her with joy.

As they often did when she rode Thunder, her thoughts strayed to the man who'd given her the horse after their ill-fated romance blew up in their faces. It was impossible, she'd discovered, to spend time with Thunder without thinking of Reid and the magical months they'd spent together.

Kate didn't believe in regrets. She was pragmatic enough by now to know that life could be incredibly sweet and just as incredibly painful. More than ten years had passed since the last time she saw Reid, the awful day he flew her home to Rhode Island after her sister Maggie was badly injured.

But not a day had gone by that she hadn't thought of him, wondered where he was, what he was doing, if he was happy. One night, about six years ago, during a lonely moment on the road, she'd searched for him on the Internet and discovered he'd sold his business and left Nashville shortly after they broke up.

She'd been unable to find a single other reference to him online in the ensuing decade. It was like he'd dropped off the face of the earth, which was why she was about to ask something of her sister that she'd hoped to handle on her own.

Kate brought Thunder to a stop outside Jill's two-story post-and-beam house. She slid off his back and tied the lead to the railing. Rubbing her hand over his flank, Kate said, "I won't be long, pal."

His nicker and nuzzle made her laugh. Sometimes she felt like the horse she rarely saw these days knew her better than any of the people in her life, except for Jill, of course. Since they were young girls, Jill had known her better than anyone, which was why Kate was so certain her sister would balk at what Kate was about to ask of her. But she was determined to ask anyway.

She rapped lightly on the front door and stepped inside. "Hello?"

"In here," Jill called from the kitchen.

Kate strolled into the kitchen, stopping short when she saw Jill dressed for business, bent over her latop with papers strewn across the table. A steaming cup of tea sat ignored next to her. "Okay, what part of *vacation* didn't you get?"

Jill glanced up at her. "You might be on vacation, but I'm still trying to keep your ass from getting sued."

Kate glanced over her shoulder, pretending to look at her ass.

"Stop being funny. It's no joke. Buddy is furious with you, and Ashton is, too."

"What else is new?" Kate asked of Reid's son, who'd given her the cold shoulder every time she saw him over the last ten years. Since he was the chief counsel for Buddy as well as Buddy's superstar wife Taylor Jones and Long Road Records, their paths crossed more often than Kate would like.

"Regardless of his ongoing feud with you, he's also moving heaven and earth to prevent a slew of lawsuits."

"He's not doing it for me. He's doing it for Buddy and the company."

"Who cares why he's doing it? The end result will save you millions."

Since Kate had been focusing on rest and relaxation since they got home two days ago, the last thing she wanted to hear about was the threat of lawsuits. "Remember those jeans we bought in the Mall of America? You must still have them around here somewhere."

"I still have them."

"So you can only be productive in a power suit."

"I have a meeting in the city in just over an hour."

Kate helped herself to a diet soda. "With who?"

"Ashton."

Here's your chance, she thought, as flutter of nerves invaded her belly. *Just say it.* "So, um…"

Without looking up from what she was doing, Jill said, "So um what?"

Kate dropped into a chair across from her sister.

Jill took off the gold-framed glasses she used for computer work and sat back in her chair. "What's on your mind?"

"I was wondering… While you're with Ashton, um…"

"Will you spit it out? I'm on a schedule."

"You're supposed to be on vacation."

"Speak. Quickly."

How to sum up years of longing and regret in one sentence?

"Is something wrong, Kate?"

Hadn't something been wrong every day that she'd spent without him? Hadn't every man she'd been with since him failed to live up to him? Hadn't she been disappointed time and again when she'd tried and failed to fall in love again? "Will you ask him for his father's contact info?"

Jill's mouth fell open, and then she quickly closed it. "You're serious."

"Yes."

"Why?"

"Because there's something I need to speak with him about. Something personal."

"And you think Ashton, who's never forgiven you for hooking up with his father in the first place, is going to just hand over that info?"

"That's where you come in. Your powers of persuasion are legendary."

Jill shook her head. "I don't feel comfortable asking him that. Our relationship is professional, and that's a very personal topic."

"I know I'm asking a lot. I know I always ask a lot of you, but I need to talk to him."

"And you won't tell me why?"

Kate shook her head.

"It's been over with him for a long time, Kate. I don't know what you're hoping to accomplish—"

"I need some closure."

Jill crossed her arms and studied her sister. "Closure."

"That's what I said." After a long pause, Kate asked, "Will you ask him?" While she awaited Jill's reply, her heart hammered. She had a feeling she was making this into too big a deal, but the need to see him, to hear his soft drawl, to feel the way she had when they were together, was getting bigger by the day. No doubt he was long over her and rarely spared her a thought. Kate told herself if that were the case, she would put the past where it belonged and get on with her life. But if there was even the slightest chance that he thought of her as often as she thought of him… "Jill?"

"If I get the chance, I'll ask him, but no promises."

"That's fair enough."

"Are you sure you want to venture into that hornet's nest again?"

"It was only a hornet's nest at the end. The rest of the time…" She met her sister's gaze. "The rest of the time it was magic."

Jill drove into the city an hour later in the white Mercedes coupe Kate had given her for Christmas last year. Her sister was endlessly generous and appreciative of everything Jill did to make her life run smoothly, but sometimes she asked too much. Like this morning… Kate had no way to know that the last thing in the world Jill would ever want to do was mention the ill-fated love affair between Reid Matthews and her sister to the man's ridiculously handsome and endlessly irritating son.

She always dreaded her one-on-one meetings with Ashton, which were far more frequent than she'd like, thanks to the fact that Kate and the attorney for her record company didn't speak to each other. So it was left to Jill to run interference between them. Sometimes she had half a mind to sit them down and tell them to stop acting like children, but she was wise enough by now to know that some hurts weren't made better by time. Some hurts were too deep to ever heal.

Ashton's office was in Green Hills, a trendy area that Jill might've preferred if close proximity to her sister didn't make her life much less complicated. Plus, she knew Kate liked having her nearby. Kate needed someone around who she could always count on—and trust. Most of the time, Jill was happy to be that person.

This was not one of those times.

She pulled into a parking space behind the restored Victorian Ashton used as an office and turned off the car. She took a moment to collect herself and gather the calm, cool façade she preferred for business dealings. No matter how much time she took to affect that cool façade, however, she could count on Ashton Matthews to have her rattled and furious within five minutes.

"Just get through this and you can be on vacation," she said out loud as she grabbed her briefcase and went inside.

"Hi, Jill," Ashton's assistant, Debi, said. "He's waiting for you in his office."

"Thank you," Jill said with a smile for Debi. She went up the stairs and took a right, heading for the huge office at the end of the hallway. Jill had been here a hundred times and had the same reaction every time. By the time she reached the closed door to Ashton's office, her heart beat hard, her palms were sweaty and her stomach fluttered with nerves. Why did the thought of seeing him always undo her? It was positively maddening!

Jill took one last moment to prepare for battle and raised her hand to knock.

"Come on in."

Oh, that voice. That accent. It was positively lethal. Jill opened the door and stepped inside, closing the door behind her. When she ventured a glance at the desk, she found him sitting back in his chair, eyeing her with what seemed to be a mixture of amusement and annoyance. Good, at least they were both annoyed.

He got up slowly and came around the desk. "Jill. Nice to see you as always."

She surreptitiously rubbed her sweaty palm on her skirt before she returned his handshake. It was appalling, really, the way she wanted to lean in for a better sniff of his cologne. He wore his blond hair short, and his dark suit had been cut to fit his broad shoulders.

"Something wrong?"

Jill snapped out of her visual perusal to realize she was still holding his hand. She released it quickly and searched for her missing composure. "Of course not."

"Have a seat. Can I get you anything to drink?"

"I'm fine."

Rather than sit behind his desk, he took the chair next to hers and crossed his long legs.

Jill's mouth went dry as she watched him move like a big cat on the prowl.

"Your sister has put us in one hell of a fix," he said in that Tennessean drawl that made her go stupid in the head, but only when it came from him. She heard that accent a hundred times a day from others, but no other voice was quite like his.

"She feels bad about it."

"Is she really sick or in need of a vacation?"

The implication that Kate was lying made Jill see red. But then she remembered the enmity between Kate and Ashton and quelled the urge to jump to her sister's defense. "She's yet to fully bounce back from the pneumonia. She went back to work too soon."

"The company's PR people are working around the clock to deal with the fallout."

"It's not Kate's fault that the press is convinced she's strung out on drugs, and besides, that's not what this meeting is about. The fact is, she wants a few months off, and it's our job to make that happen."

"It's your job to make that happen. My job is to keep Buddy's company from getting sued because your client is a flake."

"That's completely unfair and unwarranted, Ashton, and you know it. She's one of the hardest-working performers in the business, and she is *ill*. I'd like to see you try to put on a two-hour concert when you can barely breathe."

"Fine," he said begrudgingly. "If you say she's sick, she's sick. I'll do what I can to keep her from getting sued, but no promises."

"I hope you'll do as much for her as you'd do for any of Buddy's artists."

At that, his expression hardened. "What's that supposed to mean? I treat all our artists the same, but my job is to protect Long Road Records from exposure. Your sister has exposed us to tremendous liability."

"I'm going to keep saying it until you *hear* me—she is *sick*. If anyone tries to sue her for breach of contract, we can provide documentation from the hospital in Oklahoma City."

"I'd like to have that for the file."

"Fine, I'll fax it to you when I get home."

"Fine."

His sleepy-looking green eyes took a perusing journey over her that left Jill feeling naked and exposed. What the hell? "What're you looking at?"

"You."

"Why are you looking at me?"

"Because you're the only other person in the room."

He had such a way of making her feel stupid. He made her want to tell him that she'd graduated at the top of her class from both Brown University and Harvard Law, but she didn't say that. Rather, as she often did in his presence, she squirmed in her seat, sending the message that he was making her feel uncomfortable. That was probably his goal.

"And because I wonder if you ever loosen that top button and let your hair down."

Aghast, Jill stared at him as heat crept into her cheeks. "What business is that of yours?"

"Absolutely none."

"Then why would you say such a thing to me?"

His shrug was casual, as if this conversation was a normal part of their business routine. It most definitely was *not* normal. "I wonder. That's all."

She didn't want to ask. She absolutely did not want to know what he meant by that. "Wonder about what?" Clearly, her mouth was working ahead of her brain.

"I wonder what you're like when you're not playing barracuda protector for your sister. What do you like to do? What do you look like in a pair of jeans? What kind of music do you like? Who's your favorite author? That kind of stuff."

Jill had never been more shocked in her life. He wondered about *her*?

"Close your mouth before the flies get in there," he said, amusement dancing in his eyes.

She needed to get out of there before she said something she'd regret—such as, *I wonder about you, too.* "Are you..."

He waited a long beat before he said, "Am I what?"

Jill's mouth had gone totally dry. "Flirting with me?" The words came out squeaky and rough, and she immediately felt like a total fool. She was almost thirty years old, for crying out loud. She'd had her share of boyfriends, although none lately, not when she was so damned busy she didn't have time to do her laundry, let alone date. Why was her reaction to this man so different from any other?

"What if I am?"

"Why?" She said the first thing that came to mind, and damn him for laughing.

"Why not? You're a beautiful woman, or I bet you could be if you...unbuttoned...a little bit."

"Is that supposed to be flattering?"

"When was the last time you did something just for you that had nothing to do with your sister?"

"It's been a while," she said truthfully.

"You wanna have some fun?"

He was so gorgeous, far more gorgeous than any man had a right to be, and that accent absolutely undid her. "What kind of fun?"

"Any kind you want," he said in a suggestive tone that made her nipples tighten with interest. Thank God she was wearing a suit coat so he couldn't see them.

"With you."

"Yes," he said, laughing again, "that was kind of the idea."

"And how long have you been wanting to have 'fun' with me?"

"Awhile now, if I'm being truthful."

Jill couldn't believe what she was hearing.

"Nothing to say to that?" he asked, arching an eyebrow.

"Oh." *Brilliant, Counselor. Positively brilliant.*

"So what do you say? Want to get together while you're on vacation?"

Jill's mind raced as she considered all the implications, including what her sister would have to say about it.

"Don't think about what Kate would say. Think about what Jill wants."

His insight only rattled her further. All she thought about was what Kate wanted. When was the last time she gave the first consideration to what *she* wanted. Longer than she could remember. "I, um…"

"Take your time." He folded his hands behind his head. "I've got an hour until my next meeting."

"Wouldn't it be a conflict of interest for us to see each other outside of work?"

"Since we're usually on the same side, I wouldn't say so."

He was a much more seasoned attorney than she was, so she took his word for it.

"I need a favor," she said, diving in before she lost her nerve. They needed to get this issue out of the way before she could consider his very tempting offer.

"What kind of favor?"

"A personal favor that's going to make you mad."

"I'm listening."

Jill couldn't seem to form the words that would have the effect of gas thrown on a fire. Not when he'd just asked her out. She wanted to go out with him, which was the sad part. The minute she passed along Kate's request for contact info for his father, the date would probably be off the table.

"Jill?"

"Kate would like to contact your father."

He froze, staring at her with contempt stamped into his expression. "You can't be serious."

"I'm only the messenger, so don't shoot me."

"There's no way in hell I'm revisiting that issue." His hands dropped to his lap, and he stood. "The first time was more than sufficient, thank you very much."

"She only wants to see him for a minute," Jill said, making it up as she went along. "Apparently, there's something she needs to tell him."

"The last thing he needs is to hear from her. She ruined his freaking life and nearly destroyed my relationship with him. She has a lot of nerve thinking I'm going to help her get in touch with him."

"I understand," Jill said, and she did. It was a sore subject for all of them. "And for the record, I told her I was uncomfortable asking you."

Hands in pockets, he stared out the window. "Typical Kate to think of herself first and everyone else second."

"You don't give her enough credit, Ashton. She's very generous and good to the people in her life."

"I don't expect you to see her faults."

"I see them, but I love her enough to look past them."

"You'll forgive me if I don't love her that much." He turned to face her. "Tell her to leave it alone. A lot of people were hurt by what happened between them. My dad has a good life now, a life that satisfies him. I'd hate to see him hurt by her again."

"He hurt her, too."

"Maybe so, but I only saw his side of it, and it wasn't pretty. Trust me on that."

Jill nodded, sorry she'd broached the subject. She picked up her briefcase, stood and started for the door.

"Jill?"

She turned back to him.

"You never answered my question."

"Oh. I thought you were mad."

"I am mad, but not at you. I don't believe in shooting the messenger."

"Could I think about it?"

"Sure. Take all the time you need. You know where I am when you make up your mind."

Jill nodded and left, taking the stairs on wobbly legs.

"Have a good day, Jill," Debi said.

"Thanks, you too."

Jill nearly dropped her keys in her haste to get in the car. For a long time, she sat there, staring out the windshield, trying to process what'd happened. Ashton Matthews had asked her out. Her sister's sworn enemy was interested in *her*. What would she tell Kate?

Nothing, she decided. She'd keep it to herself for now.

Get *Coming Home* now. Order a signed copy from Marie's Store at *marieforce.com/store*.

OTHER TITLES BY MARIE FORCE

Other Contemporary Romances Available from Marie Force:

The Treading Water Series

Book 1: Treading Water

Book 2: Marking Time

Book 3: Starting Over

Book 4: Coming Home

The Gansett Island Series

Book 1: Maid for Love

Book 2: Fool for Love

Book 3: Ready for Love

Book 4: Falling for Love

Book 5: Hoping for Love

Book 6: Season for Love

Book 7: Longing for Love

Book 8: Waiting for Love

Book 9: Time for Love

Book 10: Meant for Love

Book 10.5: Chance for Love, *A Gansett Island Novella*

Book 11: Gansett After Dark

Book 12: Kisses After Dark

Book 13: Love After Dark

Book 14: Celebration After Dark

Book 15: Desire After Dark

Book 16: Light After Dark

Gansett Island Episodes, Episode 1: Victoria & Shannon

The Green Mountain Series

Book 1: All You Need Is Love

Book 2: I Want to Hold Your Hand

Book 4: And I Love Her

Novella: You'll Be Mine

Book 5: It's Only Love

Book 6: Ain't She Sweet

The Butler Vermont Series

(Continuation of the Green Mountain Series)

Book 1: Every Little Thing

Single Titles

Sex Machine

Sex God

Georgia on My Mind

True North

The Fall

Everyone Loves a Hero

Love at First Flight

Line of Scrimmage

Books from M. S. Force
The Erotic Quantum Trilogy
Book 1: Virtuous
Book 2: Valorous
Book 3: Victorious
Book 4: Rapturous
Book 5: Ravenous
Book 6: Delirious

Romantic Suspense Novels Available from Marie Force:
The Fatal Series
One Night With You, *A Fatal Series Prequel Novella*
Book 1: Fatal Affair
Book 2: Fatal Justice
Book 3: Fatal Consequences
Book 3.5: Fatal Destiny, *the Wedding Novella*
Book 4: Fatal Flaw
Book 5: Fatal Deception
Book 6: Fatal Mistake
Book 7: Fatal Jeopardy
Book 8: Fatal Scandal
Book 9: Fatal Frenzy
Book 10: Fatal Identity
Book 11: Fatal Threat

Single Title
The Wreck

ABOUT THE AUTHOR

Marie Force is the *New York Times* bestselling author of more than 50 contemporary romances, including the Gansett Island Series, which has sold nearly 3 million books, and the Fatal Series from Harlequin Books, which has sold 1.5 million books. In addition, she is the author of the Butler, Vermont Series, the Green Mountain Series and the erotic romance Quantum Series, written under the slightly modified name of M.S. Force. All together, her books have sold more than 5.5 million copies worldwide!

Her goals in life are simple—to finish raising two happy, healthy, productive young adults, to keep writing books for as long as she possibly can and to never be on a flight that makes the news.

Join Marie's mailing list for news about new books and upcoming appearances in your area. Follow her on Facebook at https://www.facebook.com/MarieForceAuthor, Twitter @marieforce and on Instagram at https://instagram.com/marieforceauthor/. Join one of Marie's many reader groups. Contact Marie at *marie@marieforce.com.*

Lightning Source UK Ltd.
Milton Keynes UK
UKHW02f1842100418
320835UK00016B/649/P